BOOKS BY E L JAMES

Fifty Shades of Grey

Fifty Shades Darker

Fifty Shades Freed

Grey

Darker

DARKER

DARKER

E L James

Vintage Books
A Division of Random House LLC | New York

FIRST VINTAGE BOOKS EDITION, NOVEMBER 2017

ISBN: 9780385543910
ebook ISBN: 9780385543989

Cover design by Sqicedragon and Megan Wilson
Cover photographs: front © Petar Djordjevic / Penguin Random House;
back © Shutterstock

www.vintagebooks.com

Printed in the United States of America
10 9 8 7 6 5 4 3 2 1

For my readers.
Thank you for all that you've done for me.
This book is for you.

ACKNOWLEDGMENTS

Thanks to:

Everyone at Vintage, for your dedication and professionalism. I am constantly inspired by your expertise, good humor, and love for the written word.

Anne Messitte, for your faith in me. I will forever be indebted to you.

Tony Chirico, Russell Perreault, and Paul Bogaards for your invaluable support.

The wonderful production, editorial, and design team who brought this project together: Megan Wilson, Lydia Buechler, Kathy Hourigan, Andy Hughes, Chris Zucker, and Amy Brosey.

Niall Leonard, for your love, support, and guidance, and for being less grumpy.

Valerie Hoskins, my agent—thank you for everything every day.

Kathleen Blandino, for the pre-read, and for all things Web.

Brian Brunetti, once again, for your invaluable insight into helicopter accidents.

Laura Edmonston for sharing your knowledge of the Pacific Northwest.

Professor Chris Collins, for enlightening me about soil science.

Ruth, Debra, Helena, and Liv for the encouragement and word challenges, and for making me get this done.

Dawn and Daisy, for your friendship and advice.

Andrea, BG, Becca, Bee, Britt, Catherine, Jada, Jill, Kellie,

Kelly, Leis, Liz, Nora, Raizie, QT, Susi—how many years is it now? And we're still going strong. Thank you for the Americanisms.

And all my author and book world friends—you know who you are—you inspire me every day.

And lastly, thank you to my children. I love you unconditionally. I will always be so proud of the wonderful young men you have become. You bring me such joy.

Stay golden. Both of you.

DARKER

THURSDAY, JUNE 9, 2011

I sit. Waiting. My heart is thumping. It's 5:36 and I stare through the privacy glass of my Audi at the front door of her building. I know I'm early, but I've been looking forward to this moment all day.

I'm going to see her.

I shift in my seat in the rear of the car. The atmosphere feels stifling, and though I'm trying to remain calm, the anticipation and anxiety are knotting my stomach and pressing down on my chest. Taylor sits in the driver's seat, staring straight ahead, wordless, looking his usual composed self, while I can barely breathe. It's irritating.

Damn it. Where is she?

She's inside—inside Seattle Independent Publishing. Set back beyond a wide, open sidewalk, the building is shabby and in need of renovation; the company's name is etched haphazardly in the glass, and the frosted effect on the window is peeling. The business behind those closed doors could be an insurance company or an accounting firm—they're not displaying their wares. Well, that's something I can rectify when I take control. SIP is mine. Almost. I've signed the revised heads of agreement.

Taylor clears his throat and his eyes dart to mine in the rearview mirror. "I'll wait outside, sir," he says, surprising me, and he climbs out of the car before I can stop him.

Maybe he's more affected by my tension than I thought. Am I that obvious? Maybe *he's* tense. But why? Maybe it's because he's had to deal with my ever-changing moods this past week, and I know I've not been easy.

But today has been different. Hopeful. It's the first productive day I've had since she left me, or so it feels. My optimism has driven me through my meetings with enthusiasm. Ten hours until I see her. Nine. Eight. Seven . . . My patience has been tested by the clock as it ticks closer to my reunion with Miss Anastasia Steele.

And now that I'm sitting here, alone and waiting, the determination and confidence I've enjoyed all day are evaporating.

Perhaps she's changed her mind.

Will it be a reunion? Or am I just the free ride to Portland?

I check my watch again.

5:38.

Shit. Why does time move so slowly?

I contemplate sending her an e-mail to let her know I'm outside, but as I fumble for my phone, I realize I don't want to take my eyes off the front door. Leaning back, I run through her recent e-mails in my mind. I know them by heart, all of them friendly and concise but without a hint that she's been missing me.

Maybe I *am* the free ride.

I dismiss the thought and stare at the doorway, willing her to appear.

Anastasia Steele, I'm waiting.

The door opens and my heart soars into overdrive but then quickly stutters with disappointment. It's not her.

Damn.

She has always kept me waiting. A humorless smile tugs at my lips: waiting at Clayton's, at The Heathman after the photo shoot, and again when I sent her the Thomas Hardy books.

Tess . . .

I wonder if she still has them. She wanted to give them back to me; she wanted to give them to a charity.

I don't want anything that will remind me of you.

The image of Ana leaving surfaces in my mind's eye: her sad, ashen face stricken with hurt and confusion. The memory is unwelcome. Painful.

I made her that miserable. I took everything too far, too quickly. And it fills me with a despair that has become all too familiar since she left. Closing my eyes, I try to center myself, but I'm confronted by my deepest, darkest fear: she's met someone else. She's sharing her little white bed and her beautiful body with some fucking stranger.

Damn it, Grey. Stay positive.

Don't go there. All is not lost. You'll be seeing her shortly. Your plans are in place. You are going to win her back. Opening my eyes, I stare at the front door through the window, my mood now as dark as the Audi's tinted glass. More people leave the building, but still no Ana.

Where is she?

Taylor is pacing outside and glancing toward the front door. Christ, he looks as nervous as I feel. *What the hell is it to him?*

My watch says 5:43. She'll be out in a moment. I take a deep breath and tug at my cuffs, then try to straighten my tie, only to find I'm not wearing one. *Hell.* Raking my hand through my hair, I try to dismiss my doubts, but they continue to plague me. *Am I just a free ride to her? Will she have missed me? Will she want me back? Is there someone else?* I have no idea. This is worse than waiting for her in the Marble Bar, and the irony is not lost on me. I thought that was the biggest deal I'd ever negotiate with her and that didn't turn out the way I expected. Nothing turns out as I expect with Miss Anastasia Steele. Panic knots my stomach once more. Today, I have to negotiate a bigger deal.

I want her back.

She said she loved me . . .

My heart rate spikes in response to the adrenaline that floods my body.

No. No. Don't think about that. She can't feel that way about me. Calm down, Grey. Focus.

I glance once more at the entrance to Seattle Independent Publishing and she's there, walking toward me.

Fuck.

Ana.

Shock sucks the breath from my body like a kick to the solar plexus. Beneath a black jacket she's wearing one of my favorite dresses, the purple one, and black high-heeled boots. Her hair, burnished by the early-evening sun, sways in the breeze as she moves. But it's not her clothing or her hair that holds my attention. Her face is pale, almost translucent. There are dark circles beneath her eyes, and she's thinner.

Thinner.

Guilt lances through me.

Christ.

She's suffered, too.

My concern at her appearance turns to anger.

No. Fury.

She hasn't been eating. She's lost, what, five or six pounds in the last few days? She glances at some random guy behind her and he gives her a broad smile. He's a good-looking son of a bitch, full of himself. *Asshole.* Their carefree exchange only fuels my rage. He watches her with blatant male appreciation as she walks toward the car, and my wrath increases with each of her steps.

Taylor opens the door and offers her his hand to help her climb inside. And suddenly she is sitting beside me.

"When did you last eat?" I snap, struggling to keep my composure. Her blue eyes peer up at me, stripping me bare and leaving me as raw as they did the first time I met her.

"Hello, Christian. Yes, it's nice to see you, too," she says.

What. The. Fuck.

"I don't want your smart mouth now. Answer me."

She stares at her hands in her lap, so that I've no idea what she's thinking, then trots out some lame excuse about eating a yogurt and a banana.

That's not eating!

I try, really try, to keep a rein on my temper.

"When did you last have a real meal?" I press her, but she ignores me, looking out the window. Taylor pulls away from the curb, and Ana waves to the prick who followed her out of the building.

"Who's that?"

"My boss."

So that's Jack Hyde. I recall the employee details I flipped through this morning: from Detroit, scholarship to Princeton, worked his way up at a publishing firm in New York but has moved on every few years, working his way across the country. He never retains an assistant—they don't last more than three months. He's on my watch list, and I'll have my security adviser Welch find out more.

Focus on the matter at hand, Grey.

"Well? Your last meal?"

"Christian, that really is none of your concern," she whispers.

"Whatever you do concerns me. Tell me." Don't write me off, Anastasia. *Please.*

I'm the free ride.

She sighs in frustration and rolls her eyes to piss me off. And I see it—a soft smile pulling at the corner of her mouth. She's trying not to laugh. She's trying not to laugh *at me*. After all the heartache I've suffered, it's so refreshing that it cracks through my anger. It's so Ana. I find myself mirroring her, and I try to mask my smile.

"Well?" My tone is much gentler.

"Pasta alla Vongole, last Friday," she answers, her voice subdued.

Jesus H. Christ, she's not eaten since our last meal together! I want to pull her across my knee, right now, here in the back of the SUV—but I know I can't ever touch her like that again.

What do I do with her?

She looks down, examining her hands, her face paler and sadder than it was before. And I drink her in, trying to fathom what to do. An unwelcome emotion blooms in my chest, threatening to overwhelm me but I push it aside. As I study her it becomes achingly clear that my biggest fear is unfounded. I know she didn't get drunk and meet someone. Looking at how she is now, I know she's been on her own, tucked up in her bed, weeping her heart out. The thought is at once comforting and distressing. I'm responsible for her misery.

Me.

I'm the monster. I did this to her. How can I ever win her back?

"I see." The words feel inadequate. My task suddenly feels too daunting. She will never want me back.

Get a grip, Grey.

I damp down my fear and make a plea. "You look like you've lost at least five pounds, possibly more since then. Please eat, Anastasia." I'm helpless. What else can I say?

She sits still, lost in her own thoughts, staring straight ahead, and I have time to study her profile. She's as elfin and sweet and as beautiful as I remember. I want to reach out and stroke her cheek. Feel how soft her skin is . . . check that she's real. I turn my body toward her, itching to touch her.

"How are you?" I ask, because I want to hear her voice.

"If I told you I was fine, I'd be lying."

Damn. I'm right. She's been suffering—and it's all my fault. But her words give me a modicum of hope. Perhaps she's missed me. Maybe? Encouraged, I cling to that thought. "Me, too. I miss you." I reach for her hand because I can't live another minute without touching her. Her hand feels small and ice-cold engulfed in the warmth of mine.

"Christian. I—" She stops, her voice cracking, but she doesn't pull her hand from mine.

"Ana, please. We need to talk."

"Christian. I . . . please. I've cried so much," she whispers, and her words, and the sight of her fighting back tears, pierce what's left of my heart.

"Oh, baby, no." I tug her hand and before she can protest I lift her into my lap, circling her with my arms.

Oh, the feel of her.

"I've missed you so much, Anastasia." She's too light, too fragile, and I want to shout in frustration, but instead I bury my nose in her hair, overwhelmed by her intoxicating scent. It's reminiscent of happier times: An orchard in the fall. Laughter at home. Bright eyes, full of humor and mischief . . . and desire. My sweet, sweet Ana.

Mine.

At first, she's stiff with resistance, but after a beat she relaxes against me, her head resting on my shoulder. Emboldened, I take a risk and, closing my eyes, I kiss her hair. She doesn't struggle out of my hold, and it's a relief. I've yearned for this woman. But I must be careful. I don't want her to bolt again. I hold her, enjoying the feel of her in my arms and this simple moment of tranquility.

But it's a brief interlude—Taylor reaches the Seattle downtown helipad in record time.

"Come." With reluctance, I lift her off my lap. "We're here."

Perplexed eyes search mine.

"Helipad—on the top of this building." How did she think we were getting to Portland? It would take at least three hours to drive. Taylor opens her door and I climb out on my side.

"I should give you back your handkerchief," she says to Taylor with a coy smile.

"Keep it, Miss Steele, with my best wishes."

What the hell is going on between them?

"Nine?" I interrupt, not just to remind him what time he'll pick us up in Portland, but to stop him from talking to Ana.

"Yes, sir," he says quietly.

Damn right. She's my girl. Handkerchiefs are my business, not his.

Flashes of her vomiting on the ground, me holding back her hair, run through my head. I gave her my handkerchief then. I never got it back. And later that night I watched her sleep beside me. Perhaps she still has it. Perhaps she still uses it.

Stop. Now. Grey.

Taking her hand—the chill has gone, but her hand is still cool—I lead her into the building. As we reach the elevator, I recall our encounter at The Heathman. That first kiss.

Yeah. That first kiss.

The thought wakes my body.

But the doors open, distracting me, and reluctantly I release her to usher her inside.

The elevator is small, and we're no longer touching. But I sense her.

All of her.

Here. Now.

Shit. I swallow.

Is it because she's so near? Darkening eyes look up at mine.

Oh, Ana.

Her proximity is arousing. She inhales sharply and looks at the floor.

"I feel it, too." I reach for her hand again and caress her knuckles with my thumb. She looks up at me, her fathomless eyes clouding with desire.

Fuck. I want her.

She bites her lip.

"Please don't bite your lip, Anastasia." My voice is low, full of longing. Will I always want her like this? I want to kiss her, press her into the elevator wall like I did during our first kiss. I want to fuck her here, and make her mine again. She blinks, her lips gently parted, and I suppress a groan. How does she do this? Derail me with a look? I am used to control—and I'm practically drooling over her because her teeth are pressing into her lip. "You know what it does to me." And right now, baby, I want to take you in this elevator, but I don't think you'll let me.

The doors slide open and the rush of cold air brings me back to the now. We're on the roof, and although the day has been warm, the wind has picked up. Anastasia shivers beside me. I wrap my arm around her and she huddles in to my side. She feels too slight, but her petite frame fits perfectly under my arm.

See? We fit together so well, Ana.

We head out onto the helipad toward *Charlie Tango.* The rotors are slowly spinning—she's ready for liftoff. Stephan, my pilot, runs toward us. We shake hands, and I keep Anastasia tucked under my arm.

"Ready to go, sir. She's all yours!" he roars above the sound of the helicopter engines.

"All checks done?"

"Yes, sir."

"You'll collect her around eight thirty?"

"Yes, sir."

"Taylor's waiting for you out front."

"Thank you, Mr. Grey. Safe flight to Portland. Ma'am." He salutes Anastasia and heads to the waiting elevator. We duck down under the rotors and I open the door, taking her hand to help her climb aboard.

As I strap her into the seat, her breath hitches. The sound travels straight to my groin. I cinch the straps extra-tight, trying to ignore my body's reaction to her.

"This should keep you in your place." The thought runs through my head, and I realize I've said it out loud. "I must say, I like this harness on you. Don't touch anything."

She flushes. Finally, some color stains her face—and I can't resist. I run the back of my index finger down her cheek, tracing the line of her blush.

Lord, I want this woman.

She scowls, and I know it's because she can't move. I hand her some headphones, take my seat, and buckle up.

I run through my preflight checks. All instruments are in the green with no advisory lights. I roll the throttles to "fly," set the transponder code, and confirm that the anticollision light is on. It all looks good. I don my headphones, switch on the radios, and check the rotor rpm.

When I turn to Ana, she's watching me intently. "Ready, baby?"

"Yes." She's wide-eyed and excited. I can't help my wolfish grin as I radio the tower to make sure that they're awake and listening.

Once I have permission to take off, I check the oil temperature and the rest of the gauges. They're all in normal operating range, so I increase the collective, and *Charlie Tango*, elegant bird that she is, rises smoothly into the sky.

Oh, I love this.

Feeling a little more confident as we gain altitude, I glance at Miss Steele beside me.

Time to dazzle her.

Showtime, Grey.

"We've chased the dawn, Anastasia. Now the dusk." I smile, and I'm rewarded with a shy smile that illuminates her face. Hope stirs in my chest. I have her here when I thought all was lost and she seems happier now than when she walked out of her office. I might just be the free ride, but I'm going to try and enjoy every damn minute of this flight with her.

Dr. Flynn would be proud.

I'm in the moment. And I'm optimistic.

I can do this. I can win her back.

Baby steps, Grey. Don't get ahead of yourself.

"As well as the evening sun, there's more to see this time," I say, interrupting the silence. "Escala's over there. Boeing there—and you can just see the Space Needle."

Curious as ever, she cranes her slim neck to look. "I've never been," she says.

"I'll take you. We can eat there."

"Christian, we broke up." I hear the dismay in her voice.

That is not what I want to hear, but I try not to overreact. "I know. I can still take you there. And feed you." I give her a pointed look and she blushes a lovely pale rose.

"It's very beautiful up here. Thank you." She changes the subject.

"Impressive, isn't it?" I play along—and she's right, I never get tired of the view from up here.

"Impressive that you can do this."

Her compliment surprises me. "Flattery from you, Miss Steele? But I'm a man of many talents."

"I'm fully aware of that, Mr. Grey," she responds tartly, and I suppress a smirk imagining what she's referring to. This is what I've missed: her impertinence, disarming me at every turn.

Keep her talking, Grey. "How's the new job?"

"Good, thank you. Interesting."

"What's your boss like?"

"Oh. He's okay." She sounds less than enthusiastic about Jack Hyde. Has he tried anything with her?

"What's wrong?" I want to know—has that prick done anything inappropriate? I will fire his ass if he has.

"Aside from the obvious, nothing."

"The obvious?"

"Oh, Christian, you really are very obtuse sometimes," she says with playful disdain.

"Obtuse? Me? I'm not sure I appreciate your tone, Miss Steele."

"Well, don't, then," she quips, pleased with herself. I like that she mocks and teases me. She has the ability to make me feel two feet tall or ten feet tall with just a look or a smile—it's refreshing, and unlike anything I've known before.

"I've missed your smart mouth, Anastasia." An image of her on her knees in front of me pops into my mind and I shift in my seat.

Shit. Concentrate, Grey. She looks away, concealing her smile, and stares down at the suburbs passing beneath us while I check the heading. All is well; we're on track for Portland.

She's quiet, and I steal the occasional glance at her. Her face is lit with curiosity and wonder as she gazes out at the landscape below and the opal sky. Her cheeks are soft and glowing in the evening light. And in spite of her pallor and the dark circles beneath her eyes—evidence of the suffering I've caused her—she's stunning. How could I have let her walk out of my life?

What was I thinking?

While we race above the clouds in our bubble, high in the sky, my optimism grows and the turmoil of the last week recedes. Slowly, I begin to relax, enjoying a serenity I've not felt since she left. I could get used to this. I'd forgotten how content I feel in her company. And it's refreshing to see my world through her eyes.

But as we near our destination my confidence falters. I hope to God that my plan works. I need to take her somewhere private. To dinner, maybe. *Damn it.* I should have booked a table somewhere. She needs feeding. If I get her to dinner, I'll just need to find the right words. These last few days have shown me that I need someone—I need her. I want her, but will she have me? Can I convince her to give me a second chance?

Time will tell, Grey—just take it easy. Don't frighten her off again.

WE LAND ON PORTLAND'S downtown helipad fifteen minutes later. As I bring *Charlie Tango*'s engines to idle and switch off the transponder, fuel, and radios, the uncertainty I've felt since I resolved to win her back resurfaces. I need to tell her how I feel, and that's going to be hard—because I don't understand my feelings toward her. I know that I've missed her, that I've been miserable without her, and that I'm willing to try a relationship her way. But will it be enough for her? Will it be enough for me?

Talk to her, Grey.

Once I've unbuckled my harness I lean across to undo hers and catch a trace of her sweet fragrance. As ever, she smells good. Her eyes meet mine in a furtive glance—revealing an inappropriate thought? What exactly is she thinking? As usual I'd love to know, but have no idea.

"Good trip, Miss Steele?"

"Yes, thank you, Mr. Grey."

"Well, let's go see the boy's photos." I open the door, jump down, and hold my hand out for her.

Joe, the manager of the helipad, is waiting to greet us. He's an antique: a veteran of the Korean War, but still as spry and acute as a man in his fifties. Nothing escapes his notice. His eyes light up as he gives me a craggy smile.

"Joe, keep her safe for Stephan. He'll be along around eight or nine."

"Will do, Mr. Grey. Ma'am. Your car's waiting downstairs, sir. Oh, and the elevator's out of order. You'll need to use the stairs."

"Thank you, Joe."

As we head for the emergency stairwell, I eye Anastasia's high-heeled boots and remember her less-than-dignified fall into my office.

"Good thing for you this is only three floors—in those heels." I hide my smile.

"Don't you like the boots?" she asks, looking down at her feet. A pleasing vision of them hooked over my shoulders springs to mind.

"I like them very much, Anastasia." I hope my expression doesn't betray my lascivious thoughts. "Come. We'll take it slow. I don't want you falling and breaking your neck." I'm thankful that the elevator is out of order—it gives me a plausible excuse to hold her. Putting my arm around her waist, I pull her to my side and we descend the stairs.

In the car on the way to the gallery my anxiety doubles; we're attending the opening of an exhibition by her so-called friend. The man who, last time I saw him, was trying to push his tongue into her mouth. Perhaps over the last few days they've talked. Perhaps this is a long-anticipated rendezvous between them.

Hell, I hadn't considered that before. I sure hope it's not.

"José is just a friend," Ana explains.

What? She knows what I'm thinking? Am I that obvious? Since when?

Since she stripped me of all my armor and I discovered that I needed her.

She stares at me and my stomach tightens. "Those beautiful eyes look too large in your face, Anastasia. Please tell me you'll eat."

"Yes, Christian, I'll eat." She sounds less than sincere.

"I mean it."

"Do you, now?" Her voice is laced with sarcasm, and I almost have to sit on my hands.

Fuck this.

It's time to declare myself.

"I don't want to fight with you, Anastasia. I want you back, and I want you healthy." I'm honored with her shocked, all-eyes look.

"But nothing's changed." Her expression shifts to a frown.

Oh, Ana, it has—there's been a seismic shift in me.

We pull up at the gallery and I have no time to explain before the show. "Let's talk on the way back. We're here."

Before she can say she's not interested, I exit the car, walk around to her side, and open the door. She looks mad as she climbs out.

"Why do you do that?" she exclaims, exasperated.

"Do what?" *Shit—what's this?*

"Say something like that and then just stop."

That's it—that's why you're mad?

"Anastasia, we're here. Where you want to be. Let's do this and then talk. I don't particularly want a scene in the street."

She presses her lips together in a petulant pout, then gives me a begrudging "Okay."

Taking her hand, I move swiftly into the gallery, and she scrambles behind me.

The space is brightly lit and airy. It's one of those converted warehouses that are fashionable at the moment—all wood floors and brick walls. Portland's cognoscenti sip cheap wine and chat in hushed tones while they admire the exhibition.

A young woman greets us. "Good evening, and welcome to José Rodriguez's show." She stares at me.

It's only skin deep, sweetheart. Look elsewhere.

She's flustered but seems to recover when she spies Anastasia. "Oh, it's you, Ana. We'll want your take on all this, too." She hands her a brochure and points us toward the makeshift bar. Ana's brow furrows, and that little *v* that I love forms above her nose. I want to kiss it, like I've done before.

"You know her?" I ask. She shakes her head and her frown deepens. I shrug. *Well, this is Portland.* "What would you like to drink?"

"I'll have a glass of white wine, thank you."

As I head for the bar I hear an exuberant shout. "Ana!"

Turning, I see that *that boy* has his arms wrapped around my girl.

Hell.

I can't hear what they're saying, but Ana closes her eyes, and for one horrible moment I think she's going to burst into tears. But she remains composed as he holds her at arm's length, appraising her.

Yeah, she's that thin because of me.

I fight back my guilt—though it seems she's trying to reassure him. For his part, he looks really fucking interested in her. Too interested. Anger flares in my chest. She says he's just a friend, but it's obvious he doesn't feel that way. He wants more.

Back off, buddy, she's mine.

"The work here is impressive, don't you think?" A balding young man in a loud shirt sidetracks me.

"I've not looked around yet," I answer, and turn to the barman. "Is this all you have?"

"Yep. Red or white?" he says, sounding disinterested.

"Two glasses of white wine," I grunt.

"I think you'll be impressed. Rodriguez has a unique eye," the irritating prick with the irritating shirt tells me. Tuning him out, I glance at Ana. She's staring at me, her eyes large and luminous. My blood thickens and it's impossible to look away. She's a beacon in the crowd and I'm lost in her gaze. She looks sensational. Her hair frames her face and falls in a lush cascade to curl at her breasts. Her dress, looser than I remember, still hugs her curves. She might have worn it deliberately. She knows it's my favorite. Doesn't she? Hot dress, hot boots . . .

Fuck—control yourself, Grey.

Rodriguez asks Ana a question and she's forced to break eye contact with me. I sense she's reluctant to do so, which is pleasing. But damn it, that boy's all perfect teeth, broad shoulders, and sharp suit. He's a good-looking son of a bitch, for a dope smoker, I'll give him that. She nods at something he says and gives him a warm, carefree smile.

I'd like her to smile like that at me. He leans down and kisses her cheek. *Fucker.*

I glare at the bartender.

Hurry up, man. He's taking an eternity to pour the wine, incompetent fool.

Finally, he's finished. I grab the glasses, cold-shoulder the young man beside me who's talking about another photographer or some such crap, and head back to Ana.

At least Rodriguez has left her alone. She's lost in thought, con-

templating one of his photographs. It's a landscape, a lake, and not
without merit, I suppose. She glances up at me with a guarded
expression as I hand her a glass. I take a quick sip from mine.
Christ, it's disgusting, a warm over-oaked chardonnay.

"Does it come up to scratch?" She sounds amused, but I have
no idea what she's referring to—the exhibition, the building? "The
wine," she clarifies.

"No. Rarely does at these kinds of events." I change the subject.
"The boy's quite talented, isn't he?"

"Why else do you think I asked him to take your portrait?" Her
pride in his work is obvious. It irks me. She admires him and takes
an interest in his success because she cares about him. She cares
about him too much. An ugly emotion with a bitter sting rises in
my chest. It's jealousy, a new feeling, one that I've only ever felt
around her—and I don't like it.

"Christian Grey?" A guy dressed like a vagrant thrusts a camera
in my face, interrupting my dark thoughts. "Can I have a picture,
sir?"

Damned paparazzi. I want to tell him to fuck off but decide to
be polite. I don't want Sam, my publicity guy, dealing with a press
complaint.

"Sure." I reach out and pull Ana to my side. I want everyone to
know she's mine; if she'll have me.

Don't get ahead of yourself, Grey.

The photographer takes a few snaps. "Mr. Grey, thank you." At
least he sounds appreciative. "Miss . . . ?" he asks, wanting to know
her name.

"Ana Steele," she answers, shyly.

"Thank you, Miss Steele." He slithers off and Anastasia steps
out of my grasp. I'm disappointed to let her go and fist my hands to
resist the urge to touch her again.

She peers at me. "I looked for pictures of you with dates on the
Internet. There aren't any. That's why Kate thought you were gay."

"That explains your inappropriate question." I can't help smiling as I remember her awkwardness at our first meeting: her lack

of interview skills, her questions. *Are you gay, Mr. Grey?* And my annoyance.

That seems so long ago. I shake my head and continue. "No—I don't do dates, Anastasia, only with you. But you know that."

And I'd like many, many more.

"So you never took your"—she lowers her voice and glances over her shoulder to check that no one's listening—"subs out?" She blanches at the word, embarrassed.

"Sometimes. Not on dates. Shopping, you know." Those occasional trips were just a distraction, maybe a reward for good submissive behavior. The one woman I've wanted to share more with . . . is Ana. "Just you, Anastasia," I whisper, and I want to plead my case, ask her about my proposition, see how she feels, and if she'll take me back.

However, the gallery is too public a setting. Her cheeks turn that delicious pink that I love, and she stares down at her hands. I hope it's because she likes what I'm saying, but I can't be sure. I need to get her out of here and on her own. Then we can talk seriously and eat. The sooner we've seen the boy's work, the sooner we can leave.

"Your friend here seems more of a landscape man, not portraits. Let's look around." I hold out my hand, and to my delight, she takes it.

We stroll through the gallery, stopping briefly at each photograph. Though I resent the boy and the feelings he inspires in Ana, I have to admit he's quite good. We turn the corner—and stop.

There she is. Seven full-blown portraits of Anastasia Steele. She looks jaw-droppingly beautiful, natural, and relaxed—laughing, scowling, pouting, pensive, amused, and in one of them, wistful and sad. As I scrutinize the detail in each photograph, I know, without a shadow of a doubt, that *he* wants to be much more than her friend. "Seems I'm not the only one," I mutter. The photographs are his homage to her—his love letters—and they're all over the gallery walls for any random asshole to ogle.

Ana is staring at them in stunned silence, as surprised as I am to see them. Well, there's no way anyone else is having these. I want the pictures. I hope they're for sale.

"Excuse me." I abandon Ana for a moment and head to the reception desk.

"May I help you?" the woman who greeted us when we arrived asks.

Ignoring her fluttering eyelashes and provocative, overly red smile, I inquire, "The seven portraits you have hanging at the back, are they for sale?"

A look of disappointment flits across her face but resolves into a broad smile. "The Anastasia collection? Stunning work."

Stunning model.

"Of course they're for sale. Let me check the prices," she gushes.

"I want them all." And I reach for my wallet.

"All of them?" She sounds surprised.

"Yes." *Irritating woman.*

"The collection is fourteen thousand dollars."

"I'd like them delivered as soon as possible."

"But they're due to hang for the duration of the exhibition," she says.

Unacceptable.

I give her my full-kilowatt smile, and she adds, flustered, "But I'm sure we can arrange something." She fumbles with my credit card as she swipes it.

When I return to Ana, I find a blond dude chatting with her, trying his luck. "These photographs are terrific," he says. I place a territorial hand on her elbow and give him my best fuck-off-now glare. "You're a lucky guy," he adds, taking a step back.

"That I am," I answer, dismissing him as I usher Ana over to the wall.

"Did you just buy one of these?" Ana nods toward the portraits.

"One of these?" I scoff. *One? Are you serious?*

"You bought more than one?"

"I bought them all, Anastasia." And I know I sound conde-scending, but the thought of someone else owning and enjoying these photographs is out of the question. Her lips part in astonishment, and I try not to let it distract me. "I don't want some stranger ogling you in the privacy of their home."

"You'd rather it was you?" she counters.

Her response, though unexpected, is entertaining; she's admonishing me. "Frankly, yes," I respond in kind.

"Pervert," she mouths, and bites her lip, I suspect to suppress a laugh.

Lord, she's challenging and funny and right. "Can't argue with that assessment, Anastasia."

"I'd discuss it further with you, but I've signed an NDA." With a haughty look, she turns to study the pictures once more.

And she's doing it again: laughing at me and trivializing my lifestyle. Christ, I'd like to put her in her place—preferably under me or on her knees. I lean in closer and whisper in her ear, "What I'd like to do to your smart mouth."

"You're very rude." She's scandalized, her expression prim, while the tips of her ears turn a fetching pink.

Oh, baby, that's old news.

I glance back at the pictures. "You look very relaxed in these photographs, Anastasia. I don't see you like that very often."

She examines her fingers once more, hesitating as if she's contemplating what to say. I don't know what she's thinking, so, reaching forward, I tilt her head up. She gasps as my fingers make contact with her chin.

Again, that sound; I feel it in my groin.

"I want you that relaxed with me." I sound hopeful.

Damn it. Too hopeful.

"You have to stop intimidating me if you want that," she retorts, surprising me with her depth of feeling.

"You have to learn to communicate and tell me how you feel!" I snap back.

Shit, are we doing this here, now? I want to do this in private. She clears her throat and draws herself up to full height.

"Christian, you wanted me as a submissive," she says, keeping her voice down. "That's where the problem lies. It's in the definition of a submissive—you e-mailed it to me once." She pauses, glaring at me. "I think the synonyms were, and I quote, 'compliant, pliant, amenable, passive, tractable, resigned, patient, docile, tame, subdued.' I wasn't supposed to look at you. Not talk to you, unless you gave me permission to do so. What do you expect?"

We need to discuss this in private! Why is she doing this here?

"It's very confusing being with you," she continues, in full flow. "You don't want me to defy you, but then you like my 'smart mouth.' You want obedience except when you don't so that you can punish me. I just don't know which way is up when I'm with you."

Okay, I can see that could be confusing—however, I do not want to discuss it here. We need to leave.

"Good point well made, as usual, Miss Steele." My tone is arctic. "Come, let's go eat."

"We've only been here for half an hour."

"You've seen the photos. You've spoken to the boy."

"His name is José," she asserts, louder this time.

"You've spoken to *José*—the man who, if I am not mistaken, was trying to push his tongue into your mouth the last time I met him, while you were drunk and ill." I grit my teeth.

"He's never hit me," she retaliates with fury in her eyes.

What the hell? She *does* want to do this now.

I can't believe it. *She fucking asked me how bad it could get!* Anger erupts like Mount St. Helens deep in my chest. "That's a low blow, Anastasia." I'm seething. Her face reddens, and I don't know if it's from embarrassment or anger. I run my hands through my hair to prevent myself from grabbing her and dragging her outside so we can continue this discussion in private. I take a deep breath.

"I'm taking you for something to eat. You're fading away in front of me. Find the boy, say good-bye." My tone is clipped as I struggle to control my temper, but she doesn't move.

"Please, can we stay longer?"

"No. Go. Now. Say good-bye." I manage not to shout. I recognize that stubborn, mulish set to her mouth. She's mad as hell, and in spite of all I've been through over the last few days, I don't give a shit. We are leaving if I have to pick her up and carry her. She gives me a withering look and turns with a sharp spin, her hair flying so that it hits my shoulder. She stalks off to find him.

As she moves away I struggle to recover my equilibrium. What is it about her that presses all my buttons? I want to scold her, spank her, and fuck her. Here. Now. And in that order.

I scan the room. The boy—no, Rodriguez—is standing with a flock of female admirers. He notices Ana, and, forgetting his fans, he greets her like she's the center of his whole goddamn universe. He listens intently to everything she has to say, then sweeps her into his arms, spinning her around.

Get your fat paws off my girl.

She glances at me, then weaves her hands into his hair and presses her cheek to his and whispers something in his ear. They continue talking. Close. His arms around her. And he's basking in her fucking light.

Before I'm even aware that I'm doing it, I'm striding over, ready to rip him limb from limb. Fortunately for him, he releases her as I approach.

"Don't be a stranger, Ana. Oh, Mr. Grey, good evening," the boy mumbles, sheepish and a little intimidated.

"Mr. Rodriguez, very impressive. I'm sorry *we* can't stay longer, but *we* need to head back to Seattle. Anastasia?" I take her hand.

"Bye, José. Congratulations again." She leans away from me, gives Rodriguez a tender kiss on his reddening cheek, and I'm going to have a coronary. It takes all my self-control not to haul her over my shoulder. Instead I drag her by the hand to the front door and out onto the street. She's stumbling behind me, trying to keep up, but I don't care.

Right now. I just want to—

There's an alley. I hurry us into it, and before I know what I'm doing I've pressed her against the wall. I grab her face between my hands, pinning her body with mine as rage and desire mix in a heady, explosive cocktail. I capture her lips with mine and our teeth clash, but then my tongue is in her mouth. She tastes of cheap wine and delicious, sweet, sweet Ana.

Oh, this mouth.

I have missed this mouth.

She ignites around me. Her fingers are in my hair, pulling hard. She moans into my mouth, giving me more access, and she's kissing me back, her passion unleashed, her tongue entwined with mine. Tasting. Taking. Giving.

Her hunger is unexpected. Desire bursts through my body, like a forest fire licking through dry tinder. I'm so aroused—I want her now, here, in this alley. And what I'd intended as a punishing I-own-you kiss becomes something else.

She wants this, too.

She's missed this, too.

And it's more than arousing.

I groan in response, undone.

With one hand, I hold her at the nape of her neck as we kiss. My free hand travels down her body, and I reacquaint myself with her curves: her breast, her waist, her ass, her thigh. She moans as my fingers find the hem of her dress and start tugging it higher. My goal is to pull it up, fuck her here. Make her mine, again.

The feel of her.

It's intoxicating, and I want her like I've never wanted her before.

In the distance and through the fog of my lust, I hear a police siren wail.

No! No! Grey!

Not like this. Get a grip.

I pull back, gazing down at her, and I'm panting and mad as hell.

"You. Are. Mine!" I growl, and push myself away from her, as my reason returns. "For the love of God, Ana." I bend over, hands on my knees, trying to catch my breath and calm my raging body. I'm painfully hard for her right now.

Has anyone ever affected me like this? Ever?

Christ! I nearly fucked her in a back alley.

This is jealousy. This is what it feels like: my insides gutted and raw, my self-control absent. I don't like it. I don't like it one bit.

"I'm sorry," she says, hoarse.

"You should be. I know what you're doing. Do you want the photographer, Anastasia? He obviously has feelings for you."

"No." Her voice is soft and breathless. "He's just a friend." At least she sounds contrite, and it goes some way toward pacifying me.

"I have spent all my adult life trying to avoid any extreme emotion. Yet you . . . you bring out feelings in me that are completely alien. It's very . . ." Words fail me. I cannot find the vocabulary to describe how I feel. I'm out of control and at a loss. "Unsettling" is the best I can manage. "I like control, Ana, and around you, that just"—I stand and look down at her—"evaporates."

Her eyes are wide with carnal promise, and her hair is mussed and sexy, falling to her breasts. I rub the back of my neck, thankful that I've recovered some semblance of self-control.

See how I am around you, Ana. See?

I run my hand through my hair, taking deep, thought-clearing breaths. I grab her hand. "Come, we need to talk." *Before I fuck you.* "And you need to eat."

There's a restaurant close to the alley. It's not what I would have chosen for a reunion, if that's what this is, but it will suffice. I don't have long, as Taylor will be arriving soon.

I open the door for her. "This place will have to do. We don't have much time." The restaurant looks like it caters to the gallery crowd, and maybe students. It's ironic that the walls are painted the same color as my playroom, but I don't dwell on the thought.

An obsequious waiter leads us to a secluded table; he's all smiles for Anastasia. I glance at the chalkboard menu on the wall and decide to order before the waiter retreats, letting him know we're tight for time. "So we'll each have sirloin steak cooked medium, béarnaise sauce if you have it, fries, and green vegetables, whatever the chef has—and bring me the wine list."

"Certainly, sir," he says, and rushes off.

Ana purses her lips, annoyed.

What now?

"And if I don't like steak?"

"Don't start, Anastasia."

"I am not a child, Christian."

"Well, stop acting like one."

"I'm a child because I don't like steak?" She doesn't hide her petulance.

No!

"For deliberately making me jealous. It's a childish thing to do. Have you no regard for your friend's feelings, leading him on like that?"

Her cheeks pink and she examines her hands.

Yes. You should be embarrassed. You're confusing him. Even I can see that.

Is that what she's doing to me? Leading me on?

In the time we've been apart, maybe she's finally recognized that she has power. Power over me.

The waiter returns with the wine list, giving me a chance to regain my cool. The selection is average: only one drinkable wine on the menu. I glance at Anastasia, who looks like she's sulking. I know that look. Perhaps she wanted to select her own meal. And I can't resist toying with her, aware that she has little knowledge of wine. "Would you like to choose the wine?" I ask and I know I sound sarcastic.

"You choose." She presses her lips together.

Yeah. Don't play games with me, baby.

"Two glasses of the Barossa Valley Shiraz, please," I say to the waiter, who's hovering.

"Er, we only sell that wine by the bottle, sir."

"A bottle, then." *You stupid prick.*

"Sir." He retreats.

"You're very grumpy," she says, no doubt feeling sorry for the waiter.

"I wonder why that is?" I keep my expression neutral, but even to my own ears *I'm* now sounding childish.

"Well, it's good to set the right tone for an intimate and honest discussion about the future, wouldn't you say?" She gives me a saccharine smile.

Oh, tit for tat, Miss Steele. She's called me out again and I have to admire her nerve. I realize our bickering will get us nowhere.

And I'm being an ass.

Don't blow this deal, Grey.

"I'm sorry," I say, because she's right.

"Apology accepted. And I'm pleased to inform you I haven't decided to become a vegetarian since we last ate."

"Since that *was* the last time you ate, I think that's a moot point."

"There's that word again, 'moot.'"

"Moot," I mouth. *That word, indeed.* I remember I last used it while discussing our arrangement on Saturday morning. The day my world fell apart.

Fuck. Don't think about that. Man up, Grey. Tell her what you want.

"Ana, the last time we spoke, you left me. I'm a little nervous. I've told you I want you back, and you've said . . . nothing." She bites her lip as the color drains from her face.

Oh no.

"I've missed you . . . really missed you, Christian," she says, quietly. "The past few days have been . . . difficult."

Difficult is an understatement.

She swallows and takes a steadying breath. This doesn't sound good. Perhaps my behavior over the last hour has finally driven her away. I tense. Where's she going with this?

"Nothing's changed. I can't be what you want me to be." Her expression is bleak.

No. No. No.

"You are what I want you to be." You are everything I want you to be.

"No, Christian, I'm not."

Oh, baby, please believe me. "You're upset because of what happened last time. I behaved stupidly, and you—so did you. Why didn't you safe-word, Anastasia?"

She looks surprised, as if this isn't something she's considered.

"Answer me," I urge.

This has haunted me. *Why didn't you safe-word, Ana?*

She wilts in her seat. Sad. Defeated.

"I don't know," she whispers.

What?

WHAT?

I'm rendered speechless. I've been in hell because she didn't safe-word. But before I recover, words tumble from her mouth. Soft, quiet, as if she's in a confessional, as if she's ashamed. "I was overwhelmed. I was trying to be what you wanted me to be, trying to deal with the pain, and it went out of my mind." Her look is raw, her shrug small and apologetic. "You know . . . I forgot."

What the hell?

"You forgot!" I'm dismayed. We've been through all this shit because she *forgot?*

I can't believe it. I clutch the table for something to anchor me to the now as I let this alarming information register.

Did I remind her of her safe words? *Christ.* I can't remember. The e-mail that she sent me the first time I spanked her comes to mind.

She didn't stop me then.

I'm an idiot.

I should have reminded her.

Wait. She knows she has safe words. I remember telling her more than once.

"We don't have a signed contract, Anastasia. But we've discussed limits. And I want to reiterate we have safe words, okay?"

She blinks a couple times but remains mute.

"What are they?" I demand.

She hesitates.

"What are the safe words, Anastasia?"

"Yellow."

"And?"

"Red."

"Remember those."

She raises an eyebrow in obvious scorn and is about to say something.

"Don't start with your smart mouth in here, Miss Steele. Or I will fuck it with you on your knees. Do you understand?"

"How can I trust you? Ever?" If she can't be honest with me, what hope do we have? She can't tell me what she thinks I want to hear. What kind of relationship is that? My spirits sink. This is the problem in dealing with someone who isn't in the lifestyle. She doesn't get it.

I should never have chased her.

The waiter arrives with the wine as we stare with incredulity at each other.

Maybe I should have done a better job of explaining it to her.

Damn it, Grey. Eliminate the negative.

Yes. It's irrelevant now. I'm going to try a relationship her way, if she'll let me.

The irritating prick takes too much time opening the bottle. Jesus. Is he trying to entertain us? Or is it just Ana he wants to impress? He finally pops the cork and pours a taste for me. I take a quick sip. It needs to breathe, but it's passable.

"That's fine." *Now go. Please.* He fills our glasses and leaves.

Ana and I haven't taken our eyes off each other. Each trying to discern what the other is thinking. She's the first to look away, and she takes a sip of wine, closing her eyes as if seeking inspiration. When she opens them, I see her despair. "I'm sorry," she whispers.

"Sorry for what?" *Hell.* Is she done with me? Is there no hope?

"Not using the safe word," she says.

Oh, thank God. I thought it was over.

"We might have avoided all this suffering," I mutter in response, and also in an attempt to hide my relief.

"You look fine." There's a tremor in her voice.

"Appearances can be deceptive. I'm not fine. I feel like the sun has set and not risen for five days, Ana. I'm in perpetual night here."

Her gasp is just audible.

How did she think I'd feel? She left me when I'd almost begged her to stay. "You said you'd never leave, yet the going gets tough and you're out the door."

"When did I say I'd never leave?"

"In your sleep." Before we went soaring. "It was the most comforting thing I'd heard in so long, Anastasia. It made me relax."

She inhales sharply. Her open and honest compassion is written all over her lovely face as she reaches for her wine. This is my chance.

Ask her, Grey.

Ask her the one question I haven't allowed myself to think about because I know I'll dread her answer, whatever it is. But I'm curious. I need to know.

"You said you loved me," I whisper, almost choking on the words. She can't feel that way about me still. Can she? "Is that now in the past tense?"

"No, Christian, it's not," she says, as if in the confessional again. I'm unprepared for the relief that rushes through me. But it's relief mixed with fear. It's a confounding combination because I know she shouldn't love a monster.

"Good," I mumble, confused. I want to stop thinking about that right now, and with impeccable timing, the waiter returns with our meal.

"Eat," I demand. The woman needs feeding.

She examines the contents of her plate with distaste.

"So help me God, Anastasia, if you don't eat, I will take you across my knee here in this restaurant. And it will have nothing to do with my sexual gratification. Eat!"

"Okay. I'll eat. Stow your twitching palm, please." She's trying for humor—but I'm not laughing. She's wasting away. She picks up her cutlery with stubborn reluctance but she takes one bite, closes her eyes, and licks her lips in satisfaction. The sight of her tongue is enough to provoke a response from my body—already in a heightened state from our kiss in the alley.

Hell, not again! I stop my response in its tracks. There'll be time for that later, *if* she says yes. She takes another bite and another and I know she'll continue eating. I'm grateful for the diversion that our food has provided. Slicing into my steak, I take a bite. It's not bad.

We continue to eat, watching each other but saying nothing.

She hasn't told me to fuck off. This is good. And as I study her I realize how much I'm enjoying just being in her company. Okay, so I'm tied up in all kinds of conflicting emotions . . . but she's here. She's with me and she's eating. I'm hopeful we can make my proposition work. Her reaction to the kiss in the alley was . . . visceral. She still wants me. I know I could have fucked her there and she wouldn't have stopped me.

She interrupts my reverie. "Do you know who's singing?" Over the restaurant sound system, a young woman with a soft lyrical voice can be heard. I don't know who she is, but we both agree she's good.

Listening to this singer reminds me that I have the iPad for Ana. I hope that she lets me give it to her, and that she likes it. In addition to the music I uploaded yesterday, I spent some time this morning adding more features—photographs of the glider on my desk and of the two of us at her graduation ceremony and a few apps, too. It's my apology, and I'm optimistic that the simple message I've had engraved on the back conveys my sentiment. I hope she doesn't think it's too cheesy. I just need to give it to her first, but I don't know if we'll get to that point. I suppress my sigh because she's always been difficult about accepting gifts from me.

"What?" she asks. She knows I'm up to something, and not for the first time I wonder if she can read my mind.

I shake my head. "Eat up."

Bright blue eyes regard me. "I can't manage any more. Have I eaten enough for Sir?"

Is she deliberately trying to goad me? I scrutinize her face, but she seems genuine, and she's eaten more than half of what was on her plate. If she hasn't eaten anything over the last few days she's probably had enough to eat this evening.

"I'm really full," she reiterates.

As if on cue, my phone vibrates in my jacket pocket, signaling a message. It will be from Taylor, he's probably close to the gallery by now. I glance at my watch.

"We have to go shortly. Taylor's here, and you have to be up for work in the morning." I hadn't considered that before. She's working now—she needs sleep. I may have to revise my plans and my body's expectations. The thought of deferring my desire displeases me.

Ana reminds me that I need to be up for work, too.

"I function on a lot less sleep than you do, Anastasia. At least you've eaten something."

"Aren't we going back via *Charlie Tango?*"

"No, I thought I might have a drink—Taylor will pick us up. Besides, this way I have you in the car all to myself—for a few hours, at least. What can we do but talk?" And I can put my proposition to her.

I shift uncomfortably in my chair. Stage three of the campaign has not gone as smoothly as I anticipated.

She's made me jealous.

I've lost control.

Yes. As usual, she's derailed me. But I can turn this around and close the deal in the car.

Don't give up, Grey.

Summoning the waiter, I ask for the check, then call Taylor. He answers on the second ring.

"Mr. Grey."

"We're at Le Picotin, Southwest Third Avenue," I inform him and hang up.

"You're very brusque with Taylor . . . In fact, with most people."

"I just get to the point quickly, Anastasia."

"You haven't gotten to the point this evening. Nothing's changed, Christian."

Touché, Miss Steele.

Tell her. Tell her, now, Grey.

"I have a proposition for you."

"This started with a proposition."

"A different proposition," I clarify.

She's a little skeptical, I think, but maybe she's curious, too. The waiter returns and I give him my card, but I keep my attention on Ana. Well, at least she's intrigued.

Good.

My heart rate accelerates. I hope she goes for this . . . or I really will be lost. The waiter hands me the credit card slip to sign. I enter an obscene tip and sign my name with a flourish. The waiter seems excessively grateful. And it's still irritating.

My phone buzzes and I scan the text. Taylor's arrived. The waiter gives me my card back and disappears.

"Come. Taylor's outside."

We both stand and I take her hand. "I don't want to lose you, Anastasia," I murmur, and raise her hand and brush my lips against her knuckles. Her breathing accelerates.

Oh, that sound.

I glance at her face. Her lips are parted, cheeks pink and eyes wide. The sight fills me with hope and desire. I stifle my impulses and lead her through the restaurant and outside, where Taylor is waiting at the curb in the Q7. It occurs to me that Ana might be reluctant to talk if he's in front.

I have an idea. Opening the rear door, I usher her in, and walk around to the driver's side. Taylor gets out to open the door for me.

"Good evening, Taylor. Do you have your iPod and head-phones?"

"Yes, sir, never leave home without them."

"Great. Use them on the way home."

"Of course, sir."

"What will you listen to?"

"Puccini, sir."

"Tosca?"

"La Bohème."

"Good choice." I smile. As ever, he surprises me. I'd always assumed his musical tastes leaned toward country and rock. Taking a deep breath, I climb into the car. I'm about to negotiate the deal of my life.

I want her back.

Taylor presses play on the car's sound system and the stirring notes from Rachmaninov swell quietly in the background. He regards me for a second in the mirror and pulls out into the light evening traffic.

Anastasia is watching me when I turn to face her. "As I was saying, Anastasia, I have a proposition for you."

She looks anxiously at Taylor, as I knew she would.

"Taylor can't hear you."

"What?" She looks perplexed.

"Taylor," I call. Taylor doesn't respond. I call him again, then lean over and tap his shoulder. He removes an earbud.

"Yes, sir?"

"Thank you, Taylor. It's okay—resume your listening."

"Sir."

"Happy now? He's listening to his iPod. Puccini. Forget he's here. I do."

"Did you deliberately ask him to do that?"

"Yes."

She blinks in surprise. "Okay . . . your proposition," she says, hesitant and apprehensive.

I'm nervous, too, baby. Here goes. Don't blow this, Grey.

How to begin?

I take a deep breath. "Let me ask you something first. Do you want a regular vanilla relationship, with no kinky fuckery at all?"

"Kinky fuckery?" she squeaks in disbelief.

"Kinky fuckery."

"I can't believe you said that." She looks anxiously at Taylor again.

"Well, I did. Answer me."

"I like your kinky fuckery," she whispers.

Oh, baby, so do I.

I'm relieved. Step one . . . okay. *Keep cool, Grey.*

"That's what I thought. So what don't you like?"

She's silent for a moment, and I know she's scrutinizing me in the light and shadows of the intermittent street lamps. "The threat of cruel and unusual punishment," she says.

"What does that mean?"

"Well, you have all those—" She stops, glancing at Taylor once more, and her voice lowers. "Things in your playroom, the canes, and whips, and they frighten the living daylights out of me. I don't want you to use them on me."

This, I have worked out for myself.

"Okay, so no whips or canes. Or belts, for that matter," I add, unable to keep the irony out of my voice.

"Are you attempting to redefine the hard limits?" she asks.

"Not as such. I'm just trying to understand you—get a clearer picture of what you do and don't like."

"Fundamentally, Christian, it's your joy in inflicting pain that's difficult for me to handle. And the idea that you'll do it because I have crossed some arbitrary line."

Hell. She knows me. She has seen the monster. I'm not going there, or I will blow this deal. I ignore her first comment and concentrate on her second point. "But it's not arbitrary—the rules are written down."

"I don't want a set of rules."

"None at all?"

Fuck—she might touch me. How can I protect myself from that? And suppose she does something stupid that puts herself at risk?

"No rules," she states, shaking her head for emphasis.

Okay, million-dollar question.

"But you don't mind if I spank you?"

"Spank me with what?"

"This." I hold up my hand.

She shifts in her seat, and a silent, sweet joy unfurls deep in my gut. *Oh, baby, I love it when you squirm.*

"No, not really. Especially with those silver balls . . ."

My cock stirs at the thought. *Damn.* I cross my legs. "Yes, that was fun."

"More than fun," she adds.

"So you can deal with some pain." I can't keep the hope out of my voice.

"Yes, I suppose." She shrugs.

Okay. So we may be able to structure a relationship around this.

Deep breath, Grey, give her the terms.

"Anastasia, I want to start again. Do the vanilla thing and then maybe, once you trust me more—and I trust you to be honest and to communicate with me—we could move on and do some of the things that I like to do."

That's it.

Fuck. My heart rate escalates; blood thrums through my body, pounding past my eardrums as I wait for her reaction. My well-being hangs in the balance. And she says . . . nothing! She stares at me as we pass under a streetlight and I see her clearly. She's assessing me. Her eyes still impossibly large in her beautiful, thinner, sadder face.

Oh, Ana.

"But what about punishments?" she says finally.

I close my eyes. It's not a no. "No punishments. None."

"And the rules?"

"No rules."

"None at all? But you have needs . . ." Her voice trails off.

"I need you more, Anastasia. These last few days have been hell. All my instincts tell me to let you go, tell me I don't deserve you. "Those photos the boy took—I can see how he sees you. You look untroubled and beautiful, not that you're not beautiful now, but here you sit. I see your pain. It's so hard knowing that I'm the one who has made you feel this way."

It's killing me, Ana.

"But I'm a selfish man. I've wanted you since you fell into my office. You are exquisite, honest, warm, strong, witty, beguilingly innocent; the list is endless. I am in awe of you. I want you, and the thought of anyone else having you is like a knife twisting in my dark soul."

Fuck. Flowery, Grey! Real flowery.

I'm like a man possessed. I'm going to scare her off.

"Christian, why do you think you have a dark soul?" she cries out, totally surprising me. "I would never say that. Sad maybe, but you're a good man. I can see that—you're generous, you're kind, and you've never lied to me. And I haven't tried very hard. Last Saturday was such a shock to my system. It was my wake-up call. I realized that you'd been easy on me, and that I couldn't be the person you wanted me to be. Then, after I left, it dawned on me that the physical pain you inflicted was not as bad as the pain of losing you. I do want to please you, but it's hard."

"You please me all the time." When will she understand this? "How often do I have to tell you that?"

"I never know what you're thinking."

She doesn't? Baby, you read me like one of your books; except I'm not the hero. I'll never be the hero.

"Sometimes you're so closed off, like an island state," she continues. "You intimidate me. That's why I keep quiet. I don't know which way your mood is going to go. It swings from north to south and back again in a nanosecond. It's confusing and you won't let me touch you, and I want so much to show you how much I love you."

Anxiety bursts in my chest and my heart starts hammering. She said it again; the three potent words I cannot bear. And touching. No. No. No. She can't touch me. But before I can respond, before the darkness takes hold, she unfastens her seatbelt and crawls across the seat and into my lap, ambushing me. She places her hands on either side of my head, staring into my eyes, and I stop breathing.

"I love you, Christian Grey," she says. "And you're prepared to do all this for me. I'm the one who is undeserving. And I'm just sorry that I can't do all those things for you. Maybe with time—I don't know—but yes, I accept your proposition. Where do I sign?" She curls her arms around my neck and hugs me, her warm cheek against mine.

I can't believe what I'm hearing.

Anxiety turns to joy. It expands in my chest, lighting me up from head to toe, spreading warmth in its wake. She's going to try. I get her back. I don't deserve her, but I get her back. I wrap my arms around her and hold her tightly, burying my nose in her fragrant hair, as relief and a kaleidoscope of colorful emotions fill the void that I've carried inside me since she left.

"Oh, Ana," I whisper, and I hold her, too dazed and too . . . replete to say anything else. She snuggles into my arms, her head on my shoulder, and we listen to the Rachmaninov. I go over her words.

She loves me.

I test the phrase in my head and what's left of my heart, and swallow the knot of fear that forms in my throat as those words ring through me.

I can do this.

I can live with this.

I must. I need to protect her and her vulnerable heart.

I take a deep breath.

I can do this.

Except the touching. I can't do that. I have to make her understand—manage her expectations. Gently I stroke her back. "Touching is a hard limit for me, Anastasia."

"I know. I wish I understood why." Her breath tickles my neck.

Shall I tell her? Why would she want to know this shit? My shit? Maybe I can hint at it, give her a clue.

"I had a horrific childhood. One of the crack whore's pimps . . ."

"There you are, you little shit."

No. No. No. Not the burn.

"Mommy! Mommy!"

"She can't hear you, you fucking maggot." He grabs my hair and pulls me out from under the kitchen table.

"Ow. Ow. Ow."

He's smoking. The smell. Cigarettes. It's a dirty smell. Like old and nasty. He's dirty. Like trash. Like drains. He drinks brown licker. From a bottle.

"And even if she could, she doesn't give a fuck," he shouts. He always shouts.

His hand hits me across my face. And again. And again. No.
No.

I fight him. But he laughs. And takes a puff. The end of the
cigarette shines bright red and orange.

"The burn," *he says.*

No. No.

The pain. The pain. The pain. The smell.

Burn. Burn. Burn.

Pain. No. No. No.

I howl.

Howl.

"Mommy! Mommy!"

He laughs and laughs. He has two teeth gone.

I shudder as my memories and nightmares float together like
smoke from his discarded cigarette, fogging my brain, dragging
me back to a time of fear and impotence.

I tell Ana I remember it all and she tightens her hold on me.
Her cheek on my neck. Her soft, warm skin against mine, bringing
me back to the now.

"Was she abusive? Your mother?" Ana's voice is hoarse.

"Not that I remember. She was neglectful. She didn't protect
me from her pimp."

She was a sad excuse and he was a sick fuck.

"I think it was me who looked after her. When she finally killed
herself, it took four days for someone to raise the alarm and find us.
I remember that." I close my eyes and see vague, muted images of
my mother slumped on the floor, me covering her with my blanket
and curling up beside her.

Anastasia gasps. "That's pretty fucked up."

"Fifty shades."

She kisses my neck, a soft, tender press of her lips onto my skin.
And I know it's not pity she's offering. It's comfort; maybe even
understanding. My sweet, compassionate Ana.

I tighten my hold on her and kiss her hair as she nestles in my
arms.

Baby, it was a long time ago.

My exhaustion catches up with me. Several sleepless nights plagued with nightmares have taken their toll. I'm tired. I want to stop thinking. She's my dreamcatcher. I never had nightmares when she was sleeping at my side. Leaning back, I close my eyes, saying nothing, because I have nothing more to say. I listen to the music, and when it's finished, to her soft, even breathing. She's asleep. She's weary. Like me. I realize I can't spend the night with her. She'll get no sleep if I do. I hold her, enjoying her weight on me, honored that she can sleep on me. I can't help my self-satisfied grin. I've done it. I've won her back. Now all I have to do is keep her, which will be challenging enough.

My first vanilla relationship—who would have thought? Closing my eyes, I imagine the look on Elena's face when I tell her. She'll have plenty to say, she always has . . .

> *I can tell by the way you're standing that you have something to tell me.*
> I dare a quick peek at Elena as her scarlet lips curl into a smile and she crosses her arms, flogger in hand.
> *Yes, Ma'am.*
> *You may speak.*
> *I have a place at Harvard.*
> Her eyes flash.
> *Ma'am,* I add quickly, and stare down at my toes.
> *I see.* She walks around me as I stand naked in her basement. The chill spring air caresses my skin, but it's the anticipation of what's to come that makes each of my hair follicles stand on end. That, and the smell of her expensive perfume. My body begins to respond.
> She laughs. *Control!* she snaps, and the flogger bites across my thighs. And I try, really try, to bring my body to heel.
> *Though perhaps you should be rewarded for good behavior,* she purrs. And she hits me again, across my chest this time, but soft, more playful. *It's quite the achievement to get into*

Harvard, my dear, dear pet. The flogger flies again, stinging
my ass, and my legs quiver in response.
Hold still, she warns. And I stand straight, waiting for the
next blow. *So you'll leave me,* she whispers, and the flogger
strikes my back.
My eyes spring open and I glance at her in alarm.
No. Never.
Eyes down, she commands.
And I stare at my feet as panic overwhelms me.
You'll leave me and find some young college girl.
No. No.
She grabs my face, her nails biting into my skin.
You will. Her ice-blue eyes burn into mine, scarlet lips
twisted in a snarl.
Never, Ma'am.
She laughs and pushes me away and raises her hand.
But the blow never comes.
When I open my eyes, Ana stands before me. She caresses
my cheek and smiles. *I love you,* she says.

I wake, momentarily disoriented, my heart thudding like a
klaxon, and I don't know if it's fear or excitement. I'm in the back
of the Q7 and Ana is curled up asleep in my lap.

Ana.

She's mine once more. And for a moment I feel giddy. A stupid
grin splits my face and I shake my head. Have I ever felt like this?
I'm excited for the future. I'm excited to see where our relationship
will go. What new things we'll try. There are so many possibilities.

I kiss her hair and rest my chin on her head. When I glance
out of the window I notice that we've reached Seattle. Taylor's eyes
meet mine in the rearview mirror.

"Are we heading to Escala, sir?"

"No, Miss Steele's."

The corners of his eyes crinkle. "We'll be there in five minutes," he says.

Whoa. We're nearly home.

"Thank you, Taylor." I've slept longer than I thought possible in the back of a car. I wonder what time it is, but I don't want to move my arm to check my watch as I'm holding her. I gaze down at my sleeping beauty. Her lips are gently parted, her dark lashes fanned out, shadowing her face. And I remember watching her sleep at The Heathman, that first time. She looked so peaceful then; she looks peaceful now. I'm reluctant to disturb her.

"Wake up, baby." I kiss her hair. Her eyelashes flutter and she opens her eyes. "Hey," I murmur in greeting.

"Sorry," she mumbles as she sits up.

"I could watch you sleep forever, Ana." No need to apologize.

"Did I say anything?" She looks worried.

"No," I reassure her. "We're nearly at your place."

"We're not going to yours?" She sounds surprised.

"No."

She sits up straight and glares at me. "Why not?"

"Because you have work tomorrow."

"Oh." Her pout says all I need to know about her disappointment. I want to laugh out loud.

"Why, did you have something in mind?" I tease her.

She squirms in my lap.

Ow.

I still her with my hands.

"Well, maybe," she says, looking anywhere but at me and sounding a little shy. I can't help my laugh. She's courageous in so many ways, and yet still so coy in others. And as I watch her, I realize that I've got to get her to open up about sex. If we're going to be honest with each other, she has to tell me how she feels. Tell me what she needs. I want her to be confident enough to express her desires. All of them.

"Anastasia, I am not going to touch you again, not until you beg me to."

"What!" She sounds a little upset.

"So that you'll start communicating with me. Next time we

make love, you're going to have to tell me exactly what you want in fine detail."

That will give you something to think about, Miss Steele.

I lift her off my lap when Taylor pulls up at the curb beside her apartment. I climb out of the car, walk to her door, and open it for her. She looks sleepy and adorable as she struggles out of the car.

"I have something for you."

This is it. Will she accept my gift? This is the final stage of my campaign to win her back. Opening the trunk, I grab the gift box that contains her Mac, her phone, and an iPad. She looks from the box to me with suspicion. "Open it when you get inside."

"You're not coming in?"

"No, Anastasia." As much as I'd like to. We both need to sleep.

"So when will I see you?"

"Tomorrow?"

"My boss wants me to go for a drink with him tomorrow."

What the hell does that fucker want? I must chase Welch for his report on Hyde. There's something off about him that isn't reflected in his employee records. I don't trust him one bit. "Does he, now?" I try to sound nonchalant.

"To celebrate my first week," she says, quickly.

"Where?"

"I don't know."

"I could pick you up from there."

"Okay. I'll e-mail or text you."

"Good."

We walk to the lobby door together and I watch, amused, as she rummages around in her purse for her keys. She unlocks the door and turns to say good-bye—and I can't resist her any longer. Leaning down, I cup her chin in my fingers. I want to kiss her hard, but I hold back and trace soft kisses from her temple to her mouth. She moans and the sweet sound travels straight to my cock.

"Until tomorrow," I say, failing to keep the desire out of my voice.

"Good night, Christian," she whispers, and her longing echoes my own.

Oh, baby. Tomorrow. Not now.

"In you go," I order, and it's one of the hardest things I've ever done: letting her leave knowing that she's mine for the taking. My body ignores my noble gesture and stiffens in anticipation. I shake my head, amazed as ever by my lust for Ana.

"Laters, baby," I call after her and, turning toward the street I head to the car, determined not to look back. Once I'm inside the car, I allow myself to look. She's still there, standing on the doorstep, watching me.

Good.

Go to bed, Ana, I will her. As if she hears me, she closes the door, and Taylor starts the car to head home to Escala.

I lean back in my seat.

What a difference a day makes.

I grin. She's mine, once more.

I imagine her in her apartment, opening the box. Will she be pissed? Or will she be delighted?

She'll be pissed.

She never took kindly to gifts.

Shit. Was it a step too far?

Taylor heads into the garage at Escala and we pull into the vacant parking space next to Ana's A3. "Taylor, will you deliver Miss Steele's Audi to her place tomorrow?" I hope she will accept the car, too.

"Yes, Mr. Grey."

I leave him in the garage, doing whatever he does, and head for the elevator. Once inside, I check my phone to see if she has anything to say about the gifts. Just as the elevator doors open and I step into my apartment, there's an e-mail.

From: Anastasia Steele
Subject: iPad
Date: June 9 2011 23:56
To: Christian Grey

You've made me cry again.

I love the iPad.

I love the songs.

I love the British Library app.

I love you.

Thank you.

Good night.

Ana xx

I grin at the screen. *Happy tears, great!*
She loves it.
She loves me.

*S*he loves me.

It's taken a three-hour car ride for me not to flinch at this thought. But then again, she doesn't really know me. She doesn't know what I'm capable of, or why I do what I do. No one can love a monster, no matter how compassionate they are.

I put the thought out of my mind because I don't want to dwell on the negative.

Flynn would be proud.

Quickly, I type a response to her e-mail.

From: Christian Grey
Subject: iPad
Date: June 10 2011 00:03
To: Anastasia Steele

I'm glad you like it. I bought one for myself.

Now, if I were there, I would kiss away your tears.

But I'm not—so go to sleep.

Christian Grey
CEO, Grey Enterprises Holdings, Inc.

I want her well rested for tomorrow. I stretch, feeling a contentment that's entirely unfamiliar, and wander into my bedroom. Looking forward to collapsing into bed, I put my phone on the nightstand and notice there's another e-mail from her.

From: Anastasia Steele
Subject: Mr. Grumpy
Date: June 10 2011 00:07
To: Christian Grey

You sound your usual bossy and possibly tense, possibly grumpy self, Mr. Grey.

I know something that could ease that. But then, you're not here—you wouldn't let me stay, and you expect me to beg . . .

Dream on, Sir.

Ana xx

P.S.: I also note that you included the Stalker's Anthem, "Every Breath You Take." I do enjoy your sense of humor, but does Dr. Flynn know?

And there it is. The Anastasia Steele wit. I have missed it. I sit down on the edge of the bed and compose my reply.

From: Christian Grey
Subject: Zen-Like Calm
Date: June 10 2011 00:10
To: Anastasia Steele

My Dearest Miss Steele
Spanking occurs in vanilla relationships, too, you know.
Usually consensually and in a sexual context . . . but I am
more than happy to make an exception.

You'll be relieved to know that Dr. Flynn also enjoys my sense
of humor.

Now, please go to sleep, as you won't get much tomorrow.

Incidentally—you will beg, trust me. And I look forward
to it.

Christian Grey
Tense CEO, Grey Enterprises Holdings, Inc.

I watch my phone, waiting for her reply. I know that she won't
let this go. And, sure enough, her response appears.

From: Anastasia Steele
Subject: Good Night, Sweet Dreams
Date: June 10 2011 00:12
To: Christian Grey

Well, since you ask so nicely, and I like your delicious threat,
I shall curl up with the iPad that you have so kindly given me

and fall asleep browsing in the British Library, listening to the
music that says it for you.

A xxx

She likes my threat? Lord, she's confusing. Then I remember
her squirming in the car while we talked of spanking.

Oh, baby, it's not a threat. It's a promise.

I get up and wander into my closet to take off my jacket while I
think of something to say.

She wants a softer approach; surely I can think of something.
And then it comes to me.

From: Christian Grey
Subject: One more request
Date: June 10 2011 00:15
To: Anastasia Steele

Dream of me.

x

Christian Grey
CEO, Grey Enterprises Holdings, Inc.

Yes. Dream of me. I want to be the only one in her head. Not
that photographer. Not her boss. Just me. I change quickly into PJ
bottoms and brush my teeth.

As I slip into bed, I check my phone once more, but there's
nothing from Miss Steele. She must be asleep. When I close my
eyes it occurs to me that I've not thought about Leila all evening.
Anastasia has been so diverting, beautiful, funny . . .

THE RADIO ALARM WAKES me for the first time since she left me. I've slept a soundless and dreamless sleep and I awake refreshed. My first thought is of Ana. How is she this morning? Has she changed her mind?

No. Stay positive.

Okay.

I wonder what her morning routine is?

Better.

And I get to see her this evening. I bound out of bed and into my sweats. My run will take me on my usual route to check on her building. But this time, I won't linger. I'm a stalker no more.

MY FEET POUND THE pavement. The sun is peeping through the buildings as I make my way to Ana's street. It's still quiet, but I have the Foo Fighters turned up loud and proud as I run. I wonder if I should be listening to something that's more in sync with my mood. Maybe "Feeling Good." Nina Simone's version.

Too sappy, Grey. Keep running.

I dash past Ana's building, and I don't have to stop. I'll see her later today. All of her. Feeling particularly pleased with myself, I wonder if perhaps we'll end up here tonight.

Whatever we do, it will be up to Ana. We're doing this her way.

I run up Wall Street, back home to begin my day.

"GOOD MORNING, GAIL." Even to my own ears I sound unusually hearty. Gail stops in her tracks in front of the stove and stares at me as if I've grown three heads. "I'll have scrambled eggs and toast this morning," I add, and wink at her as I head toward my study. Her chin drops, but she says nothing.

Ah, speechless Mrs. Jones. This is novel.

In my study, I check e-mails on my computer and there's nothing that can't wait until I get into the office. My thoughts stray to Ana and I wonder if she's had breakfast.

From: Christian Grey
Subject: So Help Me . . .
Date: June 10 2011 08:05
To: Anastasia Steele

I do hope you've had breakfast.

I missed you last night.

Christian Grey
CEO, Grey Enterprises Holdings, Inc.

In the car, on the way to the office, I get a response.

From: Anastasia Steele
Subject: Old books . . .
Date: June 10 2011 08:33
To: Christian Grey

I am eating a banana as I type. I have not had breakfast for several days, so it is a step forward. I love the British Library app—I started rereading *Robinson Crusoe* . . . and, of course, I love you.

Now leave me alone—I am trying to work.

Anastasia Steele
Assistant to Jack Hyde, Editor, SIP

Robinson Crusoe? A man alone, stranded on a deserted island. Is she trying to tell me something?

And she loves me.

Loves. Me. And I'm surprised that those words are getting easier to hear . . . but not *that* easy.

So I shift my focus to what irritates me most about her e-mail.

From: Christian Grey
Subject: Is that all you've eaten?
Date: June 10 2011 08:36
To: Anastasia Steele

You can do better than that. You're going to need your energy for begging.

Christian Grey
CEO, Grey Enterprises Holdings, Inc.

Taylor pulls up at the curb in front of Grey House.

"Sir, I'll take the Audi to Miss Steele's this morning."

"Great. Until later, Taylor. Thank you."

"Good day, sir."

In the elevator at Grey House, I read her response.

From: Anastasia Steele
Subject: Pest
Date: June 10 2011 08:39
To: Christian Grey

Mr. Grey—I am trying to work for a living—and it's you who will be begging.

Anastasia Steele
Assistant to Jack Hyde, Editor, SIP

Ha! I don't think so.

"Good morning, Andrea." I give her a friendly nod as I stride past her desk.

"Um," she stalls, but recovers quickly, because she's ever the adept PA. "Good morning, Mr. Grey. Coffee?"

"Please. Black." I close my office door, and when seated at my desk respond to Ana.

From: Christian Grey
Subject: Bring It On!
Date: June 10 2011 08:42
To: Anastasia Steele

Why, Miss Steele, I love a challenge . . .

Christian Grey
CEO, Grey Enterprises Holdings, Inc.

I LOVE THAT SHE'S so feisty over e-mail. Life is never boring with Ana. I lean back in my chair with my hands behind my head, trying to understand my effervescent mood. When have I ever felt this cheerful? It's frightening. She has the power to give me hope, and the power to make me despair. I know which I prefer. There's a blank space on my office wall; perhaps one of her portraits should fill the void. Before I can brood on this further, there's a knock on the door. Andrea enters, carrying my coffee.

"Mr. Grey, may I have a word?"

"Of course."

She perches on the chair opposite me, looking nervous. "Do you remember I'm not here this afternoon and I'm not in on Monday?"

I stare at her, completely blank. *What the hell?* I don't remember this. I hate it when she's not here.

"I thought I should remind you," she adds.

"Do you have someone covering for you?"

"Yes. HR is sending someone from another department. Her name is Montana Brooks."

"Okay."

"It's only a day and a half, sir."

I laugh. "Do I look that worried?"

Andrea gives me a rare smile. "Yes, Mr. Grey, you do."

"Well, whatever you're up to, I hope it's fun."

She stands. "Thank you, sir."

"Do I have anything scheduled for this weekend?"

"You have golf tomorrow with Mr. Bastille."

"Cancel it." I'd rather have fun with Ana.

"Will do. You also have the masquerade ball at your parents' place for Coping Together," Andrea reminds me.

"Oh. Damn."

"It's been in the schedule for months."

"Yes. I know. Leave that."

I wonder if Ana will come as my date?

"Okay, sir."

"Did you find someone to replace Senator Blandino's daughter?"

"Yes, sir. Her name is Sarah Hunter. She starts on Tuesday when I'm back."

"Good."

"You have a nine o'clock with Miss Bailey."

"Thanks, Andrea. Get me Welch on the line."

"Yes, Mr. Grey."

ROS IS CONCLUDING HER report on the Darfur airdrop. "Everything has gone as scheduled and early reports from the NGOs on the ground are that it's come at the right time and to the right place," Ros says. "Frankly, it's been a huge success. We're going to help so many people."

"Great. Perhaps we should do it every year where it's needed."

"It's expensive, Christian."

"I know. But it's the right thing to do. And it's only money."

She gives me a slightly exasperated look.

"Are we done?" I ask.

"For now, yes."

"Good."

She continues to regard me with curiosity.

What?

"I'm glad you're back with us," she says.

"What do you mean?"

"You know what I mean." She gets up and gathers her papers. "You've been absent, Christian." Her eyes narrow.

"I was here."

"No, you weren't. But I'm glad you're back and focused, and you seem happier." She gives me a broad smile and heads for the door.

Is it that obvious?

"I saw the photo in the paper this morning."

"Photo?"

"Yes. You and a young woman at a photo exhibition."

"Oh, yes." I can't hide my smile.

Ros nods. "I'll see you later this afternoon for the meeting with Marco."

"Sure."

She leaves, and I'm left wondering how the rest of my staff will react to me today.

BARNEY, MY TECH WIZARD and senior engineer, has produced three prototypes of the solar tablet. It's a product I hope we'll sell at a premium globally, and also underwrite philanthropically in the developing world. Democratizing technology is one of my passions—making it cheap, functional, and available in the poorest nations to help bring these countries out of poverty.

Later that morning we're gathered in the lab discussing the prototypes that are scattered over the workbench. Fred, the VP of our telecom division, is making a pitch to incorporate the solar cells into the rear casing of each device.

"Why can't we incorporate them into the entire casing of the tablet, even into the screen?" I ask.

Seven heads turn my way in unison.

"Not the screen, but a cover . . . maybe?" says Fred.

"Expense?" Barney pipes up at the same time.

"This is blue sky, people. Don't concern yourselves with the economics," I answer. "We'll sell it as a premium brand here and practically give it away in the third world. That's the point."

The room erupts in creativity and two hours later we have three ideas about how to cover the device in solar cells.

". . . Of course we'll make it WiMAX-enabled for the home market," Fred states.

"And incorporate the capability for satellite Internet access for Africa and India," Barney adds. "Provided we can get access." He looks quizzically toward me.

"That's a little down the line. I'm hoping we can piggyback on the EU GPS system Galileo." I know this will take a while to negotiate, but we have time. "Marco's team is looking into it."

"Tomorrow's technology today," Barney states proudly.

"Excellent." I nod in approval. I turn to my VP of procurement. "Vanessa, where are we with the conflict mineral issue? How are you dealing with it?"

LATER, WE'RE SITTING AROUND the table in my boardroom and Marco is running through the modified business plan for SIP and their contract stipulations following the signing of our revised heads of agreement yesterday.

"They want to embargo the acquisition news for a month," he says. "Something about not freaking out their authors."

"Really? Will their authors care?" I ask.

"This is a creative industry," Ros says gently.

"Whatever." And I want to roll my eyes.

"You and I have a call scheduled with Jeremy Roach, the owner, at four thirty today."

"Good. We can hash out remaining details then." My mind drifts to Anastasia. How is her day going? Has she rolled her eyes at anyone today? What are her work colleagues like? Her boss? I've asked Welch to investigate Jack Hyde; just reading Hyde's employee file, I know there's something odd about his career trajectory. He started in New York, and now he's here. Something doesn't add up. I need to know more about him, especially if Ana is working for him.

I'm also waiting for an update on Leila. Welch has nothing new to report on her whereabouts. It's like she's disappeared completely. I can only hope that wherever she is, she's in a better place.

"Their e-mail monitoring is almost as stringent as ours," Ros says, interrupting my reverie.

"So?" I ask. "Any company worth its equity has a rigorous e-mail policy."

"It surprises me for such a small operation. All e-mails are checked by the HR function."

I shrug. "I don't have an issue with that." Though I should warn Ana. "Let's go through their liabilities."

ONCE WE'VE DEALT WITH SIP, we move to the next item on the agenda. "We're going to make a tentative inquiry about the shipyard in Taiwan," Marco says.

"I don't see what we've got to lose," Ros agrees.

"My shirt and the goodwill of our workforce?"

"Christian, we don't have to do it," Ros says with a sigh.

"It makes financial sense. You know it. I know it. Let's see how far we can run with this."

My phone flashes, announcing an e-mail from Ana.

At last!

I've been so busy I haven't managed to contact her since this morning, but she's been hovering at the edge of my consciousness all day, like a guardian angel. My guardian angel. Ever present but not intrusive.

Mine.

Grey, get a grip.

As Ros lists next steps for the Taiwan project, I read Ana's e-mail.

From: Anastasia Steele
Subject: Bored . . .
Date: June 10 2011 16:05
To: Christian Grey

Twiddling my thumbs.

How are you?

What are you doing?

Anastasia Steele
Assistant to Jack Hyde, Editor, SIP

Twiddling her thumbs? The thought makes me smile as I
recall her fumbling with the tape recorder when she came to interview me.

Are you gay, Mr. Grey?

Ah, sweet, innocent Ana.

No. Not gay.

I love that she's thinking about me and has taken time out of
her day to make contact. It's . . . distracting. An unfamiliar warmth
seeps into my bones. It makes me uneasy. Really uneasy. Ignoring
it, I quickly type a response.

From: Christian Grey
Subject: Your thumbs
Date: June 10 2011 16:15
To: Anastasia Steele

You should have come to work for me.

You wouldn't be twiddling your thumbs.

I am sure I could put them to better use.

In fact, I can think of a number of options . . .

Fuck. Not now, Grey.
My eyes meet Ros's, and I sense her disapproval.
"Urgent response required," I tell her. She shares a look with
Marco.

I am doing the usual humdrum mergers and acquisitions.

It's all very dry.

Your e-mails at SIP are monitored.

Christian Grey
Distracted CEO, Grey Enterprises Holdings, Inc.

I can't wait to see her this evening, and she's yet to e-mail where
we'll meet. It's frustrating. But we've agreed to try our relationship
her way, so I put my phone down and turn my attention back to
my meeting.
Patience, Grey. Patience.
We've moved on to discuss the mayor of Seattle's visit to Grey
House next week, an appointment I set up when I met him earlier
this month.
"Is Sam on this?" Ros asks.
"Like a rash," I respond. Sam never misses a PR opportunity.
"Okay. If you're ready I'll get Jeremy Roach on the line from
SIP to go through those final details."
"Let's do it."

BACK IN MY OUTER office, Andrea's replacement is applying yet more lipstick to her scarlet mouth. I don't like it. And the color reminds me of Elena. One of the things I love about Ana is that she doesn't cake herself in lipstick, or any other makeup for that matter. Hiding my disgust, and ignoring the new girl, I head into my office. I can't even remember her name.

Fred's revised proposal for Kavanagh Media is open on my desktop, but I'm preoccupied and finding it hard to concentrate. Time is moving on and I've not heard from Anastasia; as ever, I'm waiting for Miss Steele. I check my e-mail once more.

Nothing.

I check my phone for texts.

Nothing.

What's keeping her? I hope it's not her boss.

There's a knock on my door.

What now?

"Come in."

Andrea's replacement pokes her head around the door and, *ping*, there's an e-mail, but it's not from Ana.

"What?" I bark, trying to remember the woman's name.

She's unfazed. "I'm just about to leave, Mr. Grey. Mr. Taylor left this for you." She holds up an envelope.

"Just leave it on the console there."

"Do you need me for anything else?"

"No. Go. Thanks." I give her a thin smile.

"Have a good weekend then, sir," she offers, simpering.

Oh, I fully intend to.

I dismiss her, but she doesn't leave. She pauses for a moment, and I realize she's expecting something from me.

What?

"I'll see you Monday," she says with an annoying, nervous giggle.

"Yes. Monday. Shut the door behind you."

Looking a little crestfallen, she does as she's told.

What was that about?

I pick up the envelope from the console. It's the key to Ana's

Audi, and written in Taylor's tidy hand are the words: *Parked in allocated parking space at rear of apartment building.*

Back at my desk, I turn my attention to my e-mails, and finally there's one from Ana. I grin like the Cheshire Cat.

From: Anastasia Steele
Subject: You'll Fit Right In
Date: June 10 2011 17:36
To: Christian Grey

We are going to a bar called Fifty's.

The rich seam of humor that I could mine from this is endless.

I look forward to seeing you there, Mr. Grey.

A. x

Is this a reference to fifty shades?
Weird. Is she making fun of me?
Okay. Let's have some fun with this.

From: Christian Grey
Subject: Hazards
Date: June 10 2011 17:38
To: Anastasia Steele

Mining is a very, very dangerous occupation.

Christian Grey
CEO, Grey Enterprises Holdings, Inc.

Let's see what she makes of that.

From: Anastasia Steele
Subject: Hazards?
Date: June 10 2011 17:40
To: Christian Grey

And your point is?

So obtuse, Anastasia? That's not like you. But I don't want to fight.

From: Christian Grey
Subject: Merely . . .
Date: June 10 2011 17:42
To: Anastasia Steele

Making an observation, Miss Steele.

I'll see you shortly.

Sooners rather than laters, baby.

Christian Grey
CEO, Grey Enterprises Holdings, Inc.

Now that she's been in contact, I relax and concentrate on the Kavanagh proposal. It's good. I send it back to Fred and tell him to send it on to Kavanagh. Idly I speculate whether Kavanagh Media might be ripe for a takeover. It's a thought. I wonder what Ros and Marco would say. I shelve the idea for now and head down to the lobby, texting Taylor to let him know where I'm meeting Ana.

50'S IS A SPORTS bar. It's vaguely familiar, and I realize I've been here before with Elliot. But then Elliot is a jock, a real guy's guy, who's the life and soul of any party. This is his type of place, a shrine to team sports. I was too hotheaded to play on a team at any of my schools. I preferred more solitary pursuits like sculling and full-contact sports like kickboxing, where I could kick the shit out of someone . . . or have the shit kicked out of me.

Inside, it's crowded with young office workers starting their weekends with a quick drink or five, and it takes me only two seconds to spot her by the bar.

Ana.

And he's there. *Hyde.* Crowding her.

Asshole.

Her shoulders are tense. She's obviously uncomfortable.

Fuck him.

With great effort I keep my walk casual, trying to maintain my cool. When I'm by her side, I drape my arm over her shoulder and pull her toward me, freeing her from his unwanted advances.

I kiss her, just behind her ear. "Hello, baby," I whisper into her hair. She melts against me as the asshole stands taller, appraising me. I want to rip the "fuck you" expression off his rugged, smug face, but I deliberately ignore him to focus on my girl.

Hey, baby. Is this guy bothering you?

She beams at me. Eyes shining, lips moist, her hair cascading over her shoulders. She's wearing the blue blouse that Taylor bought her, and it complements her eyes and skin. Leaning in, I kiss her. Her cheeks color, but she turns to the asshole who's taken the hint and stepped back a little.

"Jack, this is Christian. Christian, Jack," she says, waving between us.

"I'm the boyfriend," I state, so there's no confusion, and hold out my hand to Hyde.

See. I can play nice.

"I'm the boss," he responds as we shake. His grip is tight, so I tighten mine.

Keep your hands off my girl.

"Ana did mention an ex-boyfriend," he says, with a patronizing drawl.

"Well, no longer ex." I give him a slight fuck-off smile. "Come on, baby, time to go."

"Please, stay and join us for a drink," Hyde says, emphasizing the word "us."

"We have plans. Another time, perhaps."

Like. Never.

I don't trust him, and I want Ana far away from him. "Come," I say when I take her hand.

"See you Monday," she says as she tightens her fingers around mine. She's addressing Hyde and an attractive woman, who must be one of her colleagues. At least Ana wasn't on her own with him. The woman gives Ana a warm smile while Hyde scowls at us both. I sense his eyes boring into my back as we leave. But I don't give a fuck.

Outside, Taylor is waiting in the Q7. I open the rear door for Ana.

"Why did that feel like a pissing contest?" she asks as she gets in.

Perceptive as ever, Miss Steele.

"Because it was," I confirm, and close her door.

When I'm in the car, I reach for her hand because I want to touch her, and raise it to my lips. "Hi," I whisper. She looks so good. The dark circles beneath her eyes have disappeared. She's slept. She's eaten. Her healthy glow has returned. From her bright smile, I'd say she's brimming with happiness, and it washes over me.

"Hi," she says, all breathy and suggestive. Damn, I want to jump her now—though I'm sure Taylor wouldn't appreciate it if I did. I glance at him and his eyes dart to mine in the rearview mirror. He's waiting for instruction.

Well, we're doing this Ana's way.

"What would you like to do this evening?" I ask.

"I thought you said we had plans."

"Oh, I know what I'd like to do, Anastasia. I'm asking you what you want to do."

Her smile widens into a salacious grin that speaks directly to my cock.

Hot damn.

"I see. So . . . begging it is, then. Do you want to beg at my place or yours?" I tease.

Her face shines with humor. "I think you're being very presumptuous, Mr. Grey. But by way of a change, we could go to my apartment." She bites down on her plump lower lip and peers at me through her dark lashes.

Fuck.

"Taylor, Miss Steele's, please." And hurry!

"Sir," Taylor acknowledges, and he heads off into the traffic.

"So how has your day been?" I ask, and brush my thumb across her knuckles. Her breath hitches.

"Good. Yours?"

"Good, thank you." Yes. Really good. I've done more work today than I've done all week. I kiss her hand, because I have her to thank for that. "You look lovely."

"As do you."

Oh, baby, it's just a pretty face.

Speaking of pretty faces—"Your boss, Jack Hyde, is he good at his job?"

She frowns and the *v* I like to kiss forms above her nose. "Why? This isn't about your pissing contest?"

"That man wants into your panties, Anastasia," I warn her, trying to sound as neutral as possible. She looks shocked. Jesus, she's so innocent. It was obvious to me and anyone who was paying attention at the bar.

"Well, he can want all he likes," she says, her tone prim. "Why are we even having this conversation? You know I have no interest in him whatsoever. He's just my boss."

"That's the point. He wants what's mine. I need to know if he's good at his job." Because if not, I'll fire his sorry ass.

She shrugs but looks down at her lap.

What? Has he tried something already?

She tells me she thinks he's good at what he does, but she sounds like she's trying to convince herself.

"Well, he'd better leave you alone, or he'll find himself on his ass on the sidewalk."

"Oh, Christian, what are you talking about? He hasn't done anything wrong"

Why is she frowning? Does he make her uncomfortable? Talk to me, Ana. Please. "He makes one move, you tell me. It's called gross moral turpitude—or sexual harassment."

"It was just a drink after work."

"I mean it. One move and he's out."

"You don't have that kind of power," she scoffs, amused. But her smile fades and she regards me with skepticism. "Do you, Christian?"

I do, actually. I smile at her.

"You're buying the company?" she whispers, and she looks appalled.

"Not exactly." This is not the reaction I was expecting, nor is the conversation going the way I thought it would.

"You've bought it. SIP. Already." Her face pales.

Christ! She's pissed.

"Possibly," I answer, cautiously.

"You have or you haven't?" she demands.

Showtime, Grey. Tell her.

"Have."

"Why?" Her voice is shrill.

"Because I can, Anastasia. I need you safe."

"But you said you wouldn't interfere in my career!"

"And I won't."

She snatches her hand back. "Christian!"

Shit. "Are you mad at me?"

"Yes. Of course I'm mad at you," she yells. "I mean, what kind of responsible business executive makes decisions based on who he is currently fucking?" She glances nervously at Taylor, then glares at me, her expression full of recrimination.

And I want to admonish her for her foul mouth and for overreacting. I start to tell her so, then decide that it might not be a good idea. Her lips are set in the mulish Steele pout that I know so well . . . I have missed that, too.

She folds her arms in disgust.

Fuck.

She's really mad.

I glare back at her, wanting nothing more than to drag her across my knee—but, sadly, that's not an option.

Hell, I was only doing what I thought was best.

Taylor parks outside her apartment, and before he's stopped, it seems, she's out of the car.

Shit! "I think you'd better wait here," I say to Taylor, and I scramble after her. My evening may be about to take a radically different course than the one I'd planned. I may have blown it already.

When I reach her at the lobby door, she's rummaging around in her purse for keys; I stand behind her, helpless.

What to do?

"Anastasia," I entreat her, as I try to remain calm. She lets out an exaggerated sigh and turns to face me, her mouth pressed in a hard line.

Following up what she said in the car, I try for humor. "First, I haven't fucked you for a while—a long while, it feels—and second, I wanted to get into publishing. Of the four companies in Seattle, SIP is the most profitable." I keep talking about the company but what I really want to say is . . . *Please don't fight with me.*

"So you're my boss now?" she snaps.

"Technically, I'm your boss's boss's boss."

"And technically, it's gross moral turpitude—the fact that I am fucking my boss's boss's boss."

"At the moment, you're arguing with him." My voice is beginning to rise.

"That's because he's such an ass."

Ass. Ass!

She's calling me names! The only people who do that are Mia and Elliot.

"An ass?" Yes. Maybe I am. And suddenly I want to laugh. Anastasia called me an ass—Elliot would approve.

"Yes." She's trying to stay mad at me, but her mouth is lifting at the corners.

"An ass?" I repeat, and I cannot help my smile.

"Don't make me laugh when I'm mad at you!" she shouts, trying and failing to stay serious. I give her my best one-thousand-watt smile and she unleashes an uninhibited, spontaneous laugh that makes me feel ten feet tall.

Success!

"Just because I have a stupid damn grin on my face doesn't mean I am not mad as hell at you," she claims between giggles. Leaning forward, I nuzzle her hair and inhale deeply. Her scent and her proximity stir my libido. I want her.

"As ever, Miss Steele, you are unexpected." I gaze down, treasuring her flushed face and shining eyes. She's beautiful. "So are you going to invite me in, or am I to be sent packing for exercising my democratic right as an American citizen, entrepreneur, and consumer to purchase whatever I damn well please?"

"Have you spoken to Dr. Flynn about this?"

I laugh. Not yet. It will be a mindfuck when I do.

"Are you going to let me in or not, Anastasia?"

For a moment she looks undecided, making my heartbeat spike. But she bites her lip, then smiles and opens the door for me. I wave Taylor off and follow Ana upstairs, enjoying the fantastic view of her ass. The gentle sway of her hips as she climbs each step is beyond seductive—more so, I think, because she has no idea she's so alluring. Her innate sensuality stems from her innocence: her willingness to experiment, and her ability to trust.

Damn. I hope I still have her trust. After all, I drove her away. I will have to work hard to rebuild it. I don't want to lose her again.

Her apartment is neat and tidy, as I would expect, but it has an unused, uninhabited vibe about it. It reminds me of the gallery: it's all old brick and wood. The concrete kitchen island is a stark and novel design statement. I like it.

"Nice place," I remark with approval.

"Kate's parents bought it for her."

Eamon Kavanagh has indulged his daughter. It's a stylish place—he's chosen well. I hope Katherine appreciates it. I turn and stare at Ana as she stands by the island. I wonder how she feels living with such a well-off friend. I'm sure she pays her way . . . but it must be tough to play second fiddle to Katherine Kavanagh. Maybe she likes it, or maybe she finds it a struggle. She certainly doesn't squander her money on clothes. But I've remedied that; I have a closetful for her at Escala. I wonder what she'll think about that? She'll likely give me a hard time.

Don't think about that now, Grey.

Ana's studying me, her eyes dark. She licks her bottom lip, and my body lights up like a firework.

"Er . . . would you like a drink?" she asks.

"No thank you, Anastasia." I want you.

She clasps her hands together, seemingly at a loss and looking a little apprehensive. Do I still make her nervous? This woman can bring me to my knees, and she's the one who's nervous?

"What would you like to do, Anastasia?" I ask, and move closer to her, my eyes not leaving hers. "I know what I want to do."

And we can do it here, or in your bedroom, or your bathroom, I don't care—I just want you. Now.

Her lips part as her breath hitches and her breathing quickens.

Oh, that sound is beguiling.

You want me, too, baby.

I know it.

I feel it.

She backs up against the kitchen island with nowhere else to go.

"I'm still mad at you," she asserts, but her voice is tremulous and soft. She doesn't sound mad at all. Wanton, maybe. But not mad.

"I know," I agree, and give her a wolfish grin. Her eyes widen.

Oh, baby.

"Would you like something to eat?" she whispers.

I nod slowly. "Yes. You."

Standing over her, staring into eyes that are dark with desire, I feel the heat from her body. It's searing me. I want to be wrapped in it. Bathed in it. I want to make her scream and moan and call out my name. I want to reclaim her and wipe the memory of our breakup from her mind.

I want to make her mine. Again.

But first things first.

"Have you eaten today?" I need to know.

"I had a sandwich at lunch."

That will do. "You need to eat," I chide her.

"I'm really not hungry right now . . . for food."

"What are you hungry for, Miss Steele?" I lower my face so that our lips are almost touching.

"I think you know, Mr. Grey."

She's not wrong. I stifle my groan and it takes all my self-control not to grab her and toss her onto the concrete counter. But I was serious when I said she'd have to beg. She has to tell me what she wants. She has to vocalize her feelings, her needs, and desires. I want to learn what makes her happy. I lean down as if to kiss her, fooling her, and whisper in her ear instead.

"Do you want me to kiss you, Anastasia?"

She inhales sharply. "Yes."

"Where?"

"Everywhere."

"You're going to have to be a bit more specific than that. I told you I'm not going to touch you until you beg me and tell me what to do."

"Please," she pleads.

Oh no, baby. I'm not going to make this easy on you. "Please what?"

"Touch me."

"Where, baby?"

She reaches for me.

No.

The darkness erupts inside me and grips my throat with its claws. Instinctively, I step back, my heart pounding as fear courses through my body.

Don't touch me. Don't touch me.

Fuck.

"No. No," I mutter.

This is why I have rules.

"What?" She's confused.

"No." I shake my head. She knows this. I told her yesterday. I have to make her understand she can't touch me.

"Not at all?" She steps toward me and I don't know what she intends. The darkness stabs at my insides, so I take another step back and hold up my hands to ward her off.

With a smile, I beseech her, "Look. Ana . . ." But I can't find the right words.

Please. Don't touch me. I can't handle it.

Damn, it's frustrating.

"Sometimes you don't mind," she protests. "Perhaps I should find a marker pen, and we could map out the no-go areas."

Well, that's an approach that I've not considered before. "That's not a bad idea. Where's your bedroom?" I need to move her on from this subject.

She nods to the left.

"Have you been taking your pill?"

Her face falls. "No."

What!

After all the trouble we went to to get her on the fucking pill! I can't believe she just stopped taking it.

"I see."

This is a disaster. What the hell am I going to do with her? Damn it. I need condoms. "Come, let's have something to eat," I say, thinking that we can go out and I can replenish my supply.

"I thought we were going to bed. I want to go to bed with you."
She sounds sullen.

"I know, baby."

But with us it's two steps forward and one step back.

This evening is not going as planned. Maybe it was too much
to hope. How can she be with a fucked-up asshole who can't bear
to be touched? And how can I be with someone who forgets to take
their damned pill? I hate condoms.

Christ. Maybe we are incompatible.

Enough of the negative thinking, Grey. Enough!

She looks crestfallen, and part of me is suddenly absurdly
pleased that she does. At least she wants me. I bound forward and
grab her wrists, pinning her hands behind her and pulling her into
my arms. Her slender body against the length of mine feels good.
But she's slim. Too slim. "You need to eat and so do I." And you've
completely thrown me by trying to touch me. I need to recover my
composure, baby. "Besides . . . anticipation is the key to seduction,
and right now I'm really into delayed gratification." Especially with
no contraception.

She looks a little skeptical.

Yes, I know. I just made that up.

"I'm seduced and I want my gratification now. I'll beg. Please,"
she whimpers.

She is Eve herself: temptation incarnate. I tighten my hold and
there's definitely less of her. It's disconcerting, more so because I
know I'm to blame. "Eat. You're too slender." I kiss her forehead
and release her, wondering where we can dine.

"I'm still mad that you bought SIP, and now I'm mad at you
because you're making me wait." She purses her lips.

"You are one angry little madam, aren't you?" I state, knowing
she won't understand the compliment. "You'll feel better after a
good meal."

"I know what I'll feel better after."

"Anastasia Steele, I'm shocked." I feign outrage and hold my
palm against my heart.

"Stop teasing me. You don't fight fair." All of a sudden her stance changes. "I could cook something," she says, "except we'll have to go shopping."

"Shopping?"

"For groceries."

"You have no food here?" For heaven's sake—no wonder she hasn't eaten! "Let's go shopping, then." I stride to the door of her apartment and open it wide, gesturing for her to exit. This could work in my favor. I just need to find a pharmacy or a convenience store.

"Okay, okay," she says, and scurries out the door.

As we walk down the street hand in hand, I wonder at how, in her presence, I can run through an entire spectrum of emotion: from angry, to carnal, to fearful, to playful. Before Ana, I was calm and stable, but boy, was my life monotonous. That changed the moment she fell into my office. Being with her is like being inside a storm, my feelings colliding and crashing together, then surging and ebbing away. I hardly know which way is up. Ana's never dull. I just hope what's left of my heart can cope.

We walk two blocks to Ernie's Supermarket. It's small, and packed with too many people; mostly singles, I think, judging from the contents of their shopping baskets. And here am I, single no more.

I like that idea.

I follow in Ana's wake, holding a wire basket and enjoying the view of her ass, all tight and taut in her jeans. I especially like it when she leans over the vegetable counter and picks up some onions. The fabric stretches across her behind and her blouse rides up, revealing a sliver of pale, flawless skin.

Oh, what I'd like to do to that ass.

Ana is looking at me, perplexed and asking me questions about when I was last in a supermarket? I have no idea. She wants to cook stir-fry because it's quick. Quick, huh? I smirk and follow her through the store, enjoying how adept she is at choosing her ingredients: a squeeze of a tomato here, the sniff of a pepper there. As we walk to the checkout she asks me about my staff and how long they've been with me. *Why does she want to know?* "Taylor, four years, I think. Mrs. Jones, about the same."

I ask her a question of my own. "Why didn't you have any food in the apartment?"

Her expression clouds. "You know why."

"It was you who left me," I remind her. If you'd stayed we might have worked things out and avoided all the misery.

"I know," she says, sounding contrite.

I stand in line beside her. There's a woman in front of us, trying to wrangle two small children, one of whom is whining incessantly.

Jesus. How do people do this?

We could have gone out to eat. There are enough restaurants around here. "Do you have anything to drink?" I ask, because after this real-life experience, I'm going to need alcohol.

"Beer, I think."

"I'll get some wine."

I put as much distance as I can between me and the screaming boy, but after a brief look around the store I realize there's no alcohol or condoms for sale here.

Damn it.

"There's a good liquor store next door," Anastasia says, when I return to the line which doesn't seem to have moved and is still dominated by the wailing child.

"I'll see what they have."

Relieved to be out of the hellhole that is Ernie's, I notice a small convenience store beside Liquor Locker. Inside, I find the only two remaining packs of condoms.

Thank heavens. Two packs of two.

Four fucks if I'm lucky.

I can't help my grin. That should be enough even for the insatiable Miss Steele.

I grab them both and pay the old guy behind the counter and leave. I'm lucky in the liquor store, too. It has an excellent selection of wine and I find an above-average pinot grigio in the fridge.

Anastasia is staggering out of the grocery store when I return.

"Here, let me carry that." I take both grocery bags and we walk back to her apartment.

She tells me a little about what she's been doing during the week. She's obviously enjoying her new job. She doesn't mention my takeover of SIP, and I'm grateful. And for my part I don't mention her asshole of a boss.

"You look very domestic," she says with ill-concealed amusement when we're back in her kitchen.

She's laughing at me. Again. "No one has ever accused me of that before." I place the bags on the kitchen island and she sets to work unloading them. I grab the wine. The grocery store was enough reality for today. Now, where would she keep a corkscrew?

"This place is still so new. I think the opener is in that drawer there." She points using her chin. I smile at her multitasking and locate the corkscrew. I'm pleased that she hasn't been drowning her sorrows during my absence. I've seen what happens when she gets drunk.

When I turn to look at her, she's blushing.

"What are you thinking about?" I ask as I shrug out of my jacket and toss it on the couch. I make my way back to the waiting bottle of wine.

"How little I know you."

"You know me better than anyone." She can certainly read me like no one else. It's unsettling. I open the bottle, mimicking the cheesy flourish of the waiter in Portland.

"I don't think that's true," she responds, as she continues to unpack the bags.

"It is, Anastasia. I'm a very, very private person." It comes with the territory, doing what I do. *What I did.*

I pour two glasses and hand one to her.

"Cheers." I raise my glass.

"Cheers." She takes a sip and then starts busying herself in the kitchen. She's in her element. I remember her telling me how she used to cook for her dad.

"Can I help you with that?" I ask.

She gives me a sideways I've-got-this look. "No, it's fine. Sit."

"I'd like to help."

She can't hide her surprise. "You can chop the vegetables." It sounds like she's making a huge concession. Perhaps she's right to be wary. I know nothing about cooking. My mother, Mrs. Jones, and my submissives—some with more success than others—have all fulfilled that role.

"I don't cook," I tell her while examining the razor-sharp knife she hands me.

"I imagine you don't need to." She places a chopping board and some red peppers in front me.

What the hell am I supposed to do with these? They are such a weird shape.

"You've never chopped a vegetable?" Anastasia asks in disbelief.

"No."

She looks smug all of a sudden.

"Are you smirking at me?"

"It appears this is something that I can do and you can't. Let's face it, Christian, I think this is a first. Here—I'll show you."

She brushes past me, her arm touching mine, and my body springs to life.

Christ.

I step out of her way.

"Like this." She demonstrates, slicing into the red pepper and removing all the seeds and shit from the inside with one smooth twirl of her knife.

"Looks simple enough."

"You shouldn't have any trouble with it." Her tone is teasing but ironic. Does she think I'm not capable of chopping a vegetable? With careful precision, I start to slice.

Damn, these seeds get everywhere. It's more difficult than I thought. Ana made it look easy. She pushes past me, her thigh brushing against my leg as she collects the ingredients. It's delib-erate, I'm sure, but I try to ignore the effect she's having on my libido, and I continue to slice with care. This blade is evil. She moves past me again, this time skimming her hip against me, then again, another touch, and all below my waist. My cock approves, big-time. "I know what you're doing, Anastasia."

"I think it's called cooking," she says with disingenuous sincerity.

Oh. Playful Anastasia. Is she finally realizing the power she has over me?

Grabbing another knife, she joins me at the chopping board, peeling and slicing garlic, shallots, and French beans. She takes every opportunity to bump into me. She's not subtle.

"You're quite good at this," I concede, as I start on my second pepper.

"Chopping?" She bats her eyelashes. "Years of practice," she states, and brushes up against me with her behind.

That's it. Enough.

She takes the vegetables and places them beside the gently smoking wok.

"If you do that again, Anastasia, I'm going to take you on the kitchen floor."

"You'll have to beg me first," she counters.

"Is that a challenge?"

"Maybe."

Oh, Miss Steele. Bring it on.

I put down the knife and meander over to where she's standing, keeping her pinned with my gaze. Her lips part as I lean past her, an inch away, but I don't touch her. With a twist, I switch off the gas for the wok. "I think we'll eat later." *Because right now I'm going to fuck your brains out.* "Put the chicken in the fridge."

Swallowing hard, she picks up the bowl of diced chicken, rather clumsily places a plate over the top, and puts the whole thing in the fridge. I step up behind her silently so that when she turns I'm right in front of her.

"So, you're going to beg?" she whispers.

"No, Anastasia." I shake my head. "No begging." I look down at her, lust and need thickening my blood.

Fuck, I want to be buried in her.

I watch as her pupils dilate and her cheeks flush with desire.

She wants me. I want her. She bites her lip and I can bear it no more. Grabbing her hips, I pull her against my growing erection. Her hands are in my hair and she's pulling me down to her mouth. I push her against the fridge and kiss her hard.

She tastes so good, so sweet.

She moans into my mouth and it's like a wake-up call that makes me harder still. I move my hand into her hair, pulling her head back so I can angle my tongue deeper into her mouth. Her tongue wrestles with mine.

Fuck—it's erotic, raw, intense. I pull back.

"What do you want, Anastasia?"

"You."

"Where?"

"Bed."

Needing no further prompting, I scoop her into my arms and carry her into her bedroom. I want her naked and yearning beneath me. Putting her gently on the floor, I switch on her bedside light and draw her curtains. As I glance through the window to the street below, I realize this is indeed the room I stared at during my silent vigils, from my stalker's hideout.

She was here, alone, curled up in her bed.

When I turn, she's watching me. Wide-eyed. Waiting. Wanting.

"Now what?" I ask.

She flushes.

And I stay absolutely still.

"Make love to me," she says after a beat.

"How? You have got to tell me, baby."

She licks her lips, a nervous gesture, and lust surges through me.

Shit—focus, Grey.

"Undress me," she says.

Yes! Hooking my index finger into the top of her blouse, careful not to touch her soft skin, I tug gently, forcing her to step toward me. "Good girl."

Her breasts rise and fall as her breathing accelerates. Her dark eyes are full of carnal promise, like mine. Deftly I start to unbutton her blouse. She puts her hands on my arms—to steady herself, I think—and glances at me.

Yeah, that's fine, baby. Don't touch my chest.

I undo the last button, slip the blouse off her shoulders, and let it fall to the floor. Making a conscious effort not to touch her beautiful breasts, I reach down to the waistband of her jeans. I undo the top button and pull down the zipper.

I resist the urge to throw her onto the bed. This is going to be a waiting game. She needs to talk to me. "Tell me what you want, Anastasia."

"Kiss me from here to here." She trails her finger from the base of her ear down her throat.

My pleasure, Miss Steele.

Smoothing her hair out of the way, I gather her soft tresses in my hand and pull her head gently to the side, exposing her slender neck. Leaning in, I nuzzle her ear and she squirms as I trail soft kisses following the path of her finger and back again. She makes a soft noise in the back of her throat.

It's arousing.

Boy, I want to lose myself in her. Rediscover her.

"My jeans . . . and panties," she rasps, breathy and flustered, and I grin against her throat. She's getting the idea.

Talk to me, Ana.

I kiss her throat one final time and kneel down in front of her, taking her by surprise. I push my thumbs into the waistband of her jeans and her panties and slowly pull them down. Sitting back on my knees, I admire her long legs and delectable ass as she steps out of her shoes and pants. Her eyes meet mine, and I await my command.

"What now, Anastasia?"

"Kiss me," she answers, her voice barely audible.

"Where?"

"You know where."

I stifle my smile. She really can't say the word.

"Where?" I coax.

She blushes once more, but with a determined yet mortified expression, she points to the top of her thighs.

"Oh, with pleasure," I chuckle, enjoying her embarrassment. Slowly I let my fingers travel up her legs until my hands are at her hips, then I tug her forward, onto my mouth.

Fuck. I smell her arousal.

I'm already uncomfortable in my jeans, but suddenly they're several sizes too small. I push my tongue through her pubic hair, wondering if I'll ever persuade her to get rid of this, but I find my goal and begin tasting her.

Lord, she's sweet. So fucking sweet.

She groans and fists her fingers in my hair and I don't stop. Swirling my tongue, around and around, teasing and testing her.

"Christian, please," she begs.

I stop.

"Please what, Anastasia?"

"Make love to me."

"I am," I answer, and blow gently on her clitoris.

"No. I want you inside me."

"Are you sure?"

"Please."

No. I'm having too much fun. I continue the slow, lascivious torture of my exquisite, precious girl.

"Christian—please!" she moans. I release her and stand, my mouth wet from her arousal, and stare down at her through hooded eyes.

"Well?" I ask.

"Well what?" she pants.

"I'm still dressed."

She seems at a loss, not understanding, and I hold my arms out in surrender.

Take me—I'm yours.

She reaches for my shirt.

Shit. No. I step back.

I forget myself.

"Oh no," I protest. I mean my jeans, baby. She blinks as she realizes what I'm asking and suddenly drops to her knees.

Whoa! Ana. What are you doing?

Rather awkwardly—her usual fingers and thumbs—she undoes my waistband and fly and tugs my jeans down.

Ah! My cock has some room.

I step out of my pants and remove my socks while she stays kneeling in her submissive position on the floor. What is she trying to do to me? Once I've dropped my pants, she reaches up and grabs my erection and squeezes me tightly like I've shown her.

Fuck.

She pushes her hand back. Ah! Almost too far. Almost painfully. I groan and tense and close my eyes; the sight of her on her knees and the feel of her hand around me is nearly too much. Suddenly, her warm, wet mouth is around me. She sucks hard. "Ah. Ana. Whoa, gently." As I cup her head she pushes me deeper into her mouth, sheathing her teeth with her lips, pressing down on me.

"Fuck," I whisper in veneration, and I flex my hips so I'm deeper in her mouth. That feels so good. She does it over and over, and it's beyond arousing. She swirls her tongue around the end, repeatedly, teasing me. She's all tit for tat today. I groan, reveling in the feel of her adept mouth and tongue.

Christ. She's too good at this. She takes me deep into her mouth once more.

"Ana, that's enough. No more," I insist through clenched teeth. She's unraveling my control. I do not want to come now; I want to be inside her when I explode, but she ignores me and does it again and again.

Fucking tease.

"Ana, you've made your point. I do not want to come in your mouth." I grunt. And still she disobeys me.

Enough, woman.

Grasping her shoulders, I drag her to her feet, lift her quickly, and toss her onto her bed. I reach for my jeans and fish out a condom from the back pocket and dispense with my shirt, dragging it over my head and leaving it beside my jeans. She's lying sprawled and wanton on the bed.

"Take your bra off." She sits up and hurriedly does as she's told, for once.

"Lie down. I want to look at you."

She lies back on her sheets, eyes on me. Her hair is tousled and free, a luscious chestnut halo spilled across the pillow. Her body is flushed a delicate pink with arousal. Her nipples are hard, calling to me; her long legs are parted.

She's stunning.

I rip the foil packet open and roll on the rubber. She watches my every move, still panting. Waiting for me.

"You're a fine sight, Anastasia Steele."

And you're mine. Again.

Crawling up the bed, I kiss her ankles, the insides of her knees, her thighs, her hip, her soft belly; my tongue swirls around her navel and she rewards me with a loud moan. I lick the underside of one breast, then the other. And take her nipple in my mouth, teasing it, elongating it as it hardens between my lips. I tug hard, and she writhes brazenly beneath me, calling out.

Patience, baby.

Releasing that nipple, I lavish my attention on its twin.

"Christian, please."

"Please what?" I murmur between her breasts, enjoying her need.

"I want you inside me."

"Do you, now?"

"Please." She's all breathy and desperate, just how I like her. I push her legs apart with my knees. Oh, I want you, too, baby. I hover over her, poised and ready. I want to savor this moment, this moment when I reclaim her beautiful body, reclaim my beautiful girl. Her dark, smoky eyes meet mine and slowly, slowly, I sink into her.

Fuck. She feels so good. So tight. So right.

She tilts her pelvis up to meet me, throws her head back, her chin in the air, and her mouth is open in soundless adulation. She grasps my upper arms and groans without restraint. What a wonderful sound it is. I place my hands around her head to hold her in place, ease out of her, then slide into her again. Her fingers find my hair, tugging and twisting, and I move slowly, feeling her tight, wet warmth around me as I relish every single fucking inch of her.

Her eyes are dark, her mouth slack, as she pants beneath me. She looks gorgeous.

"Faster, Christian, faster. Please," she pleads.

Your wish is my command, baby.

My mouth finds hers, claiming that, too, and I start to move, really move, pushing and pushing. She's so damned beautiful. I have missed this. Missed everything about her. She feels like home. She *is* home. She's everything. And I lose myself, burying myself in her over and over again.

She starts building around me, reaching her peak.

Oh, baby, yes. Her legs tense. She's close. So am I.

"Come on, baby. Give it to me," I whisper through my gritted teeth. She cries out as she detonates around me, clenching and drawing me deep inside her, and I come, pouring my life and soul into her.

"Ana! Oh, fuck—Ana!"

I collapse on her, pressing her into the mattress, and bury my face in her neck, inhaling her delicious, intoxicating Ana perfume.

She's mine once more.

Mine.

No one will take her away from me, and I'll do everything in my power to keep her.

Once I've caught my breath I lean up and take her hands in mine as her eyes flutter open. They are the bluest of blue, clear and sated. She gives me a shy smile and I trail the tip of my nose down the length of hers, trying to find the words to express my gratitude. In lieu of any suitable words, I offer her a swift kiss as I reluctantly ease out of her. "I've missed this."

"Me, too," she says.

I grip her chin and kiss her once more.

Thank you, thank you, thank you for giving me a second chance.

"Don't leave me again," I whisper. *Ever.* And I'm in the confessional, disclosing a dark secret: *my need for her.*

"Okay," she answers with a tender smile that flips my heart into overdrive. With one simple word she stitches my torn soul together. I'm elated.

My fate is in your hands, Ana. It's been in your hands since I met you.

"Thank you for the iPad," she adds, interrupting my fanciful thoughts. It's the first gift I've given her that she's accepted with grace.

"You're most welcome, Anastasia."

"What's your favorite song on there?"

"Now, that would be telling," I tease her. I think it might be the Coldplay, because it's the most apt.

My stomach growls. I'm starving, and it's not a condition I tolerate well. "Come cook me some food, wench. I'm famished." I sit up and pull her onto my lap.

"Wench?" she repeats, giggling.

"Wench. Food. Now. Please," I order, like the caveman I am, while nuzzling her hair.

"Since you ask so nicely, sire, I'll get right on it."

She wriggles in my lap as she gets up.

Ow!

When she climbs off the bed she shifts her pillow. Beneath it is a rather sad, much deflated helicopter balloon. I pick it up and look at her, wondering where it's from.

"That's my balloon," she stresses.

Oh yes, Andrea sent a balloon with flowers when Ana and Katherine moved into this apartment. What is it doing here? "In your bed?"

"Yes. It's been keeping me company."

"Lucky *Charlie Tango.*"

She returns my smile as she wraps a robe around her beautiful body.

"My balloon," she warns, before she sashays out of the bedroom.

Proprietary, Miss Steele!

Once she's left I remove the condom, knot it, and toss it in the trash basket at Ana's bedside. I fall back onto the pillows, examining the balloon. She kept it and slept with it. Every time I stood outside her apartment pining for her, she was curled up in this bed and pining for me, holding this.

She loves me.

I'm suddenly awash with mixed, bewildered emotions and panic rising in my throat.

How can this be?

Because she doesn't know you, Grey.

Shit.

Don't dwell on the negative. Flynn's words fog my brain. *Focus on the positive.*

Well, she's mine once more. I just have to keep her. Hopefully we'll have the whole weekend together to get to know each other again.

Hell. I have the Coping Together Ball tomorrow.

I could skip it—but then my mother would never forgive me.

I wonder if Ana will accompany me?

She'll need a mask if she agrees.

On the floor, I find my phone and text Taylor. I know he's seeing his daughter in the morning, but I hope he can source a mask.

> I'm going to need a mask for
> Anastasia for tomorrow's event.
> Do you think you can source something?

> TAYLOR
> Yes, sir.
> I know just the place.

> Excellent.

TAYLOR
What color?

Silver or dark blue.

And as I text I have an idea, which may or may not work.

Could you get me a lipstick, too?

TAYLOR
Any particular color?

No. I'll leave that to you.

ANA CAN COOK. The stir-fry is delicious. I'm calmer now that I've
had something to eat and I can't remember being this casual or
relaxed with her. We're both sitting on the floor, listening to music
from my iPod, as we eat and sip chilled pinot grigio. What's more,
it's gratifying to see her devour her food. She's as hungry as I am.

"This is good." I'm appreciating every forkful.

She glows in response to my compliment and tucks a stray
strand of unruly hair behind her ear. "I usually do all the cooking.
Kate isn't a great cook." She's cross-legged beside me, her legs on
display. Her rather worn robe is a fetching shade of cream. When
she leans forward it hangs open and I glimpse the soft swell of her
breast.

Grey, behave.

"Did your mother teach you?" I ask.

"Not really." She laughs. "By the time I was interested in learning how to, my mom was living with Husband Number Three in
Mansfield, Texas. And Ray, well, he would've lived on toast and
takeout if it weren't for me."

"Why didn't you stay in Texas with your mom?"

"Her husband, Steve, and I—" She stops, and her face clouds
with what I assume is an unpleasant memory. I regret asking her
and want to change the subject, but she continues. "We didn't get

along. And I missed Ray. Her marriage to Steve didn't last long. She came to her senses, I think. She never talks about him," she adds quietly.

"So you stayed in Washington with your stepfather."

"I lived very briefly in Texas. Then went back to Ray."

"Sounds like you looked after him."

"I suppose," she says.

"You're used to taking care of people."

It should be the other way around.

She turns to study my face. "What is it?" she asks, concerned.

"I want to take care of you." In every way. It's a simple statement, but it says everything for me. She's taken aback.

"I've noticed," she says wryly. "You just go about it in a strange way."

"It's the only way I know how." I'm feeling my way in this relationship. It's new to me. I don't know the rules. And right now, all I want is to take care of Ana and give her the world.

"I'm still mad at you for buying SIP."

"I know, but you being mad, baby, wouldn't stop me."

"What am I going to say to my work colleagues, to Jack?" She sounds exasperated. But an image of Hyde at the bar, leaning over her, leering, crowding her, springs to mind.

"That fucker better watch himself," I grumble.

"Christian. He's my boss."

Not if I have anything to do with it.

She's scowling at me and I don't want her mad. We're having such a chill time. *What do you do to chill out?* she asked me during the interview. Well, Ana, this is what I do, eat chicken stir-fry with you while we're sitting on the floor. She's still fretting, dwelling on her work situation, no doubt, and what she should tell them about GEH acquiring SIP.

I offer a simple solution. "Don't tell them."

"Don't tell them what?"

"That I own it. The heads of agreement was signed yesterday. The news is embargoed for four weeks while the management at SIP makes some changes."

"Oh." She looks alarmed. "Will I be out of a job?"

"I sincerely doubt it." Not if you want to stay.

Her eyes narrow. "If I leave and find another job, will you buy that company, too?"

"You're not thinking of leaving, are you?" Jesus, I'm about to spend a small fortune on acquiring this firm and she's talking about leaving!

"Possibly. I'm not sure you've given me a great deal of choice."

"Yes, I will buy that company, too."

This could get expensive.

"Don't you think you're being a tad overprotective?" There's a hint of sarcasm in her voice.

Maybe . . .

She's right.

"Yes. I am fully aware of how this looks," I concede.

"Paging Dr. Flynn," she says, rolling her eyes. And I want to reprimand her for that, but she stands and holds her hand out for my empty bowl. "Would you like dessert?" she says with an insincere smile.

"Now you're talking!" I grin, ignoring her attitude.

You can be dessert, baby.

"Not me," she says quickly, as if she can read my mind. "We have ice cream. Vanilla," she adds, and smiles as if she's privy to some inside joke.

Oh, Ana. This just gets better and better.

"Really? I think we could do something with that." This is going to be fun. I rise to my feet in anticipation of what's to come and who's to come.

Her.

Me.

Both of us.

"Can I stay?" I ask.

"What do you mean?"

"The night."

"I assumed that you would."

"Good. Where's the ice cream?"

"In the oven." Her smirk is back.

Oh, Anastasia Steele, my palm is twitching.

"Sarcasm is the lowest form of wit, Miss Steele. I could still take you across my knee."

She arches a brow. "Do you have those silver ball things?"

I want to laugh. This is good news. It means she's amenable to the occasional spanking. But that's for another time. I pat down my shirt and jeans pockets as if in search for some kegel balls. "Funnily enough, I don't carry a spare set around with me. Not much call for them in the office."

She gasps with faux outrage. "I'm very glad to hear it, Mr. Grey, and I thought you said that sarcasm was the lowest form of wit."

"Well, Anastasia, my new motto is 'If you can't beat 'em, join 'em.'"

Her mouth drops open. And she's dumbfounded.

Yes!

Why is it so much fun to spar with her?

I head toward the fridge, grinning like the fool that I am, open the freezer door, and pull out a pint of vanilla ice cream. "This will do just fine." I hold up the container. "Ben. And. Jerry's. And. Ana." From the cutlery drawer, I grab a spoon.

When I look up, Ana has a greedy look and I don't know if it's for me or the ice cream. I hope it's for a combination of both.

It's playtime, baby.

"I hope you're warm. I'm going to cool you down with this. Come." I hold out my hand, and I'm thrilled when she takes it. She wants to play, too.

The light from her bedside lamp is insipid and her room's a little dark. She might have preferred this ambiance at one time, but judging by her behavior earlier this evening, she seems less shy and more comfortable with her nudity. I place the ice cream on her bedside table and drag the duvet and pillows off the bed and onto the floor. "You have a change of sheets, don't you?"

She nods, watching me from the threshold of her room. *Char-*

lie Tango lies crumpled on the bed. "Don't mess with my balloon," she warns when I pick it up. I let it go and watch as it floats to the duvet on the floor.

"Wouldn't dream of it, baby, but I do want to mess with you and these sheets." We're going to get sticky and so is her bedding.

Now to the important question: Will she or won't she? "I want to tie you up," I whisper. In the silence that stretches between us I hear her soft gasp.

Oh, that sound.

"Okay," she says.

"Just your hands. To the bed. I need you still."

"Okay," she repeats.

I stalk toward her, our eyes locked. "We'll use this." I grab the sash from her robe, tug gently, and her robe opens, revealing a naked Ana; a further tug and the sash is free. With a gentle push at the shoulders, her robe falls to the floor. She doesn't take her eyes off mine and she doesn't make any attempt to cover herself.

Well done, Ana.

My knuckles graze her cheek; her face is smooth like satin beneath my touch. I give her a quick peck on the lips. "Lie on the bed, faceup."

Showtime, baby.

I sense Ana's anticipation as she does what she's told, lying down on the bed for me. Standing over her, I take a moment to admire her.

My girl.

My stunning girl. Long legs, narrow waist, perfect tits. Her flawless skin is radiant in the dusky light and her eyes glint darkly with carnal longing as she waits.

I'm a lucky guy.

My body stiffens in agreement.

"I could look at you all day, Anastasia."

The mattress dips as I crawl onto it and straddle her. "Arms above your head," I demand. She complies immediately, and, using the sash, I fasten her wrists together, then to the metal spindles of her headboard.

There.

What a mighty fine sight she is . . .

I give her a quick and grateful peck on the lips and climb off the bed. Once I'm standing, I pull off my shirt and jeans and place a condom on the bedside table.

Now. What to do?

At the end of the bed once more, I grab her ankles and pull her down the mattress so that her arms are fully extended. The less she can move, the more intense the sensations will be.

"That's better," I mutter to myself.

Grabbing the ice cream and spoon, I straddle her again. She bites her lip as I lift the lid and try to scoop out a spoonful. "Hmm, it's still quite hard." I contemplate smearing some of this on me and inserting myself into her mouth. But as I taste how cold it is, I fear it might have a negative, shriveling effect on my body.

That would be inconvenient.

"Delicious." I lick my lips for effect as it melts in my mouth. "Amazing how good plain old vanilla can taste." I watch her and she grins at me, her expression luminous. "Want some?"

She nods—a little uncertain, I think.

I take another spoonful, and offer her the contents so that she opens her mouth. I change my mind and pop it into my mouth. *It's like taking candy from a baby.* "This is too good to share," I declare, teasing her.

"Hey," she starts.

"Why, Miss Steele, do you like your vanilla?"

"Yes," she exclaims, and surprises me by trying to buck me off, but my weight is no match for her.

I laugh. "Getting feisty, are we? I wouldn't do that if I were you."

She stills. "Ice cream," she whines, pouting in frustration.

"Well, as you've pleased me so much today, Miss Steele." I scoop some more onto the spoon and present it to her. She regards me with amused uncertainty, but she parts her lips and I acquiesce, tipping the vanilla into her mouth. My erection hardens as I imagine her lips around me.

All in good time, Grey.

Gently, I ease the spoon from her mouth and scoop up more ice cream. She takes the second spoonful greedily. It's a little runnier, as it's beginning to melt from the warmth of my hand around the tub. Slowly, I feed her another spoonful.

"Hmm, well, this is one way to ensure you eat. Force-feed you. I could get used to this."

She clamps her mouth shut when I offer her more and there's a defiant gleam in her eye as she shakes her head. She's had enough. I tip the spoon and oh-so-slowly the melted ice cream drips onto her throat and as I move the spoon the drips fall on her sternum. Her mouth opens.

Oh yes, baby.

Bending down, I lick her clean with my tongue.

"Mmm. Tastes even better off you, Miss Steele."

She tries to flex her arms, pulling against her robe tie, but it holds, keeping her in place. The next spoonful I dribble artfully over her breasts and nipples, watching with fascination as each nipple hardens under the cold assault. With the back of the spoon I spread the vanilla over each pebbled peak and she squirms beneath me.

"Cold?" I ask, and, not waiting for an answer, I gorge myself, licking and lapping wherever there are rivulets of ice cream, sucking at her breasts, elongating her nipples further. She closes her eyes and groans.

"Want some?" I take a large mouthful, swallowing some, then kissing her, thrusting my tongue and ice cream into her waiting mouth.

Ben. And. Jerry's. And. Ana.

Exquisite.

I sit up and scoot back so I'm straddling her thighs and dribble melted ice cream off the spoon from the bottom of her sternum and down the center of her abdomen. I leave a large dollop of vanilla in her navel. Her eyes spring open in heated surprise.

"Now, you've done this before," I warn. "You're going to have to stay still, or there will be ice cream all over the bed." I pop a large spoonful of vanilla into my mouth and return to her breasts, sucking each of her nipples in turn with my cool lips and tongue. I crawl down her body, following the melted ice cream, lapping it up. She writhes beneath me, her hips pulsing in a familiar rhythm.

Oh, baby, if you kept still you'd feel so much more.

I devour what's left of the ice cream in her navel using my tongue.

She's sticky. But not everywhere.

Yet.

I kneel between her thighs and trail another spoonful of ice cream down her belly and into her pubic hair, to my ultimate goal. I dribble the remaining vanilla onto her swollen clitoris. She cries out and tenses her legs.

"Hush now." Leaning down, I slowly lick and suck her clean.

"Oh. Please. Christian."

"I know, baby, I know," I whisper against her sensitive skin but continue my lascivious invasion. Her legs tense again. She's close.

Abandoning the tub of vanilla so that it falls to the floor, I ease one finger inside her, then another, enjoying how wet, warm, and welcoming her body feels, and concentrate on her sweet, sweet spot, caressing her, feeling her, knowing that she's nearly there. Her climax imminent.

"Just here," I murmur, as my fingers slowly pump in and out of her.

She lets out a strangled cry as her body convulses around my fingers.

Yes.

I withdraw my hand and reach over for the foil packet. And even though I hate these things, it takes only a second to put on. I hover over her while she's still in the throes of her orgasm and thrust into her. "Oh yes!" I moan.

She's heaven.

My heaven.

But she's sticky. All over. My skin is sticking to hers and it's disconcerting. I withdraw and flip her onto her elbows and knees. "This way," I mutter, and reach forward to undo the sash, freeing her hands. When she's free I pull her up so she's sitting astride me: her back to my front. I palm her breasts and tug on her nipples as she groans and tilts her head back so that it's resting on my shoulder. I nuzzle her neck and begin flexing my hips, driving deeper inside her. She smells of apples and vanilla and Ana.

My favorite fragrance.

"Do you know how much you mean to me?" I whisper into her ear as her head is thrown back in ecstasy.

"No," she breathes.

I gently wrap my fingers around her jaw and throat, stilling her.

"Yes, you do. I'm not going to let you go."

Never.

I love you.

"You are mine, Anastasia."

"Yes, yours."

"I take care of what's mine," I whisper, and my teeth graze her earlobe.

She cries out.

"That's right, baby, I want to hear you."

I want to take care of you.

I curl my arm around her waist, holding her against me while I grasp her hip with my other hand. And I continue to thrust inside her. She rises and falls with me, crying out, moaning, groaning. Sweat beads on my back, on my forehead, and on my chest, so we're slipping and sliding against each other as she rides me. She fists her hands and stops moving, her legs braced around me, her eyes closed as she lets out a silent cry.

"Come on, baby," I growl through clenched teeth, and she comes, screaming a garbled version of my name. I let go, coming inside her and losing all sense of self.

We sink onto the bed and I wrap her in my arms as we lie in a sticky, sugary, panting mess together. I take a deep breath as her hair brushes against my lips.

Will it always be this way?

Mind-blowing.

I close my eyes and enjoy this lucid, quiet moment of peace.

After a while she stirs. "What I feel for you frightens me," she says, a little hoarse.

"Me, too, baby." *More than you know.*

"What if you leave me?"

What? Why would I leave her? I've been lost without her. "I'm not going anywhere. I don't think I could ever have my fill of you, Anastasia."

She turns in my arms and studies me, her eyes dark and intense, and I have no idea what she's thinking. She leans up and kisses me, a soft, tender kiss.

What the hell is she thinking?

I tuck a wisp of hair behind her ear. I have to make her believe I'm here for the long haul, for as long as she'll have me. "I've never felt the way I felt when you left, Anastasia. I would move heaven and earth to avoid feeling like that again."

The nightmares. The guilt. The despair sucking me into the abyss, drowning me.

Shit. Pull yourself together, Grey.

No. I never want to feel like that again.

She kisses me once more, a gentle, beseeching kiss, comforting me.

Don't think about it, Grey. Think about something else.

I remember my parents' summer ball. "Will you come with me to my father's summer party tomorrow? It's an annual charity thing. I said I'd go." I hold my breath.

This is a date.

A real date.

"Of course I'll come." Ana's face lights up but then falls.

"What?"

"Nothing."

"Tell me," I insist.

"I have nothing to wear."

Yes. You do. "Don't be mad, but I still have all those clothes for you at home. I'm sure there are a couple of dresses in there."

"Do you, now?" She purses her lips.

"I couldn't get rid of them."

"Why?"

You know why, Ana. I caress her hair, willing her to understand. I wanted you back and I kept them for you.

She shakes her head, resigned. "You are, as ever, challenging, Mr. Grey."

I laugh because it's true and also because it's something I might say to her. Her expression lightens. "I'm gooey. I need a shower."

"We both do."

"Sadly, there's no room for two. You go and I'll change this bedding."

HER BATHROOM IS THE size of my shower, and this has to be the smallest shower cubicle I've ever been in; I'm practically face to face with the showerhead. However, I discover the source of her fragrant hair. Green apple shampoo. As the water trickles over me, I open the lid and, closing my eyes, take a long sniff.

Ana.

I may have to add this to Mrs. Jones's shopping list. When I open my eyes, Ana is staring at me, hands on hips. To my disappointment, she's wearing her robe.

"This shower is small," I complain.

"I told you. Were you smelling my shampoo?"

"Maybe." I grin.

She laughs and hands me a towel that is designed with the spines of classic books. Ana is ever the bibliophile. I wrap it around my waist and give her a swift kiss. "Don't be long. That's not a request."

Lying in her bed, waiting for her return, I look around her room. It doesn't feel lived in. Three walls are stark exposed brick, the fourth smooth concrete, but there's nothing on them. Ana's not had time to make this place home. She's been too miserable to unpack. And that's my fault.

I close my eyes.

I want her happy.

Happy Ana.

I smile.

Ana is beside me. Radiant. Lovely. Mine. She's dressed in a white satin robe. We're in *Charlie Tango*, chasing the dawn. Chasing the dusk. Chasing the dawn. The dusk. High above the clouds we fly. Night a dark shroud arching over us. Ana's hair is burnished, titian, bright from the setting sun. We have the world at our feet and I want to give her the world. She's entranced. I do a wingover and we're in my glider. See the world, Ana. I want to show you the world. She laughs. Giggling. Happy. Her braids pointing to the ground when she's upside down. Again, she calls. And I oblige. We roll and roll and roll. But this time she starts screaming. She's staring at me in horror. Her face contorted. Horrified. Disgusted. At me. Me?

No.

No.

She screams.

I WAKE AND MY heart is pounding. Ana is tossing and turning beside me, making an eerie, unworldly sound that rouses every hair follicle on my body. In the glow of the ambient streetlight I see she's still asleep. I sit up and shake her gently.

"Jesus, Ana."

She wakes suddenly. Gasping. Eyes wild. Terrified.

"Baby, are you okay? You were having a bad dream."

"Oh," she whispers, as she focuses on me, her lashes fluttering like the wings of a hummingbird. I reach over her and switch on her lamp. She squints in the half-light. "The girl," she says, her eyes searching mine.

"What is it? What girl?" I resist the urge to gather her in my arms and kiss away her nightmares.

She blinks once more, and her voice is clearer, less fearful. "There was a girl outside SIP when I left this evening. She looked like me, but not really."

My scalp tingles.

Leila.

"When was this?" I ask, sitting upright.

"When I left work this evening." She's shaken. "Do you know who she is?"

"Yes." What the hell is Leila doing confronting Ana?

"Who?" Ana asks.

I should call Welch. During our update this morning, he had nothing to report on Leila's whereabouts. His team is still trying to find her.

"Who?" Ana persists.

Damn. I know she won't stop until she has some answers. Why the hell didn't she tell me earlier?

"It's Leila."

Her frown deepens. "The girl who put 'Toxic' on your iPod?"

"Yes. Did she say anything?"

"She said, 'What do you have that I don't?' and when I asked who she was, she said, 'I'm nobody.'"

Christ, Leila, what are you playing at? I have to call Welch.

I stumble out of bed and slip on my jeans.

In the living room, I retrieve my phone from my jacket pocket. Welch answers in two rings and any hesitation I had about calling him at five in the morning disappears. He must have been awake.

"Mr. Grey," he says, his voice hoarse as usual.

"I'm sorry to call you so early." I begin pacing what space I have in the kitchen.

"Sleep's not really my thing, Mr. Grey."

"I figured. It's Leila. She accosted my girlfriend, Anastasia Steele."

"Was it at her office? Or at her apartment? When did it happen?"

"Yes. Outside SIP. Yesterday. Early evening." I turn, and Ana, dressed only in my shirt, is standing by the kitchen counter, watching me. I study her as I continue my conversation, her expression a mixture of curious and haunted. She looks beautiful.

"What time, exactly?" Welch asks.

I repeat the question to Ana.

"About ten to six?" she says.

"Did you get that?" I ask Welch.

"No."

"Ten to six," I repeat.

"So she's tracked Miss Steele to her work."

"Find out how."

"There are press photographs of the two of you together."

"Yes."

Ana tilts her head to one side and tosses her hair over her shoulder as she listens to my side of the conversation.

"Do you think we should be concerned for Miss Steele's safety?" Welch inquires.

"I wouldn't have said so, but then I wouldn't have thought she could do this."

"I think you should consider additional security for her, sir."

"I don't know how that will go down." I look at Ana as she folds her arms, accentuating the outline of her breasts as they strain against the white cotton of my shirt.

"I'd like to increase your security, too, sir. Will you talk to Anastasia? Tell her of the danger she might be in?"

"Yes, I'll talk to her."

Ana bites her lip. I wish she'd stop. It's distracting.

Welch continues, "I'll brief Mr. Taylor and Mrs. Jones at a more reasonable hour."

"Yes."

"In the meantime, I'm going to need more personnel on the ground."

"I know." I sigh.

"We'll start with the stores in the vicinity of SIP. See if anyone saw anything. This could be the lead we've been waiting for."

"Follow it up and let me know. Just find her, Welch. She's in trouble. Find her." I hang up and look at Ana. Her tangled hair tumbles over her shoulders; her long legs are pale in the dim light from the hallway. I imagine them wrapped around me.

"Do you want some tea?" she asks.

"Actually, I'd like to go back to bed." And forget all this crap about Leila.

"Well, I need some tea. Would you like to join me for a cup?" She moves to the stove, picks up the kettle, and begins to fill it with water.

I don't want fucking tea. I want to bury myself in you and forget about Leila.

Ana gives me a pointed look and I realize she's waiting for an answer about tea.

"Yes. Please." Even to my own ears I sound surly.

What does Leila want with Ana?

And why the hell hasn't Welch found her?

"What is it?" Ana asks a few minutes later. She's holding a familiar-looking teacup.

Ana. Please. I don't want you to worry about this.

"You're not going to tell me?" she persists.

"No."

"Why?"

"Because it shouldn't concern you. I don't want you tangled up in this."

"It shouldn't concern me, but it does. She found me and accosted me outside my office. How does she know about me? How does she know where I work? I think I have a right to know what's going on."

She has an answer for everything.

"Please?" she presses.

Oh, Ana. Ana. Ana. Why do you do this?

Her bright blue eyes beseech me.

Fuck. I can't say no to that look.

"Okay." You win. "I have no idea how she found you. Maybe the photograph of us in Portland, I don't know." With some reluctance I continue, "While I was with you in Georgia, Leila turned up at my apartment unannounced and made a scene in front of Gail."

"Gail?"

"Mrs. Jones."

"What do you mean made a scene?"

I shake my head.

"Tell me." She puts her hands on her hips. "You're keeping something back."

"Ana, I—" Why is she so mad? I don't want her mixed up in this. She doesn't understand that Leila's shame is my shame. Leila chose to attempt suicide in *my* apartment and I wasn't there to help her; she cried out to me for a reason.

"Please?" Ana prompts again.

She won't give up. I sigh with exasperation and tell her that Leila made a haphazard attempt at suicide.

"Oh no!"

"Gail got her to the hospital. But Leila discharged herself before I could get there. The shrink who saw her called it a typical cry for help. He didn't believe her to be truly at risk—one step from suicidal ideation, he called it. But I'm not convinced. I've been trying to track her down since then to get her some help."

"Did she say anything to Mrs. Jones?"

"Not much."

"You can't find her? What about her family?"

"They don't know where she is. Neither does her husband."

"Husband?" she exclaims.

"Yes." *That lying asshole.* "She's been married for about two years."

"So she was with you while she was married?"

"No! Good God, no. She was with me nearly three years ago. Then she left and married this guy shortly afterward." *I told you, baby, I don't share.* I've only tangled with one married woman and that didn't end well.

"So why is she trying to get your attention now?"

"I don't know. All we've managed to find out is that she ran out on her husband about four months ago."

Ana picks up a teaspoon and waves it as she talks. "Let me get this straight. She hasn't been your submissive for three years?"

"About two and a half years."

"And she wanted more."

"Yes."

"But you didn't?"

"You know this."

"So she left you."

"Yes."

"So why is she coming to you now?"

"I don't know." She wanted more, but I couldn't give her that. *Maybe she's seen me with you?*

"But you suspect—"

"I suspect it has something to do with you." *But I could be wrong.*

Now can we go back to bed?

Ana studies me, surveying my chest. But I ignore her scrutiny and ask the question that's been nagging me since she told me she'd seen Leila. "Why didn't you tell me yesterday?"

Ana has the grace to look guilty. "I forgot about her. You know, drinks after work, at the end of my first week. You turning up at the bar and your testosterone rush with Jack." She gives me a shy smile. "And then when we were here. It slipped my mind. You have a habit of making me forget things."

I'd like to forget this now. Let's go back to bed.

"Testosterone rush?" I repeat, amused.

"Yes. The pissing contest."

"I'll show you a testosterone rush." My voice is low.

"Wouldn't you rather have a cup of tea?" She offers me a cup.

"No, Anastasia, I wouldn't." *I want you. Now.* "Forget about her. Come." I hold out my hand. She sets the teacup back on the counter and puts her hand in mine.

Back in her bedroom, I slide my shirt over her head. "I like you wearing my clothes," I whisper.

"I like wearing them. They smell of you."

I grasp her head between my hands and kiss her.

I want to make her forget about Leila.

I want to forget about Leila.

I pick her up and walk her to the concrete wall.

"Wrap your legs around me, baby," I order.

WHEN I OPEN MY eyes the room is bathed with light and Ana is awake beside me, tucked in the crook of my arm. "Hi," she says, grinning as if she's up to some mischief.

"Hi," I respond, cautiously. Something is off. "What are you doing?"

"Looking at you." She skims her hand down my belly. And my body comes to life.

Whoa!

I grab her hand.

Surely she's sore after yesterday.

She licks her lips and her guilty grin is replaced with a knowledgeable, carnal smile.

Maybe not.

Waking up beside Anastasia Steele has definite advantages. Rolling on top of her, I grab her hands and pin her to the bed as she wriggles beneath me. "I think you're up to no good, Miss Steele."

"I like being up to no good near you."

She may as well be addressing my groin directly.

"You do?" I give her a quick peck on the lips. She nods.

Oh, you beautiful girl. "Sex or breakfast?"

She tilts her hips to meet me and it takes all my self-control not to take what she's offering straightaway.

No. Make her wait.

"Good choice." I kiss her throat, her clavicle, her sternum, her breast.

"Ah," she breathes.

WE LIE IN THE afterglow.

I don't remember moments like this before Ana. I didn't lie in bed just . . . being. I nuzzle her hair. All that's changed.

She opens her eyes.

"Hi."

"Hi."

"Are you sore?" I ask.

Her cheeks pink. "No. Tired."

I stroke her cheek. "You didn't get much sleep last night."

"Neither did you." Her smile is one hundred percent coy Miss Steele, but her eyes cloud. "I haven't been sleeping well, recently."

Remorse—swift and ugly, flares in my gut. "I'm sorry," I reply.

"Don't apologize. It was my—"

I place my finger on her mouth. "Hush."

She purses her lips to kiss my finger.

"If it's any consolation," I confess, "I haven't slept well this past week, either."

"Oh, Christian," she says, and, taking my hand, kisses each knuckle in turn. It's an affectionate, humble gesture. My throat constricts as my heart expands. I'm on the edge of something unknown, a plain where the horizon disappears and the territory is new and unexplored.

It's terrifying.

It's confusing.

It's exciting.

What are you doing to me, Ana?

Where are you leading me?

I take a deep breath and focus on the woman beside me. She gives me a sexy smile and I can see us spending the entire day in bed, but I realize I'm hungry. "Breakfast?" I ask.

"Are you offering to make breakfast or demanding to be fed, Mr. Grey?" she teases.

"Neither. I'll buy you breakfast. I'm no good in the kitchen, as I demonstrated last night."

"You have other qualities," she says with a playful smirk.

"Why, Miss Steele, whatever do you mean?"

She narrows her eyes. "I think you know." She's teasing me. She sits up slowly, swinging her legs out of bed. "You can shower in Kate's bathroom. It's bigger than mine."

Of course it is.

"I'll use yours. I like being in your space."

"I like you being in my space, too." She winks, gets up, and struts out of the bedroom.

Brazen Ana.

WHEN I RETURN FROM the cramped shower, I find Ana dressed in jeans and a tight T-shirt that leaves little to my imagination. She's messing with her hair.

As I yank on my jeans I feel the Audi key in my pocket. I wonder how she'll react when I give it back to her. She seemed to take the iPad well.

"How often do you work out?" she asks, and I realize she's watching me in the mirror.

"Every weekday."

"What do you do?"

"Run, weights, kickboxing." Sprinting to and from your apartment for the past week.

"Kickboxing?" she queries.

"Yes, I have a personal trainer, an ex–Olympic contender who teaches me. His name is Claude. He's very good." I tell Ana that she'd like him as a trainer.

"Why would I need a personal trainer? I have you to keep me fit."

I walk over to where she stands, still fiddling with her hair, and I embrace her. Our eyes meet in the mirror. "But I want you fit, baby, for what I have in mind. I'll need you to keep up." *That's if we ever get back into the playroom.*

She arches a brow.

"You know you want to." I mouth the words at her reflection. She toys with her lip but then breaks our eye contact.

"What?" I ask, concerned.

"Nothing," she says, and shakes her head. "Okay, I'll meet Claude."

"You will?"

That was easy!

"Yes, jeez. If it makes you that happy," she says, and laughs.

I squeeze her and give her a peck on her cheek. "You have no idea." I kiss her behind her ear. "So what would you like to do today?"

"I'd like to get my hair cut, and, um, I need to bank a check and buy a car."

"Ah."

Here goes. From my jeans pocket I fish out the Audi key. "It's here," I inform her.

She looks blank, but then her cheeks pink and I realize she's upset.

"What do you mean it's here?"

"Taylor brought it back yesterday."

She steps out of my embrace, scowling at me.

Shit. She's pissed. Why?

From the back pocket of her jeans she brandishes an envelope. "Here, this is yours." I recognize it as the envelope that I put the check in for her ancient Beetle. I lift both hands and step away. "Oh no. That's your money."

"No, it isn't. I'd like to buy the car from you."

What. The. Hell.

She wants to give *me* money! "No, Anastasia. Your money, your car."

"No, Christian. My money, your car. I'll buy it from you."

Oh. No. You. Don't.

"I gave you that car for your graduation present." And you said you'd accept it.

"If you'd given me a pen, that would be a suitable graduation present. You gave me an Audi."

"Do you really want to argue about this?"

"No."

"Good. Here are the keys." I place her keys on the dresser.

"That's not what I meant!"

"End of discussion, Anastasia. Don't push me."

The look she's giving me now says it all. If I were dry tinder I would burst into flame, and not in a good way. She's mad. Really mad. Suddenly she narrows her eyes and gives me a wicked smile. Taking the envelope, she holds it aloft and, in a rather theatrical manner, rips it in half, and in half again. She drops the contents in her trash basket and gives me a victorious fuck-you look.

Oh. Game on, Ana.

"You are, as ever, challenging, Miss Steele." I echo the words she used yesterday and turn on my heel and head into the kitchen.

Now I'm pissed. Fucking pissed.

How dare she?

I find my phone and call Andrea.

"Good morning, Mr. Grey." She sounds a little breathless when she answers.

"Hi, Andrea."

In the background, on her side of the call, I hear a woman shouting, "Doesn't he realize you're getting married today, Andrea?" Andrea's voice comes through, "Excuse me, Mr. Grey."

Married!

There's the sound of muffled fumbling. "Mom, be quiet. It's my boss." The muffling ceases. "What can I do for you, Mr. Grey?" she says.

"You're getting married?"

"Yes, sir."

"Today?"

"Yes. What is it you want me to do?"

"I wanted you to deposit twenty-four thousand dollars into Anastasia Steele's bank account."

"Twenty-four thousand?"

"Yes, twenty-four thousand dollars. Directly."

"I'll take care of it. It will be in her account on Monday."

"Monday?"

"Yes, sir."

"Excellent."

"Anything else, sir?"

"No, that's all, Andrea."

I hang up, aggravated that I've disturbed her on her wedding day and more aggravated that she didn't tell me she was getting married.

Why wouldn't she tell me? Is she pregnant?

Will I have to find a new PA?

I turn to Miss Steele, who is fuming on the threshold.

"Deposited in your bank account Monday. Don't play games with me."

"Twenty-four thousand dollars!" she shouts. "And how do you know my account number?"

"I know everything about you, Anastasia," I reply, trying to keep my cool.

"There's no way my car was worth twenty-four thousand dollars," she counters.

"I would agree with you, but it's about knowing your market, whether you're buying or selling. Some lunatic out there wanted that deathtrap and was willing to pay that amount of money. Apparently, it's a classic. Ask Taylor if you don't believe me."

We glower at each other.

Impossible woman.

Impossible. Impossible.

Her lips part. She's breathless, her pupils dilated. Drinking me in. Consuming me.

Ana.

Her tongue licks her lower lip.

And it's there in the air between us.

Our attraction, a living force. Building. Building.

Fuck.

I grab her and push her against the door, my lips seeking and finding hers. I claim her mouth, kissing her greedily, my fingers closing around the nape of her neck, holding her. Her fingers are in my hair. Pulling. Directing me while she kisses me back, her tongue in my mouth. Taking. Everything. I cup her behind and pull her against my erection and grind my body into hers. I want her. Again.

"Why, why do you defy me?" I say out loud as I kiss her neckline. She tilts her head back to give me full access to her throat.

"Because I can," she whispers.

Ah. She stole my line.

I'm panting when I lean my forehead against hers.

"Lord, I want to take you now, but I'm out of condoms. I can never get enough of you. You're a maddening, maddening woman."

"And you make me mad," she breathes. "In every way."

I take a deep breath and look down into dark, hungry eyes that promise me the world, and I shake my head.

Steady, Grey.

"Come. Let's go out for breakfast. And I know a place you can get your hair cut."

"Okay." She smiles.

And we fight no more.

WE WALK HAND IN hand up Vine Street and turn right on First Avenue. I wonder how normal it is to go from seething at each other to this casual calm I feel as we walk through the streets. Maybe most couples are like this. I look down at Ana beside me. "This feels so normal," I tell her. "I love it."

"Christian, I think Dr. Flynn would agree that you are anything but normal. Exceptional, maybe." She squeezes my hand.

Exceptional!

"It's a beautiful day," she adds.

"It is."

She briefly closes her eyes and turns her face to the morning sun.

"Come, I know a great place for brunch."

One of my favorite cafés is only a couple of blocks from Ana's on First. When we get there I open the door for Ana and pause to inhale the smell of fresh bread.

"What a charming place," she says when we sit down at a table. "I love the art on the walls."

"They support a different artist every month. I found Trouton here."

"Raising the ordinary to extraordinary," Ana says.

"You remembered."

"There's very little I could forget about you, Mr. Grey."

And I you, Miss Steele. You are extraordinary.

I chuckle and hand her a menu.

"I'LL GET THIS." Ana grabs the check before I do. "You have to be quick around here, Grey."

"You're right, I do," I grumble. Someone who owes more than fifty thousand dollars in student-loan debt should not be paying for my breakfast.

"Don't look so cross. I'm twenty-four thousand dollars richer than I was this morning. I can afford—" She inspects the bill. "Twenty-two dollars and sixty-seven cents for breakfast."

Short of wrestling the check from her, there's little I can do. "Thank you," I mutter.

"Where to now?" she asks.

"You really want your hair cut?"

"Yes, look at it."

Dark tendrils have escaped from her ponytail, framing her beautiful face. "You look lovely to me. You always do."

"There's your father's function this evening."

I remind her that it's black tie and at my parents' home. "They have a tent. You know, the works."

"What's the charity?"

"It's a drug-rehab program for parents with young kids called Coping Together." I hold my breath, hoping that she doesn't start to ask me about the Grey connection to this cause. It's personal and I don't need her pity. I've told her all I want to tell her about that time in my life.

"Sounds like a good cause," she says with compassion, and thankfully leaves it there.

"Come, let's go." I stand and hold out my hand, ending the conversation.

"Where are we going?" she asks, as we continue our walk down First Avenue.

"Surprise."

I can't tell her it's Elena's place. I know she'll freak. From our conversation in Savannah, I know the mere mention of her name is a hot button for Ana. It's Saturday and Elena doesn't work on weekends, and when she does work it's at the salon in the Bravern Center.

"Here we are." I open the door at Esclava and usher Ana in. I haven't been here for a couple of months; the last time was with Susannah.

"Good morning, Mr. Grey," Greta greets us.

"Hello, Greta."

"Is this the usual, sir?" she asks politely.

Fuck. "No." I give Ana a nervous look. "Miss Steele will tell you what she wants."

Ana's eyes are on me, burning with insight. "Why here?" she demands.

"I own this place, and three more like it."

"You own it?"

"Yes. It's a sideline. Anyway—whatever you want, you can have it here, on the house." I run through all the spa treatments available. "All that stuff that women like—everything. It's done here."

"Waxing?"

For a split second I think about recommending the chocolate wax for her pubic hair, but given our détente, I keep my suggestion to myself. "Yes, waxing, too . . . everywhere."

Ana blushes.

How will I ever convince her that penetrative sex would be more pleasurable for her without the hair?

One step at a time, Grey.

"I'd like a haircut, please," she says to Greta.

"Certainly, Miss Steele."

Greta concentrates on her computer and punches a few keys. "Franco is free in five minutes."

"Franco's fine," I confirm, but notice Ana's demeanor has suddenly changed. I'm about to ask what's wrong when I glance up and see Elena walking out of the back office.

Hell. What's she doing here?

Elena has a quick word with one of her employees, then she spies me and lights up like Christmas, her expression one of wicked delight.

Shit.

"Excuse me," I say to Ana, and hurry to meet Elena before she makes her way to us.

"Well, this is an unexpected pleasure," Elena purrs in greeting as she kisses me on both cheeks.

"Good morning, Ma'am. I wasn't expecting to see you here."

"My aesthetician called in sick. So, you *have* been avoiding me."

"I've been busy."

"I can see. Is that someone new?"

"That is Anastasia Steele."

Elena beams at Ana, who is watching us intently. She knows that we're talking about her, and she responds with a lukewarm smile.

Damn.

"Your little southern belle?" Elena asks.

"She's not southern."

"I thought you went to Georgia to see her."

"Her mom lives there."

"I see. She certainly looks like your type."

"Yeah." *Let's not go there.*

"Are you going to introduce me?"

Ana is talking to Greta—grilling her, I think. *What's she asking?*

"I don't think that's a good idea."

Elena looks disappointed. "Why not?"

"She's named you Mrs. Robinson."

"Oh, really? That's funny. Though I'm surprised someone that young knows the reference." Elena's tone is wry. "I'm also astonished you told her about us. What happened to confidentiality?" She taps a scarlet fingernail against her lips.

"She's not going to talk."

"I hope so. Look, don't worry. I'll back off." She holds her hands up in surrender.

"Thank you."

"But is this a good idea, Christian? She's hurt you once already." Elena's face is etched with concern.

"I don't know. I missed her. She missed me. I've decided I'm going to try it her way. She's willing."

"Her way? Are you sure you can? Are you sure you want to?"

Ana is still staring at us. She's alarmed.

"Time will tell," I answer.

"Well, I'm here if you need me. Good luck." She gives me a soft but calculated smile. "Don't be a stranger."

"Thanks. Are you going to my parents' soirée this evening?"

"I don't think so."

"That's probably a good idea."

She looks momentarily surprised, but says, "Let's catch up later this week when we can talk more freely."

"Sure."

She squeezes my arm and I head back to Ana, who is still waiting by the reception desk. Her face is pinched and her arms are folded across her body as she radiates her displeasure.

This is not good.

"Are you okay?" I ask, knowing full well that she isn't.

"Not really. You didn't want to introduce me?" she replies, in a tone that's both sarcastic and indignant.

Christ. She knows it's Elena. How? "But I thought—"

Ana interrupts me. "For a bright man, sometimes—" She stops midsentence, too angry to continue. "I'd like to go, please." She taps her foot against the marble floor.

"Why?"

"You know why," she snaps, and rolls her eyes as if I'm the biggest idiot she's ever met.

You are the biggest idiot she's ever met, Grey.

You know how she feels about Elena.

Everything was going so well.

Make this right, Grey.

"I'm sorry, Ana. I didn't know she'd be here. She's never here. She's opened a new branch at the Bravern Center, and that's where she's normally based. Someone was sick today."

Ana turns abruptly and storms to the door.

"We won't need Franco, Greta," I inform the receptionist, annoyed that she may have heard our exchange. Hastily, I go after Ana.

She wraps her arms around herself defensively and marches up the street with her head down. I'm forced to take longer strides to catch up with her.

Ana. Stop. You're overreacting.

She simply doesn't understand the nature of Elena's and my relationship.

As I walk beside her, I'm floundering. What do I do? What do I say? Perhaps Elena is right.

Can I do this?

I've never tolerated this kind of behavior from any submissive; what's more, none of them have been this petulant.

But I hate it when she's angry with me.

"You used to take your subs there?" she asks, and I don't know if it's a rhetorical question or not. I chance a reply.

"Some of them, yes."

"Leila?"

"Yes."

"The place looks very new."

"It's been refurbished recently."

"I see. So Mrs. Robinson met all your subs."

"Yes."

"Did they know about her?"

Not in the way you're thinking. They never knew about our D/s relationship. They just thought we were friends. "No. None of them did. Only you."

"But I'm not your sub."

"No, you most definitely are not." Because I certainly wouldn't indulge this behavior from anyone else.

She stops suddenly and whirls around to face me, her expression bleak. "Can you see how fucked up this is?" she says.

"Yes. I'm sorry." I didn't know she was going to be there.

"I want to get my hair cut, preferably somewhere where you haven't fucked either the staff or the clientele." Her voice is hoarse and she's on the verge of tears.

Ana.

"Now, if you'll excuse me." She turns to go.

"You're not running. Are you?" Panic starts to well inside me. This is it. She's out before we've even had a second chance.

Grey, you've blown it.

"No," she shouts, exasperated. "I just want a damn haircut. Somewhere I can close my eyes, have someone wash my hair, and I can forget about all this baggage that accompanies you."

She's not leaving me. I take a deep breath. "I can have Franco come to the apartment, or your place," I offer.

"She's very attractive."

Christ. Not this. "Yes, she is." So what? Give it up, Ana.

"Is she still married?"

"No. She got divorced about five years ago."

"Why aren't you with her?"

Ana! Let it go. "Because that's over between us. I've told you this." How many times do I need to tell her? My phone vibrates in my jacket pocket. I hold my finger up to stop her tirade and answer my phone. The caller ID says it's Welch. I wonder what he has to report.

"Mr. Grey."

"Welch."

"Three things. We've tracked Mrs. Leila Reed to Spokane,

where she'd been living with a man named Geoffrey Barry. He was killed in an auto accident on I-90."

"Killed in a car crash? When?"

"Four weeks ago. Her husband, Russell Reed, knew about Barry but still won't disclose where Mrs. Reed has gone."

"That's twice that bastard's not been forthcoming. He must know. Does he have no feelings for her whatsoever?" I'm staggered that her ex could be so heartless.

"He has feelings for her, but they're certainly not matrimonial."

"This is beginning to make sense."

"Did the psychiatrist give you anything to go on?" Welch asks.

"No."

"Could she be suffering a kind of psychosis?"

I agree with Welch that this might be her condition, but it still doesn't explain where she is, which is what I really want to know. I look around. *Where are you, Leila?* "She's here. She's watching us," I mutter.

"Mr. Grey, we're close. We'll find her." Welch tries to reassure me and asks if I'm at Escala.

"No." I wish Ana and I weren't so exposed here on the street.

"I'm considering how many people you need for your close protection team."

"Two or four, twenty-four-seven."

"Okay, Mr. Grey. Have you told Anastasia?"

"I haven't broached that yet." Ana's watching me, listening. Her expression is intense but inscrutable.

"You should. There's something else. Mrs. Reed has obtained a concealed-weapons license."

"What?" Fear grips my heart.

"The details came up in our search this morning."

"I see. When?"

"It's dated yesterday."

"That recently? But how?"

"She forged the papers."

"No background checks?"

"All the forms are faked. She's using a different name."

"I see. E-mail the name, address, and photos if you have them."

"Will do. And I'll organize the additional security."

"Twenty-four-seven, from this afternoon. Establish liaison with Taylor." I hang up. This is serious.

"Well?" Ana asks.

"That was Welch."

"Who's Welch?"

"My security adviser."

"Okay. So, what's happened?"

"Leila left her husband about three months ago and ran off with a guy who was killed in a car accident four weeks ago."

"Oh."

"The asshole shrink should have found that out. Grief, that's what this is."

Damn. That hospital could have done a better job.

"Come." I hold out my hand and Ana takes it without thinking. Then, just as abruptly, she snatches her hand away.

"Wait a minute. We were in the middle of a discussion about 'us.' About her, your Mrs. Robinson."

"She's not my Mrs. Robinson. We can talk about it at my place."

"I don't want to go to your place. I want to get my hair cut!" she yells.

I take my phone and call the salon. Greta answers immediately.

"Greta, Christian Grey. I want Franco at my place in an hour. Ask Mrs. Lincoln."

"Yes, Mr. Grey." She puts me on hold for a nanosecond. "That's fine. He can be there at one."

"Good." I hang up. "He's coming at one."

"Christian!" Ana glares at me.

"Anastasia, Leila is obviously suffering a psychotic break. I don't know if it's you or me she's after, or what lengths she's prepared to go to. We'll go to your place, pick up your things, and you can stay with me until we've tracked her down."

"Why would I want to do that?"

"So I can keep you safe."

"But—"

Give me strength.

"You are coming back to my apartment if I have to drag you there by your hair."

"I think you're overreacting."

"I don't. We can continue our discussion back at my place. Come."

She glowers at me. Intractable. "No," she says.

"You can walk or I can carry you. I don't mind either way, Anastasia."

"You wouldn't dare."

"Oh, baby, we both know that if you throw down the gauntlet, I'll be only too happy to pick it up."

She narrows her eyes.

Ana. You give me no choice.

I scoop her up and throw her over my shoulder, ignoring the startled look of a couple walking past us.

"Put me down!" she rages, and starts to struggle. I tighten my hold on her and slap her behind.

"Christian!" she screeches. She's mad. But I don't give a fuck. An alarmed man—a father, I presume—pulls his young children out of our path.

"I'll walk! I'll walk," she shrieks, and I put her down immediately. She whirls around so fast her hair hits my shoulder. She stomps off in the direction of her apartment and I follow, but I keep watch. Everywhere.

Where are you, Leila?

Behind a parked car? A tree?

What do you want?

Ana comes to a sudden stop. "What's happened?" she demands.

"What do you mean?" *What now?*

"With Leila."

"I've told you."

"No, you haven't. There's something else. You didn't insist that I go to your place yesterday. So what's happened?"

Perceptive, Miss Steele.

"Christian! Tell me!"

"She managed to obtain a concealed-weapons permit yesterday."

Her whole demeanor changes. Anger turns to fear. "That means she can just buy a gun," she whispers, horrified.

"Ana." I pull her into my arms. "I don't think she'll do anything stupid, but I just don't want to take that risk with you."

"Not me. What about you?" she says, her voice filled with anguish. She wraps her arms around me and hugs me hard. She's scared for me.

Me!

And a moment ago I thought she was leaving.

This is unreal.

"Let's get back." I kiss her hair. As we move on, I extend my arm around her shoulders and pull her to my side to protect her. She slips her hand into the belt loop of my jeans, holding me close, her fingers curled around my hip.

This . . . proximity is new. I could get used to it.

We walk back to her apartment and I keep an eye out for Leila.

I CONTEMPLATE THE RANGE of emotions I've experienced since waking as I watch Ana pack a small suitcase. In the alley the other day I tried to articulate how I felt. The best I could do was "unsettled." And that still describes my psyche right now. Ana is not the mild woman I remember—she's far more audacious and volatile.

Has she changed so much since she left me? *Or have I?*

It doesn't help that there's a whole new level of disquiet because of Leila. For the first time in a long time, I'm fearful. What if something were to happen to Ana because of my association with Leila? That whole situation is out of my control. And I don't like it.

Ana, for her part, is solemn and unusually quiet. She folds the balloon into her backpack.

"*Charlie Tango*'s coming, too?" I tease.

She nods and gives me a tepid smile. She's either scared or still mad about Elena. Or she's pissed for being hoisted over my shoulder in the street. Or maybe it's the twenty-four thousand dollars.

Damn, there's a great deal to choose from. I wish I knew what she was thinking.

"Ethan is back Tuesday," she says.

"Ethan?"

"Kate's brother. He's staying here until he finds a place in Seattle."

Ah, the other Kavanagh progeny. The beach bum. I met him at her graduation. He had his hands all over Ana. "Well, it's good that you'll be staying with me. Give him more room."

"I don't know that he's got keys. I'll need to be back then. That's everything," she says.

Taking her case, I have a quick look around before we lock up. I note with displeasure that the apartment has no intruder alarm.

THE AUDI IS PARKED out back where Taylor said it would be. I open the passenger door for Ana, but she stays rooted to the ground, staring at me.

"Are you getting in?" I ask, confused.

"I thought I was driving."

"No. I'll drive."

"Something wrong with my driving?" she asks, and there's that tone again. "Don't tell me you know what I scored on my driving test. I wouldn't be surprised, with your stalking tendencies."

"Get in the car, Anastasia." My patience is running thin.

Enough. You're making me crazy. I want you home where you'll be safe.

"Okay," she huffs, and climbs in. She doesn't live far from me, so our ride shouldn't take long. Normally I would enjoy driving the small Audi. It's nimble in Seattle's traffic. But I'm distracted by every pedestrian. One of them could be Leila.

"Were all your submissives brunettes?" Ana asks out of nowhere.

"Yes." But I don't really want to discuss this. Our fledgling relationship is moving into dangerous territory.

"I just wondered." She's fidgeting with a tassel on her backpack; fidgeting means she's apprehensive.

Put her at ease, Grey.

"I told you. I prefer brunettes."

"Mrs. Robinson isn't a brunette."

"That's probably why. She put me off blondes forever."

"You're kidding." Ana's disbelief is obvious.

"Yes. I'm kidding." Do we really have to talk about this? My anxiety multiplies. If she keeps digging, I'll confess my darkest secret.

No. I can never tell her. She'll leave me.

Without a backward glance.

And I recall watching her walk up the street and into the garage at The Heathman after our first coffee.

She never looked back.

Not once.

If I hadn't contacted her about the photographer's show . . . I wouldn't be with her now.

Ana's strong. If she says good-bye, she means it.

"Tell me about her," Ana interrupts my thoughts.

What now? Is she talking about Elena? Again? "What do you want to know?" More information about Mrs. Lincoln will only worsen her mood.

"Tell me about your business arrangement."

Well, that's easy enough. "I'm a silent partner. I'm not particularly interested in the beauty business, but she's built it into a successful venture. I just invested and helped get her started."

"Why?"

"I owed it to her."

"Oh?"

"When I dropped out of Harvard, she loaned me a hundred grand to start my business."

"You dropped out?"

"It wasn't my thing. I did two years. Unfortunately, my parents were not so understanding."

"You're what?" Grace scowls at me, her expression apoplectic.

"I want to leave. I'm going to start my own company."

"Doing what?"

"Investments."

"Christian, what do you know about investments? You need to finish college."

"Mom, I have a plan. I think I can do this."

"Look, son, this is a huge step that could affect your entire future."

"I know, Dad, but I can't do it anymore. I don't want to live in Cambridge for another two years."

"Transfer. Come back to Seattle."

"Mom, it's not the place."

"You just haven't found your niche."

"My niche is out in the real world. Not in academia. It's stifling."

"Have you met someone?" Grace asks.

"No," I lie smoothly. I knew Elena before I went off to Harvard. Grace narrows her eyes and the tips of my ears burn.

"We cannot condone this reckless move, son." Carrick is summoning his full-on pompous-prick dad mode, and I worry he's going to give me his signature "study hard, work hard, and family first" lecture.

Grace emphasizes her point. "Christian, you're gambling with the rest of your life."

"Mom. Dad. It's done. I'm sorry to disappoint you again. My decision is already made. I'm just informing you."

"But what about the wasted tuition?" My mother is wringing her hands.

Shit.

"I'll pay you back."

"How? And how in heaven's name are you going to start a business? You need capital."

"Don't worry about that, Mom. It's in hand. And I will pay you back."

"Christian, darling, it's not about the money . . ."

The only lesson I learned at college was how to read a balance sheet, and I found the peace that single sculls brought me.

"You don't seem to have done too badly dropping out. What was your major?" Ana says, bringing me back to our conversation.

"Politics and economics."

"So, she's rich?" Ana is fixated on Elena's loan to me.

"She was a bored trophy wife, Anastasia. Her husband was wealthy—big in timber." This always makes me smile. I give Ana a sideways smirk. Lincoln Timber. What an unpleasant asshole he turned out to be. "He wouldn't let her work. You know, he was controlling. Some men are like that."

"Really? A controlling man?" Ana sounds scornful. "Surely a mythical creature." Sarcasm drips off every word. She's in a sassy mood, but her response makes me grin.

"She lent you her husband's money?"

She sure did.

"That's terrible."

"He got his own back."

The asshole.

My thoughts take a dark turn. He nearly killed his wife because she was fucking me. I shudder to think what he'd have done to her if I hadn't shown up. Fury surges through my body and I clutch the steering wheel as we wait for the Escala garage barrier to open. Blood drains from my knuckles. Elena was in the hospital for three months and she refused to press charges.

Control yourself, Grey.

I relax my hold on the steering wheel.

"How?" asks Ana, as curious as ever, wanting to know about Linc's revenge.

I'm not telling her that story. I shake my head and park in one of my allotted spaces and turn off the ignition. "Come—Franco will be here shortly."

In the elevator, I glance down at her. The little *v* is there between her brows. She's pensive, maybe processing what I told her—or is it something else?

"Still mad at me?" I ask.

"Very."

"Okay." At least I know.

Taylor has returned from visiting Sophie, his daughter. He greets us when we arrive in the foyer.

"Good afternoon, sir," he says quietly to me.

"Has Welch been in touch?"

"Yes, sir."

"And?"

"Everything's arranged."

"Excellent. How's your daughter?"

"She's fine, thank you, sir."

"Good. We have a hairdresser arriving at one—Franco De Luca."

"Miss Steele," Taylor greets Ana.

"Hi, Taylor. You have a daughter?"

"Yes, ma'am."

"How old is she?"

"She's seven."

Ana looks confused.

"She lives with her mother," Taylor explains.

"Oh, I see," she says, and he gives her a rare smile.

I turn and head into my living room. I'm not sure I appreciate Taylor charming Miss Steele or vice versa. I hear Ana behind me.

"Are you hungry?" I ask.

She shakes her head and her eyes scan the room. She hasn't been here since the awful day she left me. I want to tell her I'm glad she's back, but she's mad at me right now.

"I have to make a few calls. Make yourself at home."

"Okay," she says.

IN MY STUDY, on my desk, I find a large cloth bag. Inside is a stunning silver mask with navy plumes for Ana. Beside it there's a small Chanel bag containing a red lipstick. Taylor has done well. However, I don't think Ana will be too impressed with my lipstick idea—at least not at the moment. I place the mask on a shelf and pocket the lipstick, then sit down at my computer.

It was an enlightening and diverting morning with Anastasia.

She's been as challenging as ever since we woke, whether it was about the check for her death trap of a Beetle, my relationship with Elena, or who pays for breakfast.

Ana's fiercely independent and still doesn't seem interested in my money. She doesn't take, she gives; but then she's always been that way. It's refreshing. All of my submissives used to love their gifts. *Grey, who are you kidding?* They said they did, but perhaps that was because of the role they were playing.

I put my head in my hands. This is difficult. I'm on an uncharted course with Ana.

Her anger toward Elena is unfortunate. Elena is a friend.

Is Ana jealous?

I can't help my past, and after all that Elena has done for me, it's going to be awkward dealing with Ana's hostility.

Is this what my life will be like from now on, mired in this uncertainty? It will make an interesting topic to discuss with Flynn the next time I see him. Perhaps he can coach me through this.

Shaking my head, I activate the iMac and check my e-mails. Welch has sent through a copy of Leila's forged concealed-weapons license. She's using the name Jeanne Barry and an address in Belltown. The photograph is her likeness, though she looks older, thinner, and sadder than she did when I knew her. It's depressing. The woman needs help.

I print out a couple of spreadsheets from SIP— P&Ls for the last three years that I will examine later. Then I review the résumés of the additional close protection team that Taylor has approved; two of them are ex-Feds and two are ex–Navy Seals. But I have yet to broach the subject of additional security with Ana.

One step at a time, Grey.

WHEN I'VE FINISHED RESPONDING to a few work e-mails, I go in search of Ana.

She's not in the living room or my bedroom but while there I collect a couple of condoms from my bedside and continue my search. I want to go upstairs to check whether she's in the sub's room, but I hear the elevator doors and Taylor greeting someone. My watch reads 12:55. Franco must have arrived.

The doors of the foyer open, and before Taylor opens his mouth I say, "I'll fetch Miss Steele."

"Very good, sir."

"Let me know as soon as the security detail gets here."

"Will do, Mr. Grey."

"And thanks for the mask and lipstick."

"You're welcome, sir." Taylor closes the door.

Upstairs, I can't see her, but I hear her.

Ana's talking to herself in the closet.

What the hell is she doing in there?

Taking a deep breath, I open the door and she's sitting cross-legged on the floor. "There you are. I thought you'd run off."

She holds up a finger and I realize that she's on the phone, and not talking to herself at all. Leaning against the doorjamb, I watch as she tucks her hair behind her ear and starts winding a strand around her index finger.

"Sorry, Mom, I have to go. I'll call again soon . . ." She's jittery. Do I make her feel that way? Perhaps she's hiding in here to get away from me. She needs some space? The thought is disheartening.

"Love you, too, Mom." She hangs up and turns to me, her expression expectant.

"Why are you hiding in here?" I ask.

"I'm not hiding. I'm despairing."

"Despairing?" Anxiety pricks my skin. She *is* thinking of running.

"Of all this, Christian." She gestures toward the dresses hanging in the closet.

The clothes? She doesn't like them?

"Can I come in?" I ask.

"It's your closet."

My closet. Your clothes, Ana.

Slowly I sink to the floor opposite her, trying to gauge her mood. "They're just clothes. If you don't like them, I'll send them back." I sound resigned rather than conciliatory.

"You're a lot to take on, you know?"

She's not wrong. Scratching my unshaved chin, I consider what to say.

Be real. Be truthful. Flynn's words ring in my head.

"I know. I'm trying," I reply.

"You're very trying," she quips.

"As are you, Miss Steele."

"Why are you doing this?" She gestures between us.

Her and me.

She and I.

Ana and Christian.

"You know why." *I need you.*

"No, I don't," she insists.

I scrape my hands through my hair, looking for inspiration. What does she want me to say? What does she want to hear? "You are one frustrating female."

"You could have a nice brunette submissive. One who'd say, 'How high?' every time you said jump, provided of course she had permission to speak. So why me, Christian? I just don't get it."

What should I tell her? Because I've woken up since I met her? Because my whole world has changed. It's rotating on a different axis. "You make me look at the world differently, Anastasia. You don't want me for my money. You give me . . ." I search for the word. "Hope."

"Hope for what?"

Everything.

"More," I answer. It's what Ana wanted. And now I want it, too.

Give her your whole pitch, Grey.

I tell her she's right. "I'm used to women doing exactly what I say, when I say, doing exactly what I want. It gets old. There's something about you, Anastasia, which calls to me on some deep level I don't understand. It's a siren's call. I can't resist you, and I don't want to lose you."

Whoa. Flowery, Grey.

I take her hand. "Don't run, please. Have a little faith in me and a little patience. Please."

And it's there in her sweet smile. Her compassion. Her love. I could bask in that look all day. Every day. She places her hands on my knees, surprising me, and leans up to plant a kiss on my lips. "Okay. Faith and patience, I can live with that," she says.

"Good. Because Franco's here."

She flips her hair over her shoulder. "About time!" Her girlish laugh is infectious, and together we stand.

Hand in hand, we make our way downstairs and I think we might be over whatever was making her mad.

FRANCO MAKES AN EMBARRASSING fuss over my girl. I leave them in my bathroom. I'm not sure Ana would appreciate me micromanaging a haircut.

Heading back to my study, I feel tension in my shoulders. I feel it everywhere. This morning has been out of my control, and though she says she's going to try faith and patience, I'll have to see if she's as good as her word.

But Ana has never given me a reason to doubt her.

Except when she left.

And she hurt me . . .

I dismiss the dark thought and quickly check my e-mails. There's one from Flynn.

From: Dr. John Flynn
Subject: Tonight
Date: June 11 2011 13:00
To: Christian Grey

Christian
Are you attending your parents' benefit this evening?

JF

I respond immediately.

From: Christian Grey
Subject: Tonight
Date: June 11 2011 13:15
To: Dr. John Flynn

Good afternoon, John.
I am indeed, and I'll be accompanied by Miss Anastasia
Steele.

Christian Grey
CEO, Grey Enterprises Holdings, Inc.

I wonder what he'll make of that. I think it's the first time I've really followed his advice—and I am trying my relationship with Ana her way.

So far, so confusing.

I shake my head and retrieve the spreadsheets I printed out and a couple of bound reports I have to read about the shipping business in Taiwan.

I'M LOST IN THE figures for SIP. They are hemorrhaging money. Their overhead is too high, their write-offs are astronomical, their production costs are rising, and their staff—

A movement out of the corner of my eye distracts me.

Ana.

She stands at the entrance of the living room, twisting one foot inward and looking awkward and shy. She's staring anxiously at me, and I know she's seeking my approval.

She's stunning. Her hair a glossy mane.

"See! I tell you he like it." Franco has followed her into the living room.

"You look lovely, Ana," I say, and my compliment induces a fetching flush on her cheeks.

"My work 'ere is done," Franco says, clapping his hands.

It's time to see him out.

"Thank you, Franco," I say, and attempt to direct him out of my living room. He grabs Ana and kisses her on both cheeks in a rather dramatic display of affection. "Never let anyone else be cutting your hair, *bellissima* Ana!"

I glare at him until he lets her go. "This way," I say to get him out.

"Mr. Grey, she is a jewel."

I know.

"Here." I hand him three hundred dollars. "Thank you for coming at such short notice."

"It was a pleasure. A real pleasure." He pumps my hand, and not a moment too soon Taylor appears to escort him to the foyer.

Thank God.

Ana is standing where I left her.

"I'm glad you kept it long." I take a strand of her hair and caress it between my fingers. "So soft," I whisper. She watches me—anxious, I think. "Are you still mad at me?" I ask.

She nods.

Oh, Ana.

"What precisely are you mad at me about?"

She rolls her eyes at me . . . and I recall a moment in her bedroom in Vancouver when she made exactly the same mistake. But that was a lifetime ago in our short relationship, and I'm sure she wouldn't let me spank her right now. Though I want to. Yes. I want to very much.

"You want the list?" she says.

"There's a list?" I'm amused.

"A long one."

"Can we discuss it in bed?" Thoughts of spanking Ana have gone to my groin.

"No."

"Over lunch, then. I'm hungry, and not just for food."

"I am not going to let you dazzle me with your sexpertise."

Sexpertise!

Anastasia, you flatter me.

And I like it.

"What is bothering you specifically, Miss Steele? Spit it out."

I've lost track.

"What's bothering me?" she scoffs. "Well, there's your gross invasion of my privacy, the fact that you took me to some place where your ex-mistress works and you used to take all your lovers to have their bits waxed, you manhandled me in the street like I was six years old." She's on a roll with a litany of all my misbehavior. I feel like I'm in first grade again. "And to cap it all, you let your Mrs. Robinson touch you!"

She didn't touch me! *Christ.* "That's quite a list. But just to clarify once more, she's not my Mrs. Robinson."

"She can touch you," she stresses, and her voice wavers, full of hurt.

"She knows where."

"What does that mean?"

"You and I don't have any rules. I have never had a relationship without rules, and I never know where you're going to touch me. It makes me nervous." She's unpredictable and she has to understand that her touch disarms me. "Your touch completely—it just means more. So much more."

You can't touch me, Ana. Please just accept this.

She steps forward, raising her hand.

No. The darkness squeezes my ribs. I step back. "Hard limit," I whisper.

She masks her disappointment. "How would you feel if you couldn't touch me?"

"Devastated and deprived."

Her shoulders fall and she shakes her head but gives me a resigned smile. "You'll have to tell me exactly why this is a hard limit, one day, please."

"One day," I answer. And I push the vision of a burning cigarette out of my head.

"So, the rest of your list. Invading your privacy. Because I know your bank account number?"

"Yes, that's outrageous."

"I do background checks on all my submissives. I'll show you." I head into my study and she follows. Wondering if this is a good idea, I pull Ana's file from the cabinet and hand it to her. She glances at her neatly typed name and gives me a withering look.

"You can keep it," I tell her.

"Well, gee, thanks," she sneers, and starts flipping through and scanning the contents.

"So, you knew I worked at Clayton's?"

"Yes."

"It wasn't a coincidence. You didn't just drop by?"

Fess up, Grey.

"No."

"This is fucked up. You know that?"

"I don't see it that way. What I do, I have to be careful."

"But this is private."

"I don't misuse the information. Anyone can get hold of it if they have half a mind to, Anastasia. To have control, I need information. It's how I've always operated."

"You do misuse the information. You deposited twenty-four thousand dollars that I didn't want into my account."

"I told you. That's what Taylor managed to get for your car. Unbelievable, I know, but there you go."

"But the Audi—"

"Anastasia, do you have any idea how much money I make?"

"Why should I? I don't need to know the bottom line of your bank account, Christian."

"I know. That's one of the things I love about you. Anastasia, I earn roughly one hundred thousand dollars an hour."

Her lips form the letter *o*.

And for once she remains silent.

"Twenty-four thousand dollars is nothing. The car, the Tess books, the clothes, they're nothing."

"If you were me, how would you feel about all this . . . largesse coming your way?" she asks.

This is irrelevant. We're talking about her, not me.

"I don't know." I shrug because it's such a ludicrous question.

She sighs as if she's had to explain a complex equation to a simpleton. "It doesn't feel great. I mean, you're very generous, but it makes me uncomfortable. I have told you this often enough."

"I want to give you the world, Anastasia."

"I just want you, Christian. Not all the add-ons."

"They're part of the deal. Part of what I am." Who I am.

She shakes her head, seeming subdued. "Shall we eat?" she asks, changing the subject.

"Sure."

"I'll cook."

"Good. Otherwise, there's food in the fridge."

"Mrs. Jones is off on the weekends?"

I nod.

"So, you eat cold cuts most weekends?"

"No."

"Oh?"

I take a deep breath, wondering how the piece of information I'm going to give Ana will go down. "My submissives cook, Anastasia." Some well, some not so well.

"Oh, of course." She fakes a smile. "What would Sir like to eat?"

"Whatever Madam can find," I reply, knowing she won't get the reference.

She nods and exits my study, leaving her file. Placing it back in the filing cabinet, I catch sight of Susannah's file. She was a hopeless cook, even worse than me. But she tried . . . and we had some fun with that.

"You've burned this?"

"Yes. Sorry, Sir."

"Well, what are we going to do with you?"

"Whatever pleases you, Master."

"Did you burn this deliberately?"

Her flush and the twitch of her lips as she masks her smile are answer enough.

Those were pleasurable and simpler times. My previous relationships were dictated by a set of rules that were followed, and if they weren't, there were consequences. I had peace. And I knew what was expected of me. They were intimate relationships, but none of my previous submissives thrilled me as Ana does, even though she's so difficult.

Maybe it's because she's so difficult.

I remember our contract negotiation. She was difficult then.

Yes. Look how that turned out, Grey.

She's had me on my toes since I met her. Is this why I like her so much? How long will I feel this way? Probably as long as she stays. Because deep down I know she'll leave me eventually.

They all do.

Music starts blaring from the living room. "Crazy in Love" by Beyoncé. Is Ana sending me a message?

I stand in the corridor that leads to my study and the TV room and watch her cook. She's whisking some eggs, but she stops suddenly, and from what I can see, she's grinning like a fool.

I creep up behind her and slip my arms around her, startling her. "Interesting choice of music," I croon in her ear and plant a kiss behind it. "Your hair smells good." She shimmies out of my arms.

"I'm still mad at you," she says.

"How long are you going to keep this up?" I ask, and rake my hand through my hair in frustration.

"At least until I've eaten." Her tone is haughty but playful.

Good.

Picking up the remote, I switch off the music. "Did you put that on your iPod?" Ana asks.

I shake my head. I don't want to say it was Leila, because she might get mad again.

"Don't you think she was trying to tell you something back then?" she says, guessing correctly that it was Leila.

"Well, with hindsight, probably," I reply. *Why didn't I see this coming?*

Ana asks why it's still on my iPod, and I offer to remove it.

"What would you like to hear?"

"Surprise me," she says, and it's a challenge.

Very well, Miss Steele. Your wish is my command. I scroll through the iPod, dismissing several tunes. I consider "Please Forgive Me" by David Gray, but that's too obvious and frankly too apologetic.

I know. What did she call it earlier? Sexpertise? Yes.

Use it. *Seduce her, Grey.*

I've had enough of her crankiness. I find the song I want, hit play. *Perfect.* The orchestra swells and music fills the room with a cool, sultry intro, and then Nina Simone sings. *"I put a spell on you."*

Ana whirls around, armed with a whisk, and I catch and hold her gaze as I move toward her.

"You're mine," Nina sings.

You're mine.

"Christian, please," Ana whispers when I reach her.

"Please what?"

"Don't do this."

"Do what?"

"This." She's breathless.

"Are you sure?" I take the whisk out of her hand before she decides to use it as a weapon.

Ana. Ana. Ana.

I'm close enough to smell her. I shut my eyes and take a deep breath. When I open them, the telltale flush of desire stains her cheeks.

And it's there between us.

That familiar pull.

Our intense attraction.

"I want you, Anastasia," I whisper. "I love and I hate, and I love arguing with you. It's very new. I need to know that we're okay. It's the only way I know how."

She closes her eyes. "My feelings for you haven't changed," she says, her voice low and reassuring.

Prove it.

Her eyelashes flutter and her eyes flit to the exposed skin above my shirt and she bites her lip. I suppress my groan as the heat radiating from her body warms us both.

"I'm not going to touch you until you say yes." My voice is thick with my hunger. "But right now, after a really shitty morning, I want to bury myself in you and just forget everything but us."

Her eyes meet mine. "I'm going to touch your face," she says, surprising me.

Okay. I ignore the frisson that runs down my spine. Her hand caresses my cheek and I close my eyes, enjoying the feel of her fingertips teasing my stubble.

Oh, baby.

No need for fear, Grey.

Instinctively, I press my face into her touch, experiencing it, luxuriating in it. I lean down, my lips close to hers, and she raises her face to mine.

"Yes or no, Anastasia?"

"Yes." The word is no more than an audible sigh.

And I lower my mouth to hers, my lips brushing hers, coaxing her. Tasting her. Teasing her until she opens up for me. I embrace her, one hand on her behind pushing her against my arousal and my other hand running up her back, into her soft hair, where I tug gently. She moans as her tongue meets mine.

"Mr. Grey." We're interrupted.

Christ.

I release Ana.

"Taylor," I acknowledge through gritted teeth as he stands on the threshold of the living room, looking suitably embarrassed but resolute.

What. The. Fuck.

We have an understanding that he makes himself scarce when

I'm not alone in the apartment. Whatever he has to say must be important. "My study," I indicate, and Taylor walks briskly across the room. "Rain check," I whisper to Ana and follow Taylor out.

"I'm sorry to interrupt you, sir," he says when we're in my office.

"You'd better have a good reason."

"Well, your mother called."

"Please don't tell me that's the reason."

"No, sir. But you should call her back sooner rather than later. It's about this evening."

"Okay. What else?"

"The security team is here, and, knowing how you feel about guns, I thought I should inform you that they're armed."

"What?"

"Mr. Welch and I both think it's a precautionary measure."

"I loathe guns. Let's hope they don't have to use them." I sound pissed—and I am—I was making out with Anastasia Steele.

When have I ever been interrupted while making out?

Never.

The thought suddenly amuses me.

I'm living the adolescence I never had.

Taylor relaxes, and I know it's because my mood has changed.

"Did you know Andrea was getting married today?" I ask him, because this has been bugging me since this morning.

"Yes," he answers with a puzzled expression.

"She didn't tell me."

"Probably just an oversight, sir."

Now I know he's patronizing me. I raise an eyebrow.

"The wedding is at The Edgewater," he says quickly.

"Is she staying there?"

"I believe so."

"Can you discreetly inquire if the happy couple has a room there and get them upgraded to the best suite available? And pay for it."

Taylor smiles. "Certainly, sir."

"Who's the lucky guy?"

"That I don't know, Mr. Grey."

I wonder why Andrea has been so mysterious about her wedding. I brush aside the thought as the aroma of something delicious filters into the room and my stomach growls in anticipation.

"I'd better get back to Anastasia."

"Yes, sir."

"Was that all?"

"Yes."

"Great." We both exit my study. "I'll brief them in ten," I say to Taylor when we're back in the living room. Ana is bending over the stove, retrieving a couple of plates.

"We'll be ready," Taylor says, and departs, leaving me alone with Anastasia.

"Lunch?" she offers.

"Please." I sit down at one of the barstools where she's laid our places for lunch.

"Problem?" she inquires, as curious as ever. I have yet to tell her about the additional security.

"No."

She doesn't push me for any answers as she busies herself plating our lunch of Spanish omelet with salad. I'm impressed she's so capable and at ease in my kitchen. She sits beside me as I take a bite and the food melts in my mouth.

Hmm. Delicious.

"This is good. Would you like a glass of wine?"

"No thank you," she replies, and gingerly starts eating her lunch.

At least she's eating.

I forgo the wine, as I know I'll be drinking this evening. Which reminds me that I have to call my mother. I wonder what she wants. She doesn't know I split up with Ana—and now we're back together. I should let her know that Ana is coming to the ball this evening.

Using the remote, I switch on some relaxing music.

"What's this?" Ana asks.

"Canteloube, *Songs of the Auvergne*. This is called 'Bailero.'"

"It's lovely. What language is it?"

"It's in old French—Occitan, in fact."

"You speak French; do you understand it?"

"Some words, yes. My mother had a mantra: 'musical instrument, foreign language, martial art.' Elliot speaks Spanish; Mia and I speak French. Elliot plays guitar, I play piano, and Mia the cello."

"Wow. And the martial arts?"

"Elliot does judo. Mia put her foot down at age twelve and refused." Ana knows I kickbox.

"I wish my mother had been that organized."

"Dr. Grace is formidable when it comes to the accomplishments of her children."

"She must be very proud of you. I would be," Ana says warmly.

Oh, baby, you couldn't be more wrong. Nothing is that simple. I've been a big disappointment to my folks: school expulsions, dropping out of college, no relationships that they knew of . . . If Grace only knew the truth about my lifestyle.

If you only knew the truth, Ana.

Don't go there, Grey.

"Have you decided what you'll wear this evening? Or do I need to come and pick something for you?"

"Um, not yet. Did you choose all those clothes?"

"No, Anastasia, I didn't. I gave a list and your size to a personal shopper at Neiman Marcus. They should fit. Just so you know, I have ordered additional security for this evening and the next few days. With Leila unpredictable and unaccounted for somewhere on the streets of Seattle, I think it's a wise precaution. I don't want you going out unaccompanied. Okay?"

She looks a little stunned but agrees, surprising me by acquiescing without argument.

"Good. I'm going to brief them. I shouldn't be long."

"They're here?"

"Yes."

She looks puzzled. But she hasn't objected to the additional security, so while I have the upper hand, I pick up my empty plate and place it in the sink and leave Ana to finish her meal in peace.

The security team is gathered in Taylor's office, seated at his round table. After our introductions I sit down and run through the evening's event.

BRIEFING FINISHED, I RETURN to my study to call my mother.

"Darling, how are you?" she enthuses into the phone.

"I'm well, Grace."

"Are you coming this evening?"

"Of course. And Anastasia is coming, too."

"She is?" She sounds surprised, but she recovers quickly. "That's wonderful, sweetheart. I'll make room at our table." She sounds too exuberant. I can only imagine her delight.

"I'll see you this evening, Mother."

"I look forward to it, Christian. Good-bye."

There's an e-mail from Flynn.

From: Dr. John Flynn
Subject: Tonight
Date: June 11 2011 14:25
To: Christian Grey

I look forward to meeting Anastasia.

JF

I bet you do, John.

It seems everyone is thrilled I have a date tonight.

Everyone, including me.

ANA IS LYING ACROSS the bed in the submissive's room, staring at her Mac. She's engrossed in reading something on the Web.

"What are you doing?" I ask.

She startles, and for some reason looks guilty. I lie down beside her and see that's she's on a website with a page titled "Multiple Personality Disorder: The Symptoms."

I understand that I have many issues, but fortunately schizophrenia is not one of them. I can't hide my amusement at her amateur psychological sleuthing. "On this site for a reason?"

"Research. Into a difficult personality."

"A difficult personality?"

"My own pet project."

"I'm a pet project now? A sideline. Science experiment, maybe. When I thought I was everything. Miss Steele, you wound me."

"How do you know it's you?"

"Wild guess," I tease.

"It's true that you are the only fucked-up, mercurial control freak that I know intimately."

"I thought I was the only person you know intimately."

"Yes. That, too," she replies, and an embarrassed flush turns her cheeks a fetching pink.

"Have you reached any conclusions yet?"

She turns to scrutinize me, her expression warm. "I think you're in need of intense therapy."

I tuck her hair behind her ear, pleased that she's kept it long and I can still do this. "I think I'm in need of you," I counter. "Here." I give her the lipstick.

"You want me to wear this?"

I laugh. "No, Anastasia, not unless you want to. Not sure it's your color."

Scarlet red is Elena's color. Though I don't tell Ana that. She'll combust. And not in a good way.

I sit up on the bed, cross my legs, and pull my shirt over my head. This is either a brilliant brain wave—or a stupid one. We'll see. "I like your road-map idea."

She looks puzzled.

"The no-go areas," I prompt.

"Oh. I was kidding," she says.

"I'm not."

"You want me to draw on you, with lipstick?" She's bewildered.

"It washes off. Eventually."

She considers my proposition and a smile tugs at her lips. "What about something more permanent, like a Sharpie?"

"I could get a tattoo."

"No to the tattoo!" She laughs, but her eyes are wide in horror.

"Lipstick, then," I retort. Her laugh is infectious and I beam at her.

She shuts the Mac and I hold out my hands. "Come. Sit on me."

She peels her shoes off and crawls over to me. I lay back, keeping my knees upright. "Lean against my legs."

She sits astride me, excited at this new challenge.

"You seem—enthusiastic for this," I note with irony.

"I'm always eager for information, Mr. Grey, and it means you'll relax, because I'll know where the boundaries lie."

I shake my head. I hope this is a good idea. "Open the lipstick," I instruct.

For once, she does as she's told.

"Give me your hand."

She holds up her free hand.

"The one with the lipstick!"

"Are you rolling your eyes at me?" she chides.

"Yep."

"That's very rude, Mr. Grey. I know some people who get positively violent at eye rolling."

"Do you, now?" My tone is wry.

She places her hand with the lipstick in mine and I sit up suddenly, surprising her, so we're nose to nose.

"Ready?" I whisper, trying to curb my anxiety, but panic starts to spread.

"Yes," she responds, the word as soft as a summer breeze.

Knowing I'm about to overstep my bounds, the darkness is circling like a vulture, waiting to consume me. Taking her hand, I move it to the top of my shoulder and fear squeezes my ribs, expelling the air from my lungs.

"Press down." I struggle to get the words out. She does, and I guide her hand around my arm socket and down the side of my chest. The darkness slides into my throat, threatening to choke me. Ana's amusement is gone, replaced by her solemn and determined concentration. I fix my eyes on hers and read every nuanced thought and emotion in the depths of her irises, each a life buoy, keeping me from drowning, holding the darkness at bay.

She is my salvation.

I stop at the bottom of my rib cage and move her hand across my abdomen, the lipstick spilling its red trail as she paints my body. I'm panting, trying desperately to hide my fear. Each muscle is tense and standing proud as the red slices my flesh. I lean back, supporting myself on flexed, straining arms as I fight my demons and surrender myself to her gentle illustration. She's halfway done when I let go and give her total control. "And up the other side," I whisper.

With the same single-minded focus, Ana draws up my right side. Eyes impossibly large. Anguished. But holding my attention. When she reaches the top of my shoulder, she stops. "There, done," she breathes, her voice husky with repressed emotion. She lifts her hand away from my body, giving me a brief respite.

"No, you're not." I draw a line with my finger around the base of my neck above my clavicle. Ana takes a deep breath and traces the lipstick along the same line. When she finishes, blue eyes meet gray.

"Now my back," I instruct, and shift so that she clambers off me. I turn around, my back to her, and cross my legs. "Follow the line from my chest, all the way around to the other side." My voice is hoarse and alien to me, like I've left my body entirely to watch a beautiful young woman tame a monster.

No. No.

Be in the moment, Grey.

Live this.

Feel this.

Conquer this.

I am at Ana's mercy.

The woman I love.

The tip of the lipstick crosses my back as I hunch over and screw my eyes shut, tolerating the pain. It disappears.

"Around your neck, too?" Her voice is plaintive. Full of reassurance. *My life buoy.* I nod and the pain is back, piercing my skin beneath my hairline.

Then, just as suddenly, it's gone again.

"Finished," she says, and I want to shout my relief from the helipad on Escala. I turn to face her and she's watching me. And I know I'll shatter like a shard of glass if I see any pity on her face . . . but there's none. She's waiting. Patient. Kind. Controlled. Compassionate.

My Ana.

"Those are my boundaries," I whisper.

"I can live with those. Right now I want to launch myself at you," she says, her eyes shining.

At last!

My relief is a wicked smile, and I hold out my hands in invitation. "Well, Miss Steele, I'm all yours."

She squeals with glee and throws herself into my arms.

Whoa!

She knocks me off balance, but I recover and twist so that she lands on the bed beneath me, grasping my biceps. "Now, about that rain check." I kiss her, hard. Her fingers curl in my hair and tug as I consume her. She moans, her tongue entwined with mine, and there's a reckless, wild abandon in our kissing. She's driving the darkness out and I'm drinking in her light. Adrenaline is fueling my passion and she's matching me kiss for kiss. I want her naked. I sit her up and drag her T-shirt over her head and toss it to the floor.

"I want to feel you." My words are feverish against her lips as I undo her bra and throw it aside. I lay her back down on the bed and kiss her breast, my lips toying with one nipple while my fingers tease the other. She cries out when I suck and tug hard.

"Yes, baby, let me hear you," I breathe against her skin.

She squirms beneath me as I continue my sensual worship of

her breasts. Her nipples respond to my touch, growing longer and harder as Ana writhes to a rhythm set by her passion.

She is a goddess.

My goddess.

I undo the button on her jeans as she twists her hands in my hair. I make short work of her zipper and slip my hand inside her panties. My fingers slide with ease to their goal.

Fuck.

She thrusts her pelvis up to meet the heel of my hand and I press against her clitoris as she mewls beneath me. She's slick and ready. "Oh, baby," I whisper, and lean up and hover over her, watching her wild expression. "You're so wet."

"I want you," she whimpers.

I kiss her again as my hand moves against and inside her. I'm greedy. I want all of her. I need all of her.

She's mine.

Mine.

I sit up and grab the hem of her jeans, and in one swift tug they're off. I hook my fingers in her panties and they follow. I stand and out of my pocket take a foil packet and toss it at her. I'm relieved to remove my jeans and underwear.

Ana rips open the packet and eyes me hungrily when I lie down beside her. Slowly she rolls the condom over me and I grab her hands and roll onto my back.

"You. On top," I insist, and I sit her astride me. "I want to see you."

Slowly I ease her down onto me.

Fuck. She. Feels. So. Good.

I close my eyes and flex my hips as she takes me, and I exhale with a long, loud groan. "You feel so good." I tighten my fingers around hers. I don't want to let her go.

And she rises and falls, her body embracing mine. Her breasts bouncing as she does. I let go of her hands, knowing she'll respect the road map, and I grab her hips. She places her hands on my arms as I rise up and thrust into her.

She cries out.

"That's right, baby, feel me," I whisper.

She tips her head back and becomes the perfect counterpoint. Up. Down. Up. Down. Up. Down.

I lose myself in our shared rhythm, reveling in every precious inch of her. She's panting and moaning. And I watch her take me, over and over. Eyes closed. Head back in ecstasy. She's magnificent. She opens her eyes.

"My Ana." My lips form the words.

"Yes. Always," she cries.

And her words call to my soul and tip me over the edge. I close my eyes and surrender to her once more.

She cries out as she finds her own release, pulling me to mine as she collapses on top of me.

"Oh, baby," I grunt, and I'm spent.

HER HEAD LOLLS ON my chest, but I don't care. She's subdued the darkness. I caress her hair and with tired fingers I stroke her back as we both catch our breath.

"You are so beautiful," I murmur, and it's only when Ana lifts her head that I realize I've said the words out loud. She eyes me with skepticism.

When will she learn to take a compliment?

I sit up quickly, catching Ana off-guard. But I hold her in place and we're face to face again.

"You. Are. Beautiful." I emphasize each word.

"And you're amazingly sweet sometimes." She leans forward and gives me a chaste kiss.

I lift her up and she winces as I ease out of her. I kiss her gently. "You have no idea how attractive you are, do you?"

She looks nonplussed.

"All those boys pursuing you, that isn't enough of a clue?"

"Boys? What boys?"

"You want the list? The photographer, he's crazy about you; that boy in the hardware store; your roommate's older brother. Your boss." That untrustworthy fucker.

"Oh, Christian, that's just not true."

"Trust me. They want you. They want what's mine." I tighten my hold on her and she rests her forearms on my shoulders, her hands in my hair. And she studies me with amused tolerance.

"Mine," I assert.

"Yes. Yours." She gives me an indulgent smile. "The line is still intact," she continues. And draws her finger over the lipstick mark on my shoulder.

I stiffen, alarmed.

"I want to go exploring," she whispers.

"The apartment?"

"No." She shakes her head. "I was thinking of the treasure map that we've drawn on you."

What?

She rubs her nose against mine, distracting me.

"And what would that entail exactly, Miss Steele?"

She raises her hand and tickles my stubble with her fingertips. "I just want to touch you everywhere I'm allowed."

Her index finger brushes my lips and I capture it between my teeth.

"Ow," she yelps when I bite down, and I grin as I growl.

So she wants to touch me. I've given her my boundaries.

Try it her way, Grey.

"Okay," I acquiesce, but I hear the uncertainty in my voice. "Wait." I lift her and remove the condom and drop it beside the bed. "I hate those things. I've a good mind to call Dr. Greene around to give you a shot."

"You think the top ob-gyn in Seattle is going to come running?"

"I can be very persuasive." I smooth her hair behind her ear. She has the most beautiful small, impish ears. "Franco's done a great job on your hair. I like these layers."

"Stop changing the subject," she warns.

I lift her so she's astride me once more. Watching her carefully, I recline onto the pillows while she rests her back against my upright knees. "Touch away," I murmur.

Her eyes never leave mine and she places her hand on my belly, beneath the lipstick line. I tense as her finger explores the valleys between my abdominal muscles. I flinch and she lifts her finger.

"I don't have to," she says.

"No, it's fine. Just takes some readjustment on my part. No one's touched me for a long time."

"Mrs. Robinson?"

Shit. Why did I allude to her?

Warily, I nod. "I don't want to talk about her. It will sour your good mood."

"I can handle it."

"No, you can't, Ana. You see red whenever I mention her. My past is my past. It's a fact. I can't change it. I'm lucky that you don't have one, because it would drive me crazy if you did."

"Drive you crazy? More than you are already?"

"Crazy for you," I declare.

She grins, a large, genuine grin. "Shall I call Dr. Flynn?"

"I don't think that will be necessary."

She wriggles on top of me and I drop my legs. With her eyes on mine, she places her fingers on my belly.

I tense.

"I like touching you," she says, and her hand slips down to my navel, teasing the hair there. Her fingers quest lower.

Whoa.

My cock twitches in approval.

"Again?" she says with a carnal smile.

Oh, Anastasia, you insatiable woman.

"Oh yes, Miss Steele, again."

I sit up and clasp her head in my hands and kiss her, long and hard. "You're not too sore?" I whisper against her lips.

"No."

"I love your stamina, Ana."

SHE DOZES BESIDE ME. Replete, I hope. After all of today's arguments and recriminations, I'm now feeling more at peace.

Perhaps I can do this vanilla thing.

I look down at Ana. Her lips are parted and her lashes leave little shadows across her pale cheek. She looks serene and beautiful, and I could watch her sleep forever.

Yet she can be really fucking difficult.

Who knew?

And the irony is—I think I like it.

She makes me question myself.

She makes me question everything.

She makes me feel alive.

BACK IN THE LIVING room, I gather my papers from the sofa and head into my study. I've left Anastasia asleep. She must be exhausted after last night, and we have a long night ahead at the ball.

At my desk I fire up my computer. One of Andrea's many virtues is that she keeps my contacts up-to-date and synced across all my devices. I look up Dr. Greene and, sure enough, I have her e-mail address. I'm so over condoms—I'd like her to see Ana as soon as possible. I send her an e-mail, but I don't imagine I'll hear from her until Monday—after all, it's the weekend.

I send a couple of e-mails to Ros and make some notes on the reports I read earlier. Opening a drawer to put away my pen, I spy the red box with the earrings I bought Ana for the gala that we never attended.

She left me.

Taking out the box, I examine the earrings once more. They are perfect for her. Elegant. Simple. Stunning. I wonder if she'd accept them today. After the fight about the Audi and the twenty-four thousand dollars, it seems unlikely. But I'd like to give them to her. I put the box in my pocket and check my watch. It's time to wake Ana, as I'm sure she'll need a while to get ready for tonight.

SHE'S CURLED UP IN the middle of the bed, looking small and lonely. She's in the sub's room. I wonder why she's up here. She's not my submissive. She should be asleep in my bed, downstairs.

"Hey, sleepyhead." I kiss her temple.

"Mmm," she grumbles, and her eyelids flicker open.

"Time to get up," I whisper, and kiss her quickly on the lips.

"Mr. Grey." Her fingers caress my stubble. "I've missed you."

"You've been asleep." How can she have missed me?

"I missed you in my dreams."

Her simple, sleepy statement floors me. She is so unpredictable and bewitching. I grin as an unexpected warmth spreads through my body. It's becoming familiar but I don't want to put a name to the feeling. It's too new. Too scary.

"Up," I order, and I leave her to get ready before I'm tempted to join her.

AFTER A QUICK SHOWER, I shave. Usually I try to avoid eye contact with the asshole in the mirror, but today he looks happier, though somewhat ridiculous with a smeared red lipstick line around his neck.

My thoughts turn to the night ahead. I usually loathe these events and find them intensely dull, but this time I'll have a date. Another first with Ana. I hope having her on my arm will ward off the flocks of Mia's friends who try desperately to get themselves noticed. They have never learned that I'm just not interested.

I wonder how Ana will find it—perhaps she'll think it's dull, too. I hope not. Maybe I should liven up the evening.

As I finish shaving, an idea comes to mind.

A few minutes later, wearing my dress pants and shirt, I head upstairs, pausing outside my playroom.

Is this a good idea?

Ana can always say no.

I unlock the door and step inside.

I've not been in my playroom since she left me. It's quiet, and ambient light glows on the red walls, giving the place an illusion of warmth. But today this room is not my sanctuary. It hasn't been since she left me alone and in darkness. It holds the memory of her tearstained face, her anger, and her bitter words. I close my eyes.

You need to sort your shit out, Grey.

I'm trying, Ana. I'm trying.

You are one fucked-up son of a bitch.

Fuck.

If she only knew. She'd leave. Again.

I discard the unpalatable thought and from the chest fetch what I need.

Will she go for this?

I like your kinky fuckery. Her hushed words from the night of our reconciliation give me some consolation. With Ana's confession in mind, I turn to leave. For the first time ever, I don't want to linger in here.

As I lock the door I wonder when or if Ana and I will revisit this room. I know I'm not ready. How Ana will feel about the—what does she call it?—Red Room of pain, we'll have to see. The thought that I may never use it again depresses me. Brooding on this, I walk to her room. Perhaps I should get rid of the canes and belts. Maybe that would help.

I open the submissive's room door and stop.

A startled Ana whirls around to face me. She's dressed in a black corset, tiny lace panties, and thigh-highs.

All thought is erased from my mind.

My mouth dries as I stare.

She's a walking wet dream.

She's Aphrodite.

Thank you, Caroline Acton.

"Can I help you, Mr. Grey? I assume there is some purpose to your visit other than to gawk mindlessly at me." There's a haughty edge to her voice.

"I am rather enjoying my mindless gawk, thank you, Miss Steele." I step into the room. "Remind me to send a personal note of thanks to Caroline Acton."

Ana gestures with her hands. She's wondering what I'm talking about.

"The personal shopper at Neiman's," I clarify.

"Oh."

"I'm quite distracted."

"I can see that. What do you want, Christian?" she says, sounding impatient, but I think she's teasing me. I pull the kegel balls out of my pocket for her to see, and her expression changes from playful to alarmed.

She thinks I want to spank her.

I do . . .

But.

"It's not what you think," I reassure her.

"Enlighten me."

"I thought you could wear these, tonight."

She blinks several times. "To this event?"

I nod.

"Will you spank me later?"

"No."

Her face falls and I can't help but laugh. "You want me to?"

I watch her swallow, indecision plain on her face.

"Well, rest assured I am not going to touch you like that, not even if you beg me." I pause and let that information sink in before I continue. "Do you want to play this game?" I hold them up. "You can always take them out if it's too much."

Her eyes darken and a small, wicked smile teases her lips. "Okay," she says.

And once again I'm reminded that Anastasia Steele is not a woman to back away from a challenge.

I spy the Louboutins on the floor. "Good girl. Come here, and I'll put them in once you've put your shoes on."

Ana in fine lingerie and Louboutins—all my dreams are coming true.

I hold out my hand to help her into her shoes. She steps into them, and turns from elfin and gamine to tall and willowy.

She's gorgeous.

Man, what they do for her legs.

I lead her to the bedside and fetch the bedroom chair and place it in front of her.

"When I nod, you bend down and hold on to the chair. Understand?"

"Yes."

"Good. Now open your mouth."

She does, and I slide my index finger between her lips.

"Suck," I order. She clasps my hand, and, with a lustful glance at me, she does exactly as I ask.

Christ.

Her look is scorching. Wanton. Unwavering. And her tongue teases and pulls at my finger.

I might as well have my cock in her mouth.

I'm hard.

Instantly.

Oh, baby.

I've known very few women who have had this instant effect on me, but none as instant as Ana . . . and given her naïveté it surprises me. But she's had this hold on me since I met her.

Get to the matter in hand, Grey.

To lubricate the balls, I slip them into my mouth while she continues to pleasure my finger. When I try to withdraw it, her teeth clamp down and she gives me a winsome smile.

No you don't, I warn, shaking my head, and she loosens her grip, releasing me.

I nod, indicating she should bend over the chair, and she obliges.

Kneeling behind her, I move her panties to one side and slide my fellated finger inside her and circle slowly, feeling the tight, wet walls of her vagina. She moans and I want to tell her to be quiet and to stay still, but that's not the relationship we have anymore.

We're doing things her way.

I withdraw my finger, then gently ease each ball inside her, carefully pushing them as deep as they can go. As I slip her panties back in place, I kiss her delectable derrière. I sit back on my heels and run my hands up her legs and kiss each thigh where her stockings stop.

"You have fine, fine legs, Miss Steele." I stand and grasp her hips, pulling her against my arousal. "Maybe I'll have you this way when we get home, Anastasia. You can stand now."

She does, her breath quickening once she's upright, and she shimmies in front of me, her ass brushing my erection. I kiss her shoulder and extend my arm around her, palm up, holding out the Cartier box.

"I bought these for you to wear to last Saturday's gala. But you left me, so I never had the opportunity to give them to you." I take a deep breath. "This is my second chance."

Will she accept them?

It seems symbolic somehow. If she's serious about us, she'll accept them. I hold my breath. She reaches for the box and opens it and stares at the earrings for the longest time.

Please take them, Ana.

"They're lovely," she whispers. "Thank you."

She *can* play nice. I grin as I relax, knowing I won't have to fight to get her to keep them. I kiss her shoulder and spot the silver satin dress on the bed. I ask her if that's what she's chosen to wear.

"Yes. Is that okay?"

"Of course. I'll let you get ready."

I'VE LOST COUNT OF the number of these events I've attended, but for the first time I'm excited. I get to show Ana off to my family and all of their well-heeled friends.

I finish tying my bow tie with ease and grab my jacket. Slipping it on, I take one last look in the mirror. The asshole looks happy, but he needs to straighten his tie.

"Keep still," Elena snaps.

"Yes, Ma'am." I stand before her, getting ready for prom. I've told my parents I'm not going and that I'm seeing a friend. It will be our own personal prom. Just Elena and I. She moves, and I hear the rustle of expensive silk and inhale the provocative scent of her perfume.

"Open your eyes."

I do as I'm instructed. She's poised behind me and we're facing a mirror. I look at her, not at the idiot boy standing in front of her.

She takes the ends of my bow tie. "And this is how you do this." Slowly, she moves her fingers. Her nails are bright scarlet. I watch. Fascinated.

She pulls the ends and I'm wearing a most respectable bow tie.
"Now, let's see if you can do it. And if you do, I'll reward you."
She smiles her secret I-so-own-you smile and I know it will be good.

I'M REHASHING THE NIGHT'S arrangements with the security team when I hear her footfalls behind me. All four men are suddenly distracted. Taylor smiles. When I turn around, Ana is standing at the bottom of the stairs.

A vision. Wow.

She's stunning in her silver gown and reminiscent of a silent-movie siren.

I saunter over to her, feeling a disproportionate sense of pride, and kiss her hair. "Anastasia. You look breathtaking." I'm delighted that she's wearing the earrings. She flushes.

"A glass of champagne before we go?" I offer.

"Please."

I nod to Taylor, who leads his three colleagues out to the foyer, and with my arm around my date we head into the living room. From the fridge, I take a bottle of Cristal Rosé and open it.

"Security team?" Ana asks, as I pour the bubbling liquid into champagne flutes.

"Close protection. They're under Taylor's control. He's trained in that, too." I hand her a glass.

"He's very versatile."

"Yes, he is. You look lovely, Anastasia. Cheers." I raise my glass to meet hers. She takes a sip and closes her eyes, savoring the wine.

"How are you feeling?" I ask, noting the pink flush on her cheeks, the same blush of the champagne, and I wonder how long she'll tolerate the balls.

"Fine, thank you." She gives me a coy smile.

Tonight will be entertaining.

"Here, you're going to need this." I give her the velvet bag that contains her mask. "Open it."

Ana does and pulls out the delicate silver masquerade mask and runs her fingers through the plumes.

"It's a masked ball."

"I see." She examines the mask in wonder.

"This will show off your beautiful eyes, Anastasia."

"Are you wearing one?"

"Of course. They're very liberating, in a way."

She grins.

I have one more surprise for her. "Come. I want to show you something." I hold out my hand and lead her back out to the corridor and into my library. I can't believe I haven't shown her this room.

"You have a library!" she exclaims.

"Yes, the balls room, as Elliot calls it. The apartment is quite spacious. I realized today, when you mentioned exploring, that I've never given you a tour. We don't have time now, but I thought I'd show you this room and maybe challenge you to a game of billiards in the not-too-distant future."

Her eyes are bright with wonder as she takes in the collection of books and the billiard table. "Bring it on," she says with a self-satisfied grin.

"What?" She's hiding something. Can she play?

"Nothing," she says quickly, and I know that's probably the answer. She really is a hopeless liar.

"Well, maybe Dr. Flynn can uncover your secrets. You'll meet him this evening."

"The expensive charlatan?"

"The very same. He's dying to meet you. Shall we go?"

She nods, and excitement shines in her eyes.

WE TRAVEL IN COMPANIONABLE silence in the back of the car. I skim my thumb across her knuckles, sensing her growing anticipation. She crosses and uncrosses her legs, and I know the balls are taking their toll.

"Where did you get the lipstick?" she asks out of the blue.

I point to Taylor and mouth his name.

She laughs. Then stops abruptly.

And I know it's the kegel balls.

"Relax," I whisper. "If it's too much . . ." I kiss each of her knuckles and suck the tip of her little finger, rolling my tongue around it, as she did with my finger earlier. Ana closes her eyes, tips her head back, and inhales. Her smoldering eyes meet mine when she opens them again. She rewards me with a wicked grin and I respond in kind.

"So what can we expect at this event?" she asks.

"Oh, the usual stuff."

"Not usual for me."

Of course. When would she have been to an event like this? I kiss her knuckles once more as I explain. "Lots of people flashing their cash. Auction, raffle, dinner, dancing—my mother knows how to throw a party."

The Audi joins the line of cars arriving at my parents' house. Ana strains to have a look. I glance out of the back window to see Reynolds from the security detail following us in my other Audi Q7.

"Masks on." I retrieve mine from the black silk bag beside me.

When we pull up into the driveway, we are both in disguise. Ana looks spectacular. She's dazzling, and I want to show her off to the world. Taylor comes to a stop and one of the valets opens my door.

"Ready?" I ask Ana.

"As I'll ever be."

"You look beautiful, Anastasia." I kiss her hand and climb out of the car.

I put my arm around my date, and we walk alongside the house on a green carpet my mother has rented for the occasion. I glance once over my shoulder and observe our four security personnel walking behind us, looking everywhere. It's reassuring.

"Mr. Grey!" A photographer calls out to me, and I pull Ana close and we pose.

"Two photographers?" Ana observes, curious.

"One is from *The Seattle Times*; the other is for a souvenir. We'll be able to buy a copy later."

We pass a line of servers holding flutes of champagne and I hand a glass to Ana.

My parents have gone all-out, like they do every year. Pavilion, pergolas, lanterns, checkered dance floor, ice swans, and a string quartet. I watch Ana as she takes in the surroundings with awe. It's gratifying to see my parents' generosity through her eyes. It's not often that I get the opportunity to stand back and appreciate how lucky I am to be part of their world.

"How many people are coming?" she asks, sizing up the elaborate tent next to the shoreline.

"I think about three hundred. You'll have to ask my mother."

"Christian!" I hear the shrill, not-so-dulcet tones of my sister; then she's throwing her arms around my neck in a melodramatic display of affection. She's a vision in pink.

"Mia." I return her enthusiastic hug. She spies Ana, and I'm forgotten.

"Ana! Oh, darling, you look gorgeous! You must come and meet my friends. None of them can believe that Christian finally has a girlfriend." She hugs Ana and takes her hand. Ana gives me a quick apprehensive look before Mia drags her to a group of women who coo over her. All except one.

Shit. I recognize Lily, Mia's friend since kindergarten. Spoiled, wealthy, gorgeous, but spiteful, she embodies all the worst attributes of privilege and entitlement. And there was a time when she thought she was entitled to me. I shudder.

I watch Ana as she's gracious with Mia's friends, but she steps back suddenly looking uncomfortable. I think Lily is being an asshole. This will never do. I walk over and put my arm around Ana's waist. "Ladies, if I could claim my date back, please?"

"Lovely to meet you," Ana says to the throng as I pull her away. "Thank you," she mouths.

"I saw that Lily was with Mia. She is one nasty piece of work."

"She likes you," Ana observes.

"Well, the feeling is not mutual. Come, let me introduce you to some people."

Ana is impressive—the perfect date. Gracious, elegant, and

sweet, she listens attentively to anecdotes, she asks intelligent questions, and I love the way she defers to me.

Yes. I especially love that. It's novel and unexpected.

But then she's always unexpected.

What's more, she's oblivious to the many, many admiring glances she receives from both men and women, and she stays close to my side. I attribute her rosy glow to the champagne and maybe the kegel balls, and if the latter are bothering her, she hides it well.

The master of ceremonies announces that dinner is served, and we follow the green carpet across the lawn to the pavilion. Ana is looking toward the boathouse.

"Boathouse?" I ask.

"Maybe we can go there later."

"Only if I can carry you over my shoulder."

She laughs, then stops abruptly.

I grin. "How are you feeling?"

"Good," she says with a superior air, and my grin broadens.

Game on, Miss Steele.

Behind us, Taylor and his men follow at a discreet distance and, once in the tent pavilion, position themselves so they have a good view of the crowd.

My mother and Mia are already at our table with a friend of Mia's.

Grace welcomes Ana warmly. "Ana, how delightful to see you again! And looking so beautiful, too."

"Mother." I greet Grace and kiss her on both cheeks.

"Oh, Christian, so formal!" she chides.

My maternal grandparents join us, and after the obligatory hugs I introduce them both to Ana.

"Oh, he's finally found someone, how wonderful, and so pretty! Well, I do hope you make an honest man of him," my grandmother enthuses.

Inappropriate, Grandma.

Fuck. I stare at my mother. *Help. Mom. Stop her.*

"Mother, don't embarrass Ana," Grace admonishes her mom.

"Ignore the silly old coot, m'dear. She thinks because she's so old, she has a God-given right to say whatever nonsense pops into that woolly head of hers." My grandfather gives me a wink.

Theodore Trevelyan is my hero. We have a special bond. This man has patiently taught me how to plant, cultivate, and graft apple trees, and in doing so has won my eternal affection. Quiet. Strong. Kind. Patient with me. Always.

"Here, kiddo," Grandpa Trev-yan says. "You don't talk much, do you?"

I shake my head. No. I don't talk at all.

"That's no problem. Folks around here talk too much anyway. Do you want to help me in the orchard?"

I nod. I like Grandpa Trev-yan. He has kind eyes and a loud laugh. He holds out his hand, but I tuck my hands under my arms.

"As you like, Christian. Let's go make some green apple trees make red apples."

I like red apples.

The orchard is big. There are trees. And trees. And trees. But they are small trees. Not big. And they have no leaves. And no apples. Because of winter. I have big boots on and a hat. I like my hat. I'm warm.

Grandpa Trev-yan looks at a tree.

"See this tree, Christian? It makes bitter green apples. But we can fool the tree to make sweet red apples for us. These twigs are from the red apple tree. And here are my pruning shears."

Prew-nig sheers. They are sharp.

"Do you want to cut this one?"

I say yes with my head.

"We're going to graft this twig you've cut. It's called a scion."

Si-yon. Si-yon. I say the word in my head. He takes a knife and makes one end of the twig sharp. And he cuts a branch on the tree and sticks the si-yon in the cut.

"Now we tape it up."

He takes green tape and ties the twig to the branch.

"And we put melted beeswax on the wound. Here. You take this brush. Steady now. That's right."

We make many grafts.

"You know, Christian, apples are second only to oranges as the most valuable fruit grown in the U.S. of A. Here in Washington, though, there's not really enough sun for oranges."

I'm sleepy.

"Tired? You want to head back to the house?"

I say yes with my head.

"We've done a lot of grafting. This tree will yield a huge crop of sweet red apples come autumn. You can help me pick them."

He smiles and holds out a big hand and I take it. It's big and rough but warm and gentle.

"Let's go have some hot chocolate."

Grandpa gives me a crinkled smile and I turn my attention to Mia's date, who seems to be checking out mine. His name is Sean and I think he's from Mia's old high school. I shake his hand, squeezing hard.

Keep your eyes on your own date, Sean. And by the way, you're with my sister. Treat her well or I will end you. I think I manage to convey all of that information in my pointed look and the tight grip I have on his hand.

He nods and swallows. "Mr. Grey."

I pull out Ana's chair and we sit.

My dad is standing on the stage. He taps the mic and rattles off a welcome and an introduction to the great and the good gathered before him. "Welcome, ladies and gentlemen, to our annual charity ball. I hope that you enjoy what we have laid out for you tonight and that you'll dig deep into your pockets to support the fantastic work that our team does with Coping Together. As you know, it's a cause that is very close to my wife's heart, and mine."

The plumes on Ana's mask quiver as she turns to look at me, and I wonder if she's thinking about my past. Should I answer her unspoken question?

Yes. This charity exists because of me.

My parents formed it because of my miserable start in life. And now they help hundreds of addicted parents and their kids by offering them refuge and rehabilitation.

But she says nothing and I remain impassive, as I'm not sure how I should feel about her curiosity.

"I'll hand you over now to our master of ceremonies. Please be seated, and enjoy," Dad says, and he hands the microphone to the MC, then wanders over to our table, making a beeline for Ana. He greets her with a kiss on each cheek. She blushes. "Good to see you again, Ana," he says.

"Ladies and gentlemen: please nominate a table head," the MC calls out.

"Ooh. Me, me!" cries Mia, bouncing like a child in her seat. "In the center of the table you will find an envelope," the MC continues. "Would everyone find, beg, borrow, or steal a bill of the highest denomination you can manage, write your name on it, and place it inside the envelope? Table heads, please guard these envelopes carefully. We will need them later."

"Here." I give a hundred-dollar bill to Ana.

"I'll pay you back," she whispers.

Sweetheart.

I don't want that argument again. Saying nothing because a scene would be unseemly, I hand her my Mont Blanc so she can sign her name on the note.

Grace signals a couple of servers standing at the front of the pavilion and they pull back the canvas, revealing a picture-postcard view of Seattle and Meydenbauer Bay at dusk. It's a great view, especially at this time of the evening, and I'm glad the weather has remained fine for my parents.

Ana gazes at the cityscape and its reflection in the water with delight.

And I examine it anew. It's stunning. The darkening sky ablaze with the setting sun mirrored in the water, the lights of Seattle twinkling in the distance. Yeah. Stunning.

Seeing all this through Ana's eyes is humbling. For years I've taken it for granted. I glance at my parents. My father clasps his wife's hand as she laughs at something her friend says. The way he looks at her . . . the way she looks at him.

They love each other.

Still.

I shake my head. Is it weird that I'm having a strange and new appreciation for my upbringing?

I was lucky. Very lucky.

Our servers arrive, ten of them in total, and as one they present the table with our first course. Ana peeks at me from behind her mask.

"Hungry?"

"Very," she replies, with serious intent.

Damn. All other thoughts evaporate as my body responds to her bold statement and I know she's not referring to the food. My grandfather diverts her and I shift in my seat, trying to bring my body to heel.

The food is good.

But then it always is at my parents' place.

I have never been hungry here.

I'm startled by the direction of my thoughts and I'm glad when Lance, my mother's friend from college, engages me in a conversation about what GEH is developing.

I'm acutely aware of Ana's eyes on me as Lance and I debate the economics of technology in the developing world.

"You can't just give this technology away!" Lance scoffs.

"Why not? Ultimately, whose benefit is it for? As human beings, we all have to share finite space and resources on this planet. The smarter we are, the more efficiently we'll use them."

"Democratizing tech is not what I'd expect from someone like you." Lance laughs.

Dude. You don't know me very well.

Lance is engaging enough, but I'm distracted by the beautiful Miss Steele. She moves beside me as she listens to our conversation, and I know the kegel balls are having the desired effect.

Perhaps we should go to the boathouse.

My conversation with Lance is interrupted a few times by various business associates offering a handshake and the odd anecdote. I don't know if they're checking out Ana or trying to ingratiate themselves with me.

By the time dessert is served, I'm ready to leave.

"If you'll excuse me," Ana says suddenly, breathless. And I know she's had enough.

"Do you need the powder room?" I ask.

She nods, and in her eyes I see a desperate plea.

"I'll show you," I offer.

She stands and I start to get up, but Mia stands, too. "No, Christian! You're not taking Ana—I will."

And before I can say anything, she grabs Ana's hand.

Ana gives me an apologetic shrug and follows Mia out of the pavilion. Taylor signals that he's on it and trails behind them both; I'm sure Ana is unaware of her shadow.

Fuck. I wanted to go with her.

My grandmother leans in to talk to me. "She's delightful."

"I know."

"You look happy, dear."

Do I? I thought I was sulking at a missed opportunity.

"I don't think I've ever seen you so relaxed." She pats my hand; it's an affectionate gesture, and for once I don't withdraw from her touch.

Happy?

Me?

I test the word to see if it fits, and an unexpected warmth flares in my gut.

Yes. She makes me happy.

It's a new feeling. I've never described myself in those terms.

I smile at my grandmother and squeeze her hand. "I think you're right, Grandmother."

Her eyes twinkle and she squeezes mine back. "You should bring her to the farm."

"I should. I think she'd like that."

Mia and Ana return to the pavilion, giggling. It's a pleasure to watch them together and to witness my whole family embrace my girl. Even my grandmother has concluded that Ana makes me happy.

She's not wrong.

As Ana takes her seat, she gives me a swift carnal look.

Ah. I mask my smile. I want to ask if she's still wearing the kegel balls, but I presume she's removed them. She's done well to wear them this long. Taking Ana's hand in mine, I give her a list of auction prizes.

I think Ana will enjoy this part of the evening—Seattle's elite flashing their cash.

"You own property in Aspen?" she asks, and everyone at the table turns to look at her. I nod and put my finger to my lips.

"Do you have property elsewhere?" she whispers.

I nod. But I don't want to disturb everyone at the table with conversation. This is the part of the evening when we raise a sizable sum for the charity.

As everyone applauds a sale price of $12,000 for a signed Mariners baseball bat, I lean over and say, "I'll tell you later."

She licks her lips and my earlier frustration returns. "I wanted to come with you."

She shoots me a quick aggrieved look, which I think means that she's of the same mind, but she settles down to listen to the bidding.

I watch her get caught up in the excitement of the auction, turning her head to see who's bidding on what and applauding at the conclusion of each lot.

"And up next is a weekend stay in Aspen, Colorado. What are my starting bids, ladies and gentlemen, for this generous prize courtesy of Mr. Christian Grey?" There's a smattering of applause and the master of ceremonies continues. "Do I hear five thousand dollars?"

The bidding begins.

I contemplate taking Ana to Aspen. I don't even know if she

skis. The thought of her on skis is unsettling. She's not a coordinated dancer, so she might be a disaster on the slopes. I wouldn't want her to get hurt.

"Twenty thousand dollars, we are bid. Going once, going twice," the MC calls. Ana puts her hand up and calls.

"Twenty-four thousand dollars!"

And it's like she's kicked me in the solar plexus.

What. The. Fuck.

"Twenty-four thousand dollars, to the lovely lady in silver, going once, going twice. Sold!" the master of ceremonies declares, to rapturous applause. Everyone at our table gapes at her while my anger spirals out of control. That money was for her. Taking a deep breath, I lean forward and kiss her cheek. "I don't know whether to worship at your feet or spank the living shit out of you," I hiss in her ear.

"I'll take option two, please," she says quickly. Breathlessly.

What?

For a moment I'm confused, and then I realize the kegel balls have done their work. She's needy, really needy, and my anger is forgotten. "Suffering, are you?" I whisper. "We'll have to see what we can do about that." I run my fingers along her jaw.

Make her wait, Grey.

That should be punishment enough.

Or perhaps we could prolong the agony. A wicked thought comes to mind.

She wriggles beside me as my family congratulates her on her win. I drape my arm over her chair and begin to stroke her naked back with my thumb. With my other hand I take hers and kiss her palm, then rest her hand on my thigh. Slowly, I ease her hand up my thigh until her fingers are resting on my erection.

I hear her gasp, and from beneath her mask her shocked eyes meet mine.

I will never tire of shocking sweet Ana.

As the auction continues, my family returns their attention to the next prize. Ana, emboldened, no doubt, by her need, surprises me and starts to caress me through my pants.

Hell.

I keep my hand over hers so no one will be the wiser as she fondles me and I continue to stroke her neck.

My pants are becoming uncomfortable.

She's turned the tables on you, Grey. Again.

"Sold, for one hundred and ten thousand dollars!" the MC declares, bringing me back into the room. The prize is a week in my parents' place in Montana, and it's a colossal amount of money.

The whole room erupts with cheers and applause, and Ana takes her hands off me and joins in the clapping.

Damn.

Reluctantly, I applaud, too, and now that the auction is over, I plan to give Ana a tour of the house.

"Ready?" I mouth to her.

"Yes," she says, her eyes shining through her mask.

"Ana!" Mia says. "It's time!"

Ana looks confused. "Time for what?"

"The First Dance Auction. Come on!" Mia stands and holds out her hand.

Fucking hell. My annoying little sister.

I glower at Mia. Cockblocker extraordinaire.

Ana looks at me and starts to giggle.

It's infectious.

I stand, grateful for my jacket. "The first dance will be with me, okay? And it won't be on the dance floor," I murmur against the pulse beneath her ear.

"I look forward to it." She kisses me in full view of everyone.

I grin and then notice that the entire table is staring at us.

Yes, people. I have a girlfriend. Get used to it.

They, as one, look away, embarrassed to be caught gawking.

"Come on, Ana." Mia is persistent and leads Ana toward the small stage, where several women are assembled.

"Gentlemen, the highlight of the evening!" the MC booms over the PA system and the excited hum of the crowd. "The moment you've all been waiting for! These twelve lovely ladies have all agreed to auction their first dance to the highest bidder!"

Ana is uncomfortable. She looks down at the ground, then at her knotted fingers. She looks anywhere but at the group of young men approaching the stage.

"Now, gentlemen, pray gather around and take a good look at what could be yours for the first dance. Twelve comely and compliant wenches."

When did Mia get Ana involved in this fucking charade?

It's a meat market.

I know it's for a good cause, but still.

The MC announces the first young woman, giving her a hyperbolic introduction. Her name is Jada, and her first dance is quickly sold off for $5,000. Mia and Ana are talking. Ana looks engaged in what Mia is saying.

Shit.

What is Mia telling her?

Mariah is up for sale next. She seems embarrassed by the MC's introduction, and I don't blame her. Mia and Ana continue to talk—and I know it's about me.

For fuck's sake, Mia, shut up.

Mariah's first dance is sold for $4,000.

Ana glances at me, then back at Mia, who appears to be in full flow.

Jill is up next, and her first dance is sold for $4,000.

Ana stares at me, and I see her eyes glitter inside her mask, but I have no idea what she's thinking.

Shit. What did Mia say?

"And now, allow me to introduce the beautiful Ana."

Mia ushers Ana to the center of the stage and I make my way to the front of the crowd. Ana does not like to be the center of attention.

Damn Mia for making her do this.

But Anastasia is beautiful.

The MC makes another overblown and ridiculous introduction. "Beautiful Ana plays six musical instruments, speaks fluent Mandarin, and is keen on yoga . . . well, gentlemen—"

Enough. "Ten thousand dollars," I shout.

"Fifteen." There's a call from some random guy.

What the hell?

I turn to look at who is bidding on my girl, and it's Flynn, the expensive charlatan, as Ana calls him. I'd recognize his gait anywhere. He gives me a polite nod.

"Well, gentlemen! We have high rollers in the house this evening," the MC announces to the assembled patrons.

What is Flynn's game? How far does he want to take this?

The chatter in the pavilion dies as the crowd watches us and waits to hear my reaction.

"Twenty," I offer, my voice low.

"Twenty-five," counters Flynn.

Ana looks anxiously from me to Flynn. She's mortified. And, frankly, so am I. I've had enough of whatever game Flynn is playing.

"One hundred thousand dollars," I call, so that the entire audience can hear me.

"What the fuck?" one of the women behind Ana calls out, and I hear gasps from people in the crowd around me.

Come on, John.

I give Flynn a level stare and he laughs and graciously holds up both his hands. He's done.

"One hundred thousand dollars for the lovely Ana! Going once. Going twice." The MC invites Flynn to bid again, but he shakes his head and bows.

"Sold!" the MC cries out triumphantly, and the applause and cheering are deafening. I step forward and hold out my hand to Ana.

I've won my girl.

She beams at me with relief when she places her hand in mine. I help her down from the stage and kiss the back of her hand, then tuck it under my arm. We make our way to the exit of the pavilion, ignoring the catcalls and the shouts of congratulations.

"Who was that?" she asks.

"Someone you can meet later. Right now, I want to show you something. We have about twenty minutes until the First Dance

Auction finishes. Then we have to be back on the dance floor so that I can enjoy that dance I've paid for."

"A very expensive dance," she observes dryly.

"I'm sure it'll be worth every single cent."

At last. I have her. Mia is still on the stage and unable to stop me now. I guide Ana across the lawn toward the dance floor, aware that two of the close protection guys are tailing us. The sounds of revelry fade behind us as I take her through the French doors that lead into the sitting room. I leave the doors open so the guys can follow us. From there we head into the hall and up two flights of stairs to my childhood bedroom.

It will be another first.

Inside, I lock the door. Security can wait outside. "This was my room."

Ana stands in the center, drinking it all in: my posters, my bulletin board. Everything. Her eyes scan it all, then settle on me.

"I've never brought a girl in here."

"Never?"

I shake my head. There's an adolescent thrill running through me. A girl. In my room. What would my mom say?

Ana's lips part in invitation. Her eyes are dark beneath her mask and they don't leave mine. I saunter over to her.

"We don't have long, Anastasia, and the way I'm feeling right this moment, we won't need long. Turn around. Let me get you out of that dress."

She spins around immediately.

"Keep the mask on," I whisper in her ear.

She groans and I haven't even touched her. I know that she'll be craving relief after wearing the kegel balls for so long. I unzip her dress and help her out of it. I step back, drape it over a chair, and remove my jacket.

She's wearing the corset.

And thigh-highs.

And heels.

And the mask.

She's driven me to distraction during dinner.

"You know, Anastasia." I move toward her, undoing my bow tie and then the shirt buttons at the collar. "I was so mad when you bought my auction lot. All manner of ideas ran through my head. I had to remind myself that punishment is off the menu. But then you volunteered." Standing close, I stare down at her. "Why did you do that?"

I need to know.

"Volunteer?" Her voice is husky, revealing her desire. "I don't know. Frustration. Too much alcohol. Worthy cause."

She shrugs, and her eyes move to my mouth.

"I vowed to myself I would not spank you again, even if you begged me."

"Please."

"But then I realized you're probably very uncomfortable at the moment, and it's not something you're used to."

"Yes," she answers, breathy and sexy and pleased, I think, that I know how she feels.

"So there might be a certain latitude. If I do this, you must promise me one thing."

"Anything."

"You will safe-word if you need to, and I will just make love to you, okay?"

She agrees readily.

I lead her to the bed, throw the comforter aside, and sit down as she stands before me in her mask and corset.

She looks sensational.

I grab a pillow and place it beside me. Taking her hand, I tug so that she falls across my lap, her chest on the pillow. I sweep her hair off her face and the mask.

There.

She looks glorious.

Now, to spice this up. "Put your hands behind your back."

She scrambles to do my bidding and squirms on top of me.

Eager. I like that.

I tie her wrists with my tie. She's helpless. In my power.

It's exhilarating.

"You really want this, Anastasia?"

"Yes," she stresses, clarifying her need.

But I still don't get it. I thought all this was off the table.

"Why?" I ask as I caress her behind.

"Do I need a reason?"

"No, baby, you don't. I'm just trying to understand you."

Be in the moment, Grey.

She wants this. And so do you.

I stroke her ass once more, preparing myself. Preparing her.

Leaning over, I hold her down with my left hand and I smack her once with the other, just at the junction of her fine, fine ass and her thighs.

She moans an incoherent word.

It's not a safe word.

I smack her again.

"Two. We'll go with twelve." I start counting.

I smooth her behind and spank her twice, once on each cheek. And I pull off her lacy panties, trailing them down her thighs, her knees, her calves, and over her Louboutins, where I discard them on the floor.

It's arousing.

In every way.

Noting she's no longer wearing the kegel balls, I spank her again, numbering each blow. She groans and writhes across my knees, her eyes shut beneath her mask. Her ass is a lovely shade of pink.

"Twelve," I whisper when I'm done.

I caress her glowing ass and sink two fingers into her.

She's wet.

So fucking wet.

So ready.

She moans as I rotate my fingers inside her and she comes, loudly, frantically, around them.

Wow. That's quick. She's such a sensual creature.

"That's right, baby," I murmur, and I untie her wrists. She's panting, trying to catch her breath. "I've not finished with you yet, Anastasia."

I'm now uncomfortable. I want her.

Badly.

Lowering her so that her knees touch the floor, I kneel behind her. I undo my zipper and yank down my underwear, freeing my eager erection. From my pants pocket, I extract a condom and pull my fingers out of my girl.

She whimpers.

I wrap my cock in latex. "Open your legs." She complies and I ease into her. "This is going to be quick, baby," I whisper. I hold her hips and slowly pull out of her, then I slam into her.

She cries out. With joy. With abandon. With ecstasy.

This is what she wants, and I'm only too happy to oblige. I thrust and thrust, and then she's meeting me. Thrusting back.

Shit.

This is going to be even quicker than I thought. "Ana, no," I warn. I want to prolong her pleasure. But she's a greedy girl and she takes all she can. A voracious counterpoint to me.

"Ana, shit." It's a strangled cry as I come and it sets her off. She screams as her orgasm rips through her, pulling on me as I sink on to her.

Man, that was good.

I'm spent.

After all the teasing and the anticipation during that meal . . . this was inevitable. I kiss her shoulder and pull out of her and remove the condom, tossing it into the wastebasket by the bed. That will give my mother's housekeeper something to think about.

Ana's still in her mask, panting, smiling. She looks satiated. I kneel over her, resting my forehead on her back as we both find our equilibrium.

"Mmm," I murmur in satisfaction, and plant a kiss on her flawless back. "I believe you owe me a dance, Miss Steele."

She hums a contented response from somewhere deep in her throat. I sit back and pull her onto my lap.

"We don't have long. Come on." I kiss her hair. She moves off
my lap and sits on the bed, beginning to dress as I do up my shirt
and redo my bow tie.

Ana gets up and walks over to where I've placed her dress.
Wearing only her mask, corset and shoes, she embodies sensuality.
I knew she was a goddess, but this . . . She's beyond all my expecta-
tions.

I love her.

I turn away, feeling suddenly vulnerable, and straighten the
comforter on my bed.

The uneasy feeling ebbs like a receding tide as I finish and see
Ana examining the photographs on my bulletin board. There are
many—from all over the world. My parents were fond of a foreign
vacation.

"Who's this?" Ana asks, pointing to an old black-and-white
photograph of the crack whore.

"No one of consequence." I slip on my jacket and straighten my
mask. I'd forgotten about that picture. Carrick gave it to me when
I was sixteen. I'd tried several times to throw it away, but I could
never quite bring myself to dispose of it.

"Son, I have something for you."

*"What?" I'm in Carrick's study, expecting a dressing down. But
for what I don't know. I hope he hasn't found out about Mrs. Lincoln.*

"You seem calmer, more collected, more yourself these days."

I nod, hoping that my expression gives nothing away.

*"I was going through some old files and I found this." He hands
me a black-and-white photograph of a sad young woman. It's like a
gut punch.*

The crack whore.

*He studies my reaction. "We were given this at the time of the
adoption."*

"Oh," I manage to say through my closing throat.

"I thought you might want to see it. Do you recognize her?"

"Yes." I squeeze the word out.

He nods, and I know he has something else to say.

What more does he have?

"I don't have any information on your biological father. By all accounts he wasn't part of your mother's life in any way."

He's trying to tell me something . . . It wasn't her fucking pimp? Please tell me it wasn't him.

"If you want to know anything else . . . I'm here."

"That man?" I whisper.

"No. Nothing to do with you," my dad says, to reassure me.

I close my eyes.

Thank fuck. Thank fuck. Thank fuck.

"Is that all, Dad? Can I go?"

"Of course." Dad looks troubled, but he nods.

Clutching the photo, I leave his office. And I run. Run. Run. Run . . .

The crack whore was a sad and pathetic creature. She looks every bit the victim in this old black-and-white. I think it's a police mug shot but with the numbers cut off. I wonder if things would have ended up differently for her if my parents' charity had existed then. I shake my head. I don't want to talk about her with Ana. "Shall I zip you up?" I ask, to change the subject.

"Please," Ana says, and turns her back to me so I can zip up her dress. "Then why is she on your bulletin board?"

Anastasia Steele, you have an answer and a question for everything.

"An oversight on my part. How's my tie?"

She examines my tie and her eyes soften. She reaches up and straightens it, pulling on both ends. "Now it's perfect," she says.

"Like you." I fold her in my arms and kiss her. "Feeling better?"

"Much, thank you, Mr. Grey."

"The pleasure was all mine, Miss Steele."

I'm feeling grateful. Content.

I hold out my hand and she takes it with a shy but satisfied grin. I unlock the door and we head downstairs and back out to the gardens. I don't know at which point our security joins us, but they follow us onto the terrace through the sitting room's French doors. A few smokers are gathered there, puffing away, and they watch us with interest, but I ignore them and lead Ana toward the dance floor.

The MC announces, "And now, ladies and gentlemen, it's time for the first dance. Mr. and Dr. Grey, are you ready?" Carrick nods, my mother in his arms. "Ladies and gentlemen of the First Dance Auction, are you ready?" I circle Ana's waist and peer down at her, and she grins.

"Then we shall begin," the MC declares with gusto. "Take it away, Sam!" The band leader bounds across the stage, turns to the band and snaps his fingers, and the band begins a cheesy version of "I've Got You Under My Skin." I pull Ana close as we start to dance and she falls easily into step with me. She's captivating as I twirl her around the dance floor, and we grin at each other like the lovesick fools we are . . .

Have I ever felt like this?

Buoyant?

Happy?

Master of the fucking universe.

"I love this song," I tell her. "Seems very fitting."

"You're under my skin, too. Or you were in your bedroom."

Ana! I'm shocked.

"Miss Steele, I had no idea you could be so crude."

"Mr. Grey, neither did I. I think it's all my recent experiences," she says with a mischievous smile. "They've been an education."

"For both of us." I take her for a spin around the dance floor once more. The song finishes, and reluctantly I release her to applaud.

"May I cut in?" Flynn asks, appearing from nowhere. He has some explaining to do after the charade at the auction, but I step aside.

"Be my guest. Anastasia, this is John Flynn. John, Anastasia."

Ana shoots me a nervous look and I retreat to the sidelines to watch. Flynn opens his arms and Ana takes his hand as the band strikes up "They Can't Take That Away from Me."

Ana is animated in John's arms. I wonder what they are talking about.

Me?

Shit.

My anxiety returns in full force.

I have to face the reality that once Ana knows all my secrets, she'll leave, and that trying things her way is just prolonging the inevitable.

But John wouldn't be so indiscreet, surely.

"Hello, darling," Grace says, interrupting my dark thoughts.

"Mother."

"Are you enjoying yourself?" She's also watching Ana and John.

"Very much."

Grace has taken off her mask. "What a generous donation from your young friend," she says, but there's a slight edge to her voice.

"Yes," I respond dryly.

"I thought she was a student."

"Mom, it's a long story."

"I figured as much."

Something is off. "What is it, Grace? Spit it out."

She tentatively reaches out to touch my arm. "You look happy, darling."

"I am."

"I think she's good for you."

"I think so, too."

"I hope she doesn't hurt you."

"Why would you say that?"

"She's young."

"Mother, what are you—"

A female guest wearing the most garish gown I've ever seen approaches Grace.

"Christian, this is my friend Pamela, from book club."

We exchange pleasantries, but I want to grill my mother. What the hell is she trying to imply about Ana? The music is coming to an end, and I know I need to rescue Anastasia from my psychiatrist.

"This conversation isn't over," I warn Grace and head over to where Ana and John have stopped dancing.

What is my mother trying to tell me?

"It's been a pleasure to meet you, Anastasia," Flynn says to Ana.

"John." I nod in greeting.

"Christian." Flynn acknowledges me and excuses himself—to find his wife, no doubt. I'm confounded by the exchange I've just had with my mother. I sweep Ana into my arms for the next dance.

"He's much younger than I expected," Ana says. "And terribly indiscreet."

Fuck. "Indiscreet?"

"Oh yes, he told me everything," she discloses.

Shit. Did he really do this? I test Ana to see how much damage he's done. "Well, in that case, I'll get your bag. I'm sure you want nothing more to do with me."

Ana stops dancing. "He didn't tell me anything!" she exclaims, and I think she wants to shake me.

Oh, thank God.

I place my hand on the small of her back as the band launches into "The Very Thought of You." "Then let's enjoy this dance."

And I'm an idiot. Of course Flynn wouldn't break any professional confidences. And as Ana matches me step for step, my spirit soars and my anxiety dissipates. I had no idea I could enjoy dancing so much.

It amazes me how poised Ana is tonight on the dance floor, and for a moment I'm back in the apartment after our first night together, watching her doing a little jig with her headphones on. She was so uncoordinated then—such a contrast to the Ana who's here with me now, following my lead perfectly and enjoying herself.

The band segues into "You Don't Know Me."

It's slower. It's melancholy. It's bittersweet.

It's a warning.

Ana. *You don't know me.*

And as I hold her and we sway together, I silently beg her forgiveness for a sin she knows nothing about. For something she must never know about.

She doesn't know me.

Baby, I'm sorry. I inhale her scent and it offers me some solace. Closing my eyes, I commit it to my memory so I'll always be able to recall it once she's gone.

Ana.

The song finishes and she gives me a winsome smile.

"I need to go to the restroom," she says. "I won't be long."

"Okay." I watch her leave with Taylor following and note the other three security officers standing at the edges of the dance floor. One of them peels off to trail after Taylor.

I spot Dr. Flynn talking with his wife.

"John."

"Hello again, Christian. You've met my wife, Rhian."

"Of course. Rhian," I say as we shake hands.

"Your parents know how to throw a party," she says.

"That they do," I respond.

"If you'll excuse me, I'm going to run to the powder room. John. Behave," she warns, and I have to laugh.

"She knows me well," Flynn remarks dryly.

"So what the fuck was all that about?" I ask. "Are you having some fun at my expense?"

"Definitely at your expense. I love to see you parted with your money."

"You're lucky that she's worth every single penny."

"I had to do something to make you see that you're not afraid of commitment." Flynn shrugs.

"That was the reason you bid against me, to test me? It's not my lack of commitment that scares me." I give him a bleak look.

"She seems well equipped to deal with you," he says.

I'm not so sure.

"Christian, just tell her. She knows you have issues. It's not because of anything I've said." He holds his hands up. "And this isn't really the time or the place to have this discussion."

"You're right."

"Where is she?" Flynn glances around.

"Powder room."

"She's a lovely young woman."

I nod in agreement.

"Have some faith," he says.

"Mr. Grey." We're interrupted by Reynolds, from the security team.

"What is it?" I ask him.

"Could I have a private word?"

"You can speak freely," I answer. This is my shrink, for fuck's sake.

"Taylor wanted you to know that Elena Lincoln is talking to Miss Steele."

Shit.

"Go," says Flynn, and from the look he gives me, I know he'd like to be a fly on the wall for that conversation.

"Laters," I mutter, and follow Reynolds to the pavilion.

Taylor is standing by the tented doorway. Beyond him, inside the large tent, Ana and Elena are in a tense discussion. Ana suddenly whirls around and storms toward me.

"There you are," I say, trying to gauge her mood when she reaches us. She completely ignores me and brushes past both Taylor and me.

This is not good.

I give Taylor a quick look, but he remains impassive.

"Ana," I call, and hurry to catch up with her. "What's wrong?"

"Why don't you ask your ex?" she seethes. She's furious.

I check to make sure that no one is in listening distance. "I'm asking you," I persist.

She glares at me.

What the hell have I done?

She squares her shoulders. "She's threatening to come after me if I hurt you again—probably with a whip," she snarls.

And I don't know if she's being intentionally funny, but the image of Elena threatening Ana with a riding crop is ridiculous. "Surely the irony of that isn't lost on you," I tease Ana in an attempt to lighten her mood.

"This isn't funny, Christian!" she snaps.

"No, you're right. I'll talk to her."

"You will do no such thing." She crosses her arms.

What the hell am I supposed to do?

"Look," she says, "I know you're tied up with her financially, forgive the pun, but—" She stops and huffs because she seems at a sudden loss for words. "I need the restroom," she growls. Ana is pissed. Again.

I sigh. What can I do? "Please don't be mad," I urge. "I didn't know she was here. She said she wasn't coming." I reach up and Ana lets me run my thumb across her bottom lip. "Don't let Elena ruin our evening, please, Anastasia. She's really old news." I tip her chin up and plant a gentle kiss on her lips.

She relents with a sigh and I think our fight is over. I take her elbow. "I'll accompany you to the powder room so you don't get interrupted again."

I fish out my phone as I wait for her outside the portable luxury restrooms that my mother has rented for the event. There's an e-mail from Dr. Greene saying she can see Ana tomorrow.

Good. I'll deal with that later.

I punch Elena's number into my phone and walk several steps away to a quiet corner of the backyard. She answers on the first ring.

"Christian."

"Elena, what the hell are you doing?"

"That girl is unpleasant and rude."

"Well, maybe you should leave her alone."

"I thought I should introduce myself," Elena says.

"What for? I thought you said you weren't coming. Why did you change your mind? I thought we'd agreed."

"Your mother called and begged me to come, and I was curious about Anastasia. I need to know she's not going to hurt you again."

"Well, leave her alone. This is the first regular relationship I've ever had, and I don't want you jeopardizing it through some misplaced concern for me. Leave. Her. Alone."

"Chris—"

"I mean it, Elena."

"Have you turned your back on who you are?" she asks.

"No, of course not." I look up, and Ana is watching me. "I have to go. Good night." I hang up on Elena, probably for the first time in my life.

Ana raises a brow. "How's the old news?"

"Cranky." I decide a change of subject is for the best. "Do you want to dance some more? Or would you like to go?" I check my watch. "The fireworks start in five minutes."

"I love fireworks," she says, and I know she's being conciliatory.

"We'll stay and watch them, then." I fold her in my arms and pull her close. "Don't let her come between us, please."

"She cares about you," Ana says.

"Yes, and I her, as a friend."

"I think it's more than a friendship to her."

"Anastasia, Elena and I—" I stop. What can I tell Ana to reassure her? "It's complicated. We have a shared history. But it is just that, history. As I've said to you time and time again, she's a good friend. That's all. Please, forget about her." I kiss her hair and she says no more.

I take her hand, and we wander back to the dance floor.

"Anastasia," my father says in his smooth tone. He's standing behind us. "I wondered if you'd do me the honor of the next dance." Carrick holds his hand out to her.

I give him a smile and watch him lead my date onto the dance floor as the band starts "Come Fly with Me."

They're soon enjoying a spirited conversation and I wonder again if it's about me.

"Hello, darling." My mother sidles up to me, holding a glass of champagne.

"Mother, what were you trying to say?" I ask without any preamble.

"Christian, I—" She stops and looks anxiously at me, and I know she's prevaricating. She never likes to give bad news.

My anxiety level rises. "Grace. Tell me."

"I spoke with Elena. She told me that you and Ana had split up and that you were heartbroken."

What?

"Why didn't you tell me?" she continues. "I know you run a business together, but I was upset hearing it from her."

"Elena is exaggerating. I wasn't heartbroken. We had a falling-out. That's all. I didn't tell you because it was temporary. It's fine now."

"I hate to think of you being hurt, darling. I hope she's with you for the right reasons."

"Who? Ana? What are you implying, Mother?"

"You're a wealthy man, Christian."

"You think she's a gold-digger?" And it's like she's struck me. *Fuck.*

"No, that's not what I said—"

"Mom. She's not like that at all." I'm trying not to lose my temper.

"I hope so, darling. I'm just watching out for you. Be careful. Most young people experience heartbreak during their adolescence." She gives me a knowing look.

Oh, please. My heart was broken way, way before I hit puberty.

"Darling, you know we only want you happy, and I have to say, on the evidence of this evening, I've never seen you happier."

"Yeah. Mother, I appreciate the concern, but it's all good." I almost cross my fingers behind my back. "Now I'm going to rescue my gold-digging girlfriend from the clutches of my father." My voice is arctic.

"Christian—" My mother tries to call me back, but frankly she can fuck off. How dare she think that of Ana. And why the hell is Elena gossiping about me and Ana to Grace?

"That's enough dancing with old men," I announce to Ana and my dad.

Carrick laughs. "Less of the 'old,' son. I've been known to have my moments." He winks at Ana and swaggers away to join his distressed-looking wife.

"I think my dad likes you," I mutter, feeling murderous.

"What's not to like?" Ana says with a coy smile.

"Good point well made, Miss Steele." I pull her into an embrace as the band starts to play "It Had to Be You."

"Dance with me." My voice is low and husky.

"With pleasure, Mr. Grey," she replies. We dance and my thoughts of gold-diggers, overanxious parents, and interfering ex-Dommes are forgotten.

At midnight, the MC declares that we can remove our masks. We stand on the banks of the bay and watch the astonishing fireworks display, Ana in front of me, cloaked in my arms. Her face is lit by a kaleidoscope of colors as the fireworks explode in the sky above us. She marvels at each dazzling burst, a huge grin on her face. The display is perfectly timed to the music, Handel's "Zadok the Priest."

It's stirring.

My parents have gone overboard for their guests, and it makes me feel a little less annoyed with them. The final volley of rockets bursts into golden stars that light up the bay. The crowd spontaneously applauds as sparks rain down from the sky, illuminating the black water.

It's spectacular.

"Ladies and gentlemen," the MC calls out as the cheers and whistles fade. "Just one note to add at the end of this wonderful evening: your generosity has raised a total of one million eight hundred and fifty-three thousand dollars!" The news is met with rousing cheers from the crowd. It's an impressive total. I imagine my mother has been busy all evening extracting money from her wealthy friends and guests. My contribution of $600,000 has helped. The applause is deafening, and on the pontoon where the fireworks technicians have been busy, the words "Thank You from Coping Together" light up in silver sparklers and shimmer over the dark mirror of the bay.

"Oh, Christian, that was wonderful," Ana exclaims, and I kiss her. I suggest to her that it's time to go. I can't wait to get home and curl up with her. It's been a long day. I'm hoping that I don't need to persuade her to stay the night. For a start, Leila is still at large. Also, in spite of everything, I've enjoyed today, and I want more. I want her to stay through Sunday, and maybe next week, too.

Tomorrow Ana can see Dr. Greene and, depending on the weather, we could either go soaring or go sailing. I could show her *The Grace*.

Spending more time with Ana is appealing.

Very appealing.

Taylor approaches, shaking his head, and I know he wants us to stay put until the crowd disperses. He's been vigilant all evening and must be exhausted. I follow his direction and ask Ana to wait with me.

"So, Aspen?" I ask, to divert her.

"Oh, I haven't paid for my bid," she says.

"You can send a check. I have the address."

"You were really mad."

"Yes, I was."

"I blame you and your toys."

"You were quite overcome, Miss Steele. A most satisfactory outcome, if I recall. Incidentally, where are they?"

"The silver balls? In my bag."

"I'd like them back. They are far too potent a device to be left in your innocent hands."

"Worried I might be quite overcome again, maybe with somebody else?" she says, with a wicked gleam in her eye.

Ana, don't tease me about these things.

"I hope that's not going to happen. But no, Ana, I want all your pleasure."

Always.

"Don't you trust me?" she asks.

"Implicitly. Now, can I have them back?"

"I'll think about it."

Miss Steele is playing hardball.

In the distance, the DJ has started his set.

"Do you want to dance?" I ask.

"I'm really tired, Christian. I'd like to go, if that's okay."

I motion to Taylor. He nods and talks into his sleeve micro-phone to the other security personnel, and we make our way across the lawn. Mia gallops toward us with her shoes in hand. "You're not going, are you? The real music's just beginning. Come on, Ana." She grabs Ana's free hand.

"Mia, Anastasia's tired. We're going home. Besides, we have a big day tomorrow."

Ana looks at me in surprise.

Mia pouts because she's not getting her way, but she doesn't push it. "You must come by sometime next week. Maybe we can hit the mall?"

"Sure, Mia," Ana replies, and I hear the fatigue in her voice. I must get her home. Mia kisses Ana good-bye, then grabs me and hugs me, hard. Her face shines as she stares up at me.

"I like seeing you this happy," she says, and she kisses me on the cheek. "Bye. You guys have fun." She runs off to her waiting friends, who start making their way to the dance floor.

My parents are nearby, and I'm now feeling guilty about the outburst with my mother. "We'll say good night to my parents before we leave. Come." We stroll toward them. Grace's face lights up when she sees us. Reaching up, she touches my face, and I try not to scowl at her. She smiles. "Thank you for coming and bring-ing Anastasia. It was wonderful watching the two of you together."

"Thanks for a great evening, Mom," I manage. I don't want to bring up our earlier conversation in front of Ana.

"Good night, son. Ana," says Carrick.

"Please do come again, Anastasia, it's been lovely having you here," Grace enthuses. She seems sincere, and the sting of her gold-digger comment begins to fade. Perhaps she is just looking out for me. But they don't know Ana at all. She's the least acquisi-tive woman I've ever met.

We walk around to the front of the house. Ana runs her hands up and down her arms. "Are you warm enough?" I ask.

"Yes, thank you."

"I really enjoyed this evening, Anastasia. Thank you."

"Me, too . . . Some parts more than others." And clearly she's thinking about our tryst in my childhood bedroom.

"Don't bite your lip," I warn.

"What did you mean about a big day tomorrow?" she asks. I tell her that Dr. Greene will make a house call and that I have a surprise for her.

"Dr. Greene?"

"Yes."

"Why?"

"Because I hate condoms."

"It's my body," she grumbles.

"It's mine, too," I whisper.

Ana. Please. I. Hate. Them.

Her eyes shine in the soft glow of paper lanterns that are strung up over the front yard, and I wonder if she's going to continue this argument. She raises her hand, and I still. She tugs the corner of my bow tie, and it unravels. With gentle fingers, she undoes the top button of my shirt. Fascinated, I watch her, and stay rooted to the ground.

"You look hot like this," she says quietly, surprising me.

I think she's moved on from Dr. Greene. "I need to get you home. Come."

The Q7 pulls up, and the valet gets out and gives the keys to Taylor. One of our security guys, Sawyer, hands me an envelope. It's addressed to Ana.

"Where did this come from?" I ask him.

"One of the servers gave it to me, sir."

Is it from an admirer? The handwriting seems familiar. Taylor ushers Ana into the car and I slide in beside her, handing her the note. "It's addressed to you. One of the staff gave it to Sawyer. No doubt from yet another ensnared heart."

Taylor follows the line of cars out of my parents' driveway. Ana rips the envelope open and casts her eyes over the note inside.

"You told her?" she exclaims.

"Told who what?"

"That I call her Mrs. Robinson."

"It's from Elena? This is ridiculous." I told Elena to leave Ana alone. Why is she ignoring me? And what has she said to Ana? What the hell is her problem? "I'll deal with her tomorrow. Or Monday." I want to read the note, but Ana doesn't give me the opportunity. She stuffs it in her purse but fishes out the kegel balls.

"Until next time," she says, handing them back to me.

Next time?

Now, that is good news. I squeeze her hand and she returns the gesture as she stares out of the window into the darkness.

Midway across the 520 bridge, she's asleep. I take a moment to relax. So much has happened today. I'm tired, so I put my head back and close my eyes.

Yeah. It's been quite a day.

Ana and the check. Her bad temper. Her willfulness. The lipstick. The sex.

Yes. The sex.

And of course I will have to deal with my mother's anxiety and her offensive concern that Ana is an opportunist who's after my fortune.

And then there's Elena, interfering, behaving badly. What the hell am I going to do about her?

I look at my image reflected in the car window. The sallow, ghoulish figure stares back at me and disappears only when we exit I-5 onto a well-lit Stewart Street. We are close to home.

Ana is still asleep when we pull up outside. Sawyer jumps out of the car and opens my door.

"Do I need to carry you in?" I ask Ana, squeezing her hand. She wakes and sleepily shakes her head. With Sawyer in front of us, keeping vigil, we walk into the building together as Taylor takes the car into the garage.

Ana leans on me in the elevator and closes her eyes.

"It's been a long day, eh, Anastasia?"

She nods.

"Tired?"

She nods.

"You're not very talkative," I observe.

She nods once more, making me smile.

"Come. I'll put you to bed." My fingers curl around hers, and we follow Sawyer out of the elevator and into the foyer. Sawyer halts in front of us and holds up his hand. I tighten my grip on Ana's fingers.

What the hell?

"Will do, T," Sawyer says, and turns to face us. "Mr. Grey, the tires on Ms. Steele's Audi have been slashed and paint thrown all over it."

Ana gasps.

What?

My immediate thought is that some mindless vandal has broken into the garage . . . then I remember Leila.

What the hell has she done?

Sawyer continues. "Taylor is concerned that the perp may have entered the apartment and may still be there. He wants to make sure."

How can anyone be in the apartment?

"I see. What's Taylor's plan?"

"He's coming up in the service elevator with Ryan and Reynolds. They'll do a sweep, then give us the all-clear. I'm to wait with you, sir."

"Thank you, Sawyer." I tighten my hold on Ana. "This day just gets better and better." There's no way Leila could be in the apartment. Is there?

And I recall those moments when I thought I saw something move at the periphery of my vision . . . and when I woke because I thought someone had ruffled my hair, only to find Ana fast asleep beside me. A shiver of doubt runs down my spine.

Shit.

If Leila's here, I need to know. I don't think she'll hurt me. I kiss Ana's hair. "Listen, I can't stand here and wait. Sawyer, take care of

Miss Steele. Don't let her in until you have the all-clear. I'm sure Taylor is overreacting. She can't get into the apartment."

"No, Christian." Ana tries to stop me, her fingers clasping my lapels. "You have to stay with me."

"Do as you're told, Anastasia. Wait here." I sound sterner than I mean to, and she releases me. "Sawyer?" He's standing in my way, uncertain. I raise a brow, and after a moment's hesitation he opens the double doors into the apartment and lets me go through. He closes them behind me.

In the hallway outside the living room it's dark and quiet. I stand and listen, straining my ears for anything unusual. All I hear is the sigh of the wind as it wraps itself around the building, and the hum of the electrical appliances from the kitchen. Far below in the street there's a police siren, but apart from that, Escala is still and quiet, as it should be.

If Leila were here, where would she go?

My first thought is the playroom, and I'm about to dash upstairs when there's a rumble and a ping from the service elevator, and Taylor and the two other security guys spill out into the corridor wielding guns, as if they're in some macho action movie.

"Are those strictly necessary?" I ask Taylor, who's leading the charge.

"We're taking the necessary precautions, sir."

"I don't think she's here."

"We'll do a quick sweep."

"Okay," I reply, resigned. "I'll check upstairs."

"I'll come with you, Mr. Grey." I suspect that Taylor is being unduly concerned for my safety.

He issues swift instructions to the other two and they scatter to search the apartment. I switch on all the lights so that the living room and corridor are well lit and bright, and I head upstairs with Taylor.

He's thorough. He checks under the four-poster bed, the table, and even the couch in the playroom. He does the same in the sub's room and in each of the spare rooms. No sign of any intruder. He proceeds into his and Mrs. Jones's quarters, and I head downstairs. My bathroom and walk-in closet are clear, as is my bedroom. Standing in the middle of the room, I feel like a fool, but I squat down and check under the bed.

Nothing.

Not even dust. Mrs. Jones is doing a stellar job.

The balcony door is locked, but I open it. Outside, the breeze is cool and the city is laid out, dark and somber, at my feet. There's the hum of distant traffic and the faint moan of the wind, but that's it. Inside again, I lock the door.

Taylor comes back downstairs. "She's not here," he says.

"You think it's Leila?"

"Yes, sir." His mouth forms a hard, flat line. "Do you mind if I search your room?"

Though I've already done this, I'm too tired to argue. "Sure."

"I want to check all the closets and cupboards, sir," he says.

"Fine." I shake my head at the preposterous situation we're in, and I open the foyer doors to find Ana. Sawyer brandishes his gun but lowers it when he sees it's me.

"All clear," I tell him. He holsters his pistol and stands aside. "Taylor is overreacting," I say to Ana. She looks exhausted, and she doesn't move—she just stares at me pale-faced, and I realize she's scared. "It's all right, baby." I fold her in my arms and kiss her hair. "Come on, you're tired. Bed."

"I was so worried," she says.

"I know. We're all jumpy."

Sawyer has disappeared, presumably into the apartment.

"Honestly, your exes are proving to be very challenging, Mr. Grey," she asserts.

"Yes. They are." They really are. I lead her into the living room. "Taylor and his crew are checking all the closets and cupboards. I don't think she's here."

"Why would she be here?" Ana sounds bewildered, and I reassure her that Taylor is thorough and that we've searched everywhere, including the playroom. To calm her, I offer her a drink, but she declines. She's tired. "Come. Let me put you to bed. You look exhausted."

In my bedroom, she empties the contents of her evening bag on top of the chest of drawers. "Here." She passes Elena's note to me. "I don't know if you want to read this. I want to ignore it."

I scan the note.

Anastasia,
I may have misjudged you. And you have definitely
misjudged me. Call me if you need to fill in any of
the blanks — we could have lunch. Christian doesn't
want me talking to you, but I would be more than
happy to help. Don't get me wrong, I approve,
believe me — but so help me, if you hurt him . . .
He's been hurt enough. Call me: (206) 279-6261.
                                        Mrs. Robinson

It provokes my temper.

Is this one of Elena's games?

"I'm not sure what blanks she can fill in." I put the note in my pants pocket. "I need to talk to Taylor. Let me unzip your dress."

"Are you going to call the police about the car?" she asks, as she turns around. I move her hair out of the way and pull down the zipper.

"No. I don't want the police involved. Leila needs help, not police intervention, and I don't want them here. We just have to double our efforts to find her." I kiss her shoulder. "Go to bed."

IN THE KITCHEN, I pour myself a glass of water.

What the hell is going on? My world seems to be imploding. Just when I'm beginning to get back on track with Ana, my past is coming back to haunt me: Leila and Elena. I wonder for a moment if they might be colluding with each other, but then I realize that I'm being paranoid. What an absurd notion. Elena is not that crazy.

I rub my face.

Why would Leila be targeting me?

Is it jealousy?

She wanted more. I didn't.

But I would have been happy to continue our relationship as it was . . . She was the one who ended it.

"Master. May I speak freely?" Leila says. She's sitting at my right at the dinner table, wearing a fetching lacy La Perla one-piece.

"Of course."

"I have developed feelings for you. I had hoped you would collar me and that I would stay by your side forevermore."

Collar? Forevermore? I think to myself. What's this once-upon-a-time bullshit?

"But I think that is beyond my dreams," she continues.

"Leila. You know that's not for me. We've discussed this."

"But you're lonely. I can see it."

"Lonely? Me? I don't feel that way. I have my work. My family. I have you."

"But I want more, Master."

"I can't give you more. You know this."

"I see." She raises her face to look at me, her amber eyes scrutinizing me. She's broken the fourth wall—she has never looked at me without permission. But I don't scold her.

"I can't. It's not within me." I've always been honest with her. This is nothing that she doesn't know.

"It is within you, Sir. But maybe I'm not the person to make you realize it." She sounds sad. She looks back down at her clean plate. "I'd like to terminate our relationship."

She's caught me by surprise. "Are you sure? Leila, this is a big step. I'd like to continue our arrangement."

"I can't do this anymore, Master." Her voice cracks on the last word, and I don't know what to say. "I can't," she whispers, clearing her throat.

"Leila—" I stop, bewildered by the emotion I hear in her voice. She's been an impeccable sub. I thought we were compatible. "I'll be sorry to see you go," I say, because it's true. "I've really enjoyed our time together. I hope you have, too."

"I'll be sorry, too, Sir. I've more than enjoyed everything. I had hoped . . ." Her voice trails off and she gives me a sad smile.

"I wish I felt differently." But I don't. I have no need of a permanent relationship.

"You've never given me any indication that you would." Her voice is quiet.

"I'm sorry. You're right. Let's end this as you wish. It's for the best, especially if you've developed feelings for me."

TAYLOR AND THE SECURITY team arrive back in the kitchen. "There's no sign of Leila in the apartment, sir," Taylor says.

"I didn't think there would be, but I appreciate you checking. Thanks."

"We're going to monitor the cameras in turn. Ryan first. Sawyer and Reynolds are going to sleep."

"Good. As you should."

"Yes, Mr. Grey. Gentlemen." Taylor dismisses the three men. "Good night."

Once they've left, Taylor turns to me. "The car's a mess, sir."

"Write-off?"

"I think so. She's done a real number on it."

"That's if it's Leila."

"I'll speak to the building security in the morning and check their CCTV. Do you want to involve the police?"

"Not yet."

"Okay." Taylor nods.

"I'll need to get Ana another car. Can you talk to Audi tomorrow?"

"Yes, sir. I'll have the wreck collected in the morning."

"Thanks."

"Is there anything else, Mr. Grey?"

"No. Thanks. Get some rest."

"Good night, sir."

"Good night."

Taylor leaves and I head into my study. I'm wired. I can't possibly sleep. I contemplate calling Welch just to keep him up-to-date, but it is too late. Slipping off my jacket, I hang it on my chair, then sit down at my computer and write him an e-mail.

As I press send my phone buzzes. Elena Lincoln's name flashes up on the screen.

What now?

I answer. "What do you think you're doing?"

"Christian!" She's surprised.

"I don't know why you're calling at this hour. I have nothing to say to you."

She sighs. "I just wanted to tell you—" She stops and changes tack. "I was hoping to leave a message."

"Well, you can tell me now. You don't have to leave a message." I'm finding it impossible to keep my composure.

"You're angry. I can tell. If it's about the note, listen—"

"No, you listen. I asked you, and now I am telling you. Leave her alone. She has nothing to do with you. Do you understand?"

"Christian, I only have your best interests at heart."

"I know you do. But I mean it, Elena. Leave her the fuck alone. Do I need to put it in triplicate for you? Are you hearing me?"

"Yes. Yes. I'm sorry." I've never heard her so contrite. It goes some way to cooling my anger.

"Good. Good night." I slam my phone down on the desk. Interfering woman. I put my head in my hands.

I'm so fucking tired.

There's a knock on my door.

"What?" I shout. I look up. It's Ana. She's dressed in my T-shirt, and she's all legs and big fearful eyes. She's bearding the lion in his den.

Oh, Ana.

"You should be in satin or silk, Anastasia. But even in my T-shirt you look beautiful."

"I missed you. Come to bed." Her voice is sexy and cajoling.

How can I sleep with all this shit going on? I stand and walk around my desk to gaze down at her. What if Leila wants to hurt her? What if she succeeds? How could I live with that?

"Do you know what you mean to me? If something happened to you, because of me . . ." I'm overwhelmed by a familiar, uncomfortable feeling that expands in my chest, becoming a lump in my throat that I have to swallow.

"Nothing's going to happen to me," she says in a soothing tone. She strokes my cheek, her fingers scratching my stubble. "Your beard grows quickly." There's wonder in her voice. I love her tender touch on my cheek. It's soothing and sensual. It tames the darkness. She caresses my bottom lip with her thumb, her eyes following her fingers. Her pupils are large and the small *v* has appeared between her brows as she concentrates. She traces a line from my bottom lip, down my chin, down my throat, to the base of my neck, where my shirt is open.

What is she doing?

She runs her finger along what I can only assume is the lipstick line. I close my eyes, waiting for the darkness to constrict my chest. Her finger touches my shirt.

"I'm not going to touch you. I just want to undo your shirt," she says.

Opening my eyes, I keep my panic in check and focus on her face. I don't stop her. The material of my shirt lifts and she unfastens a second button. Keeping the fabric off my skin, her fingers move to the next button down and she undoes that one, then the next. I don't move. I daren't. My breathing is shallow as I suppress my fear; my whole body is tense and waiting.

Don't touch me.

Please, Ana.

She opens the next button down and smiles up at me. "Back on home territory," she says, and her fingers trail along the line she made much, much earlier in the day and I tense my diaphragm as her fingers skim across my skin.

She undoes the final button and opens my shirt fully and I let out the breath I'm holding. Next she grabs my hand and, grasping my shirt cuff, removes my left cuff link, followed by the right. "Can I take your shirt off?" she asks.

I nod, totally disarmed, and she lifts my shirt up off my shoulders and pulls it from my body. She's done. She looks pleased with herself, and I'm standing half naked in front of her.

Slowly I relax.

That wasn't so bad.

"What about my pants, Miss Steele?" I manage a lascivious smirk.

"In the bedroom. I want you in your bed."

"Do you, now? Miss Steele, you are insatiable."

"I can't think why," she says, taking my hand. I let her lead me across the living room, through the corridor, and into my bedroom. It's cold. My nipples pucker against the chill in the room.

"You opened the balcony door?" I ask.

"No," Ana replies, looking at the open door with a bewildered expression. Then she turns to me, her face ashen. She's alarmed.

"What?" I ask, as every hair on my body stands on end—not from cold but from fear.

"When I woke," she whispers, "there was someone in here. I thought it was my imagination."

"What?" I scan the room quickly, then dash to the balcony and look outside. No one there—but I distinctly remember locking this door during the search. And I know Ana's never been on the balcony. I lock it again.

"Are you sure?" I ask her. "Who?"

"A woman, I think. It was dark. I'd only just woken up."

Fuck!

"Get dressed. Now!" I order. Why the hell didn't she tell me when she came into my office? I have to get her out of here.

"My clothes are upstairs," she whimpers.

From my chest of drawers I pull out some sweatpants. "Put these on." I toss them at her, pull out a T-shirt, and dress quickly.

I pick up the phone at my bedside.

"Mr. Grey?" Taylor answers.

"She's still fucking here," I bark.

"Shit," says Taylor, and he hangs up.

Moments later he barrels into the bedroom with Ryan.

"Ana says she saw someone in the room. A woman. She came to see me in my study and neglected to tell me this." I give her a pointed look. "Then when we got back here the balcony door was open. I remember closing and locking it myself during the search. It's Leila. I know it is."

"How long ago?" Taylor asks Ana.

"About ten minutes," she answers.

"She knows the apartment like the back of her hand. I'm taking Anastasia away now. She's hiding here somewhere. Find her. When is Gail back?"

"Tomorrow evening, sir."

"She's not to return until this place is secure. Understand?"

"Yes, sir. Will you be going to Bellevue?"

"I'm not taking this problem to my parents. Book me somewhere."

"Yes. I'll call you."

"Aren't we all overreacting slightly?" Ana asks.

"She may have a gun," I growl.

"Christian, she was standing at the end of the bed. She could have shot me then if that's what she wanted to do."

I take a deep breath, because now isn't the time to lose it. "I'm not prepared to take the risk. Taylor, Anastasia needs shoes." Taylor leaves, but Ryan stays to watch over Ana.

I hurry into my closet, strip out of my pants, and pull on some jeans and my jacket. From my dress-pants pocket I grab the condoms I'd slipped in there earlier and stuff them into my jeans pocket. I pack some clothes, and as an afterthought grab my denim jacket.

Ana is where I left her, looking lost and anxious. My sweatpants are far too big on her, but there's no time for her to change. I place the denim jacket over her shoulders and grab her hand.

"Come."

I lead her into the living room to wait for Taylor.

"I can't believe she could hide somewhere in here," Ana says.

"It's a big place. You haven't seen it all yet."

"Why don't you just call her? Tell her you want to talk to her?"

"Anastasia, she's unstable, and she may be armed," I stress, irritated.

"So we just run?"

"For now, yes."

"Supposing she tries to shoot Taylor?"

Jesus. I hope she doesn't.

"Taylor knows and understands guns. He'll be quicker with a gun than she is." I hope.

"Ray was in the army. He taught me to shoot."

"You, with a gun?" I scoff. I'm shocked. I loathe guns.

"Yes." She sounds offended. "I can shoot, Mr. Grey, so you'd better beware. It's not just crazy ex-subs you need to worry about."

"I'll bear that in mind, Miss Steele."

Taylor comes down the stairs and we join him in the foyer. He gives Ana a carry-on suitcase and her Chucks. She hugs him, taking him and me by surprise.

"Be careful," she says.

"Yes, Miss Steele," Taylor replies, embarrassed yet pleased by her concern and her spontaneous affection. I give him a look and he adjusts his tie.

"Let me know where I'm going."

Taylor takes out his wallet and passes me his credit card. "You might want to use this when you get there."

Whoa. He's really taking this seriously. "Good thinking."

Ryan joins us. "Sawyer and Reynolds found nothing," he tells Taylor.

"Accompany Mr. Grey and Miss Steele to the garage," Taylor says.

The three of us enter the elevator, where Ana has a chance to pull on her Chucks. She looks a little comical in my jacket and sweatpants. But as cute as she looks, I can't find the funny in our situation; the fact is I've placed her in harm's way.

Ana blanches when she sees her car in the garage. It's a mess— the windshield is shattered and the bodywork is covered in dents and cheap white paint. My blood boils at the sight, but for Ana's sake I control my rage. I usher her quickly into the R8. She's staring straight ahead when I climb into the car beside her, and I know it's because she can't bear to look at her car.

"A replacement will arrive on Monday," I assure her, hoping that might make her feel better. I start the engine and put on my seatbelt.

"How could she have known it was my car?"

I sigh. This is not going to go down well. "She had an Audi A3. I buy one for all my submissives. It's one of the safest cars in its class."

"So, not so much a graduation present, then," she says quietly.

"Anastasia, despite what I hoped, you have never been my submissive, so technically it is a graduation present." I back out of the parking space and head to the garage exit where we pause, waiting for the barrier to lift.

"Are you still hoping?" she asks.

What?

The in-car phone rings. "Grey," I answer.

"Fairmont Olympic. In my name," Taylor informs me.

"Thank you, Taylor. And Taylor, be careful."

"Yes, sir," he says, and hangs up.

It's eerily quiet in downtown Seattle. That's one of the advantages of driving at nearly three in the morning. I take a detour on I-5 just in case Leila is following us. Every few minutes I check the rearview mirror, anxiety gnawing at my gut.

Everything is out of control. Leila might be dangerous. Yet, she had the opportunity to harm Ana and didn't. She was a gentle soul when I knew her, artistic, bright, mischievous. And when she ended our relationship as a means of self-preservation, I admired her for that. She was never destructive, not even to herself, until she turned up at Escala and cut herself in front of Mrs. Jones, and tonight when she vandalized Ana's car.

She's not herself.

And I don't trust her not to hurt Ana.

How could I live with myself if that happened?

Ana is swimming in my clothes, looking small and miserable, staring out of the car window. She asked me a question and I was interrupted. She wanted to know if I'm still hoping for a submissive.

How can she ask that?

Reassure her, Grey.

"No. It's not what I hope for, not anymore. I thought that was obvious."

She turns to look at me, huddling down in my jacket, so that she looks even smaller. "I worry that, you know, that I'm not enough."

Why is she bringing this up now? "You're more than enough. For the love of God, Anastasia, what do I have to do?"

She fiddles with a button on my denim jacket. "Why did you think I'd leave when I told you Dr. Flynn had told me all there was to know about you?"

Is this what she's brooding about?

Keep it vague, Grey.

"You cannot begin to understand the depths of my depravity, Anastasia. And it's not something I want to share with you."

"And you really think I'd leave if I knew? Do you think so little of me?"

"I know you'll leave," I answer, and the thought is untenable.

"Christian, I think that's very unlikely. I can't imagine being without you."

"You left me once. I don't want to go there again."

She pales and begins fiddling with the drawstring on my sweatpants.

Yeah. You hurt me.

And I hurt you . . .

"Elena said she saw you last Saturday," she whispers.

No. That's bullshit. "She didn't." Why the hell would Elena lie?

"You didn't go to see her when I left?"

"No. I just told you I didn't, and I don't like to be doubted." And I realize I'm taking my anger out on her. In a gentler tone I add, "I didn't go anywhere last weekend. I sat and made the glider you gave me. Took me forever."

Ana looks down at her fingers. She's still fiddling with the drawstring.

"Contrary to what Elena thinks," I continue, "I don't rush to her with all my problems, Anastasia. I don't rush to anybody. You may have noticed, I'm not much of a talker."

"Carrick told me you didn't talk for two years."

"Did he, now?" Why can't my family keep quiet?

"I kind of pumped him for information," she confesses.

"So what else did Daddy say?"

"He said your mom was the doctor who examined you when you were brought into the hospital. After you were discovered in your apartment. He said learning the piano helped. And Mia."

A vision of Mia as a baby, a shock of black hair and a gurgling smile, comes to mind. She was someone I could take care of, someone I *could* protect. "She was about six months old when she arrived. I was thrilled, Elliot less so. He'd already had to contend with my arrival. She was perfect. Less so now, of course."

Ana giggles. And it's so unexpected. I immediately feel more at ease.

"You find that amusing, Miss Steele?"

"She seemed determined to keep us apart."

"Yes, she's quite accomplished." And annoying. She is . . . Mia. My baby sister. I squeeze Ana's knee. "But we got there in the end." I offer her a brief smile, then check the rearview mirror. "I don't think we've been followed."

I take the next off-ramp and head back into downtown Seattle.

"Can I ask you something about Elena?" Ana asks, when we're stopped at a red light.

"If you must." But I really wish she wouldn't.

"You told me ages ago that she loved you in a way you found acceptable. What did that mean?"

"Isn't it obvious?"

"Not to me."

"I was out of control. I couldn't bear to be touched. I can't bear it now. For a fourteen-, fifteen-year-old adolescent boy with hormones raging, it was a difficult time. She showed me a way to let off steam."

"Mia said you were a brawler."

"Christ, what is it with my loquacious family?" We're stopped at the next red. I glare at her. "Actually, it's you. You inveigle information out of people."

"Mia volunteered that information. In fact, she was very forthcoming. She was worried you'd start a brawl in the tent if you didn't win me at the auction," she says.

"Oh, baby, there was no danger of that. There was no way I would let anyone else dance with you."

"You let Dr. Flynn."

"He's always the exception to the rule."

I turn into the driveway of the Fairmont Olympic Hotel. A valet scrambles out to meet us and I pull up toward him.

"Come," I say to Ana and get out of the car to retrieve our luggage. I toss the keys to the enthusiastic young man. "Name of Taylor," I inform him.

The lobby is quiet, save for some random woman and her dog. At this time? Odd.

The receptionist checks us in. "Do you need a hand with your bags, Mr. Taylor?" she asks.

"No, Mrs. Taylor and I can manage."

"You're in the Cascade Suite, Mr. Taylor, eleventh floor. Our bellboy will help with your bags."

"We're fine. Where are the elevators?"

She directs us, and as we wait, I ask Ana how she's holding up. She looks worn out.

"It's been an interesting evening," she says, with her usual gift for understatement.

Taylor has booked us into the largest suite in the hotel. I'm surprised to discover it has two bedrooms. I wonder if Taylor is expecting us to sleep apart, as I do with my submissives. Maybe I should tell him this doesn't apply to Ana.

"Well, Mrs. Taylor, I don't know about you, but I'd really like a drink," I say, as Ana follows me into the master bedroom, where I set our overnight bags on the ottoman.

Back in the main living room there's a fire burning in the hearth. Ana warms her hands while I fix a drink at the bar. She looks gamine, adorable, and her dark hair shines coppery and bright in the firelight.

"Armagnac?"

"Please," she says.

By the fire, I hand her a brandy glass. "It's been quite a day, huh?" I gauge her reaction. I'm amazed, given all the drama of the evening, that she hasn't broken down and wept by now.

"I'm okay," she says. "How about you?"

I'm wired.

Anxious.

Angry.

I know of one thing that will give me relief.

You, Miss Steele.

My panacea.

"Well, right now I'd like to drink this, and then, if you're not too tired, take you to bed and lose myself in you." I'm really chancing my luck. She must be exhausted.

"I think that can be arranged, Mr. Taylor," she says, and rewards me with a shy smile.

Oh, Ana. You're my heroine.

I slip out of my shoes and socks. "Mrs. Taylor, stop biting your lip," I murmur. She takes a sip of her Armagnac and closes her eyes. She hums her appreciation for her drink. The sound soft and mellow and oh so sexy.

I feel it in my groin.

She really is something else.

"You never cease to amaze me, Anastasia. After a day like today, or yesterday, rather, you're not whining or running off into the hills screaming. I am in awe of you. You're very strong."

"You're a very good reason to stay," she whispers.

That strange feeling swells in my chest. Scarier than the darkness. Bigger. More potent. It has the power to wound.

"I told you, Christian, I'm not going anywhere, no matter what you've done. You know how I feel about you."

Oh, baby, you'd run if you knew the truth.

"Where are you going to hang José's portraits of me?" she asks, throwing me for a loop.

"That depends," I respond, bemused that she can change tack so quickly.

"On what?"

"Circumstances." It'll depend on whether she stays. I don't think I could bear to look at them when she's no longer mine.

If. If she's no longer mine.

"His show's not over yet, so I don't have to decide straightaway." I still don't know when the gallery will deliver them, in spite of my request.

She narrows her eyes, studying me, as if I'm hiding something.

Yeah. My fear. That's what I'm hiding.

"You can look as sternly as you like, Mrs. Taylor. I'm saying nothing," I tease.

"I may torture the truth from you."

"Really, Anastasia, I don't think you should make promises you can't fulfill."

She narrows her eyes once more, but this time, she's amused. She places her glass on the mantelpiece, then takes mine and sets it beside hers. "We'll just have to see about that," she says with cool determination in her voice. Grasping my hand, she guides me into the bedroom.

Ana is taking the lead.

This hasn't happened since that time in my study when she jumped me.

Go with it, Grey.

At the foot of the bed, she stops.

"Now that you have me in here, Anastasia, what are you going to do with me?"

She looks up at me, eyes shining, full of love, and I swallow, awed at the sight of her. "I'm going to start by undressing you. I want to finish what I started earlier."

All the breath leaves my body.

She grasps the lapels of my jacket and gently eases it off my shoulders. She turns and places it on the ottoman and I catch a trace of her fragrance.

Ana.

"Now your T-shirt," she says. I feel bolder. I know she won't touch me. Her road-map idea was a good one, and I still have the smudged remains of the lipstick on my chest and back. I raise my arms and take a step back as she tugs my T-shirt over my head.

Her lips part as she surveys my torso, and I itch to touch her, but I'm loving her slow, sweet seduction.

We're doing it her way.

"Now what?" I murmur.

"I want to kiss you here." She runs a fingernail across my belly from hipbone to hipbone.

Fuck.

I tense everywhere as all the blood in my body heads south. "I'm not stopping you," I whisper.

Grabbing my hand, she instructs me to lie down.

With my pants on?

Okay.

I remove the covers on the bed and sit down, my eyes on Ana, waiting to see what she'll do next. She shrugs out of my denim jacket and lets it fall to the floor; my sweatpants follow, and it takes all my self-control not to grab her and toss her onto the bed.

Squaring her shoulders, her gaze fixed on mine, she grips the hem of my T-shirt and tugs it over her head, wiggling to get it free.

Naked before me, she's beautiful. "You are Aphrodite, Anastasia."

She cradles my face in her hands and stoops to kiss me, and I can resist her no more. When her lips touch mine, I reach for her hips and pull her onto the bed so that she's beneath me. As we kiss, I push her legs apart so I'm resting at the junction of her thighs:

my favorite place. She kisses me back with a ferocity that fires my blood, her mouth voracious, her tongue wrestling with mine. She tastes of Armagnac and Ana. My hands are on her. With one, I cup her head and I trail the other up her body, kneading and squeezing as I go. Palming her breast, I tweak her nipple and marvel as it hardens between my fingers.

I need this. I crave this contact.

She groans and tilts her pelvis, compressing my hardening denim-clad cock.

Fuck.

I suck in my breath. And stop kissing her.

What are you doing?

She's panting, gazing up at me with a scorching, imploring expression.

She wants more.

I flex my hips, pushing my erection against her while watching her reaction. She closes her eyes and moans with carnal appreciation and tugs at my hair. I do it again, and this time she slides against me.

Whoa.

The feeling's exquisite.

Her teeth scrape my chin and she claims my lips and my tongue in a passionate wet kiss as she and I grind against each other, moving in perfect opposition, creating a sweet, sweet friction that is delicious torture. The heat builds and burns between us, concentrated at our point of connection. Her fingers grasp my arms as her breathing accelerates. Panting, she moves her hand to my lower back and into the waistband of my jeans, where she cups my ass and urges me on.

I'm going to come.

No.

"You're going to unman me, Ana." I kneel up and tug down my pants, freeing my erection, and grab a condom from my pocket. I hand it to Ana, who lies, breathless, on the bed.

"You want me, baby, and I sure as hell want you. You know what to do."

With greedy fingers she rips open the foil packet and unfurls the condom over my straining dick.

She's so keen. I grin at her when she lies back down.

Insatiable Ana.

I run my nose along hers and slowly, slowly sink into her, claiming her.

She's mine.

She grasps my arms and tilts her chin up, her mouth open in a wide *o* of pleasure. Gently, I slide into her again, my arms and hands on either side of her face.

"You make me forget everything. You are the best therapy." I ease out of her again, and ease back inside her.

"Please, Christian, faster." She pushes her pelvis up to meet me.

"Oh no, baby. I need this slow."

Please. Let's do this slowly.

I kiss her and tug her bottom lip. She twines her fingers in my hair and holds me and lets me continue at my slow, tender pace. On and on and on. She begins to build, her legs stiffening, and she throws her head back as she comes, taking me with her.

"Oh, Ana," I call, and her name is a prayer on my lips. That unfamiliar feeling is back, swelling in my chest, fighting to get out. And I know what it is. I've known forever. I want to tell her I love her.

But I can't.

The words burn to ashes in my throat.

I swallow and rest my head on her belly, my arms coiled around her. Her fingers tangle in my hair. "I will never get enough of you. Don't leave me." I kiss her belly.

"I'm not going anywhere, Christian, and I seem to remember that I wanted to kiss your belly," she says. And she sounds a little grumpy.

"Nothing stopping you now, baby."

"I don't think I can move. I'm so tired."

I stretch out beside her and pull the comforter over us. She looks radiant but exhausted.

Let her sleep, Grey.

"Sleep now, sweet Ana." I kiss her hair and hold her.

I never want to let her go.

I WAKE TO BRILLIANT sunshine filtering through the sheers that shroud the windows and Ana soundly asleep beside me. In spite of our late night I feel refreshed; I sleep well when I'm with her.

I climb out of bed, grab my jeans and my T-shirt, and drag them on. If I stay in bed, I know I'll wake her. She's too tempting to leave alone, and I know she needs sleep.

In the main room, I sit down at the escritoire and take my laptop out of the bag. My first job is to e-mail Dr. Greene. I ask her if she can come to the hotel to attend to Ana. She responds that the only time she can do is ten fifteen.

Great.

I confirm the time and then call Mac, who's the first mate on my yacht.

"Mr. Grey."

"Mac. I'd like to take *The Grace* out this afternoon."

"You'll have fine weather."

"Yes. I'd like to head out to Bainbridge Island."

"I'll get her ready, sir."

"Great. We'll see you at around lunchtime."

"We?"

"Yes, I'm bringing my girlfriend, Anastasia Steele."

There's a slight hesitation in Mac's voice before he says, "Look forward to it."

"Me, too."

I hang up, excited that I can show *The Grace* to Ana. I think she'll love sailing. She loved the soaring and the flight in *Charlie Tango*.

I call Taylor for an update, but his phone goes to voice mail. I hope he's getting some well-deserved sleep or having Ana's wrecked Audi removed from the garage as he promised. It reminds me that I need to replace her car. I wonder if Taylor has spoken to the Audi dealership. It's a Sunday, so maybe not.

My phone buzzes. It's a text from my mother.

GRACE

Darling, it was so lovely to see you and
Anastasia last night.
As ever, thank you, and Ana, for your
generosity.
Mom X

I'm still smarting over her gold-digger comments. It's obvious
she doesn't know Ana well. But then, she's only met Ana three
times. It was Elliot who was always bringing girls around . . . not
me. Grace couldn't keep up.

"Elliot, darling, we get attached to them and then they're
history. It's heartbreaking."
"Don't get attached." He shrugs, chewing with his mouth open.
"I don't," he mutters so only I can hear him.
"One day someone will break your heart, Elliot," Grace says as
she hands Mia a plate of mac and cheese.
"Whatever, Mom. At least I bring girls home." He eyes me with
disdain.
"Lots of my friends want to marry Christian. Ask them," Mia
pipes up in my defense.
Ugh. What an unpleasant thought—her poisonous little eighth-
grade friends.
"Don't you have exams to study for, douchebag?" I give Elliot
the finger.
"Study. Not me, dickless. I'm out tonight," he brags.
"Boys! Enough! This is your first night home from college. You
haven't seen each other in ages. Stop arguing. Eat up."
I take a bite of mac and cheese. Tonight I get to see Mrs.
Lincoln . . .

It's 9:40 so I order breakfast for Ana and me, knowing it will
take at least twenty minutes. I turn back to my e-mails and decide
to ignore my mother's text for now.
Room service arrives just after ten. I ask the young man to keep

everything in the cart's warming drawers and, after he's set the table, I dismiss him.

Time to wake Ana.

She's still fast asleep. Her hair is a mess of mahogany on the pillow, her skin luminous in the light, and her face soft and sweet in repose. I lie down beside her and watch her, drinking in every detail. She blinks and opens her eyes.

"Hi."

"Hi." She tugs the comforter up to her chin as her cheeks turn rosy. "How long have you been watching me?"

"I could watch you sleep for hours, Anastasia. But I've only been here about five minutes." I kiss her temple. "Dr. Greene will be here shortly."

"Oh."

"Did you sleep well?" I ask. "Certainly seemed like it to me, with all that snoring."

"I do not snore!"

I put her out of her misery, grinning. "No. You don't."

"Did you shower?" she asks.

"No. Waiting for you."

"Oh. Okay."

"What time is it?"

"Ten fifteen. I didn't have the heart to wake you earlier."

"You told me you didn't have a heart at all."

That at least is true. But I ignore her comment.

"Breakfast is here. Pancakes and bacon for you. Come, get up, I'm getting lonely out here." I swat her behind, clamber off the bed, and leave her to get up.

In the dining room I remove the dishes from the cart and lay out the plates. I sit down and within moments my toast and scrambled eggs are history. I pour myself some coffee, wondering whether to hurry Ana along, but decide against it and open *The Seattle Times*.

She shuffles into the dining room wearing an oversized robe and sits down beside me.

"Eat up. You're going to need your strength today," I say.

"And why is that? You going to lock me in the bedroom?" she teases.

"Appealing as that idea is, I thought we'd go out today. Get some fresh air." I'm excited about *The Grace*.

"Is it safe?" she quips.

"Where we're going it is," I mutter, unamused by her comment. "And it's not a joking matter," I add.

I want to keep you safe, baby.

Her mouth sets in that stubborn way she has and she stares down at her breakfast.

Eat, Ana.

As if she can read my mind, she grabs her fork and starts picking at her breakfast, allowing me to relax a little.

A few minutes later there's a knock on the door. I glance at my watch.

"That'll be the good doctor," I say, and stroll to the door to answer it.

"Good morning, Dr. Greene, come in. Thank you for coming at such short notice."

"Again, Mr. Grey, thank you for making it worth my while. Where's the patient?" Dr. Greene is all business.

"She's having her breakfast and will be ready in a minute. Do you want to wait in the bedroom?"

"That'll be fine."

I show her into the master, and soon after Ana wanders in and gives me a disapproving look. I choose to ignore it and close the door, leaving her with Dr. Greene. She can be as annoyed as she likes, but she stopped taking her pills. And she knows I hate condoms.

My phone buzzes.

At last.

"Good morning, Taylor."

"Good morning, Mr. Grey. You called?"

"What news?"

"Sawyer has been through the CCTV footage from the garage and I can confirm it was Leila who vandalized the car."

"Shit."

"Quite, sir. I've updated Welch on the situation, and the Audi has been removed."

"Good. Have you checked the apartment CCTV?"

"We're doing that now, but we haven't found anything yet."

"We need to know how she got in."

"Yes, sir. She's not here now. We've done a thorough check, but I understand that until we're certain that she can't get in again you should stay away. I'm having all the locks changed. Even on the fire escape."

"The fire escape. I always forget about that."

"It's easily done, sir."

"I'm taking Ana to *The Grace*. We'll stay on board if we need to."

"I'd like to do a security check of *The Grace* before you get there," Taylor says.

"Okay. I can't imagine we'll be there before one."

"We can collect your luggage from the hotel after that."

"Great."

"And I've e-mailed Audi about a replacement vehicle."

"Okay. Let me know how that goes."

"Will do, sir."

"Oh, and Taylor, in the future, we only need a one-bedroom suite."

Taylor hesitates. "Very good, sir," he says. "Will that be all for now?"

"No, one more thing. When Gail returns, can you ask her to move all of Miss Steele's clothes and belongings into my room?"

"Certainly, sir."

"Thanks."

I hang up and sit back down at the dining table to finish the newspaper. I note with displeasure that Ana has hardly touched her breakfast.

Plus ça change, Grey. Plus ça change.

HALF AN HOUR LATER Ana and Dr. Greene emerge from the
bedroom. Ana looks subdued. We exchange good-byes with the
doctor and I close the suite door behind her.

"Everything okay?" I ask Ana as she stands, looking sullen, in
the hallway. She nods but won't look at me. "Anastasia, what is it?
What did Dr. Greene say?"

She shakes her head. "You're good to go in seven days."

"Seven days?"

"Yes."

"Ana, what's wrong?"

"It's nothing to worry about. Please, Christian, just leave it."

Normally I have no idea what she's thinking, but something
is troubling her, and because it's troubling her, it's troubling me.
Maybe Dr. Greene warned her away from me. I tilt her chin back
so we're eye to eye. "Tell me," I persist.

"There's nothing to tell. I'd like to get dressed." She jerks her
chin out of my hand.

Fuck. What's wrong?

I run my hands through my hair in an effort to remain calm.

Perhaps it's the Leila scare?

Or maybe the doctor gave her some bad news?

She gives nothing away.

"Let's shower," I suggest eventually. She agrees but is hardly
enthusiastic. "Come." I take her hand and move into the bathroom
with a reluctant Ana trailing behind me. I turn on the shower and
strip out of my clothes while she stands in the middle of the bathroom sulking.

Ana, what the hell is wrong?

"I don't know what's upset you, or if you're just bad-tempered
through lack of sleep," I say quietly as I unfasten her robe. "But I
want you to tell me. My imagination is running away with me, and
I don't like it."

She rolls her eyes, but before I can rebuke her she says, "Dr.
Greene scolded me about missing the pill. She said I could be
pregnant."

"What?"

Pregnant!

And I'm free-falling. Fuck.

"But I'm not," she says. "She did a test. It was a shock, that's all. I can't believe I was that stupid."

Oh, thank God.

"You're sure you're not?"

"Yes."

I exhale. "Good. Yes, I can see that news like that would be very upsetting."

"I was more worried about your reaction."

"My reaction? Well, naturally, I'm relieved. It would be the height of carelessness and bad manners to knock you up."

"Then maybe we should abstain," she snaps.

What the hell?

"You are in a bad temper this morning."

"It was just a shock, that's all," she says, sullen again.

I haul her into my embrace. She's tense and stiff with indignation. I kiss her hair and hold her. "Ana, I'm not used to this," I whisper. "My natural inclination is to beat it out of you, but I seriously doubt you want that."

She could cry it out if I did. In my experience, women feel better after a good cry.

"No, I don't," she responds. "This helps." And she puts her arms around me and hugs me tighter, her warm cheek against my chest. I rest my chin on the top of her head. We stand like this for an age and slowly she relaxes in my arms.

"Come, let's shower." I strip her out of her robe and she follows me into the hot water. It's welcome. I've felt grimy all morning. I shampoo my hair and hand the bottle to Ana. She looks happier now, and I'm glad the showerhead is big enough for both of us. She surrenders herself to the water, tipping up her lovely face, and begins to wash her hair.

I take the body wash, lather up my hands, then begin washing Ana. Her earlier bad mood has rattled me. I feel responsible. She's tired and she had a trying evening. As she rinses her hair, I massage and wash her shoulders, arms, underarms, back, and her beautiful breasts. Turning her around, I continue with her stomach and belly, between her legs, and her ass. She makes a noise of approval deep in her throat.

My smile is broad.

That's better.

I turn her to face me. "Here." I give her the body wash. "I want you to wash off the remains of the lipstick."

Her eyes flicker open and her expression is serious and earnest.

"Don't stray far from the line, please," I add.

"Okay."

She squeezes soap onto her palm and rubs her hands together to make a frothy lather. Placing her hands on my shoulders, she begins to wash away the line with a gentle circular motion. I close my eyes and take a deep breath.

Can I do this?

My breathing shallows, and panic wells in my throat. She continues down my side, her nimble fingers tenderly administering to me. But it's unbearable. Like tiny razor blades on my skin. Every muscle in my body is tense. I stand like a hollow bronze, counting the seconds until she's finished.

It's taking an eternity.

My teeth are clenched.

Suddenly her hands are no longer on my body and that alarms me more. I open my eyes and she's soaping her hands again. She glances up at me and I see my pain reflected in her eyes and on her sweet, anxious face. And I know it's not pity but compassion. My agony is her agony.

Oh Ana.

"Ready?" she asks, her voice hoarse.

"Yes," I whisper, determined not to let the fear win, and I close my eyes.

She touches my side and I freeze, as fear fills my gut, my chest, and my throat, leaving nothing but the darkness. It's a gaping, aching void that consumes me, all of me.

Ana sniffles and I open my eyes.

She's crying, her tears lost in the cascade of hot water, her nose pink. Her compassion is spilling down her face—her compassion and her anger as she washes away my sins.

No. Don't cry, Ana.

I'm just a fucked-up man.

Her lip trembles.

"No. Please, don't cry." I fold her into my arms and hold her. "Please don't cry for me."

She starts sobbing. Really sobbing. And I cradle her head in my hands and lean down to kiss her. "Don't cry, Ana, please," I whisper against her mouth. "It was long ago. I am aching for you to touch me, but I just can't bear it. It's too much. Please, please don't cry."

"I . . . want to touch you, too . . ." she stutters between sobs. "More than you'll ever know. To see you like this. So hurt and afraid, Christian. It wounds me deeply. I love you so much."

I run my thumb across her bottom lip. "I know. I know."

And she squints at me with a look of dismay, because she knows my words have no conviction.

"You're very easy to love. Don't you see that?" she says, as the water falls around us.

"No, baby, I don't."

"You are. And I do," she stresses. "And so does your family. So do Elena and Leila. They have a strange way of showing it, but they do. You are worthy."

"Stop."

I can't bear it. I put my finger over her lips and shake my head. "I can't hear this. I'm nothing, Anastasia." I'm a lost boy, standing before you. Unloved. Abandoned by the one person who was supposed to protect me, because I'm a monster.

That's me, Ana.

That's all I am.

"I'm a husk of a man. I don't have a heart."

"Yes, you do," she cries passionately. "And I want it, all of it. You're a good man, Christian, a really good man. Don't ever doubt that. Look at what you've done. What you've achieved." She continues to sob. "Look what you've done for me. What you've turned your back on, for me. I know. I know how you feel about me." Her blue, blue eyes, filled with love, filled with compassion, leave me as raw and exposed as they did the first time I met her.

She sees me. She thinks she knows me.

"You love me," she says.

Every ounce of oxygen evaporates from my lungs.

Time suspends and all I can hear is my own blood thrumming in my ears and the splash of the water as it washes the darkness away.

Answer her, Grey. Tell her the truth.

"Yes," I whisper, "I do."

It's a deep, dark confession wrenched from my soul. And yet as I say the words out loud it all becomes clear. Of course I love her. Of course she knows. I've loved her since I met her. Since I watched her sleep. Since she gave herself to me and only me. I'm addicted. I can't get enough. That's why I tolerate her attitude.

I'm in love. This is what it feels like.

Her reaction is instant. Her smile is dazzling, lighting up her beautiful face. She's breathtaking. She clasps my head, bringing my mouth to hers, and kisses me, pouring all her love and sweetness into me.

It's humbling.

It's overwhelming.

It's hot.

And my body responds. The only way it knows how.

Groaning against her lips, I encircle her with my arms. "Oh, Ana, I want you, but not here."

"Yes," she says feverishly against my mouth.

I switch off the water and lead her out of the shower. I wrap her in her bathrobe and secure a towel around my waist. Taking a smaller one, I begin to dry her hair.

This is what I love. Taking care of her.

And what's more, for a change, she's letting me.

She stands patiently while I squeeze the water from her hair and rub her head. When I look up she's watching me in the mirror above the sink. Our eyes meet and I'm lost in her loving look.

"Can I reciprocate?" she asks.

What does she have in mind?

I nod and Ana reaches for another towel. Standing on tiptoe, she wraps it around my head and starts to rub. I lower my head, giving her easier access.

Mmm. This feels good.

She uses her nails, rubbing hard.

Oh, man.

I grin like a fool, feeling . . . cherished. When I raise my head to look at her she's peeking at me through the towel, and she grins, too. "It's a long time since anyone did this to me. A very long time," I tell her. "In fact, I don't think anyone's ever dried my hair."

"Surely Grace did? Dried your hair when you were young?"

I shake my head. "No. She respected my boundaries from day one, even though it was painful for her. I was very self-sufficient as a child."

Ana stills for a moment and I wonder what she's thinking. "Well, I'm honored," she says.

"That you are, Miss Steele. Or maybe it is I who am honored."

"That goes without saying, Mr. Grey."

She tosses the damp towel onto the vanity unit in front of us and reaches for a new one. As she stands behind me our eyes meet once more in the large mirror.

"Can I try something?" she asks.

We're doing this your way, baby.

I nod, giving her permission, and she runs the towel down my left arm, removing all the drops of water that cling to my skin. She looks up, watching me intently, and leans forward, and kisses my biceps.

My breathing stalls.

She dries my other arm and leaves a trail of feather-light kisses over my right biceps. Dodging behind me so I can no longer see what she's doing. She wipes my back, respecting the lipstick lines.

"Whole back," I offer, feeling brave, "with the towel." I take a deep breath and shut my eyes.

Ana does as she's told and briskly dries my back. When she finishes she gives me a swift kiss on my shoulder.

I exhale. That wasn't so bad.

She puts her arms around me and dries my belly.

"Hold this," she says, and hands me a face towel. "Remember in Georgia? You made me touch myself using your hands," she explains. She wraps her arms around me and stares at me in the mirror. With the towel draped over her head, she looks like a biblical character.

The Virgin.

She's soft enough and sweet enough, but a virgin no more.

Grasping my hand that holds the face towel, she guides it across my chest, drying a spot. As soon as the towel touches me, I freeze. My mind empties and I will my body to endure this touch. I stand tense before her, unmoving. We're doing this her way. I start to pant with a strange mixture of fear, love, and fascination, and my eyes follow her fingers as she gently guides my hand, and wipes my chest dry.

"I think you're dry now," she says, and drops her hand.

In the mirror's reflection we fix our eyes on each other.

I want her. I need her. I tell her.

"I need you, too," she says, her eyes darkening.

"Let me love you."

"Yes," she replies, and I scoop her up in my arms, my lips on hers, and carry her into the bedroom. I lay her down on the bed, and with infinite care and tenderness I show her how much I honor her, cherish her, and treasure her.

And love her.

I AM A NEW being. A new Christian Grey. I am in love with Anastasia Steele, and what's more, she loves me. Of course, the girl needs to have her head examined, but right now I'm grateful, spent, and happy.

I lie beside her, imagining a world of possibility. Ana's skin is soft and warm. I cannot stop touching her while we gaze at each other in the calm after the storm.

"So, you can be gentle." Her eyes are alight with amusement.

Only with you.

"Hmm. So it would seem, Miss Steele."

She grins, showing perfect white teeth. "You weren't particularly the first time we, um, did this."

"No?" I take a strand of her hair and wind it around my index finger. "When I robbed you of your virtue."

"I don't think you robbed me. I think my virtue was offered up pretty freely and willingly. I wanted you, too, and if I remember correctly, I rather enjoyed myself." Her smile is shy but warm.

"So did I, if I recall, Miss Steele. We aim to please. And it means you're mine, completely."

"Yes, I am. I wanted to ask you something."

"Go ahead."

"Your biological father, do you know who he was?"

Her question is completely unexpected. I shake my head. She surprises me again. I never know what's going on in that smart brain of hers. "I have no idea. Wasn't the savage who was her pimp, which is good."

"How do you know?"

"Something my dad—something Carrick said to me."

Her look is expectant, urging me on. "So hungry for information, Anastasia." I sigh and shake my head. I don't like thinking about this time in my life. It's difficult to separate the memories from the nightmares. But she's persistent. "The pimp discovered the crack whore's body and phoned it in to the authorities. Took him four days to make the discovery, though. He shut the door when he left. Left me with her. Her body."

Mommy is asleep on the floor.
She has been asleep for a long time.
She doesn't wake up.
I call her. I shake her.
She doesn't wake up.

I shudder and continue. "Police interviewed him later. He denied flat-out I had anything to do with him, and Carrick said he looked nothing like me."

Thank God.

"Do you remember what he looked like?"

"Anastasia, this isn't a part of my life I revisit very often. Yes, I remember what he looked like. I'll never forget him." Bile rises in my throat. "Can we talk about something else?"

"I'm sorry. I didn't mean to upset you."

"It's old news, Ana. Not something I want to think about."

She looks guilty and, knowing she's gone too far with these questions, changes the subject. "So, what's this surprise, then?"

Ah. She remembered. Now, this I can deal with. "Can you face going out for some fresh air? I want to show you something."

"Of course."

Great! I swat her behind. "Get dressed. Jeans will be good. I hope Taylor's packed some for you."

I leap out of bed, excited to take Ana sailing, and she watches me pull on my underwear.

"Up," I nag, and she grins.

"Just admiring the view," she says.

"Dry your hair," I tell her.

"Domineering as ever," she observes, and I bend down to kiss her.

"That's never going to change, baby. I don't want you sick."

She rolls her eyes.

"My palms still twitch, you know, Miss Steele."

"I am glad to hear it, Mr. Grey. I was beginning to think you were losing your edge."

Oh. Mixed signals from Miss Steele.

Don't tempt me, Ana. "I could easily demonstrate that is not the case, should you so wish." I grab a sweater from my bag, fetch my phone, and pack the rest of my belongings.

Once I'm done, I find Ana dressed and drying her hair.

"Pack your things. If it's safe, we'll go home tonight; if not, we can stay again."

ANA AND I STEP into the elevator. An elderly couple moves aside for us. Ana looks up at me and smirks. I squeeze her hand and grin, remembering that kiss.

Oh, fuck the paperwork.

"I'll never let you forget that," she says so only I can hear. "Our first kiss."

I'm tempted to do a repeat performance and scandalize the elderly couple, but I settle for a discreet peck on her cheek that makes her giggle.

We check out at reception and walk hand in hand through the foyer to the valet.

"Where are we going, exactly?" Ana asks as we wait for my car.

I tap the side of my nose and wink, trying to hide my excitement. Her face lights up with a huge smile, matching mine. Leaning down, I kiss her. "Do you have any idea how happy you make me feel?"

"Yes. I know exactly. Because you do the same for me."

The valet appears with my R8.

"Great car, sir," he says, as he gives me my keys. I tip him and he opens Ana's door.

As I turn onto Fourth Avenue, the sun is shining, my girl is beside me, and there's good music playing on my car stereo.

I overtake an Audi A3 and suddenly remember Ana's wrecked car. I realize I've not thought about Leila and her crazy behavior for the last few hours. Ana's a good distraction.

She's more than a distraction, Grey.

Perhaps I should buy her something else.

Yes. Something different. Not an Audi.

A Volvo.

No. My dad has one.

A BMW.

No. My mom has one.

"I need to make a detour. It shouldn't take long," I inform her.

"Sure."

We pull into the Saab dealership. Ana looks perplexed. "We need to get you a new car," I say.

"Not an Audi?"

No. I'm not getting you the car I've bought all my subs. "I thought you might like something else."

"A Saab?" She's amused.

"Yeah. A 9-3. Come."

"What is it with you and foreign cars?"

"The Germans and the Swedes make the safest cars in the world, Anastasia."

"I thought you'd already ordered me another Audi A3?"

"I can cancel that. Come." I climb out of the car, walk to her side, and open the door. "I owe you a graduation present."

"Christian, you really don't have to do this."

I make it clear to her that I do and we stroll into the car show-room where a salesman greets us with a well-rehearsed smile. "My name's Troy Turniansky. Are you after a Saab, sir? Pre-owned?" He rubs his hands, sensing a sale.

"New," I inform him.

"Did you have a model in mind, sir?"

"9-3 2.0T Sport Sedan."

Ana shoots a questioning look at me.

Yeah. I've been meaning to test drive one of these.

"An excellent choice, sir."

"What color, Anastasia?" I ask.

"Er, black?" she says with a shrug. "You really don't need to do this."

"Black's not easily seen at night."

"You have a black car."

This is not about me. I give her a pointed look.

"Canary yellow, then," she says, and flips her hair over her shoulder—irritated, I think.

I scowl at her.

"What color do you want me to have?" She crosses her arms.

"Silver or white."

"Silver, then," she says, but reiterates that she'd be fine with the Audi.

Now, sensing the loss of a sale, Turniansky pipes up. "Perhaps you'd like the convertible, ma'am?"

Ana lights up and Turniansky claps his hands.

"Convertible?" I ask, raising a brow. And her cheeks redden with embarrassment.

Miss Steele would like a convertible, and I'm beyond pleased that I've found something she wants. "What are the safety stats on the convertible?" I ask the salesman, and he's prepared, reeling off a brochure's worth of stats and other information. I glance at Ana, and she's all smiles and teeth. Turniansky hurries to his desk to consult his computer on the availability of a brand-new convertible 9-3.

"Whatever you're high on, I'd like some, Miss Steele." I pull her close.

"I'm high on you, Mr. Grey."

"Really? Well, you certainly look intoxicated." I kiss her. "And thank you for accepting the car. That was easier than last time."

"Well, it's not an Audi A3."

"That's not the car for you."

"I liked it."

"Sir, the 9-3? I've located one at our Beverly Hills dealership. We can have it here for you in a couple of days." Turniansky is bursting at the seams with his achievement.

"Top of the range?" I ask.

"Yes, sir."

"Excellent." I hand him my credit card.

"If you'll come this way, Mr. . . ." Turniansky glances at the name on the card. "Grey." I follow him to his desk.

"Can you get it here tomorrow?"

"I can try, Mr. Grey." He nods and we begin to fill out the paperwork.

"THANK YOU," ANA SAYS as we set off.

"You're most welcome, Anastasia."

The soulful, sad voice of Eva Cassidy fills the R8 when I turn on the engine.

"Who's this?" Ana asks, and I tell her.

"She has a lovely voice."

"She does. She did."

"Oh."

"She died young." Too young.

"Oh." Ana gives me a wistful look.

I remember that she didn't finish her breakfast earlier and I ask her if she's hungry.

I'm keeping track, Ana.

"Yes."

"Lunch first, then."

I speed along Elliott Avenue, heading to Elliott Bay Marina. Flynn was right. I like trying things her way. I look at Ana, who's lost in the music, staring out at the passing scenery. I feel content and excited for what I have planned this afternoon.

The car lot is crowded at the marina, but I find a space. "We'll eat here. I'll open your door," I say, as Ana makes a move to get out of the car. Together we walk toward the waterfront, arms around each other.

"So many boats," she says.

And one of them is mine.

We stand on the promenade and watch the sailboats out in the Sound. Ana tugs her jacket around herself.

"Cold?" I tuck her under my arm, closer to my side.

"No, just admiring the view."

"I could stare at it all day. Come, this way."

We head into SP's, the waterfront restaurant and bar, for lunch. Inside, I search for Dante, Claude Bastille's brother.

"Mr. Grey!" He sees me before I see him. "What can I get you this afternoon?"

"Dante, good afternoon." I usher Ana onto one of the stools at the bar. "This lovely lady is Anastasia Steele."

"Welcome to SP's Place." Dante grins at Ana, his dark eyes intrigued. "What would you like to drink, Anastasia?"

"Please, call me Ana," she says, then, eyeing me, adds, "and I'll have whatever Christian's drinking."

Ana is deferring to me, like she did at the ball. I like it.

"I'm going to have a beer. This is the only bar in Seattle where you can get Adnams Explorer."

"A beer?"

"Yes. Two Explorers, please, Dante."

Dante nods and sets up the drinks on the bar and I tell Ana that the seafood chowder that's served here is delicious. Dante writes down our food order and gives me a wink.

Yes, I'm here with a woman I'm not related to. It's a first, I know.

I turn my attention to Ana. "How did you get started in business?" she asks, and takes a sip of her beer.

I give her the executive summary: With Elena's money and some shrewd but risky investments I was able to build a capital fund. The first company I acquired was about to go under; it had been developing power units for cell phones using graphene technology, but the R&D had exhausted the company's capital. The patents they held were worth exploiting, and I kept their key talent, Fred and Barney, who are now my two chief engineers.

I tell Ana about our work on solar and wind-up technology for the home market and the developing world, and our innovative research to develop battery storage. All critical initiatives, given the depletion of fossil fuels.

"You still with me?" I ask when our chowder arrives. I love that she's interested in what I do. Even my parents struggle not to glaze over when I tell them about my work.

"I'm fascinated," she says. "Everything about you fascinates me, Christian."

Her words are encouraging, so I continue my story, of how I bought and sold more companies, keeping those that shared my ethos, breaking up and selling the others.

"Mergers and acquisitions," she muses.

"The very same. I moved into shipping two years ago, and from there into improving food production. Our test sites in Africa are pioneering new agricultural techniques for higher crop yields."

"Feed the world," Ana teases me.

"Yeah, something like that."

"You're very philanthropic."

"I can afford to be."

"This is delicious," Ana says, as she takes another spoonful of chowder.

"One of my favorites," I respond.

"You told me you like sailing." Ana motions to the boats outside.

"Yes. I've been coming here since I was a kid. Elliot and I learned to sail at the sail school here. Do you sail?"

"No."

"So what does a young woman from Montesano do to keep herself amused?" I take a sip of my beer.

"Read."

"It always comes back to books with you, doesn't it?"

"Yes."

"What happened between Ray and your mom?"

"I think they drifted apart. My mom is such a romantic, and Ray, well, he's more practical. She'd been in Washington all her life. She wanted adventure."

"Did she find any?"

"She found Steve." Her expression darkens, as if the mention of his name leaves a nasty taste in her mouth. "But she never talks about him."

"Oh."

"Yes. I don't think that was a happy time for her. I wondered if she regretted leaving Ray after that."

"And you stayed with him."

"Yes. He needed me more than my mom did."

We talk freely and easily. Ana is a good listener and much more forthcoming about herself this time. Perhaps it's because she now knows that I love her.

I love Ana.

There. That's not so painful, is it, Grey?

She's explaining how much she disliked living in Texas and Vegas because of the heat. She prefers the cooler climate in Washington.

I hope she stays in Washington.

Yes. With me.

Like moving in?

Grey, you're getting way ahead of yourself here.

Take her sailing.

I glance at my watch and drain my beer. "Shall we go?"

We settle up for lunch and we head outside into the mild summer sunshine. "I wanted to show you something."

Holding hands, we amble past the smaller boats anchored in the marina. I spot *The Grace*'s mast towering above the smaller boats as we near her mooring. My anticipation escalates. I haven't been sailing for a while, and now I get to take my girl. Leaving the main promenade, we step onto the dock, then down onto a narrower pontoon. At *The Grace*, I stop. "I thought we'd go sailing this afternoon. This is my boat."

My catamaran. My pride and joy.

Ana's impressed.

"Built by my company. She's been designed from the ground up by the very best naval architects in the world and constructed here in Seattle at my yard. She has hybrid electric drives, asymmetric dagger boards, a square-topped mainsail—"

"Okay!" Ana says, holding up her hands. "You've lost me, Christian."

Don't get carried away, Grey.

"She's a great boat." I can't conceal my admiration.

"She looks mighty fine, Mr. Grey."

"That she does, Miss Steele."

"What's her name?"

I take her hand and show her *"The Grace"* written in an elaborate scroll on the side. "You named her after your mom?" Ana sounds surprised.

"Yes. Why do you find that strange?"

She shrugs, at a loss for words.

"I adore my mom, Anastasia. Why wouldn't I name a boat after her?"

"No, it's not that. It's just—"

"Anastasia, Grace Trevelyan-Grey saved my life. I owe her everything."

Her smile is uncertain, and I wonder what's going through her head, and what I might have done to make her think I don't love my mother.

Okay, so I once told Ana I didn't have a heart—but there's always been room for my family in what's left of it. Even Elliot.

I didn't know there was space for anyone else.

But there's an Ana-shaped space.

And she's filled it to overflowing.

I swallow as I try to contain the depth of feeling I have for her. She's bringing my heart back to life, bringing me back to life.

"Do you want to come aboard?" I ask, before I say something sappy.

"Yes, please."

Taking my hand, she follows me as I stride up the gangplank onto the aft deck. Mac appears, startling Ana when he opens the sliding doors to the main saloon.

"Mr. Grey! Welcome back." We shake hands.

"Anastasia, this is Liam McConnell. Liam, my girlfriend, Anastasia Steele."

"How do you do?" she says to Liam.

"Call me Mac. Welcome aboard, Miss Steele."

"Ana, please."

"How's she shaping up, Mac?" I ask.

"She's ready to rock and roll, sir," he says with a huge grin.

"Let's get under way, then."

"You going to take her out?" he asks.

"Yep," I reply. I wouldn't miss this for the world. "Quick tour, Anastasia?"

We go through the sliding doors. Ana scans the inside, and I know she's impressed. The interior has been created by a Swedish designer based in Seattle, all clean lines and light oak that give the saloon a bright and airy feel. I've adopted the same look throughout *The Grace*. "This is the main saloon. Galley beside." I wave in its direction. "Bathrooms on either side." I point them out, then lead her through the small door to my cabin. Ana gasps at the sight of the bed. "This is the master cabin. You're the first girl in here, apart from family." I hold her and kiss her. "They don't count. Might have to christen this bed," I whisper against her lips. "But not right now. Come, Mac will be casting off." I lead Ana back into the main saloon. "Office in there, and at the front here, two more cabins."

"So how many can sleep on board?"

"It's a six-berth cat. I've only ever had the family on board, though. I like to sail alone. But not when you're here. I need to keep an eye on you." From the chest by the sliding door I extract a bright red life jacket.

"Here." I slip it over her head and tighten the straps.

"You love strapping me in, don't you?"

"In any form." I wink at her.

"You are a pervert."

"I know."

"My pervert," she teases.

"Yes, yours."

Once I've fastened the buckles I grab the side of the life jacket and kiss her quickly. "Always," I say, and release her before she can respond. "Come." We go outside and up the steps to the top deck and the cockpit.

Below, at the dock, Mac is casting off the bow line. He leaps back on board.

"Is this where you learned all your rope tricks?" Ana is pretending to be naïve.

"Clove hitches have come in handy. Miss Steele, you sound curious. I like you curious. I'd be more than happy to demonstrate what I can do with a rope."

Ana goes quiet, and I think I've upset her.

Damn.

"Gotcha." She giggles, pleased with herself.

Well, that's not fair. I narrow my eyes. "I may have to deal with you later, but right now I've got to drive my boat." I sit down at the captain's chair and fire up the twin fifty-five-horsepower engines. I switch off the blower and Mac scoots along the top deck, grabbing the guardrail, then bounces down to the aft deck to release the stern lines. He waves at me and I radio the Coast Guard to get the all-clear.

I take *The Grace* out of idle, move the shifter forward, and ease the throttle. And my beautiful boat glides out of her berth.

Ana is waving to the small crowd that has gathered on the dock to witness our departure. I tug her back between my legs.

"See this." I point to the VHF. "That's our radio. Our GPS, our AIS, the radar."

"What's the AIS?"

"That identifies us to shipping. This is our depth gauge. Grab the wheel."

"Aye, aye, Captain." She salutes me.

I pilot us slowly out of the marina, Ana's hands beneath mine on the wheel. We turn into open water and we sweep across the Sound in a large arc until we're heading northwest toward the Olympic Peninsula and Bainbridge Island. The wind is moderate at fifteen knots, but I know once we get the sheets up *The Grace* will fly. I love this. Challenging myself against the elements in a boat I've helped design, using the skills I've spent a lifetime perfecting. It's thrilling.

"Sail time," I say to Ana, and I cannot contain my excitement. "Here, you take her. Keep her on this course."

Ana looks freaked out.

"Baby, it's really easy. Hold the wheel and keep your eye on the horizon over the bow. You'll do great; you always do. When the sails go up, you'll feel the drag. Just hold her steady. I'll signal like this"—I make a slashing motion with my hand across my throat—"and you can cut the engines. This button here." I point to the engines' kill button. "Understand?"

"Yes." But she looks uncertain. I know she's got this. She always does. I give her a quick kiss and bound onto the top deck to prep and hoist the main sail. Mac and I crank in unison, making light work of it. When the wind catches the sheet we lurch forward, and I glance at Ana, but she's holding us steady. Mac and I work on the headsail and it flies up the mast, welcoming the wind and harnessing its power.

"Hold her steady, baby, and cut the engines!" I shout over the roar of the wind and the waves, and I motion to her. Ana presses the button and the roar of the engines ceases as we whip across the sea, flying northwest.

I join Ana at the wheel. The wind is lashing her hair around her face; she's exhilarated, her cheeks flushed with joy. "What do you think?" I yell, above the call of the sea and the wind.

"Christian! This is fantastic."

"You wait until the spinney's up." With my chin I point to Mac, who is raising the spinnaker.

"Interesting color," Ana shouts.

I give her a knowing wink. Yep, the color of my playroom.

The wind pumps up the spinney and *The Grace* charges ahead, unleashing her power and giving us a thrilling ride. Ana looks from the spinnaker to me. "Asymmetrical sail. For speed," I call out. I've pushed *The Grace* to twenty knots, but the wind has to be in our favor for that kind of speed.

"It's amazing!" she shouts. "How fast are we going?"

"She's doing fifteen knots."

"I have no idea what that means."

"It's about seventeen miles an hour."

"Is that all? It feels much faster."

Ana is radiant. Her joy is infectious. I squeeze her hands on the wheel. "You look lovely, Anastasia. It's good to see some color in your cheeks, and not from blushing. You look like you do in José's photos."

She turns in my arms and kisses me. "You know how to show a girl a good time, Mr. Grey."

"We aim to please, Miss Steele." She turns back to face the bow and I smooth the hair away from her neck and kiss her. "I like seeing you happy," I murmur in her ear, and we careen across Puget Sound.

WE ANCHOR IN THE cove near Hedley Spit on Bainbridge Island. Together, Mac and I lower the dinghy so he can go ashore and visit a friend in Point Monroe. "I'll see you in about an hour, Mr. Grey." He descends into the small boat, gives Ana a wave, and fires up the outboard motor.

I vault up to the aft deck where Ana is standing and grab her hand. I don't need to watch Mac speed toward the lagoon; I have more pressing business to attend to.

"What are we going to do now?" Ana asks, as I take her into the saloon.

"I have plans for you, Miss Steele." And with indecent haste, I drag her into my cabin. She's smiling as I make quick work of her life jacket and toss it to the floor. Once it's off, she stares at me, remaining mute, but her teeth tease her bottom lip, and I don't know if it's deliberate or an unconscious lure.

I want to make love to her.

On my boat.

It will be another first.

Caressing her face with the tips of my fingers, I slowly move them down to her chin, her neck, and her sternum to the first closed button on her blouse. Her eyes never waver from mine. "I want to see you." With my thumb and forefinger, I undo the button. She stands absolutely still, her breathing accelerated.

I know she's mine to do with as I please. My girl.

I stand back to give her some room. "Strip for me," I whisper. Her lips part and eyes blaze with desire. Slowly she brings her fingers up to her next fastened button, and at a snail's pace undoes it, then moves at the same infuriating pace to the next one.

Fuck.

She's taunting me. Minx.

When the final button is undone she pulls her shirt apart and shrugs out of it, letting it fall to the floor.

She's wearing a white lacy bra, her nipples taut against the lace, and she's a fine, fine sight. Her fingers run down past her navel and toy with the top button of her jeans.

Sweetheart, you need to take your shoes off.

"Stop. Sit." I point to the edge of the bed and she complies.

I fall to my knees and undo the laces of first one and then the other sneaker, pulling them off, followed by her socks.

I pick up her foot and kiss the soft pad of her big toe, then graze it with my teeth.

"Ah," she breathes, and the sound is music to my dick.

Let her do this her way, Grey.

Standing, I hold out my hand and pull her up from the bed. "Continue." I give her the floor and step back to enjoy the show.

With a wanton look at me, she undoes the button and tugs down her zipper at the same slow pace. She hooks her thumbs into her waistband and slowly shimmies out of her jeans, sliding them down her legs.

She's wearing a thong.

A thong.

Wow.

She unfastens her bra and slides the straps down her arms before dropping it on the floor.

I want to touch her.

And I clench my fists to stop myself.

She slips off her thong and lets it fall to her ankles, where she steps out of it and stands before me.

She is all woman.

And I want her.

All of her.

Her body, her heart, and her soul.

You have her heart, Grey. She loves you.

I grab the hem of my sweater and pull it over my head, then my T-shirt. I slip out of my shoes and socks. Her eyes never leave mine.

Her look is scorching.

I move to undo my jeans. She puts her hand over mine. "Let me," she whispers.

I'm impatient to get out of my jeans, but I give her a big smile. "Be my guest."

She steps forward and slips her hand over the waistband of my jeans and tugs so I'm forced to take a step closer to her. She undoes the top button, but she doesn't undo the zipper. Instead, her intrepid fingers meander from the zipper to trace the straining outline of my cock. Instinctively, I flex my hips, pushing my erection into her hand. "You're getting so bold, Ana, so brave." I cradle her face with my hands and kiss her, easing my tongue into her mouth while she places her hands on my hips and circles her thumbs against my skin, just above the waistband of my jeans.

"So are you," she breathes against my lips.

"Getting there," I answer.

She tugs down my fly, pushes her hand inside my pants, and takes hold of my cock. I growl in appreciation and my lips find hers as I fold her in my arms, feeling her soft skin against mine.

The darkness is gone.

She knows where to touch me.

And how to touch me.

Her hand tightens around me, squeezing hard, and her hand moves up and down, pleasuring me. I tolerate a few moves, then whisper, "Oh, I want you so much, baby." I step back and remove my pants and underwear and stand before her naked, ready.

Her eyes scan my body, but as she does that *v* appears between her brows.

"What's wrong, Ana?" I ask, and gently stroke her cheek. Is she reacting to my scars?

"Nothing. Love me, now," she says.

Embracing her, I kiss her with fervor, my fingers tangling in her hair. I'll never get enough of her mouth. Her lips. Her tongue. I walk her backward and gently lower both of us onto the bed. Lying by her side, I run my nose along her jawline, inhaling deeply.

Orchards. Apples. Summer and a mellow fall.

She's all of those things.

"Do you have any idea how exquisite your scent is, Ana? It's irresistible." With my lips, I trace a line down her throat, across her breasts, kissing her as I go, breathing in her essence as I travel down her body.

"You are so beautiful." I suck gently on a nipple.

She moans and her body bows off the bed.

The sound makes me harder. "Let me hear you, baby." I cup her breast, then move to her waist, enjoying the feel of her smooth skin under my fingers. I move past her hip, her ass, down to her knee while I kiss and suckle her breasts. Holding her knee, I hitch up her leg and curl it over my hips.

She gasps, and I revel in her reaction.

Rolling over, I take her with me so she's on top of me. I hand her a condom from the side table.

Her delight is clear and she scoots down so that she's sitting on my thighs. She grabs my erection and leans down and kisses the tip. Her hair falls, forming a curtain around my cock as she takes me into her mouth.

Fuck. It's erotic.

She consumes me, sucking hard, skimming her teeth over me. I groan and flex my hips so I'm deeper in her mouth.

She lets me go, tears open the foil packet, and unrolls the condom on my rigid dick. I hold out my hands to help her balance, and she takes them both, and slowly, oh-so-slowly, sinks down on me.

Oh, God.

It's so good.

I close my eyes and tip my head back as she takes me. And I give myself over to her.

She moans and I place my hands on her hips and move her up and then down as I push up, consuming her. "Oh, baby," I whisper, and I want more. So much more.

I sit up so we're nose to nose and I'm cradling her ass with my thighs, and I'm buried deep inside her. She gasps and grabs my arms as I hold her head and stare into her beautiful eyes, eyes that shine with her love and desire.

"Oh, Ana. What you make me feel," I say, and kiss her with unbridled passion.

"Oh, I love you," she says, and I close my eyes.

Ana loves me.

I roll her over, her legs locked around my waist, and look down at her in wonder.

I love you, too. More than you'll ever know.

Slowly, tenderly, gently, I start to move, relishing every treasured inch of her.

This is me, Ana.

All of me.

And I love you.

I place my arm around her head, cocooning her in my embrace while she touches my arms, my hair, and my ass with her fingers. I kiss her mouth, her chin, her jaw. I push her higher and higher until she's on the brink. Her body starts to tremble. She's panting, she's ready.

"That's right, baby. Give it up for me. Please. Ana."

"Christian!" she cries out as she comes around me, and I let go.

THE AFTERNOON SUN FILTERS through the portholes, casting watery reflections over the cabin ceiling. It's so peaceful out here on the water. Maybe we could sail around the world, just Ana and me.

She dozes beside me.

My beautiful, passionate girl.

Ana.

I remember thinking those three letters had the power to wound, but now I know they also have the power to heal.

She doesn't know the real you.

I frown at the ceiling. This thought keeps plaguing me. Why?

It's because I want to be honest with her. Flynn thinks I should trust her and tell her, but I don't have the nerve.

She'll leave.

No. I banish the thought and enjoy lying with her for a few

more minutes. "Mac will be back soon." I'm sorry to have broken the peaceful silence between us.

"Hmm," she mumbles, but her eyes open and she smiles.

"As much as I'd like to lie here with you all afternoon, he'll need a hand with the dinghy." I kiss her lips. "Ana, you look so beautiful right now, all mussed up and sexy. Makes me want you more."

She strokes my face.

She sees me.

No. Ana, you don't know me.

Reluctantly, I clamber out of bed, and she turns and lies on her stomach.

"You ain't so bad yourself, Captain," she says with appreciation as I dress.

I sit down beside her to put on my shoes.

"Captain, eh?" I muse. "Well, I am master of this vessel."

"You are master of my heart, Mr. Grey."

I wanted to be your master in a different way, but this is good. I think I can do this. I kiss her. "I'll be on deck. There's a shower in the bathroom if you want one. Do you need anything? A drink?"

She's amused, and I know it's at my expense.

"What?" I ask.

"You."

"What about me?"

"Who are you and what have you done with Christian?"

"He's not very far away, baby," I answer, and anxiety knots like ivy around my heart. "You'll see him soon enough, especially if you don't get up." I smack her ass so that she laughs and yelps at once.

"You had me worried." She feigns concern.

"Did I, now? You do give off some mixed signals, Anastasia. How's a man supposed to keep up?" I give her a swift kiss. "Laters, baby." I leave her to get dressed.

Mac arrives five minutes later, and together we get the dinghy fastened onto its rig at the stern.

"How was your friend?" I ask.

"In good spirits."

"You could have stayed longer," I say.

"And miss the trip back?"

"Yes."

"Nah, I can't stay away from this lady too long," Mac says, and he pats the hull of *The Grace*.

I grin. "I get it."

My phone buzzes.

"Taylor," I answer, and Ana opens the sliding doors to the saloon. She's holding her life jacket.

"Good afternoon, Mr. Grey. The apartment is clear," Taylor says.

I pull Ana close and kiss her hair. "That's great news."

"We've been through every room."

"Good."

"We've also been through all the CCTV footage of the last three days."

"Yes."

"It's been illuminating."

"Really?"

"Miss Williams was coming through the stairwell."

"The fire-escape stairwell?"

"Yes. She had a key and climbed all those floors to get there."

"I see." Wow, that's some climb.

"The locks have been changed and it's safe for you to return. We have your luggage. Will you be coming back this evening?"

"Yes."

"When can we expect you?"

"Tonight."

"Very good, sir."

I hang up and Mac fires up the engines.

"Time to head back." I give Ana a swift kiss and strap her into her life jacket.

ANA IS A KEEN and willing deckhand. Between us, we hoist and stow the mainsail, the headsheet, and the spinney while Mac steers. I teach her how to tie three knots. This she's not so good at, and I find it hard to keep a straight face.

"I may tie you up one day," she promises.

"You'll have to catch me first, Miss Steele." It's a long time since anyone tied me up, and I'm not sure I'd like it anymore. I shudder, thinking how defenseless I'd be against her touch. "Shall I give you a more thorough tour of *The Grace*?"

"Please, she's so beautiful."

ANA STANDS IN MY arms at the wheel, just before we make the turn into the marina. She looks so happy.

And that makes me happy.

She's been fascinated by *The Grace* and all that I've shown her. Even the engine room.

It's been fun. I take a deep breath, the salt water in the air cleansing my soul. And I'm reminded of a quote from one of my favorite books—a memoir, *Wind, Sand and Stars*. "'There is a poetry of sailing as old as the world,'" I murmur in her ear.

"That sounds like a quote."

"It is. Antoine de Saint-Exupéry."

"Oh, I adore *The Little Prince*."

"Me, too."

I pilot us into the marina, then slowly turn *The Grace* and reverse into the berth. The crowd that gathered to watch has dispersed by the time Mac jumps onto the dock and ties the stern lines to two dock cleats.

"Back again," I say to Ana, and, as usual, I'm a little reluctant to leave *The Grace*.

"Thank you. That was a perfect afternoon."

"I thought so, too. Perhaps we can enroll you in sailing school, so we can go out for a few days, just the two of us."

Or we could sail around the world, Ana, just you and me.

"I'd love that. We can christen the bedroom again and again."

I kiss her under her ear. "Hmm, I look forward to it, Anastasia." She squirms with pleasure. "Come, the apartment is clean. We can go back."

"What about our things at the hotel?"

"Taylor has collected them already. Earlier today, after he did a sweep of *The Grace* with his team."

"Does that poor man ever sleep?"

"He sleeps. He's just doing his job, Anastasia, which he's very good at. Jason is a real find."

"Jason?"

"Jason Taylor."

Ana's smile is tender.

"You're fond of Taylor," I observe.

"I suppose I am. I think Taylor looks after you very well. That's why I like him. He seems kind, reliable, and loyal. He has an avuncular appeal to me."

"Avuncular?"

"Yes."

"Okay, avuncular."

Ana laughs. "Oh, Christian, grow up, for heaven's sake."

What?

She's scolding me.

Why?

Because I'm possessive? Maybe that's childish.

Maybe. "I'm trying," I respond.

"That you are. Very," she says, looking toward the ceiling.

"What memories you evoke when you roll your eyes at me, Anastasia."

"Well, if you behave yourself, maybe we can relive some of those memories."

"Behave myself? Really, Miss Steele—what makes you think I want to relive them?"

"Probably the way your eyes lit up like Christmas when I said that."

"You know me so well already," I say.

"I'd like to know you better."

"And I you, Anastasia. Come, let's go." Mac has lowered the gangplank, allowing me to lead Ana onto the dock. "Thanks, Mac." I shake his hand.

"Always a pleasure, Mr. Grey, and good-bye. Ana, great to meet you."

"Good day, Mac, and thank you," Ana replies, and she looks a little shy.

Together Ana and I walk up to the promenade, leaving Mac on *The Grace*.

"Where's Mac from?" Ana asks.

"Ireland. Northern Ireland."

"Is he your friend?"

"Mac? He works for me. Helped build *The Grace*."

"Do you have many friends?"

What would I need friends for?

"Not really. Doing what I do. I don't cultivate friendships. There's only—" *Shit.* I stop myself. I don't want to mention Elena. "Hungry?" I ask, feeling food might be a safer topic.

Ana nods.

"We'll eat where I left the car. Come."

ANA AND I ARE seated at a table in Bee's, an Italian bistro next to SP's. She reads the menu while I take a sip of a fine chilled Frascati. I like watching her read.

"What?" Ana asks when she looks up.

"You look lovely, Anastasia. The outdoors agrees with you."

"I feel rather windburned, to tell the truth. But I had a lovely afternoon. A perfect afternoon. Thank you."

"My pleasure."

"Can I ask you something?"

"Anything, Anastasia. You know that."

"You don't seem to have many friends. Why is that?"

"I told you, I don't really have time. I have business associates, though that's very different from friendships, I suppose. I have my family, and that's it." I shrug. "Apart from Elena."

Thankfully, she ignores my Elena comment. "No male friends your own age that you can go out with and let off steam?"

No. Just Elliot.

"You know how I like to let off steam, Anastasia." My voice is low. "And I've been working, building up the business. That's all I do, except sail and fly occasionally." *And fuck, of course.*

"Not even in college?"

"Not really."

"Just Elena, then?"

I nod. *Where is she going with this?*

"Must be lonely."

Leila's words come back to me: *"But you're lonely. I can see it."* I frown. The only time I felt lonely was when Ana left me.

It was crippling.

I never want to feel like that again.

"What would you like to eat?" I ask, hoping to move the subject on.

"I'm going for the risotto."

"Good choice." I beckon the waiter over.

We place our order. Risotto for Ana, penne for me.

The waiter scurries off and I notice Ana staring down at her lap, knotting her fingers. Something is on her mind. "Anastasia, what's wrong? Tell me."

She looks at me, continuing to fidget, and I know there's something bothering her. "Tell me," I demand. I hate it when she's anxious.

She sits up, straightening her back. She means business.

Shit. Now what?

"I'm just worried that this isn't enough for you. You know, to let off steam."

What? Not this again. "Have I given you any indication that this isn't enough?" I ask.

"No."

"Then why do you think that?"

"I know what you're like. What you, um, need." Her voice is hesitant, and she rounds her shoulders and crosses her arms like she's folding in on herself. I close my eyes and rub my forehead. I don't know what to say. I thought we were having a good time.

"What do I have to do?" I whisper.

I'm trying, Ana. I'm really trying.

"No, you misunderstand," she says, suddenly animated. "You have been amazing, and I know it's just been a few days, but I hope I'm not forcing you to be someone you're not."

Her response is reassuring, but I think she's missing the point. "I'm still me, Anastasia, in all my fifty shades of fucked up . . . ness," I say, searching for the word. "Yes, I have to fight the urge to be controlling, but that's my nature, how I've dealt with my life. Yes, I expect you to behave a certain way, and when you don't it's both challenging and refreshing. We still do what I like to do. You let me spank you after your outrageous bid yesterday."

The thought of last night's arousing encounter preoccupies me for a moment.

Grey!

Keeping my voice low, I try to unravel how I feel. "I enjoy punishing you. I don't think the urge will ever go, but I'm trying, and it's not as hard as I thought it would be."

"I didn't mind that," Ana says quietly, and she's referring to our assignation in my childhood bedroom.

"I know. Neither did I."

I take a deep breath and tell her the truth. "But let me tell you, Anastasia, this is all new to me, and these last few days have been the best in my life. I don't want to change anything."

Her face brightens. "They've been the best in my life, too, without exception."

I'm sure my relief is reflected in my smile.

She persists. "So, you don't want to take me into your playroom?"

Fuck. I swallow. "No, I don't."

"Why not?" she asks.

Now I'm really in the confessional. "The last time we were in there you left me. I will shy away from anything that could make you leave me again. I was devastated when you left. I explained that. I never want to feel like that again. I've told you how I feel about you."

"But it hardly seems fair. It can't be very relaxing for you to be constantly concerned about how I feel. You've made all these changes for me, and I—I think I should reciprocate in some way. I don't know, maybe try some role-playing games." She's blushing.

"Ana, you do reciprocate, more than you know. Please, please don't feel like this. Baby, it's only been one weekend. Give us some time. I thought a great deal about us when you left. We need time. You need to trust me, and I you. Maybe in time we can indulge, but I like how you are now. I like seeing you this happy, this relaxed and carefree, knowing that I had something to do with it. I have never—" I stop.

Don't give up on me, Ana.

I hear Dr. Flynn's voice, nagging me. "We have to walk before we can run," I say out loud.

"What's so funny?" she asks.

"Flynn. He says that all the time. I never thought I'd be quoting him."

"A Flynnism."

I laugh. "Exactly."

The waiter arrives with the appetizers and our heavy conversation ceases, turning to the much lighter subject of travel. We discuss all the countries Ana would love to visit, and the places I've been. Talking to Ana reminds me how lucky I am. My parents took us all over the world: to Europe, to Asia, and to South America. My father in particular considered travel a vital part of our education. Of course, they could afford it. Ana's never left the U.S. and has always longed to visit Europe. I'd like to take her to all these places; I wonder how she'd feel about sailing the world with me.

Don't get ahead of yourself, Grey.

TRAFFIC IS LIGHT DURING our drive back to Escala. Ana admires the passing sights, her foot tapping in time to the music that fills the car.

I can't help thinking about our earlier intense conversation about our relationship. The truth is, I don't know if I can maintain a vanilla relationship, but I'm willing to try. I don't want to push her into something she doesn't want to do.

But she's willing, Grey.

She said so.

She wants the Red Room, as she calls it.

I shake my head. I think, for once, I'm going to take Dr. Flynn's advice.

Walk before we run, Ana.

I glance out of the window and catch sight of a young woman with long brown hair and she reminds me of Leila. It's not her, but as we near Escala I begin to scan the streets, searching for her.

Where the fuck is she?

By the time I pull into the garage at Escala, my hands are gripping the steering wheel and tension has tightened every muscle in my body. I'm wondering if it was a good idea to come back to the apartment with Leila still at large.

Sawyer is in the garage, prowling around my parking spaces like a caged lion. This is overkill surely, but I'm relieved to see the Audi A3 is gone. He opens Ana's car door as I switch off the engine.

"Hello, Sawyer," she says.

"Miss Steele. Mr. Grey," he says in greeting.

"No sign?" I ask him.

"No, sir," he responds, and even though I knew that would be the answer, it's vexing. I grasp Ana's hand and we step into the elevator.

"You are not allowed out of here alone. You understand?" I caution Ana.

"Okay," she says as the doors close, and her lips twitch in amusement.

"What's so funny?" I'm floored that she agreed so readily.

"You are."

"Me?" My tension starts to dissolve. She's laughing at me? "Miss Steele? Why am I funny?" I purse my lips, trying to stop my smile.

"Don't pout," she says.

I'm pouting?

"Why?"

"Because it has the same effect on me as I have on you when I do this." She lets her teeth toy with her bottom lip.

"Really?" I do it once more and lean down to give her a swift kiss. When my lips touch hers, it sparks my desire. I hear her sharp intake of breath, then her fingers are twisting in my hair. Holding my lips to hers, I grab her and push her against the elevator wall, my hands cradling her face. Her tongue is in my mouth and mine in hers as she takes what she wants and I give her all that I have.

It's explosive.

I want to fuck her. Now.

I pour all my anxiety into her, and she takes everything.

Ana . . .

The elevator doors open with the familiar ping and I pull my face away from her, but I'm still pinning her to the wall with my hips and my hardening erection.

"Whoa," I whisper, dragging air into my lungs.

"Whoa," she answers, panting.

"What you do to me, Ana." I trace my thumb across her lower lip. Ana's eyes flit to the foyer and I sense rather than see Taylor.

She kisses the corner of my mouth. "What you do to me, Christian," she says. I step back and take her hand. I haven't jumped her in an elevator since that day at The Heathman.

Get a grip, Grey.

"Come," I say.

As we exit the elevator, Taylor is standing to one side.

"Good evening, Taylor."

"Mr. Grey, Miss Steele."

"I was Mrs. Taylor yesterday," Ana says, all smiles for Mr. Taylor.

"That has a nice ring to it, Miss Steele," Taylor responds.

"I thought so, too."

What the hell is going on?

I scowl at Ana and Taylor. "If you two have quite finished, I'd like a debriefing." Ana and Taylor exchange a look. "I'll be with you shortly. I just want a word with Miss Steele," I say to Taylor.

He nods.

And I take Ana into my bedroom and close the door. "Don't flirt with the staff, Anastasia."

"I wasn't flirting. I was being friendly. There is a difference."

"Don't be friendly with the staff or flirt with them. I don't like it."

She sighs. "I'm sorry." She tosses her hair over her shoulder and looks down at her fingernails. I cup her chin and lift her head so I can see into her eyes. "You know how jealous I am."

"You have no reason to be jealous, Christian. You own me body and soul." She looks at me as if I've lost my mind, and suddenly I feel foolish.

She's right.

I'm completely overreacting.

I give her a chaste kiss. "I won't be long. Make yourself at home." I go to find Taylor in his office. He stands when I enter.

"Mr. Grey, about—"

I hold up my hand. "Don't. It's I who should apologize."

Taylor looks surprised.

"What's occurring?" I ask.

"Gail will return later tonight."

"Good."

"I've informed the facilities management at Escala that Miss Williams had a key. I felt they should know."

"How did they respond?"

"Well, I stopped them from calling the police."

"Good."

"The locks have all been changed and a contractor is coming to look at the emergency stairwell door. Miss Williams shouldn't have been able to get in from the outside even with a key."

"And you found nothing in your sweep?"

"Nothing, sir. I couldn't tell you where she was hiding. But she's not here now."

"Have you spoken to Welch?"

"I've briefed him."

"Thank you. Ana's going to stay here tonight. I think it's safer."

"Agreed, sir."

"Cancel the Audi. I've decided on a Saab for Ana. It should be here soon. I have asked them to expedite delivery."

"Will do, sir."

When I return to my bedroom, Ana is standing on the threshold of my closet. She looks a little stunned. I poke my head around the closet door. Her clothes are here.

"Oh, they managed the move." I thought Gail was going to handle Ana's clothes. I shrug it off.

"What's wrong?" she asks.

I give her a quick rundown of what Taylor has just told me about the apartment and Leila. "I wish I knew where she was. She's evading all our attempts to find her, when she needs help."

Ana puts her arms around me, holding me, calming me. And I embrace her and kiss the top of her head.

"What will you do when you find her?" she asks.

"Dr. Flynn has a place."

"What about her husband?"

"He's washed his hands of her." *Asshole.* "Her family is in Connecticut. I think she's very much on her own out there."

"That's sad."

Ana's compassion knows no bounds. I tighten my hold on her. "Are you okay with all your stuff being here? I want you to share my room."

"Yes."

"I want you sleeping with me. I don't have nightmares when you're with me."

"You have nightmares?"

"Yes." She squeezes me tighter, and we stand in my closet wrapped around each other.

A few moments later, she says, "I was just getting my clothes ready for work tomorrow."

"Work?" I release her.

"Yes, work," she says, confused.

"But Leila, she's out there." Doesn't she get the risk? "I don't want you to go to work."

"That's ridiculous, Christian. I have to go to work."

"No, you don't."

"I have a new job, which I enjoy. Of course I have to go to work."

"No, you don't." *I can look after you.*

"Do you think I am going to stay here twiddling my thumbs while you're off being master of the universe?"

"Frankly, yes," I respond.

Ana closes her eyes and rubs her forehead as if she's calling on all her inner strength. She doesn't understand. "Christian, I need to go to work," she says.

"No, you don't."

"Yes. I. Do." Her tone is forthright and determined.

"It's not safe." *Suppose something happens to you?*

"Christian, I need to work for a living, and I'll be fine."

"No, you don't need to work for a living, and how do you know you'll be fine?"

Fuck. This is why I like having submissives. This would not be an argument if she'd signed the fucking contract.

"For heaven's sake, Christian, Leila was standing at the end of your bed, and she didn't harm me, and yes, I do need to work. I don't want to be beholden to you. I have my student loans to pay." She places her hands on her hips.

"I don't want you going to work."

"It's not up to you, Christian. This is not your decision to make."

Fuck.

She's made up her mind.

And of course she's right.

I run my hand through my hair, trying to hold on to my temper, and eventually I have an idea. "Sawyer will come with you."

"Christian, that's not necessary. You're being irrational."

"Irrational?" I snap. "Either he comes with you or I will be really irrational and keep you here."

"How, exactly?"

"Oh, I'd find a way, Anastasia. Don't push me." I'm about to explode.

"Okay!" she shouts, holding up both her hands. "Okay, Sawyer can come with me if it makes you feel better."

I want to kiss her or spank her or fuck her. I step forward and she immediately takes a step back, watching me.

Grey! You're frightening the poor girl.

I take a deep cleansing breath and offer Ana a tour of my apartment. If she's going to stay, she should really get to know this place.

She gives me an uncertain look, as if I've caught her off guard. But she agrees and takes my outstretched hand. I give her hand a squeeze.

"I didn't mean to frighten you," I offer as an apology.

"You didn't. I was just getting ready to run," she says.

"Run?"

You've pushed her too far again, Grey.

"I'm joking!" she cries.

That's not funny, Ana.

I sigh and lead her through the apartment. I show her the spare room next to mine, then take her upstairs to the additional spare rooms, the gym, and the staff quarters.

"Are you sure you don't want to go in here?" she asks coyly, as we walk past the playroom door.

"I don't have the key." I'm still smarting from our argument. I hate arguing with her. But as usual, she's calling me out on my shit.

But what if something happens to her?

It will be my fault.

All I can do is hope Sawyer will protect her.

Downstairs, I show her the TV room.

"So you *do* have an Xbox." She laughs. I love her laugh. It immediately makes me feel better.

"Yes, but I'm crap at it. Elliot always beats me. That was funny, when you thought I meant this room was my playroom."

"I'm glad you find me amusing, Mr. Grey," she says.

"That you are, Miss Steele, when you're not being exasperating, of course."

"I'm usually exasperating when you're being unreasonable."

"Me? Unreasonable?"

"Yes, Mr. Grey. 'Unreasonable' could be your middle name."

"I don't have a middle name."

"Unreasonable would suit, then."

"I think that's a matter of opinion, Miss Steele."

"I would be interested in Dr. Flynn's professional opinion."

Lord, I love sparring with her.

"I thought Trevelyan was your middle name," she asks.

"No. Surname. Trevelyan-Grey."

"But you don't use it."

"It's too long. Come."

Next I take her to Taylor's office. He stands when we enter. "Hi, Taylor. I'm just giving Anastasia a tour." He nods at both of us. Ana looks around, surprised, I think, by the size of the room and the bank of CCTV monitors. We move on. "And, of course, you've been in here." I open the door to the library, where Ana spies the billiards table.

"Shall we play?" she challenges.

Miss Steele is up for a game. "Okay. Have you played before?"

"A few times," she says, avoiding eye contact.

She's lying.

"You're a hopeless liar, Anastasia. Either you've never played before or—"

"Frightened of a little competition?" she interrupts me.

"Frightened of a little girl like you?" I scoff.

"A wager, Mr. Grey."

"You're that confident, Miss Steele?" This is a new side to Ana I've not seen before.

Game on, Ana.

"What would you like to wager?"

"If I win, you'll take me back into the playroom."

Shit. She's serious.

"And if I win?" I ask.

"Then it's your choice." She shrugs, trying to act nonchalant, but her eyes shine with mischief.

"Okay, deal." How hard could this be? "Do you want to play pool, English snooker, or carom billiards?"

"Pool, please. I don't know the others."

I retrieve the pool balls from a cupboard under the bookshelves and rack them on the green baize. I choose a cue for Ana that should be right for her height. "Would you like to break?" I ask, as I hand her the chalk.

She is so going down.

Hmm. Maybe that could be my prize.

An image of her on her knees in front of me, hands bound, servicing my cock, comes to mind. *Yeah. That would work.*

"Okay," she says, her voice breathy and soft as she chalks her cue. She purses her lips, and while watching me through her lashes, she slowly, deliberately blows off the excess.

I feel it in my dick.

Damn.

She lines up the cue ball, then hits it with such force and mastery that it scatters the rack. The corner ball, the yellow striped number nine, dives into the top right pocket.

Oh, Anastasia Steele, you are so full of surprises.

"I choose stripes," she says, and has the gall to give me a coy smile.

"Be my guest." This is going to be fun.

She prowls around the table, seeking her next victim. I like this new Ana. Predatory. Competitive. Confident. Sexy as hell. She leans over the table, stretching out her arm, so that her blouse rides up, showing a little skin between the hem and the top of her jeans. She hits the cue ball and the maroon stripe bites the dust. Circling the table again, she gives me a cursory glance before leaning over, stretching across the table again, ass in the air, as she pockets the purple.

Hmm. I may need to revise my plans.

She's good.

She makes short work of the blue but misses the green.

"You know, Anastasia, I could stand here and watch you leaning and stretching across this billiard table all day," I tell her.

She flushes.

Yes!

That's the Ana I know.

I slip off my sweater and examine what's left on the table.

Showtime, Grey.

I proceed to pocket as many solids as I can; I have some catching up to do. I sink three and line up to pocket the orange. I hit the cue ball and the orange hurtles into the bottom left pocket, followed by the white.

Shit.

"A very elementary mistake, Mr. Grey."

"Ah, Miss Steele, I am but a foolish mortal. Your turn, I believe." I wave my hand in the direction of the table.

"You're not trying to lose, are you?" She cocks her head to one side.

"Oh no. For what I have in mind as the prize, I want to win, Anastasia. But then, I always want to win."

Blow job on her knees or . . .

I could stop her from going to work. Hmm . . . A wager that could cost her her job. I don't think that would be a popular choice.

She narrows her eyes, and I would pay good money to know what she's thinking. At the top of the table she bends down to take a closer look at the lie of the balls. Her blouse gapes and I catch sight of her breasts.

She stands and there's a little smile on her lips. She moves next to me and bends over, and shifts her ass first left, then right. She walks back to the top of the table and leans over again, showing me all she has to offer. As she bends over, she peeks up at me.

"I know what you're doing," I whisper.

And my cock approves, Ana.

Big-time.

I adjust my stance to accommodate my growing erection.

She straightens up and tilts her head to one side while running her hand up and down the cue, slowly. "Oh. I am just deciding where to take my next shot."

Fuck. She's a temptress.

She leans over, taps the orange stripe with the cue ball so it aligns with the pocket, then takes the rest from under the table and lines up the shot. As she takes aim at the white, I can see the swell of her breasts down her blouse. I inhale, sharply.

She misses.

Good.

I stroll around to stand behind her while she's still bent over the table, and place my hand on her behind. "Are you waving this around to taunt me, Miss Steele?" I smack her hard.

Because she deserves it.

She gasps.

"Yes," she whispers.

Oh, Ana. "Be careful what you wish for, baby."

I aim the cue ball at the red, and it sinks into the left top pocket. Then I try for the top right with the yellow. I hit the cue ball gently. It kisses the yellow, but the ball stops just short of its destination.

Shit. Miss.

Ana grins at me. "Red Room, here we come," she crows.

I like your kinky fuckery.

She really does.

It's confusing. I signal to her to continue, knowing that I don't want to take her to the playroom. The last time we were there, she left me.

She pockets the green stripe. She gives me a triumphant smile and sinks the orange.

"Name your pocket," I mutter.

"Top left-hand," she says as she wiggles her ass in front of me. She takes the shot and the black skirts wide of its target.

Oh, joy.

Quickly I dispatch the remaining two solids, and now I'm left with the black. I chalk my cue, gazing at Ana. "If I win, I am going to spank you, then fuck you over this billiard table."

Her lips part.

Yes. She's excited by the idea. That's what she's been asking me for all day. She thinks I've lost my edge?

Well, we'll see.

"Top right," I announce, and bend to take the shot. My cue taps the white and it sails up the table and pecks the black, which rolls toward the top-right pocket. It balances on the edge for a moment, and I stop breathing until it drops with a satisfying clunk into its goal.

Yes!

Anastasia Steele, you are mine.

I swagger over to where she stands with her mouth open, look-ing a little crestfallen. "You're not going to be a sore loser, are you?" I ask.

"Depends how hard you spank me," she murmurs. Taking the cue from her, I place it on the table, hook my finger into the top of her blouse, and tug so she steps toward me.

"Well, let's count your misdemeanors, Miss Steele." Holding up my fingers, I number her misdeeds. "One, making me jealous of my own staff." Her eyes widen. "Two, arguing with me about working. And three, waving your delectable derrière at me for the last twenty minutes."

Leaning down, I rub my nose against hers. "I want you to take your jeans and this very fetching shirt off. Now." I kiss her gently on her lips, stroll over to the library door, and lock it.

When I turn, she's frozen to the spot. "Clothes, Anastasia. You appear to still be wearing them. Take them off, or I will do it for you."

"You do it," she breathes, and her voice is as soft as a summer breeze.

"Oh, Miss Steele. It's a dirty job, but I think I can rise to the challenge."

"You normally rise to most challenges, Mr. Grey." She bites her lip.

Innuendo from Ana.

"Why, Miss Steele, whatever do you mean?" On the library desk I spy a Perspex ruler.

Perfect.

All day long she's been making not-so-veiled remarks about missing this side of me. Let's see how she fares with this. I hold it up so she can see it and flex it between my hands, then slip it into my back pocket and stroll over to her.

Shoes off, I think.

I drop to my knees and undo both her Chucks, removing them and her socks. I undo the top button of her jeans and pull down her zipper. I look up at her as I slowly tug them off. Her eyes don't leave mine. She steps out of her pants, and she's wearing her white thong.

That thong.

I'm a fan.

So is my cock . . .

I grab the back of her thighs and run my nose up the front of her panties. "I want to be quite rough with you, Ana. You'll have to tell me to stop if it's too much," I whisper, and through the lace plant a kiss on her clitoris.

She moans.

"Safe word?" she says.

"No, no safe word, just tell me to stop and I'll stop. Understand?" I kiss her again and swirl my nose around the potent little bud at the apex of her thighs. I stand before I get carried away. "Answer me."

"Yes, yes, I understand."

"You've been dropping hints and giving me mixed signals, Anastasia. You said you were worried I'd lost my edge. I'm not sure what you meant by that, and I don't know how serious you were, but we are going to find out. I don't want to go back into the playroom yet, so we can try this now, but if you don't like it, you must promise to tell me."

"I'll tell you. No safe word," she says—to reassure me, I think.

"We're lovers, Anastasia. Lovers don't need safe words." I frown. "Do they?" This is something I know nothing about.

"I guess not," she responds. "I promise."

I need to know she will communicate with me if I go too far. Her expression is earnest and full of desire. I unbutton her shirt and let it fall open, and the sight of her breasts is arousing. Very arousing. She looks amazing. From behind her I pick up the cue.

"You play well, Miss Steele. I must say I'm surprised. Why don't you sink the black?"

She purses her lips, then with a defiant look, she reaches for the cue ball and, bending over the table, lines up the shot. As she does I go and stand behind her and place my hand on her right thigh.

She tenses as I run my fingers to her ass and back down her thigh, lightly teasing her.

"I am going to miss if you keep doing that," she complains, her voice husky.

"I don't care if you hit or miss, baby. I just wanted to see you like this, partially dressed, stretched out on my billiard table. Do you have any idea how hot you look at this moment?"

She blushes and toys with the white as she tries to line it up. I caress her ass. Her beautiful ass, visible because she's wearing a thong.

"Top left," she says, and hits the cue ball with the tip of the cue. I smack her hard and she yelps. The white kisses the black, but the black bounces off the cushion, missing the pocket.

I caress her ass again. "Oh, I think you need to try that again. You should concentrate, Anastasia."

She wiggles her behind beneath my hand, like she's begging for more.

She's enjoying this far too much, so I stroll to the end of the table to reset the black ball, and, picking up the white, I run it along the table back to her.

She catches the ball and starts lining it up once more.

"Uh-uh," I warn. "Just wait."

Not so fast, Miss Steele.

I wander back and stand behind her again, but this time I stroke my hand over her left thigh, and her ass.

I love her ass.

"Take aim," I whisper.

She moans and puts her head on the table.

Don't give up yet, Ana.

She takes a deep breath and, raising her head, moves to her right and I follow her. She bends, stretches over the table again, and hits the cue ball. As the ball flies up the baize, I smack her again. Hard. The black misses.

"Oh no," she says and groans.

"Once more, baby. And if you miss this time, I'm really going to let you have it." I set up the black again and wander back until

I'm standing behind her and caressing her beautiful behind again. "You can do it," I breathe.

She pushes her backside into my hand and I give her a playful smack.

"Eager, Miss Steele?" I ask.

She moans in reply.

"Well, let's get rid of these." I slide the thong down her legs, removing it and dropping it on her discarded jeans. While kneeling behind her, I kiss each cheek of her ass. "Take the shot, baby."

She's agitated, all fingers and thumbs, and she fumbles for the cue ball, lines it up, hits it, but in her impatience misses the shot. She scrunches up her eyes, waiting for me to spank her, but instead I lean over her, pressing her onto the baize. I take the cue from her hand and push it to the side.

Now for some real fun.

"You missed," I whisper in her ear. "Put your hands flat on the table."

My erection is fighting with my fly.

"Good. I'm going to spank you now, and next time, maybe you won't." I move beside her so I have a better aim. She groans and closes her eyes, and her breathing is getting louder. I caress her behind with one hand. With the other I hold her down and twist my fingers in her hair.

"Open your legs," I tell her, and reach for the ruler in my pocket. She hesitates, so I smack her with the ruler. It makes a really satisfying noise as it cracks across her ass, and she gasps but says nothing, so I hit her again.

"Legs," I order. She complies and I strike her again. She scrunches up her eyes as she takes the pain, but she doesn't ask me to stop.

Oh, baby.

I spank her again, and again, and she moans. Her skin is turning pink beneath the ruler and my jeans are becoming impossibly tight as they restrict my arousal. I smack her again and again. And I'm lost. Lost in her. Owned by her. She's doing this for me. And I love it. I love her.

"Stop," she says.

And I drop the ruler without thinking and release her.

"Enough?" I ask.

"Yes."

"I want to fuck you now," I whisper, my voice hoarse.

"Yes," she pleads.

She wants this, too.

Her ass is pink and she's dragging air into her lungs.

I tug my fly open, allowing my cock some room, and then insert two fingers inside her, moving them in circles, reveling in her readiness.

I make quick work of putting on a condom, then steady myself behind her and slowly ease myself into her. *Oh yes.* This is without a doubt my favorite place in the world.

I ease out of her, holding her hips, then slam into her hard so that she cries out.

"Again?" I ask.

"Yes," she breathes. "I'm fine. Lose yourself. Take me with you."

Oh, Ana, with pleasure.

I slam into her once more and set up a slow but grueling rhythm, taking her again and again and again. She moans and cries out as I claim her. Every inch. Mine.

She starts to quicken—she's nearly there—and I increase the pace, listening to her cries until she orgasms around me, crying out and taking me with her, so I call out her name and empty my soul inside her.

I collapse on top of her as I catch my breath. I'm filled with gratitude and humility. I love her. I want her. Always.

I pull her into my arms and we sink to the floor, where I cradle her against my chest. I never want to let her go. "Thank you, baby," I whisper, and cover her face in soft kisses. She opens her eyes and gives me a drowsy, sated smile. I tighten my hold on her and stroke her cheek. "Your cheek is pink from the baize."

Matches your ass, baby.

Her smile widens under my tender ministration. "How was that?" I ask.

"Teeth-clenchingly good," she says. "I like it rough, Christian, and I like it gentle, too. I like that it's with you."

I close my eyes and marvel at the beautiful young woman in my arms. "You never fail, Ana. You're beautiful, bright, challenging, fun, sexy, and I thank Divine Providence every day that it was you who came to interview me and not Katherine Kavanagh." I kiss her hair and she yawns, making me smile. "I'm wearing you out. Come. Bath, then bed."

I stand and pull her to her feet. "Do you want me to carry you?"

She shakes her head.

"I'm sorry, but you'd better get dressed—we don't know who we'll meet in the hallway."

IN THE BATHROOM, I turn on the faucet and pour a copious amount of bath oil into the streaming water.

I help Ana out of her clothes and hold her hand as she steps in. I follow her quickly and we sit at opposite ends while the bath fills with hot water and fragrant foam.

I grab some body wash and with it begin to massage Ana's left foot, my thumbs rubbing her instep.

"Oh, that feels so good." She closes her eyes and tips back her head.

"Good." I'm enjoying her pleasure. Her hair is tied in a ponytail that sits precariously in a loose bun on top of her head. A few tendrils escape, and her skin looks dewy and a little sun-kissed from our afternoon on *The Grace*.

She's stunning.

It's been a bewildering couple of days; Leila's aberrant behavior, Elena's interference, and Ana, steadfast and strong through it all. It's been humbling. She humbles me. Most of all I've enjoyed sharing her happiness. I like to see her happy. Her joy is my joy.

"Can I ask you something?" she murmurs, cocking one eye open.

"Of course. Anything, Ana, you know that."

She sits up and squares her shoulders.

Oh no.

"Tomorrow, when I go to work, can Sawyer just deliver me to the front door of the office, then pick me up at the end of the day? Please, Christian. Please," she says quickly.

I stop my massage. "I thought we agreed."

"Please."

Why does she feel so passionately about this?

"What about lunchtime?" I ask, anxious once more about her safety.

"I'll make myself something to take from here so I don't have to go out. Please."

"I find it very difficult to say no to you," I admit, kissing her instep. I want her safe and, until Leila's apprehended, I'm not sure that she will be.

Ana's giving me the big blue eyes.

"You won't go out?" I ask.

"No."

"Okay."

She smiles, grateful, I think. "Thank you," she says, spilling water over the side of the bath as she moves to her knees. She places her hands on my upper arms and kisses me.

"You're most welcome, Miss Steele. How's your behind?"

"Sore. But not too bad. The water is soothing."

"I'm glad you told me to stop," I say.

"So is my behind."

I grin. "Let's go to bed."

I BRUSH MY TEETH and wander back into my bedroom, where Ana is in bed.

"Didn't Ms. Acton provide any nightwear?" I ask. I'm sure she has some silk and satin nightgowns.

"I have no idea. I like wearing your T-shirts," she replies, and her eyelids droop.

Boy, she's exhausted. I lean forward and kiss her forehead.

I still have some work to do, but I want to stay with Ana. I've been in her company all day, and it's been lovely.

I never want this day to end.

"I need to work. But I don't want to leave you alone. Can I use your laptop to log in to the office? Will I disturb you if I work from here?"

"S'not my laptop," she mumbles, and closes her eyes.

"Yes, it is," I whisper, and I sit down beside her and open her MacBook Pro. I click on Safari, log in to my e-mail, and begin to work through them.

Once that's done, I e-mail Taylor and let him know that I'd like Sawyer to accompany Ana tomorrow. The only outstanding detail is deciding where Sawyer will be while Ana is at work.

This we will figure out in the morning.

I check my schedule. I have a meeting at 8:30 with Ros and Vanessa in procurement to discuss the conflict mineral issue.

I'm tired.

Ana is fast asleep as I lay down beside her. I watch her chest rise and fall with each breath. Over such a short time she has become so dear to me.

"Ana, I love you," I whisper. "Thank you for today. Please stay." And I close my eyes.

MONDAY, JUNE 13, 2011

Seattle's morning news wakes me with a report about the Angels' upcoming game with the Mariners. When I turn my head, Ana is awake and watching me. "Good morning," she says with a bright smile. She caresses my stubbly cheek with her fingers and kisses me.

"Good morning, baby." I'm surprised that I've slept so long. "I usually wake before the alarm goes off."

"It's set so early," Ana whines.

"That it is, Miss Steele. I have to get up." I kiss her and bound out of bed.

In my closet, I pull on my sweats and grab my iPod. I check on Ana before I leave; she's gone back to sleep.

Good. She's had an action-packed weekend. As have I.

Yes. What a weekend.

I resist the urge to kiss her good-bye, and let her sleep. Glancing through the windows, I see that the sky is overcast, but I don't think it's raining. I'll chance a run, rather than my gym.

"Mr. Grey?" Ryan accosts me in the foyer.

"Good morning, Ryan."

"Sir. You're going out?" He probably thinks he needs to join me.

"I'll be fine, Ryan. Thank you."

"Mr. Taylor—"

"I'll be fine." I step into the elevator and leave Ryan in the foyer looking uncertain, probably second-guessing his decision. Leila was never one for an early morning . . . just like Ana. I think I'll be safe.

It's drizzling outside. But I don't care. With "Bittersweet Symphony" blasting in my ears I set off, sprinting down Fourth Avenue.

My mind clouds with chaotic images of all that has happened over the last few days: Ana at the ball, Ana on my boat, Ana at the hotel.

Ana. Ana. Ana.

My life has been completely overturned to the point that I'm not sure I recognize myself.

Elena's words come back to me: *"Have you turned your back on who you are?"*

Have I?

"I can't change—" The words from the song echo through my head.

The truth is, I like being in her company. I like having her in my home. I'd like her to stay. Permanently. She's brought humor, restful sleep, vitality, and love into my monochrome existence. I didn't know I was lonely until I met her.

But she won't want to move in, will she? While Leila is still at large it makes sense for her to stay, but once she's found, Ana will go. I can't make her stay, though part of me would like to. But in the interim, if she ever finds out the truth about me, she'll leave and never want to see me again.

No one can love a monster.

And when she leaves . . .

Hell.

I run harder and faster, trying to clear my confusion until I'm conscious only of my bursting lungs and my Nikes hitting the ground.

MRS. JONES IS IN the kitchen when I get back from my run. "Good morning, Gail."

"Mr. Grey, good morning."

"Did Taylor tell you about Leila?"

"Yes, sir. I hope you find her. She needs help." Gail's face is full of concern.

"She does."

"I understand Miss Steele is still here." She gives me that weird little smile she has whenever we talk about Ana.

"I think she'll be staying as long as Leila is a threat. She'll need a packed lunch today."

"Okay. What would you like for breakfast?"

"Scrambled eggs, toast."

"Very good, sir."

ONCE I'M SHOWERED AND dressed, I decide to wake Ana. She's still fast asleep. I kiss her temple. "Come on, sleepyhead, get up." Her eyes open and close again, and she takes a deep breath.

"What?" I ask.

"I wish you'd come back to bed."

Don't tempt me, baby.

"You are insatiable, Miss Steele. As much as that idea appeals, I have an eight-thirty meeting, so I have to go shortly."

Startled, Ana looks at the clock, pushes me aside to leap out of bed, and dashes into the bathroom. Shaking my head, amused at her sudden burst of energy, I pop a few condoms into my pants pocket, then saunter into the kitchen for some breakfast.

You never know, Grey. I've learned that it's good to be prepared around Anastasia Steele.

Mrs. Jones is making coffee.

"Your scrambled eggs will be ready in a moment, Mr. Grey."

"Great. Ana will join me shortly."

"Shall I make her scrambled eggs?"

"I think she likes pancakes and bacon."

Gail places a coffee and my breakfast at one of the places she's set at the kitchen counter.

Ana appears about ten minutes later, wearing some of the clothes I bought her.

A silk blouse and a gray skirt. She looks different.

Sophisticated.

Elegant.

She's beautiful. Not a gauche student but a confident young working woman.

I approve and I wrap my arm around her. "You look lovely,"

I say, kissing her behind her ear. My only misgiving about her appearance is that she has to spend time, looking like this, with her boss.

Don't dwell, Grey. This is her choice. She wants to work.

I release her when Gail places her breakfast on the bar. "Good morning, Miss Steele," she says.

"Oh, thank you. Good morning," Ana replies.

"Mr. Grey says you'd like to take lunch with you to work. What would you like to eat?"

Ana shoots me a look.

Yeah, baby. I was serious. No going out.

"A sandwich. Salad. I really don't mind." She gives Gail an appreciative smile.

"I'll rustle up a packed lunch for you, ma'am."

"Please, Mrs. Jones, call me Ana."

"Ana," Gail says.

"I have to go, baby. Taylor will come back and drop you at work with Sawyer."

"Only to the door," she reiterates.

"Yes. Only to the door." That's what we agreed. "Be careful, though," I add in a hushed tone. Standing, I grasp her chin and give her a swift kiss. "Laters, baby."

"Have a good day at the office, dear," she calls after me, and though it's a corny thing to say—it delights me.

This feels so *normal.*

In the elevator Taylor greets me with an update. "Sir, there's a coffee shop opposite SIP. I think Sawyer can station himself there during the day."

"If he needs backup? You know, bathroom breaks."

"I'll send Reynolds or Ryan."

"Okay."

I'D FORGOTTEN THAT ANDREA is out for her wedding but she won't be having much of a honeymoon if she's back at work tomorrow. The woman who's replaced her and whose name I still can't remember is browsing the *Vogue* Facebook page when I arrive. "No social media during office hours," I say with a grunt.

Rookie mistake. But she should know this. She's already an employee here.

She's startled. "I'm so sorry, Mr. Grey. I didn't hear you arrive. Can I get you some coffee?"

"Yes. You may. A macchiato."

I shut my office door and, at my desk, switch on my computer. There's an e-mail from the Saab dealership: Ana's car will arrive today. I forward the e-mail to Taylor so he can organize delivery, thinking that it will be a nice surprise for Ana this evening. Next, I e-mail Ana.

From: Christian Grey
Subject: Boss
Date: June 13 2011 08:24
To: Anastasia Steele

Good morning, Miss Steele
I just wanted to say thank you for a wonderful weekend in spite of all the drama.

I hope you never leave, ever.

And just to remind you that the news of SIP is embargoed for four weeks.

Delete this e-mail as soon as you've read it.

Yours

Christian Grey
CEO, Grey Enterprises Holdings, Inc. & your boss's boss's boss

I check Andrea's notes. The replacement's name is Montana Brooks. She knocks and brings in my coffee.

"Ros Bailey is running a little late, but Vanessa Conway is here."

"Let her wait for Ros."

"Yes, Mr. Grey."

"I need some ideas for wedding presents."

Ms. Brooks looks taken aback. "Well, it depends how well you know the person and how much you'd like to spend and—"

I don't need a lecture. I hold up my hand. "Write them down. It's for my PA."

"Does she have a bridal registry?"

"A what?"

"A bridal registry at a store?"

"I don't know. Find out."

"Yes, Mr. Grey."

"That will be all."

She leaves. *Thank God Andrea's back tomorrow.*

Welch's report on Jack Hyde is in my inbox. While I wait for Ros, I take the opportunity to look it over.

MY MEETING WITH ROS and Vanessa is brief. Vanessa and her team are conducting a thorough audit of all our supply chains, and they are proposing we source our cassiterite and wolframite from Bolivia and our tantalum from Australia to avoid the conflict mineral problem. It will be more expensive but will keep us on the right side of the U.S. Securities and Exchange Commission. And it's what we, as a company, should be doing.

When they leave, I check my e-mail. There's one from Ana.

From: Anastasia Steele
Subject: Bossy
Date: June 13 2011 09:03
To: Christian Grey

Dear Mr. Grey
Are you asking me to move in with you? And, of course,
I remembered that the evidence of your epic stalking
capabilities is embargoed for another four weeks. Do I make
a check out to Coping Together and send to your dad?
Please don't delete this e-mail. Please respond to it.

ILY xxx

Anastasia Steele
Assistant to Jack Hyde, Editor, SIP

Am I asking her to move in with me?
Shit.
Grey, this is a bold, sudden move.
I could look after her. Full-time.
She'd be mine. Really mine.
And deep down I know there is only one answer.
A resounding yes.
I ignore all her other questions and respond.

From: Christian Grey
Subject: Me, Bossy?
Date: June 13 2011 09:07
To: Anastasia Steele

Yes. Please.

Christian Grey
CEO, Grey Enterprises Holdings, Inc.

While I wait for her response I read through the rest of the report on Jack Hyde. On the surface, his background check seems fine. He's successful and earns a decent salary. He's from humble beginnings and seems bright and ambitious, but there's something unusual about his career path. Who, in publishing, starts in New York, then works at various publishers across the U.S., ending up in Seattle?

It makes no sense.

He doesn't seem to have had any long-term relationships, and he never keeps an assistant for more than three months.

That means Ana's time with him is limited.

From: Anastasia Steele
Subject: Flynnisms
Date: June 13 2011 09:20
To: Christian Grey

Christian
What happened to walking before we run?

Can we talk about this tonight, please?

I've been asked to go to a conference in New York on
Thursday.

It means an overnight stay on Wednesday.

Just thought you should know.

A x

Anastasia Steele
Assistant to Jack Hyde, Editor, SIP

She doesn't want to move in with me. This is not the news I
wanted.

What did you expect, Grey?

At least she wants to discuss it this evening, so there's hope. But
then she also wants to fuck off to New York.

Well, that sucks.

I wonder if this is a conference on her own.

Or with Hyde?

From: Christian Grey
Subject: WHAT?
Date: June 13 2011 09:21
To: Anastasia Steele

Yes. Let's talk this evening.

Are you going on your own?

Christian Grey
CEO, Grey Enterprises Holdings, Inc.

Jack Hyde must be a prick to work for if he doesn't keep an assistant for more than three months. I know I'm an asshole, but Andrea's worked for me for nearly a year and a half.

I didn't know she was getting married.

Yes. That's pissed me off, but before her there was Helena. She was with me for two years, and now she works in HR, recruiting our engineers.

While I wait for Ana's answer, I read the final page of the report.

And there it is. Three hushed-up harassment claims at his previous publishers and two official warnings at SIP.

Three?

He's a fucking creep. *I knew it*. Why wasn't this in his employee file?

He was all over Ana at the bar. Invading her space. Like the photographer.

From: Anastasia Steele

Subject: No Bold Shouty Capitals on a Monday Morning!

Date: June 13 2011 09:30

To: Christian Grey

Can we talk about this tonight?

A x

Anastasia Steele

Assistant to Jack Hyde, Editor, SIP

Evasive, Miss Steele.

It's a trip with him.

I know it.

She looked sensational this morning.

He's planned it, I bet.

From: Christian Grey
Subject: You Haven't Seen Shouty Yet.
Date: June 13 2011 09:35
To: Anastasia Steele

Tell me.

If it's with the sleazeball you work with, then the answer is
no, over my dead body.

Christian Grey
CEO, Grey Enterprises Holdings, Inc.

I hit send and then buzz Ros.

"Christian," she answers immediately.

"There's a lot of unnecessary expenditure at SIP. They're hemorrhaging money and we need to put a stop to it. I want a moratorium on all nonessential peripheral spending. Travel. Hotels.
Hospitality. All the T&E. Especially for junior staff. You know the
drill."

"Really? I don't think we'll save much money."

"Just call Roach. Make it happen. Immediately."

"What's brought this on?"

"Just do it, Ros."

She sighs. "If you insist. Do you want me to add it to the contract?"

"Yes."

"Okay."

"Thanks." I hang up.

There. Now, that should put a stop to Ana and New York.
Besides, I'd like to take her there myself. She told me yesterday
that she's never been there.

There's a ping and Ana has responded.

From: Anastasia Steele
Subject: No YOU haven't seen shouty yet.
Date: June 13 2011 09:46
To: Christian Grey

Yes. It is with Jack.

I want to go. It's an exciting opportunity for me.

And I have never been to New York.

Don't get your knickers in a twist.

Anastasia Steele
Assistant to Jack Hyde, Editor, SIP

I'm about to reply when I hear a knock. "What?" I bark.

Montana pokes her head around the door and lingers, which is especially irritating—either come in or don't. "Mr. Grey, the registry for Andrea . . ."

For a moment I have no idea what she's talking about.

"It's at Crate and Barrel," she continues, simpering.

"Okay." What the hell am I supposed to do with that information?

"I've made a list of the items still available and their prices."

"E-mail it to me," I say through gritted teeth. "And get me another coffee."

"Yes, Mr. Grey." She smiles as if we're discussing the fucking weather and shuts the door.

Now I can respond to Miss Steele.

From: Christian Grey
Subject: No YOU haven't seen shouty yet.
Date: June 13 2011 09:50
To: Anastasia Steele

Anastasia
It's not my fucking knickers I am worried about.

The answer is NO.

Christian Grey
CEO, Grey Enterprises Holdings, Inc.

Montana places another macchiato on my desk. "You have a meeting at ten with Barney and Fred in the lab," she says.

"Thanks, I'll take my coffee with me." I know I sound surly. But right now a certain blue-eyed woman is getting under my skin. Montana leaves and I take a sip of coffee.

Fuck. Shit.

It's scalding hot.

I drop the cup, the coffee, everything.

Hell.

Fortunately, it misses me and my keyboard, but it's all over the damn floor.

"Ms. Brooks!" I yell. Jesus, I wish Andrea was here.

Montana pops her head around the door. Neither in. Nor out. And still wearing too much freshly applied lipstick.

"I've just dropped my coffee all over the floor because it was scalding hot. Get it cleaned up, please."

"Oh, Mr. Grey. I'm so sorry."

She scurries in to survey the mess and I leave her to deal with it. For a moment I wonder whether she might have done this on purpose.

Grey, you're paranoid.

I grab my phone and decide to take the stairs.

Barney and Fred are sitting at the lab table.

"Good morning, gentlemen."

"Mr. Grey," Fred says. "Barney's cracked it."

"Oh?"

"Yes. The cover."

"We put this through the 3D printer, and voila."

He hands me a compact, hinged plastic cover that's attached to the tablet. "This is great," I say. "This must have taken you all weekend." I stare at Barney.

He shrugs. "Nothing better to do."

"You need to get out more, Barney. But this is good work. Is that all you wanted to show me?"

"We could easily adapt it and put this on a mobile phone cover, too."

"I'd like to see that."

"I'll get on it."

"Great. Anything else?"

"That's it for now, Mr. Grey."

"Might be worth showing the 3D printer to the mayor when he visits."

"We've got quite the show planned for him," says Fred.

"Without giving anything away," adds Barney.

"Sounds great. Thanks for the show-and-tell. I'll head back upstairs."

Waiting for the elevator, I check my e-mail. There's a reply from Ana.

From: Anastasia Steele
Subject: Fifty Shades
Date: June 13 2011 09:55
To: Christian Grey

Christian
You need to get a grip.

I am NOT going to sleep with Jack—not for all the tea in China.

I LOVE you. That's what happens when people love each other.

They TRUST each other.

I don't think you are going to SLEEP WITH, SPANK, FUCK, or WHIP anyone else.

I have FAITH and TRUST in you.

Please extend the same COURTESY to me.

Ana

Anastasia Steele
Assistant to Jack Hyde, Editor, SIP

What the hell! I told her the e-mails at SIP were monitored.

We stop at several floors and I try, really try, to contain my anger. There's that irritating, expectant hush within the elevator as my staff enter and exit, because I'm in there.

"Good morning, Mr. Grey."

"Good morning, Mr. Grey."

I nod my hellos.

But I'm not in the mood.

Beneath my polite smile, my blood is simmering.

As soon as I'm back in my office I check her work number and call her.

"Jack Hyde's office, Ana Steele speaking," she answers.

"Will you please delete the last e-mail you sent me and try to be a little more circumspect in the language you use in your work e-mail? I told you, the system is monitored. I will endeavor to do some damage limitation from here," I snarl and hang up.

I call Barney.

"Mr. Grey."

"Can you delete Miss Anastasia Steele's e-mail to me at nine fifty-five from the SIP server and all mine to her?"

There's silence at the other end of the phone.

"Barney?"

"Um. Sure, Mr. Grey, I was just working out how I can do it. I have an idea."

"Great. Let me know when it's done."

"Yes, sir."

My phone lights up. *Anastasia.*

"What?" I answer, and I think she can tell I'm more than grumpy.

"I am going to New York whether you like it or not."

"Don't count on it."

Silence.

"Ana?"

She's hung up on me.

Fuck. Again.

Who does that?

Well, I might have just done it to her, but that's not the point.

And I remember she did it when she drunk-dialed me.

I put my head in my hands.

Ana. Ana. Ana.

My office phone buzzes.

"Grey."

"Mr. Grey, Barney. It was much easier than I thought. Those e-mails are no longer on the SIP server."

"Thanks, Barney."

"No worries, Mr. Grey."

At least something is going right.

There's a knock on the door.

What now?

Montana opens the door; she's holding a can of carpet cleaner and some tissue.

"Later," I snap. I've had enough of her. She quickly reverses out of the office. I take a deep breath. Today is turning into a shit day and it's not even lunchtime. There's another e-mail from Ana.

From: Anastasia Steele
Subject: What have you done?
Date: June 13 2011 10:43
To: Christian Grey

Please tell me you won't interfere with my work.

I really want to go to this conference.

I shouldn't have to ask you.

I have deleted the offending e-mail.

Anastasia Steele
Assistant to Jack Hyde, Editor, SIP

I respond immediately.

From: Christian Grey
Subject: What have you done?
Date: June 13 2011 10:46
To: Anastasia Steele

I am just protecting what is mine.

The e-mail that you so rashly sent is wiped from the SIP server now, as are my e-mails to you.

Incidentally, I trust you implicitly. It's him I don't trust.

Christian Grey
CEO, Grey Enterprises Holdings, Inc.

Her response is almost as immediate.

From: Anastasia Steele
Subject: Grown Up
Date: June 13 2011 10:48
To: Christian Grey

Christian
I don't need protecting from my own boss.

He may make a pass at me, but I would say no.

You cannot interfere. It's wrong and controlling on so many levels.

Anastasia Steele
Assistant to Jack Hyde, Editor, SIP

"Controlling" is my middle name, Ana. I think I've told you this already, along with "unreasonable" and "weird."

From: Christian Grey
Subject: The Answer is NO
Date: June 13 2011 10:50
To: Anastasia Steele

Ana

I have seen how "effective" you are at fighting off unwanted attention. I remember that's how I had the pleasure of spending my first night with you. At least the photographer has feelings for you. The sleazeball, on the other hand, does not. He is a serial philanderer, and he will try to seduce you. Ask him what happened to his previous PA and the one before that.

I don't want to fight about this.

If you want to go to New York, I'll take you. We can go this weekend. I have an apartment there.

Christian Grey
CEO, Grey Enterprises Holdings, Inc.

She doesn't reply immediately, and I distract myself with phone calls.

Welch has nothing new on Leila. We discuss whether or not to involve the police at this stage; I'm still reluctant to do it.

"She's close, Mr. Grey," Welch says.

"She's clever. She's managed to evade us so far."

"We're watching your place, SIP, Grey House. She won't slip past us again."

"I hope she doesn't. And thanks for the report on Hyde."

"You're welcome. I can dig deeper if you wish."

"It's fine for now. But I may get back to you."

"Okay, sir."

"Bye." I hang up.

My phone buzzes before I've let go of the receiver. "I have your mother on the line," Montana chirps in a singsong voice.

Shit. That's all I need. I'm still a little pissed at my mom and her comment about Ana being after my money.

"Put her through," I mutter.

"Christian, darling," Grace says.

"Hello, Mother."

"Darling, I just wanted to apologize for what I said on Saturday. You know I think the world of Ana, it's just . . . all of this is so sudden."

"It's fine." But it's not fine.

She's quiet for a moment and I think she's doubting the sincerity of my response.

However, I'm already arguing with one woman in my life; I don't want to argue with another. "Grace?"

"Sorry, darling. It's your birthday on Saturday and we wanted to organize a party."

On my computer screen an e-mail from Ana appears.

"Mom, I can't talk now. I have to go."

"Okay, call me." She sounds melancholy, but I don't have time for her right now.

"Yes. Sure."

"Bye, Christian."

"Bye." I hang up.

From: Anastasia Steele
Subject: FW Lunch date or Irritating Baggage
Date: June 13 2011 11:15
To: Christian Grey

Christian
While you have been busy interfering in my career and saving
your ass from my careless missives, I received the following
e-mail from Mrs. Lincoln. I really don't want to meet with
her—even if I did, I am not allowed to leave this building. How
she got hold of my e-mail address, I don't know. What would
you suggest I do? Her e-mail is below:

Dear Anastasia, I would really like to have lunch with you. I
think we got off on the wrong foot, and I'd like to make that
right. Are you free sometime this week?
Elena Lincoln

Anastasia Steele
Assistant to Jack Hyde, Editor, SIP

Oh, this day just gets better and better. What the hell is Elena
doing now? And Ana is calling me out on my shit as usual.

I didn't know arguing could be so tiresome. And discouraging.
And worrying. She's mad at me.

From: Christian Grey
Subject: Irritating Baggage
Date: June 13 2011 11:23
To: Anastasia Steele

Don't be mad at me. I have your best interests at heart.

If anything happened to you, I would never forgive myself.

I'll deal with Mrs. Lincoln.

Christian Grey
CEO, Grey Enterprises Holdings, Inc.

Irritating baggage? I smile for the first time since I left Ana this morning. She has a way with words.

I call Elena.

"Christian," she answers on the fifth ring.

"Do I have to get a banner and attach it to a plane and fly it over your office?"

She laughs. "My e-mail?"

"Yes, Ana sent it to me. Please. Leave her alone. She doesn't want to see you. And I understand and respect that. You're making my life really difficult."

"You understand her?"

"Yes."

"I think she needs to know how hard you are on yourself."

"No. She doesn't need to know anything."

"You sound exhausted."

"I'm just tired of you going behind my back and chasing my girlfriend."

"Girlfriend?"

"Yes. Girlfriend. Get used to it."

She sighs long and hard.

"Elena. Please."

"Okay, Christian, it's your funeral."

What the fuck?

"I have to go," I answer.

"Good-bye," she says, and she sounds annoyed.

"Bye." I hang up.

The women in my life are vexing. I turn in my chair and stare out of the window. The rain is relentless. The sky is dark and drab, reflecting my mood. Life has become complicated. It used to be easier when everything and everyone stayed where I placed them, in their designated compartments. Now, with Ana, everything's changed. This is all new, and so far everyone, including my mother, seems to be pissed at me or pissing me off.

When I turn to face my computer there's another e-mail from Ana.

From: Anastasia Steele
Subject: Laters
Date: June 13 2011 11:32
To: Christian Grey

Can we please discuss this tonight?

I am trying to work, and your continued interference is very distracting.

Anastasia Steele
Assistant to Jack Hyde, Editor, SIP

Okay. I'll leave you alone.

What I really want to do is go over to her office and take her somewhere splendid for lunch. But I don't think she'd appreciate that.

With a heavy sigh, I open the e-mail that lists Andrea's bridal registry. Pots, pans, dishes—nothing appeals to me. And again I wonder why she didn't tell me about her nuptials.

Feeling morose, I call Flynn's office and make an appointment to see him later this afternoon. It's overdue. Then I summon Montana and ask her to go and buy me a wedding card and some lunch. Surely she can't screw that up.

AS I'M EATING MY lunch, Taylor calls.

"Taylor."

"Mr. Grey, everything's okay."

My heart goes into overdrive as adrenaline powers through my body.

Ana.

"What is it? Is Ana okay?"

"She's fine, sir."

"Do you have news on Leila?"

"No, sir."

"Then what is it?"

"I'm just letting you know that Ana went to the deli on Union Square. She's back in the office. She's fine."

"Thank you for letting me know. Anything else?"

"The Saab will be here this afternoon."

"Great." I put the phone down and try, really try, not to be mad as hell. I fail. She told me she'd stay put.

Leila could put a bullet through her.

Doesn't she understand that?

I call her.

"Jack Hyde's office—"

"You assured me you wouldn't go out."

"Jack sent me out for some lunch. I couldn't say no. Are you having me watched?" She sounds incredulous.

I ignore her question. "This is why I didn't want you going back to work."

"Christian, please. You're being so suffocating."

"Suffocating?"

"Yes. You have to stop this. I'll talk to you this evening. Unfortunately, I have to work late because I can't go to New York."

"Anastasia, I don't want to suffocate you."

"Well, you are. I have work to do. I'll talk to you later." She sounds as miserable as I feel and she hangs up.

I'm suffocating her?

Maybe I am . . .

I just want to protect her. I saw what Leila did to her car.

Don't push her too far, Grey.

She'll leave.

FLYNN HAS A REAL log fire burning in his office. It's June. It spits and crackles as we talk.

"You bought the company where she works?" Flynn asks with raised eyebrows.

"Yes."

"I think Ana has a point. I'm not surprised she feels suffocated."

I shift in my chair. This is not what I want to hear. "I wanted to get into publishing."

Flynn remains impassive, giving nothing away, waiting for me to speak.

"It's over the top, isn't it?" I concede.

"Yes."

"She wasn't impressed."

"Did you set out to impress her?"

"No. That wasn't my intention. Anyway, SIP is mine now."

"I understand that you're trying to protect her, and I know why you're trying to do that. But this is an out-of-the-ordinary reaction. You have a bank account that allows you to do this, but you will drive her away if you continue on this path."

"That's what I'm worried about."

"Christian, you have a great deal to contend with at the moment. Leila Williams—and yes, I will help you when you find her—Anastasia's animosity toward Elena . . . I think you can understand why Ana feels that way." He gives me a pointed look.

I shrug, unwilling to agree with him.

"But there's something much bigger you're not telling me, and I've been waiting for you to tell me since you arrived here. I saw it on Saturday."

I stare at him, wondering what he's talking about. He sits patiently. Waiting.

He saw it on Saturday?

The bidding?

The dancing?

Shit.

"I'm in love with Ana."

"Thank you. I know."

"Oh."

"I could have told you that when you came to see me after she left you. I'm glad you worked it out for yourself."

"I didn't know I was capable of feeling like this."

"Of course you're capable." He sounds exasperated. "That's why I was so interested in your reaction when she told you that she loved you."

"It's getting easier to hear."

He smiles. "Good. I'm glad."

"I've always been able to separate the different aspects of my life. My work. My family. My sex life. I understood what each of these meant to me. But since I met Ana, it's not as simple anymore. It's entirely unfamiliar and I feel out of my depth and out of control."

"Welcome to falling in love." Flynn smiles. "And don't be too hard on yourself. You have an ex on the loose with a gun who has already tried to get your attention by attempting suicide in front of your housekeeper. And she's vandalized Ana's car. You've put measures in place to keep Ana and you safe. You've done all you can. You can't be everywhere, and you can't keep Ana locked up."

"I want to."

"I know you do. But you can't. Simple."

I shake my head, but deep down I know John's right.

"Christian, I've long held the belief that you never really had an adolescence—emotionally speaking. I think you're experiencing it now. I can see how agitated you are," he continues, "and since you won't let me prescribe you any anti-anxiety medication, I'd like you to try the relaxation techniques we discussed."

Oh, not that shit. I roll my eyes, but I know I'm behaving like a sulky teenager. He just said as much.

"Christian, it's your blood pressure. Not mine."

"Okay." I hold my hands up in surrender. "I'll try my *happy* place." I sound sarcastic, but it will appease John, who's looking at the clock.

Where is my happy place?

My childhood in the orchard.

Sailing or soaring. Always.

It used to be with Elena.

But now my happy place is with Ana.

In Ana.

Flynn stifles a smile. "Time's up," he says.

FROM THE BACK OF the Audi, I call Ana.

"Hi," she says, her voice quiet and breathy.

"Hi. When will you be finished?"

"By seven thirty, I think."

"I'll meet you outside."

"Okay."

Thank God—I thought she might say she wanted to go back to her own apartment.

"I'm still mad at you, but that's all," she whispers. "We have a lot to talk about."

"I know. See you at seven thirty."

"I have to go. See you later." She hangs up.

"Let's sit here and wait for her," I say to Taylor, and glance at the front door of SIP.

"Okay, sir."

And I sit and listen to the rain as it drums an uneven tattoo on the roof of the car, drowning out my thoughts. Drowning out my happy place.

AN HOUR LATER, the door to SIP opens and there she is. Taylor climbs out of the car and opens the door as Ana hurries toward us, head down to avoid the rain.

I have no idea what she's going to do or say as she shuffles in beside me, but she's shaking her head and scattering droplets of water over me and the backseat.

I want to hold her.

"Hi," she says, and her anxious eyes meet mine.

"Hi," I respond and, reaching over, I grasp her hand and squeeze it.

"Are you still mad?" I ask.

"I don't know," she says.

I bring her hand to my lips and kiss each knuckle in turn. "It's been a shitty day."

"Yes, it has." Her shoulders slump and she seems to relax into the car seat as she lets out a deep breath.

"It's better now that you're here." I run my thumb across her knuckles, craving the contact. As Taylor drives us home, the day's woes seem to dissipate and at last I start to relax.

She's here. She's safe.

She's with me.

Taylor stops outside Escala and I'm not sure why. But Ana is already opening the door, so I jump out after her and we run into the building and out of the rain. I grasp her hand as we wait for the elevator, surveying the street through the plate glass. Just in case.

"I take it you haven't found Leila yet," Ana says.

"No. Welch is still looking for her."

We step into the elevator and the doors close. Ana looks up at me, elfin-faced, and wide-eyed—I can't look away. Our gaze holds my longing and her need. She licks her lips. A come-on.

And suddenly our attraction is in the air between us, like static, surrounding us.

"Do you feel it?" I whisper.

"Yes."

"Oh, Ana." I cannot bear the distance between us. I reach for her so she's in my arms and angle her head. My lips seek and find hers. She groans into my mouth, her fingers in my hair as I push her against the elevator wall. "I hate arguing with you." I want every inch of her. Right here. Right now. To know that we're okay.

Ana's response is immediate. Her hunger and passion are unleashed in our kiss, her tongue demanding and urgent. Her body rises and presses against mine, seeking relief as I lift up her skirt, my fingertips skimming her thigh and feeling lace and warm, warm flesh. "Sweet Jesus, you're wearing stockings." My voice is hoarse as I slide my thumb across her stocking line. "I want to see this." And I pull her skirt right up so I can see the tops of her thighs.

I step back to enjoy the view and press the elevator's emergency stop button. I'm panting. I'm wanting, and she stands there like the fucking goddess she is, staring me down, her eyes dark, carnal, her breasts rising and falling as she drags air into her lungs.

"Take your hair down."

Ana yanks at her hair tie and her hair spills down over her shoulders and curls at her breasts. "Undo the top two buttons of your shirt," I whisper, growing harder and harder. Her lips parted, she reaches up and slowly, too slowly, undoes the first one. Pausing for a beat, she lowers her fingers to the second button and undoes it. Unhurried. Tantalizing me further and finally revealing the soft swell of her breasts.

"Do you have any idea how alluring you look right now?" I hear the need in my voice.

She sinks her teeth into her bottom lip and shakes her head.

I think I'm going to explode. I close my eyes and try to bring my body to heel. Stepping forward, I place my hands on the wall on either side of her face. She tilts her face up, and her eyes meet mine.

I lean closer. "I think you do, Miss Steele. I think you like to drive me wild."

"Do I drive you wild?"

"In all things, Anastasia. You are a siren, a goddess." I reach down and grasp her leg above her knee and hitch it up around my waist. Slowly I lean down, pressing my body into hers. My erection sitting at the sacred junction of her thighs. I kiss her throat, my tongue tasting and savoring her. She wraps her arms around my neck and she arches her back, pressing into me.

"I'm going to take you now." I groan and lift her higher. Grabbing a condom from my pocket, I undo my fly. "Hold tight, baby."

She tightens her arms around my neck and I show her the condom. She bites down on the corner and I tug, and together we rip open the foil packet.

"Good girl."

I step back a little and manage to slide on the damn condom. "God, I can't wait for the next six days."

No more condoms.

I run my thumb over her underwear.

Lace. Good.

"I do hope you're not overly fond of these panties." And the only reply is her heavy breathing in my ear. I push my thumbs through the seam at the back and they tear apart, allowing me access to my happy place.

With my eyes on hers, I take her, slowly.

Fuck, she feels good.

She arches her back and closes her eyes and groans.

I pull back and sink slowly into her once more.

This is what I want.

This is what I needed.

After such a shitty day.

She didn't run.

She's here.

For me.

With me.

"You're mine, Anastasia." The words wash against her throat.

"Yes. Yours. When will you accept that?" Her words are a sigh. And it's what I want to hear. What I need to hear. I take her, fast, furious. I need her. With each little cry, each pant, each tug of my hair, I know she needs me, too. I lose myself in her and I feel her spiral out of control. "Oh, baby," I moan, and she comes around me, crying out, and I follow, whispering her name.

I kiss her, holding her, as my composure returns. We are forehead to forehead and her eyes are closed. "Oh, Ana, I need you so much." I close my eyes and kiss her forehead, thankful that I've found her.

"And I you, Christian," she whispers.

I release her and straighten her skirt and I do up the top two buttons of her shirt. I punch the override code into the elevator keypad and it jolts to life. "Taylor will be wondering where we are." I give her a wicked grin and she tries in vain to smooth out her hair. After a few futile attempts she gives up and opts for a ponytail.

"You'll do," I reassure her, and zip up my fly and slip the condom and her ruined panties into my pocket for disposal later.

Taylor is waiting when the doors open.

"Problem with the elevator," I say as we step out, but I avoid eye contact with him. Ana scampers off to the bedroom, no doubt to freshen up, and I make my way into the kitchen, where Mrs. Jones is preparing dinner.

"The Saab is here, Mr. Grey," Taylor says, having followed me into the kitchen.

"Great. I'll let Ana know."

"Sir." He smiles. He and Gail exchange a look before he turns to leave.

"Good evening, Gail," I say, ignoring their look, as I slip off my jacket. I hang it on the barstool and sit down at the counter.

"Good evening, Mr. Grey. Dinner will be ready shortly."

"Smells good."

Damn, I'm hungry.

"Coq au vin, for two." She gives me a fond sideways glance as she takes two plates out of the warming drawer. "I'm just checking that Miss Steele will be with us tomorrow."

"Yes."

"I'll fix lunch for her again."

"Great."

Ana returns to join me at the kitchen counter and Mrs. Jones serves us our dinner.

"Enjoy, Mr. Grey, Ana," she says, and exits the kitchen.

I fetch a bottle of Chablis from the fridge and pour each of us a glass. Ana tucks into her food. She's hungry.

"I like to see you eat."

"I know." She pops a piece of chicken into her mouth. I grin and take a sip of wine. "Tell me something good about your day," she says when she's finished chewing.

"We had a breakthrough today with the design of our solar-powered tablet. It has so many different applications. We'll be able to make solar-powered phones, too."

"You're excited about that?"

"Very. And they'll be cheap to produce and distribute in developing countries."

"Careful, your philanthropy is showing," she teases, but her expression is warm. "So is it just in New York and Aspen that you have property?"

"Yes."

"Where in New York?"

"TriBeCa."

"Tell me about it."

"It's an apartment. I rarely use it. In fact, my family uses it more than I do. I'll take you, whenever you want to go."

Ana stands and collects my plate and puts it in the sink. I think she's about to wash up. "Leave that. Gail will do it." She looks happier than when she got into the car.

"Well, now that you are more docile, Miss Steele, shall we talk about today?"

"I think you're the one who's more docile. I think I'm doing a good job in taming you."

"Taming me?" I snort, amused that she thinks I need taming.

She nods. She's serious.

Taming me.

Well, I'm certainly more docile since our assignation in the elevator. And she was more than happy to contribute to that encounter. Is that what she means?

"Yes. Maybe you are, Anastasia."

"You were right about Jack," she says, and leans across the kitchen counter, regarding me seriously.

My blood runs cold. "Has he tried anything?"

She shakes her head. "No, and he won't, Christian. I told him today that I'm your girlfriend, and he backed right off."

"You're sure? I could fire the fucker."

He's history. I want him out.

Ana sighs. "You really have to let me fight my own battles. You can't constantly second-guess me and try to protect me. It's stifling, Christian. I'll never flourish with your incessant interference. I need some freedom. I wouldn't dream of meddling in your affairs."

"I only want you safe, Anastasia. If anything happened to you, I—"

"I know," she says, "and I understand why you feel so driven to protect me. And part of me loves it. I know that if I need you, you'll be there, as I am for you. But if we are to have any hope of a future together, you have to trust me and trust my judgment. Yes, I'll get it wrong sometimes—I'll make mistakes, but I have to learn." It's a passionate plea, and I know she's right.

It's just . . . it's just . . .

Flynn's words come to mind. *You will drive her away if you continue on this path.*

She comes toward me with quiet determination and, taking my hands, places them around her waist. Gently, she puts her hands on my arms. "You can't interfere in my job. It's wrong. I don't need you charging in like a white knight to save the day. I know you want to control everything, and I understand why, but you can't. It's an impossible goal. You have to learn to let go." She strokes my face. "And if you can do that—give me that—I'll move in with you."

"You'd do that?"

"Yes," she says.

"But you don't know me," I blurt, suddenly panicked. I have to tell her.

"I know you well enough, Christian. Nothing you tell me about yourself will frighten me away."

I doubt that. She doesn't know why I do what I do.

She doesn't know the monster.

She touches my cheek again, trying to reassure me. "But if you could just ease up on me."

"I'm trying, Anastasia. I couldn't just stand by and let you go to New York with that sleazeball. He has an alarming reputation.

None of his assistants have lasted more than three months, and they're never retained by the company. I don't want that for you, baby. I don't want anything to happen to you. You being hurt, the thought fills me with dread. I can't promise not to interfere, not if I think you'll come to harm." I take a deep breath. "I love you, Anastasia. I will do everything in my power to protect you. I cannot imagine my life without you."

Quite the speech, Grey.

"I love you, too, Christian." She folds her arms around my neck and kisses me, her tongue teasing my lips.

Taylor coughs in the background, and I stand with Ana by my side.

"Yes?" I ask Taylor, a little more sharply than intended.

"Mrs. Lincoln is on her way up, sir."

"What?"

Taylor gives me an apologetic shrug.

I shake my head.

"Well, this should be interesting," I mutter, and give Ana a contrite smile. Ana looks from me to Taylor and I don't think she quite believes him. He gives her a nod and leaves.

"Did you talk to her today?" she asks me.

"Yes."

"What did you say?"

"I said that you didn't want to see her, and that I understood your reasons why. I also told her that I didn't appreciate her going behind my back."

"What did she say?"

"She brushed it off in a way that only Elena can."

"Why do you think she's here?"

"I have no idea."

Taylor returns to the living room. "Mrs. Lincoln," he says, and Elena stands staring at the two of us. I pull Ana closer to my side.

"Elena?" I say, wondering why the hell she's here.

She looks from me to Ana. "I'm sorry. I didn't realize you had company, Christian. It's Monday," she says.

"Girlfriend," I clarify.

Submissives only on the weekend, Mrs. Lincoln. You know this.

"Of course. Hello, Anastasia. I didn't know you'd be here. I know you don't want to talk to me. I accept that."

"Do you?" Ana's tone is deadly.

Hell.

Elena walks toward us. "Yes, I get the message. I'm not here to see you. Like I said, Christian rarely has company during the week." She pauses and addresses Ana directly. "I have a problem, and I need to talk to Christian about it."

"Oh? Do you want a drink?" I ask.

"Yes, please," she says.

I fetch a glass. When I turn they are both sitting in awkward silence at the kitchen island.

Shit.

This day. This day. This day. It just gets better and better.

I pour wine into both of their glasses and take a seat between them.

"What's up?" I ask Elena.

Elena's eyes dart to Ana.

"Anastasia's with me now." I reach across and give Ana's hand a reassuring squeeze in the hope that she keeps quiet. The sooner Elena says her piece, the sooner she'll be gone.

Elena looks nervous, unlike her usual self. She twists her ring, a sure sign that something is agitating her. "I'm being blackmailed."

"How?" I ask, appalled. She pulls a note out of her purse. I don't want to touch it. "Put it down, lay it out." I point with my chin at the marble top and tighten my hold on Ana's hand.

"You don't want to touch it?" Elena asks.

"No. Fingerprints."

"Christian, you know I can't go to the police with this." She puts the note on the counter. It's written in capital letters.

MRS LINCOLN
FIVE THOUSAND
OR I TELL ALL.

"They're only asking for five thousand dollars?" That doesn't seem right. "Any idea who it might be? Someone in the community?"

"No," she responds.

"Linc?"

"What—after all this time? I don't think so."

"Does Isaac know?"

"I haven't told him."

"I think he needs to know."

Ana tugs at her hand. She wants out.

"What?" I ask Ana.

"I'm tired. I think I'll go to bed," she says.

I search her face to see what she's really thinking, and as usual I have no idea.

"Okay," I answer. "I won't be long." I release her hand and she gets up.

"Good night, Anastasia," Elena says.

Ana responds, her voice frigid, and she stalks out of the room. I turn my attention back to Elena.

"I don't think there's a great deal I can do, Elena. If it's a question of money . . ." I stop. She knows I'd give her the money. "I could ask Welch to investigate?"

"No, Christian, I just wanted to share. You look very happy," she adds, changing the subject.

"I am." Ana just agreed to move in.

"You deserve to be."

"I wish that were true."

"Christian." Elena's tone is chastising. "Does she know how negative you are about yourself? About all your issues?"

"She knows me better than anyone."

"Ouch! That hurts."

"It's the truth, Elena. I don't have to play games with her. And I mean it, leave her alone."

"What is her problem?"

"You. What we were. What we did. She doesn't understand."

"Make her understand."

"It's in the past, Elena, and why would I want to taint her with our fucked-up relationship? She's good and sweet and innocent, and by some miracle she loves me."

"It's no miracle, Christian. Have a little faith in yourself. You really are quite a catch. I've told you often enough. And she seems lovely, too. Strong. Someone to stand up to you."

"She's stronger than both of us."

Elena's eyes cool. She looks thoughtful. "Don't you miss it?"

"What?"

"Your playroom."

"That really is none of your fucking business."

"I'm sorry." Her sarcasm is irritating. She's anything but sorry.

"I think you'd better go. And please, call before you come again."

"Christian, I am sorry," she says again, sincerely this time. "Since when are you so sensitive?"

"Elena, we have a business relationship that has profited us both immensely. Let's keep it that way. What was between us is part of the past. Anastasia is my future, and I won't jeopardize it in any way, so cut the fucking crap."

"I see." Elena gives me a hard stare, as if she's trying to get under my skin. It makes me uncomfortable.

"Look, I'm sorry for your trouble. Perhaps you should ride it out and call their bluff."

"I don't want to lose you, Christian."

"I'm not yours to lose, Elena."

"That's not what I meant."

"What did you mean?" I snap.

"Look, I don't want to argue with you. Your friendship means a lot to me. I'll back off from Anastasia. But I'm here if you need me. I always will be."

"Anastasia thinks that you saw me last Saturday. You called, that's all. Why did you tell her otherwise?"

"I wanted her to know how upset you were when she left. I don't want her to hurt you."

"She knows. I've told her. Stop interfering. Honestly, you're like a mother hen."

Elena laughs, but it's hollow, and I really want her to go. "I know. I'm sorry. You know I care about you. I never thought you'd end up falling in love, Christian. It's very gratifying to see. But I couldn't bear it if she hurt you."

"I'll take my chances," I state wryly. "Now, are you sure you don't want Welch to sniff around?"

"I suppose it wouldn't do any harm."

"Okay. I'll call him in the morning."

"Thank you, Christian. And I am sorry. I didn't mean to intrude. I'll go. Next time I'll call."

"Good."

I stand and she takes the hint and gets up, too. We walk into the foyer and she gives me a peck on the cheek. "I'm just watching out for you," she says.

"I know. Oh, and another thing, can you not gossip to my mother about my relationship with Ana?"

"Okay," she says, but her mouth is pinched. She's irritated now.

The elevator doors open and she steps inside.

"Good night."

"Good night, Christian."

The doors close and Ana's words from her e-mail earlier today come to mind.

Irritating baggage.

I chuckle, in spite of myself. *Yes, Ana. You are so right.*

Ana is sitting on my bed. Her look is inscrutable. "She's gone," I say, anxious about Ana's reaction. I don't know what she's thinking.

"Will you tell me all about her? I am trying to understand why you think she helped you." She glances down at her fingernails, then up at me, her eyes clear with conviction. "I loathe her, Christian. I think she did you untold damage. You have no friends. Did she keep them away from you?"

Oh, Christ. I've really had enough of this. I do not need this now. "Why the fuck do you want to know about her? We had a very long-standing affair, she beat the shit out of me often, and I fucked her in all sorts of ways you can't even imagine, end of story."

She's taken aback. Eyes flashing, she tosses her hair over her shoulder. "Why are you so angry?"

"Because all of that shit is over!" And I'm shouting.

Ana looks away, her mouth a hard line.

Damn it.

Why am I so volatile around her . . . ?

Calm down, Grey.

I sit down beside her. "What do you want to know?"

"You don't have to tell me. I don't mean to intrude."

"Anastasia, it's not that. I don't like talking about this shit. I've lived in a bubble for years with nothing affecting me and not having to justify myself to anyone. She's always been there as a confidante. And now my past and my future are colliding in a way I never thought possible. I never thought I had a future with anyone, Anastasia. You give me hope and have me thinking about all sorts of possibilities."

You've said you'd move in with me.

"I was listening," she whispers, and I think she's embarrassed.

"What? To our conversation?" *Christ. What did I say?*

"Yes."

"Well?"

"She cares for you."

"Yes, she does. And I for her in my own way, but it doesn't come close to how I feel about you. If that's what this is about."

"I'm not jealous," she says quickly, and tosses her hair over her shoulder again.

I'm not sure I believe her.

"You don't love her?"

I sigh. "A long time ago, I thought I loved her."

"When we were in Georgia you said you didn't love her."

"That's right."

She's perplexed.

Oh, baby, do I have to spell it out for you?

"I loved you then, Anastasia. You're the only person I'd fly three thousand miles to see. The feelings I have for you are very different from any I ever had for Elena." Ana asks me when I knew this. "Ironically, it was Elena who pointed it out to me. She encouraged me to go to Georgia."

Ana's expression changes. She looks wary. "So you desired her? When you were younger."

"Yes. She taught me a great deal. She taught me to believe in myself."

"But she also beat the shit out of you."

"Yes, she did."

"And you liked that?"

"At the time I did."

"So much that you wanted to do it to others?"

"Yes."

"Did she help you with that?"

"Yes."

"Did she sub for you?"

"Yes."

Ana's shocked. *Don't ask me if you don't want to know.*

"Do you expect me to like her?"

"No. Though it would make my life a hell of a lot easier. I do understand your reticence."

"Reticence! Jeez, Christian—if that were your son, how would you feel?"

What a ridiculous question.

Me. With a son?

Never.

"I didn't have to stay with her. It was my choice, too, Anastasia."

"Who's Linc?"

"Her ex-husband."

"Lincoln Timber?"

"The very same."

"And Isaac?"

"Her current submissive. He's in his mid-twenties, Anastasia. You know—a consenting adult."

"Your age," she says.

Enough. Enough.

"Look, Anastasia, as I said to her, she's part of my past. You are my future. Don't let her come between us, please. And quite frankly, I'm really bored of this subject. I'm going to do some work." I stand and look down at her. "Let it go. Please."

She sticks her chin out in that obstinate way she does. I choose to ignore it.

"Oh, I almost forgot," I add. "Your car arrived a day early. It's in the garage. Taylor has the key."

Her eyes light up. "Can I drive it tomorrow?"

"No."

"Why not?"

"You know why not."

Leila. Do I have to spell it out?

"And that reminds me," I continue. "If you're going to leave your office, let me know. Sawyer was there, watching you. It seems I can't trust you to look after yourself at all."

"Seems I can't trust you, either," she says. "You could have told me Sawyer was watching me."

"Do you want to fight about that, too?" I ask.

"I wasn't aware we were fighting. I thought we were communicating," she replies, glaring at me.

I close my eyes, struggling to keep my temper. This is getting us nowhere. "I have to work." I walk out, leaving her sitting on the bed, before I say something I'll regret.

All these questions.

If she doesn't like the answers, why does she ask me?

Elena is pissed, too.

I sit down at my desk and already there's an e-mail from her.

From: Elena Lincoln
Subject: Tonight
Date: June 13 2011 21:16
To: Christian Grey

Christian
I'm sorry. I don't know what possessed me to come over.

I feel that I'm losing you as a friend. That's all.

I value your friendship and advice so much.

I wouldn't be where I am without you.

Just know that.

Ex

ELENA LINCOLN
ESCLAVA
For The Beauty That Is You™

I think she's also telling me that I wouldn't be where I am without her. And that's true.

She grabs a handful of my hair, tugging my head back.

"What do you want to tell me?" she purrs, icy blue eyes boring into mine.

I'm broken. My knees are sore. My back is covered in welts. My thighs ache. I can't take any more. And she's looking directly into my eyes. Waiting.

"I want to leave Harvard, Ma'am," I say. And it's a dark

*confession. Harvard had always been a goal. For me. For my folks.
Just to show them I could do it. Just to prove to them I wasn't the
fuckup they thought I was.*

"*Leave? School?*"

"*Yes, Ma'am.*"

She lets go of my hair and swings the flogger from side to side.

"*What will you do?*"

"*I want to start my own business.*"

*She runs a scarlet fingernail down my cheek, to my mouth. "I
knew something was bothering you. I always have to beat it out of
you, don't I?*"

"*Yes, Ma'am.*"

"*Get dressed. Let's talk about this.*"

I shake my head. Now is not the time to think about Elena. I
turn to other e-mails.

WHEN I LOOK UP, it's ten thirty.

Ana.

I've been lost in the final SIP contract. I wonder if I should
make it a condition of sale to get rid of Hyde, but that might be
actionable.

I get up, stretch, and head into the bedroom.

Ana's not there.

She wasn't in the living room. I run upstairs to the submissive's
room, but it's empty. *Shit.*

Where could she be? Library?

I hurtle back down the stairs.

I find her curled up asleep in one of the wing-backed library
chairs. She's dressed in pale pink satin, her hair spilling down over
her chest. On her lap is an open book.

Daphne du Maurier's *Rebecca.*

I smile. My grandfather Theodore's family comes from Corn-
wall, hence my Daphne du Maurier collection.

I lift Ana into my arms. "Hey. You fell asleep. I couldn't find you." As I kiss her hair she puts her arms around my neck and says something I don't understand. I carry her through to my bedroom and tuck her into bed.

"Sleep, baby." Softly I kiss her forehead and head for the shower. I want to wash this day off my body.

S uddenly I'm awake; my heart is pounding and a deep unease tightens my gut. I'm lying naked beside Ana, and she's fast asleep. Lord, I envy her ability to sleep. My bedside light is still on, the clock reads 1:45, and I cannot shake my disquiet.

Leila?

I dart into my closet and drag on pants and a T-shirt. Back in the bedroom I check under the bed. The balcony door is locked. I hurry down the corridor to Taylor's office. The door is open, so I knock and look in. Ryan stands, surprised to see me. "Good evening, sir."

"Hi, Ryan. Everything okay?"

"Yes, sir. All's quiet."

"Nothing on the—" I point to the CCTV monitors.

"Nothing, sir. The place is secure. Reynolds just did a walk-through."

"Good. Thanks."

"You're welcome, Mr. Grey."

I shut his door and go into the kitchen for a glass of water. Looking out across the living room toward the windows and the darkness beyond, I take a sip.

Where are you, Leila?

I see her in my mind's eye, head bowed. Willing. Waiting. Wanting. Kneeling in my playroom, asleep in her room, kneeling by my side as I work in my study. And now for all I know she's wandering the streets of Seattle, cold and lonely and acting crazy.

Maybe I'm uneasy because Ana's agreed to move in.

I can protect her. But she doesn't want that.

I shake my head. Anastasia is challenging.

She's very challenging.

Welcome to falling in love. Flynn's words haunt me. So this is what it's like. Confusing, exhilarating, exhausting.

I walk over to my grand piano and lower the top board to cover the strings as quietly as I can. I don't want to wake her. I sit down and stare at the keys. I haven't played for a few days. I place my fingers on the keys and start to play. As Chopin's nocturne in B-flat minor quietly fills the room, I'm alone with the melancholy music and it soothes my soul.

A movement in my peripheral vision distracts me. Ana is standing in the shadows. Her eyes glint from the light in the hallway, and I continue to play. She walks toward me, dressed in the pale pink satin robe. She's stunning: a diva who's stepped off the silver screen.

When she reaches me, I take my hands off the keys. I want to touch her.

"Why did you stop? That was lovely," she says.

"Do you have any idea how desirable you look at this moment?"

"Come to bed," she says.

I offer her my hand, and when she takes it I pull her into my lap and embrace her, kissing her exposed neck and tracing my lips to the pulse point at her throat. She trembles in my arms.

"Why do we fight?" I ask, as my teeth tease her earlobe.

"Because we're getting to know each other, and you're stubborn and cantankerous and moody and difficult." She tilts her head to give me better access to her neck. I smile against her skin as I run my nose down her throat.

Challenging.

"I'm all those things, Miss Steele. It's a wonder you put up with me." I graze her earlobe with my teeth.

"Mmm . . ." She lets me know it feels good.

"Is it always like this?" I whisper against her skin. I cannot get enough of her?

"I have no idea," she says, her voice little more than a sigh.

"Me neither." I untie the sash on her robe and it falls open, revealing the gown beneath. It clings to her body, showing every curve, every dip, every hollow. My hand skims from her face to her breast and her nipples harden, crowning against the satin when I circle them with my fingers. I move my hand to her waist, then to her hip.

"You feel so fine under this material, and I can see everything— even this." I tug gently on her pubic hair, visible as a slight mound beneath the fabric.

She gasps and I cradle her neck and coil my hand in her hair, drawing her head back. I kiss her, coaxing open her mouth and testing her tongue with mine.

She moans once more and her fingers curl around my face, stroking my stubble as her body rises beneath my touch.

Gently I lift up her nightgown, enjoying the feel of rich, soft satin as it inches up her beautiful body, revealing her long lovely legs. My hands find her ass. She's naked. I cup her in my hand, then move and run my thumbnail down the length of her inner thigh.

I want her. Here. On my piano.

Abruptly I stand, surprising Ana, and I lift her onto the piano so she's sitting on the front of the top board, her feet on the keys. Two discordant chords ring through the room as she gazes at me. Standing between her legs, I take her hands. "Lie back." I ease her down onto the piano. The satin spills like fluid over the edge of the gleaming black wood and onto the keys.

Once she's on her back I let go, strip off my T-shirt, and push her legs apart. Ana's feet play a staccato melody on the low and high keys. I kiss the inside of her right knee and trail kisses and soft nips up her leg to her thigh. Her nightgown inches up, revealing more and more of my beautiful girl. She groans. She knows what I have in mind. Her feet flex, and the dissonant sounds from the keys resonate through the room, an uneven accompaniment to her accelerated breathing.

I reach my goal: her clitoris. And I kiss her once, relishing the jolt that shoots through her body. Then I blow on her pubic hair to make a small space for my tongue. I push her knees wider and hold her in place. She's mine. Exposed. At my mercy. And I love it. Slowly, I start circling my tongue around her sensitive sweet spot. She cries out and I continue over and over and over, while she's writhing beneath me, tilting her pelvis up for more.

I don't stop.

I consume her.

Until my face is soaked.

From me.

From her.

Her legs start to tremble.

"Oh, Christian, please."

"Oh no, baby, not yet." Pausing, I take a deep breath. She's laid out before me in satin, her hair spilling over the polished ebony; she's gorgeous, lit only from the reading light.

"No," she whimpers. She doesn't want me to stop.

"This is my revenge, Ana. Argue with me and I am going to take it out on your body somehow." I kiss her belly, feeling her muscles tighten beneath my lips.

Oh, baby, you are so ready.

My hands travel up her thighs, stroking, kneading, teasing.

With my tongue I circuit her navel while my thumbs reach the junction of her thighs.

"Ah!" she lets out a gargled cry as I push one thumb inside her while the other teases her clitoris, around and around and around.

She arches off the piano.

"Christian!" she cries.

Enough, Grey.

I lift her feet off the keys and push them so she slides effort-lessly over the top board. I undo my fly, grab a condom, and let my pants fall to the floor. I climb up and kneel between her legs as I put on the condom. She watches me, her expression intense and filled with longing. I crawl up her body until we are face to face. My love and desire are reflected in her dark, dark eyes.

"I want you so badly," I whisper, and slowly claim her.

And ease back.

And ease in.

She clutches my biceps and tips her head, her mouth open wide.

She's so close.

I build up speed and her legs flex beneath me and she lets out a strangled cry as she comes and I let go. Losing myself in the woman I love.

I STROKE HER HAIR as she rests her head on my chest.

"Do you drink tea or coffee in the evening?" Ana asks.

"What a strange question."

"I thought I could bring you tea in your study, and then I realized I didn't know what you would like."

"Oh, I see. Water or wine in the evening, Ana. Though maybe I should try tea." I move my hand from her hair to her back, stroking, touching, caressing her.

"We really know very little about each other," she whispers.

"I know." She doesn't know me. And when she does . . .

She leans up, frowning. "What is it?"

I wish I could tell you. But if I do, you'll leave.

I cup her beautiful, sweet face. "I love you, Ana Steele."

"I love you, too, Christian Grey. Nothing you tell me will drive me away."

We'll see, Ana. We'll see.

I move her to my side, sit up and vault off the piano, and lift her down.

"Bed," I whisper.

Grandpa Trev-yan and I are picking apples.

See these red apples on this green apple tree.

I nod.

We put these here. You and me. Remember?

We fooled this old apple tree.

It thought it would make bitter green apples.

But it makes these sweet red apples.

Remember.

I nod.

He holds the apple to his nose and sniffs.

Smell it.

It smells of good. It smells of full.

He rubs the apple against his shirt and gives it to me.

Taste it. I take a bite.

It is crunchy and yummy and apple pie.

I smile. My tummy is happy.

These apples are called fu-gee.

Here, you want to try the green one?

I don't know.

Grandpa takes a bite and his shoulders shake.

He makes a yuk face. *That's nasty.*

He offers it to me. He smiles. I smile and take a bite.

A shiver goes from my head to my toes.

NASTY.

I make a yuk face, too. He laughs. I laugh.

We pick the red apples and put them in the bucket.

We fooled the tree.

It's not nasty. It's sweet.

Not nasty. Sweet.

The smell is evocative. My grandfather's orchard. I open my eyes and I'm wrapped around Ana like swaddling. Her fingers are in my hair and she's smiling shyly at me.

"Good morning, beautiful," I murmur.

"Good morning, beautiful, yourself."

My body has another greeting in mind. I give her a swift kiss before disentangling my legs from hers. Balanced on one elbow, I look down at her. "Sleep okay?"

"Yes, despite the interruption to my sleep last night."

"Hmm. You can interrupt me like that anytime." I kiss her again.

"How about you? Did you sleep well?"

"I always sleep well with you, Anastasia."

"No more nightmares?"

"No."

Only dreams. Pleasant dreams.

"What are your nightmares about?"

Her question catches me off-guard, and suddenly I'm thinking of my four-year-old self—helpless, lost, lonely, hurting, and filled with rage. "They're flashbacks of my early childhood, or so Dr. Flynn says. Some vivid, some less so."

I was a neglected, abused child.

My mother didn't love me.

She didn't protect me.

She killed herself and abandoned me.

The crack whore dead on the floor.

The burn.

Not the burn.

No. Don't go there, Grey.

"Do you wake up crying and screaming?" Ana's question brings me back, and I'm running my finger along her collarbone, keeping contact with her. My dreamcatcher.

"No, Anastasia. I've never cried. As far as I can remember."

Even that evil fucking bastard couldn't make me cry.

"Do you have any happy memories of your childhood?"

"I recall the crack whore baking. I remember the smell. A birthday cake, I think. For me."

Mommy is in the kitchen.

It smells of nice.

Nice and warm and chocolate.

She sings.

Mommy's Happy song.

She smiles. "This is for you, Maggot."

For me!

"And then there's Mia's arrival with my mom and dad. My mom was worried about my reaction, but I adored baby Mia immediately. My first word was 'Mia.' I remember my first piano lesson. Miss Kathie, my tutor, was awesome. She kept horses, too."

"You said your mom saved you. How?"

Grace? Isn't it obvious?

"She adopted me. I thought she was an angel when I first met her. She was dressed in white and so gentle and calm as she examined me. I'll never forget that. If she'd said no, or if Carrick had said no . . ."

Fuck. I'd be dead by now.

I glance at my alarm clock: 6:15. "This is all a little deep for so early in the morning."

"I have made a vow to get to know you better," Ana says, looking both earnest and mischievous at once.

"Did you, now, Miss Steele? I thought you wanted to know if I preferred coffee or tea. Anyway, I can think of one way you can get to know me." I nudge her with my erection.

"I think I know you quite well enough that way."

I grin. "I don't think I'll ever get to know you well enough that way. There are definite advantages to waking up beside you." I nuzzle her ear.

"Don't you have to get up?"

"Not this morning. Only one place I want to be up right now, Miss Steele."

"Christian!"

I roll on top of her and grab her hands so they are above her head, and kiss her throat. "Oh, Miss Steele." Holding both her hands in one of mine, I skim my other hand down her body and at a leisurely pace hitch up her satin nightgown, until my arousal is cradled against her sex. "Oh, what I'd like to do to you," I whisper.

She smiles and tilts her pelvis up to meet me.

Naughty girl.

First, we need a condom.

I reach over to my bedside table.

ANA JOINS ME AT the breakfast bar. She's wearing a light blue dress and high-heeled pumps. Again, she looks stunning. I watch her devour her breakfast. I'm relaxed. Happy, even. She's said she'll move in with me and I started my day with a bang. I smirk and wonder if Ana would find that funny. She turns to me. "When am I going to meet your trainer, Claude, and put him through his paces?"

"Depends if you want to go to New York this weekend or not—unless you'd like to see him early one morning this week. I'll ask Andrea to check on his schedule and get back to you."

"Andrea?"

"My PA."

She's back today. What a relief.

"One of your many blondes?"

"She's not mine. She works for me. You're mine."

"I work for you."

Oh yes! "So you do."

"Maybe Claude can teach me to kickbox," Ana says, but she's grinning like a fool, too.

Clearly she wants to improve her odds against me. Now, this could be interesting. "Bring it on, Miss Steele."

Ana takes a bite of her pancake and glances behind her. "You put the lid of the piano back up."

"I closed it last night so as not to disturb you. Guess it didn't work, but I'm glad it didn't."

Ana blushes.

Yes. There's a lot to be said for piano sex. And sex first thing in the morning. It's great for my mood.

Mrs. Jones interrupts our moment. She leans over and places a paper bag with Ana's lunch inside in front of her. "For later, Ana. Tuna, okay?"

"Oh yes. Thank you, Mrs. Jones." Ana gives her a broad smile, which Gail reciprocates, and then Gail leaves the room to give us some privacy. This is new to Gail, too. It's unusual for me to have anyone here during the week. The only other time has been with Ana.

"Can I ask you something?" Ana interrupts my thoughts.

"Of course."

"And you won't be angry?"

"Is it about Elena?"

"No."

"Then I won't be angry."

"But I now have a supplementary question."

"Oh?"

"Which is about her."

My sense of humor evaporates. "What?"

"Why do you get so mad when I ask you about her?"

"Honestly?" I ask.

"I thought you were always honest with me."

"I endeavor to be."

"That sounds like a very evasive answer."

"I am always honest with you, Ana. I don't want to play games. Well, not those sorts of games," I add.

"What sort of games do you want to play?" Ana blinks, pretending to be clueless.

"Miss Steele, you are so easily distracted."

She laughs, and the sight and sound of her doing so restore my good humor. "Mr. Grey, you are distracting on so many levels."

"My favorite sound in the whole world is your giggle, Anastasia. Now—what was your original question?"

"Oh yes. You only saw your subs on the weekends?"

"Yes, that's correct." *Where is she going with this?*

"So no sex during the week." She glances at the living room entrance; she's checking that no one can hear.

I laugh. "Oh, that's where we're going with this. Why do you think I work out every weekday?"

Today is different. Sex on a workday. Before breakfast. The last time that happened was on a desk in my study with you, Anastasia.

"You look very pleased with yourself, Miss Steele."

"I am, Mr. Grey."

"You should be. Now eat your breakfast."

WE RIDE DOWN IN the elevator with Taylor and Sawyer, and our collective good mood continues in the car. Taylor and Sawyer are up front when we set off for SIP.

Yes, I could definitely get used to this.

Ana is buoyant. She steals glances at me, or is it me who's stealing glances at her?

"Didn't you say your roommate's brother was arriving today?" I ask her.

"Oh, Ethan," she exclaims. "I forgot. Oh, Christian, thank you for reminding me. I'll have to go back to the apartment."

"What time?"

"I'm not sure what time he's arriving."

"I don't want you going anywhere on your own."

She gives me a pained look. "I know," she says. "Will Sawyer be spying, um, patrolling today?"

"Yes." I stress the word.

Leila's still out there.

"If I were driving the Saab it would be easier," she mutters, sounding sullen.

"Sawyer will have a car, and he can drive you to your apartment, depending on what time." I glance at Taylor in the rearview mirror. He nods.

Ana sighs. "Okay. I think Ethan will probably contact me during the day. I'll let you know what the plans are then."

This arrangement leaves a great deal to chance.

But I don't want an argument.

I'm having too good a day.

"Okay. Nowhere on your own. Do you understand?" I waggle a finger at her.

"Yes, dear," she says, each word dripping with sarcasm.

Oh, what I'd give to spank her right now.

"And maybe you should just use your BlackBerry—I'll e-mail you on it. That should prevent my IT guy having a thoroughly interesting morning, okay?"

"Yes, Christian." She rolls her eyes.

"Why, Miss Steele, I do believe you're making my palm twitch."

"Ah, Mr. Grey, your perpetually twitching palm. What are we going to do with that?"

I laugh. She's funny.

My phone vibrates.

Shit. It's Elena.

"What is it?"

"Christian. Hi. It's me. I'm sorry to disturb you. I wanted to make sure you didn't call your guy. That note was from Isaac."

"You're kidding."

"Yes. This is so embarrassing. It was for a scene."

"For a scene."

"Yes. And he didn't mean five thousand in cash."

I laugh. "When did he tell you this?"

"This morning. I called him first thing. I told him I'd been to see you. Oh, Christian, I'm sorry."

"No, don't worry. You don't have to apologize. I'm glad there's a logical explanation. It did seem a ridiculously low amount of money."

"I'm mortified."

"I have no doubt you've something evil and creative planned for your revenge. Poor Isaac."

"Actually, he's furious with me. So I may have to make it up to him."

"Good."

"Anyway. Thank you for listening yesterday. Talk soon."

"Good-bye." I hang up and turn to Ana, who's watching me.

"Who was that?" she asks.

"You really want to know?"

She shakes her head and stares out the window, the corners of her mouth turning down. "Hey." I take her hand and kiss each knuckle, then take her little finger, slip it into my mouth, and suck it. Hard. Then bite down gently.

She wriggles beside me and gives a nervous look to Taylor and Sawyer in the front seat. I have her attention.

"Don't sweat it, Anastasia. She's in the past." I plant a kiss in the center of her palm and release her hand. She opens the door and I watch her stride into SIP.

"Mr. Grey, I'd like to do a sweep of Miss Steele's apartment if she's returning there today," Taylor says, and I agree it's a good idea.

ANDREA GIVES ME A broad smile when I step out of the elevator at Grey House. A mousy-looking young woman stands beside her.

"Good morning, Mr. Grey. This is Sarah Hunter. She'll be interning with us."

Sarah looks me squarely in the eye and holds out her hand. "Good morning, Mr. Grey. Pleased to meet you."

"Hello, Sarah. Welcome." We exchange firm handshakes.

Her grip is surprising.

Not so mousy, then.

I extract my hand.

"Could I see you in my office, Andrea?"

"Of course. Would you like Sarah to make you a coffee?"

"Yes. Black. Please."

Sarah sashays off toward the kitchen with an enthusiasm that I hope I won't find irritating, and I hold the door to my office open for Andrea. Once she's inside, I close the door.

"Andrea—"

"Mr. Grey—"

We both stop talking.

"Go," I say.

"Mr. Grey, I just wanted to say thank you for the suite. It was gorgeous. You really didn't—"

"Why didn't you tell me you were getting married?" I sit down at my desk.

Andrea blushes. This I do not see often, and she seems at a loss for what to say.

"Andrea?"

"Well. Um. There's a non-fraternization clause in my contract."

"You married someone who works here!"

How the hell did she keep that to herself?

"Yes, sir."

"Who's the lucky guy?"

"Damon Parker; he works in engineering."

"The Australian."

"He needs a green card. He's on an H1 visa at the moment."

"I see." A marriage of convenience. For some strange reason, I'm disappointed for and in her. She sees the censure on my face and hurries on.

"That's not the reason I married him. I love him," she says in a most uncharacteristic way, and she blushes. The stain on her cheeks restores my faith in her.

"Well, congratulations. Here you go." I hand her the "happily ever after" card I signed yesterday and hope she doesn't open it in front of me. "How's married life so far?" I ask, to prevent her from doing just that.

"I recommend it, sir." She's glowing. I recognize that look. It's how I feel myself. And now I'm at a loss as to what to say.

Andrea shifts back into work mode. "Shall we go through your schedule?" she asks.

"Please."

MARRIAGE. I CONTEMPLATE THE institution when Andrea leaves. It obviously agrees with her. It's what most women want. Isn't it? I wonder what Ana would do if I asked her to marry me. I shake my head, feeling ambushed by the thought.

Don't be ridiculous, Grey.

In my mind I replay this morning. I could wake up every day beside Anastasia Steele and I could close my eyes beside her every night.

You're smitten, Grey.

You've got it bad.

Enjoy this while it lasts.

I e-mail her.

From: Christian Grey
Subject: Sunrise
Date: June 14 2011 09:23
To: Anastasia Steele

I love waking up with you in the morning.

Christian Grey
Completely & Utterly Smitten CEO, Grey Enterprises
Holdings, Inc.

I grin when I press send.

I hope she'll read this on her BlackBerry.

Sarah brings me my coffee and I open the latest draft of the SIP agreement and start to read.

My phone buzzes. It's a text from Elena.

> ELENA
> Thank you for being so understanding.

I ignore it and go back to my document. When I look up, there's a response from Ana. I take a swig of coffee.

From: Anastasia Steele
Subject: Sundown
Date: June 14 2011 09:35
To: Christian Grey

Dear Completely & Utterly Smitten
I love waking up with you, too. But I love being in bed with you and in elevators and on pianos and billiard tables and boats and desks and showers and bathtubs and strange

wooden crosses with shackles and four-poster beds with red
satin sheets and boathouses and childhood bedrooms.

Yours

Sex Mad and Insatiable xx

Shit. Laughing and choking at the same time, I spit coffee onto
my keyboard at "Sex Mad and Insatiable." I can't believe she's written that in an e-mail. Fortunately, I have tissues left over from yesterday's coffee fiasco.

From: Christian Grey
Subject: Wet Hardware
Date: June 14 2011 09:37
To: Anastasia Steele

Dear Sex Mad and Insatiable
I've just spat coffee all over my keyboard.

I don't think that's ever happened to me before.

I do admire a woman who concentrates on geography.

Am I to infer you just want me for my body?

Christian Grey
Completely & Utterly Shocked CEO, Grey Enterprises
Holdings, Inc.

I continue my read of the SIP agreement but don't get very far
before there's a new e-mail from her.

From: Anastasia Steele
Subject: Giggling—and wet too
Date: June 14 2011 09:42
To: Christian Grey

Dear Completely & Utterly Shocked
Always.

I have work to do.

Stop bothering me.

SM&I xx

From: Christian Grey
Subject: Do I have to?
Date: June 14 2011 09:50
To: Anastasia Steele

Dear SM&I
As ever, your wish is my command.

Love that you are giggling and wet.

Laters, baby.

x

Christian Grey
Completely & Utterly Smitten, Shocked, and Spellbound
CEO, Grey Enterprises Holdings, Inc.

LATER, I'M IN MY monthly meeting with Ros and Marco—my M&A guy—and his team. We're going through a list of companies that Marco's people have identified as potential targets for take-overs.

He is discussing the last on the list. "They are floundering, but they have four patents pending, which might be useful in the fiber-optic division."

"Has Fred reviewed them?" I ask.

"He's excited," Marco replies with an avaricious grin.

"Let's do it."

My phone buzzes and Ana's name flashes on my screen.

"Excuse me," I say as I pick up the phone. "Anastasia."

"Christian, Jack has asked me to get his lunch."

"Lazy bastard."

"So I'm going to get it. It might be handy if you gave me Saw-yer's number, so I don't have to bother you."

"It's no bother, baby."

"Are you on your own?"

I look around the table. "No. There are six people staring at me right now wondering who the hell I'm talking to." Everyone looks away.

"Really?" she squeaks.

"Yes. Really," I pause. "My girlfriend." I tell the room. Ros shakes her head.

"They probably all thought you were gay, you know."

I laugh as Ros and Marco exchange a look. "Yeah, probably."

"Er—I'd better go."

"I'll let Sawyer know." I laugh at the reactions around the table. "Have you heard from your friend?"

"Not yet. You'll be the first to know, Mr. Grey."

"Good. Laters, baby."

"Bye, Christian."

I get up. "I just need to make a quick call."

Outside the boardroom, I call Sawyer.

"Mr. Grey."

"Ana's leaving to get some lunch. Please stick close."

"Yes, sir."

Back in the room, the meeting is wrapping up. Ros approaches me.

"Your private merger?" she says with a curious look.

"The very same."

"No wonder you're so upbeat. I approve," she says.

I grin, feeling smug.

BASTILLE IS ON FIRE. He's knocked me down three fucking times. "So Dante told me you brought a beautiful girl into the bar. This why you're soft today, Grey?"

"Maybe." I grin. "And she needs a trainer."

"Your PA spoke to me this morning. I can't wait to meet her."

"She wants to learn to kickbox."

"Keep your ass in line?"

"Yeah. Something like that." I lunge for him, but he feints left, his dreads flying, and he knocks me down with a swift roundhouse kick.

Shit. I'm on the floor again.

Bastille's pumped up. "She'll have no trouble punishing your sorry ass if you fight like this, Grey," he crows.

Enough is enough. He's going down.

I RETURN TO MY office showered after my bout with Bastille, and Andrea is waiting for me.

"Mr. Grey. Thank you. You really are too generous."

I dismiss her gratitude with a wave as I head into my office. "You're welcome, Andrea. If you use it for a proper honeymoon, make sure I'm away, too." She gives me a rare smile and I close my office door.

I notice a new e-mail from Ana when I sit down at my desk.

From: Anastasia Steele
Subject: Visitors from Sunny Climes.
Date: June 14 2011 14:55
To: Christian Grey

Dearest Completely & Utterly SS&S
Ethan is back, and he's coming here to collect keys to the
apartment.

I'd really like to make sure he's settled in okay.

Why don't you pick me up after work? We can go to the
apartment, then we can ALL go out for a meal maybe?

My treat?

Your

Ana x
Still SM&I

Anastasia Steele
Assistant to Jack Hyde, Editor, SIP

She's still using her work computer.
Damn it. Ana.

From: Christian Grey
Subject: Dinner Out
Date: June 14 2011 15:05
To: Anastasia Steele

I approve of your plan. Except the part about you paying!

My treat.

I'll pick you up at 6:00.

x

P.S.: Why aren't you using your BlackBerry!!!

Christian Grey
Completely and Utterly Annoyed, CEO, Grey Enterprises
Holdings, Inc.

From: Anastasia Steele
Subject: Bossiness
Date: June 14 2011 15:11
To: Christian Grey

Oh, don't be so crusty and cross.

It's all in code.

I'll see you at 6:00.

Ana x

Anastasia Steele
Assistant to Jack Hyde, Editor, SIP

From: Christian Grey
Subject: Maddening Woman
Date: June 14 2011 15:18
To: Anastasia Steele

Crusty and cross!

I'll give you crusty and cross.

And look forward to it.

Christian Grey
Completely and Utterly More Annoyed, but Smiling
for Some Unknown Reason, CEO, Grey Enterprises
Holdings, Inc.

From: Anastasia Steele
Subject: Promises. Promises.
Date: June 14 2011 15:23
To: Christian Grey

Bring it on, Mr. Grey

I look forward to it too. ;D

Ana x

Anastasia Steele
Assistant to Jack Hyde, Editor, SIP

Andrea buzzes me. "I have Professor Choudury on the phone from WSU." The professor is the head of the environmental sciences department. It's rare that he calls. "Put him through."

"Mr. Grey. I wanted to give you some good news."

"Please, go ahead."

"Professor Gravett and her team have made a breakthrough with regard to the microbes that are responsible for nitrogen fixation. I wanted to give you a heads-up because she'll be presenting her findings to you on Friday."

"That sounds impressive."

"As you know, our research has been directed at making soils more productive. And this is a game-changer."

"I'm pleased to hear it."

"It's thanks to you, Mr. Grey, and the funding from GEH."

"I look forward to hearing more about it on Friday."

"Good day, sir."

AT 5:55 P.M. I'M outside SIP's offices, in the back of the Audi, looking forward to seeing Ana.

I call her.

"Crusty and Cross here."

"Well, this is Sex Mad and Insatiable. I take it you're outside?" she answers.

"I am indeed, Miss Steele. Looking forward to seeing you."

"Ditto, Mr. Grey. I'll be right out."

I sit and wait, reading a report on the fiber-optic patents Marco was talking about earlier today.

Ana appears a few minutes later. Her hair, shining in the late-afternoon sun, bounces in thick waves over her shoulders as she walks toward me. My spirits lift, and I'm completely under her spell.

She's everything to me.

I climb out of the car to open the door for her. "Miss Steele, you look as captivating as you did this morning." Embracing her, I plant a kiss on her lips.

"Mr. Grey, so do you."

"Let's go get your friend."

I open her door and, as she climbs in, I acknowledge Sawyer, who's standing outside the SIP office, unseen by Ana. He nods and heads to the SIP parking lot.

TAYLOR STOPS OUTSIDE ANA'S apartment and I reach for the door handle of the Q7, but I'm stopped by the buzz of my phone.

"Grey," I answer, as Ana reaches for the door.

"Christian."

"Ros, what is it?"

"Something's come up."

"I'll go and get Ethan. I'll be two minutes," Ana mouths to me as she exits the car.

"Hold on a moment, Ros." I watch Ana as she presses the entry phone and speaks to Ethan. The door buzzes and in she goes.

"What is it, Ros?"

"It's Woods."

"Woods?"

"Lucas Woods."

"Oh yes. The idiot who ran his fiber-optic company into the ground and then blamed everyone else."

"The same. He's doing some rather negative press."

"And?"

"Sam is concerned about the PR fallout. Woods has gone public about the takeover. How we came in and didn't let him continue to run the company the way he wanted."

I snort my derision. "There's a good reason for that. He'd be bankrupt by now if he'd continued the way he was going."

"True."

"Tell Sam that I know Woods sounds convincing to those who don't know his story, but those who know him realize that he reached a level beyond his ability and made some really bad decisions. He's got no one to blame but himself."

"So you're not worried."

"About him? No. He's a pretentious asshole. The community knows."

"We could go after him for defamation, and he's breached his NDA."

"Why would we do that? He's the kind that feeds off publicity. He's been given enough rope to hang himself. Though he should grow some balls and let it go."

"I thought you'd say that. Sam is agitated."

"Sam just needs some perspective. He always overreacts to bad press."

As I glance out of the window, there's a young man with a duffel bag walking with purpose toward the apartment door.

Ros is continuing to talk, but I ignore her. The man looks familiar. He's sporting the beach-bum look: long blond hair, tanned. Recognition and apprehension hit me at once.

It's Ethan Kavanagh.

Shit. *Who let Ana into the apartment?*

"Ros, I have to go," I bark into the phone as fear grips my chest. *Ana.*

I fly out of the car. "Taylor, follow me," I shout, and we rush toward Ethan Kavanagh, who's about to put the key in the lock. He turns in alarm to see us barreling toward him.

"Kavanagh. I'm Christian Grey. Ana's upstairs with someone who could be armed. Wait here." There's a spark of recognition in his expression, but wordlessly—confused I think—he relinquishes hold of the key. I'm through the door and running up the stairs, taking two steps at a time.

I burst into the apartment and there they are.

A face-off.

Ana and Leila.

And Leila's holding a gun.

No. No. No. A fucking gun.

And Ana is here. Alone. Vulnerable. Panic and fury burst inside me.

I want to lunge at Leila. Take the gun. Bring her down. But I freeze and check Ana. Her eyes are wide with fright and something I can't name. Compassion, maybe? But to my relief, she's unharmed.

The sight of Leila is a shock. Not only does she have her fingers wrapped around a gun, but she's lost so much weight. She's filthy. Her clothes are in tatters and her clouded brown eyes are expressionless. A lump forms in my throat and I don't know if it's fear or empathy.

But my biggest concern is that she's still holding a gun with Ana in the room.

Does she mean to harm her?

Does she mean to harm me?

Leila's eyes are on me. Her stare intensifies, no longer lifeless. She's drinking in every detail, as if she can't believe I'm real. It's unnerving. But I stand my ground and return her look.

Her eyelashes flutter as she collects herself. But her grip tightens around the gun.

Shit.

I wait. Ready to pounce. My heart thumping, the metallic taste of fear in my mouth.

What are you going to do, Leila?

What are you going to do with that gun?

She stills and lowers her head a fraction, but her eyes stay on me, gazing at me through her dark lashes.

I sense a movement behind me.

Taylor.

I hold up my hand, warning him to be still.

He's agitated. Furious. I can feel it. But he doesn't move.

My eyes never leave Leila.

She looks like a wraith; there are dark circles beneath her eyes, her skin is translucent like parchment, and her lips are chapped and flaking.

Christ, Leila, what have you done to yourself?

Time passes. Seconds. Minutes. And we stare at each other.

Slowly, the light in her eyes changes; the brightness increases, from dull brown to hazel. And I see a flash of the Leila I knew. There's a spark of connection. A kindred spirit who enjoyed everything we shared. Our old bond, it's there. I sense it between us.

She's giving this to me.

Her breathing quickens and she licks her chapped lips, yet her tongue leaves no moisture.

But it's enough.

Enough to tell me what she needs. What she wants.

She wants me.

Me at what I do best.

Her lips part, her chest rises and falls, and a trace of color appears in her cheeks.

Her eyes brighten, her pupils enlarging.

Yes. This is what she wants.

To cede control.

She wants a way out.

She's had enough.

She's weary. She's mine.

"Kneel," I whisper, for her ears only.

She drops to her knees like the natural submissive she is. Immediate. Unquestioning. Her head bowed. The gun falls from her hand and skids across the wooden floor with a clatter that breaks the silence around us.

Behind me I hear Taylor breathe a sigh of relief.

And it's echoed in mine.

Oh, thank God.

Slowly I move toward her and pick up the gun, slipping it into my jacket pocket.

Now that she's no longer an immediate threat, I need to get Ana out of the apartment and away from her. Deep down I know I will never forgive Leila for this. I know she's unwell—broken, even. But to threaten Ana?

Unforgivable.

I stand over Leila, putting myself between her and Ana. Still not taking my eyes off Leila as she kneels with quiet grace on the floor.

"Anastasia, go with Taylor," I say.

"Ethan?" she whispers, and there's a tremor in her voice.

"Downstairs," I inform her.

Taylor is waiting for Ana, who doesn't move.

Please, Ana. Go.

"Anastasia," I prompt.

Go.

She remains rooted to the floor.

I step beside Leila—and still Ana won't move. "For the love of God, Anastasia, will you do as you're told for once in your life and go!" Our eyes lock and I implore her to leave. I can't do this with her here. I don't know how stable Leila is; she needs help, and she might hurt Ana.

I try to convey this to Ana with my beseeching look.

But she's ashen. She's in shock.

Shit. She's had a fright, Grey. She can't move.

"Taylor. Take Miss Steele downstairs. Now."

Taylor nods and makes a move to Ana.

"Why?" Ana whispers.

"Go. Back to the apartment. I need to be alone with Leila."

Please. I need you out of harm's way.

She looks from me to Leila.

Ana. Go. Please. I need to take care of this problem.

"Miss Steele. Ana." Taylor holds his hand out to Anastasia.

"Taylor," I urge. Without hesitation, he scoops Ana into his arms and leaves the apartment.

Thank fuck.

I let out a deep breath and caress Leila's filthy, matted hair as the door to the apartment closes.

We are on our own.

I step back. "Get up."

Awkwardly, Leila rises to her feet, but her eyes remain on the floor.

"Look at me," I whisper.

Slowly, she lifts her head, and her pain is visible on her face. Tears spring to her eyes and start to trickle down her cheeks.

"Oh, Leila," I whisper, and I embrace her.

Fuck.

The smell.

She stinks of poverty and neglect and homelessness.

And I'm back in a small, badly lit apartment above a cheap liquor store in Detroit.

She smells of him.

His boots.

His unwashed body.

His squalor.

Saliva pools in my mouth and I gag. Once. It's hard to bear.

Hell.

But she doesn't notice. I hold her as she weeps and weeps and weeps, snot-sobbing all over my jacket.

I hold her.

Trying not to retch.

Trying to banish the stench.

A stench so achingly familiar. And so unwelcome.

"Hush," I whisper. "Hush."

When she's gasping for air and her body is racked with dry sobs, I release her. "You need a bath."

Taking her hand, I lead her to Kate's bedroom and the ensuite. It's roomy like Ana said. There's a shower, a bath, and a selection of expensive toiletries on display. I shut the door and I'm tempted to lock it; I don't want her to run. But she stands, meek and quiet, as she shudders with each dry sob. "It's okay," I murmur. "I'm here."

I turn on the faucet and hot water buckets into the spacious bath. I squirt some bath oil into the cascade, and soon the stifling fragrance of lilies is overcoming Leila's stench.

She begins to shiver.

"Do you want a bath?" I ask.

She looks down at the foaming suds and then at me. She nods.

"Can I take off your coat?"

She nods once more. And, using only the tips of my fingers, I peel it from her body. It's beyond salvation. It'll need burning.

Beneath, her clothes hang off her. She's wearing a grubby pink blouse and a pair of grungy slacks of an indeterminate color.

They're also beyond rescue. Around her wrist is a tattered, soiled bandage.

"These clothes, they need to come off. Okay?"

She nods.

"Arms up."

Dutifully she complies, and I pull off her blouse and try not to register my shock at her appearance. She's emaciated, all jutting bones and pointed angles, a sharp contrast to the Leila of old. It's sickening.

This is my fault; I should have found her earlier.

I tug down her slacks.

"Step out." I hold her hand.

She does, and I add her slacks to the pile of rags.

She's shaking.

"Hey. It's okay. We're going to get you some help. Okay?"

She nods but remains impassive.

I take her hand and undo the bandage. I think it should have been changed; the smell is putrid. I retch but don't vomit. The scar on her wrist is livid but miraculously looks clean. I discard the bandage and dressing.

"You'll need to take those off." I'm referring to her grubby underwear. She looks at me. "No. You do it," I say and turn around to give her a modicum of privacy. I hear her move, a scraping of her flats on the bathroom floor, and when she stops I turn around and she's naked.

Gone are her lush curves.

She must not have eaten for weeks.

It's galling.

"Here." I give her my hand, which she takes, and with the other I test the temperature of the water. It's hot but not too hot.

"Get in."

She steps into the bath and slowly sinks into the foaming, fragrant water. I strip off my jacket and roll up the sleeves of my shirt and sit down on the floor beside the bath. She turns her small, sad face toward me but remains mute.

I reach across for the body wash and a nylon scrubber that Kavanagh must use. Well, she won't miss it—I spy another on the shelf.

"Hand," I say. Leila gives me her hand, and methodically and gently I start to wash her.

She's grimy. She hasn't washed for weeks, it seems. There's grime. Everywhere.

How does someone get this dirty?

"Lift your chin up."

I scrub under her neck and down her other arm, leaving her skin clean and a little pinker. I wash her torso and her back.

"Lie down."

She lies down in the bath and I wash her feet and her legs in turn.

"Do you want me to wash your hair?"

She nods. And I reach for the shampoo.

I've bathed her before. Several times. Usually as a reward for her behavior in the playroom. It was always a pleasure.

This, not so much.

I make brisk work of her hair and use the handheld shower to rinse out the suds.

By the time I'm finished, she looks a little better.

I sit back on my heels.

"Long time since you did this," she says. Her voice low and bleak, devoid of all emotion.

"I know." I reach over and pull the plug to empty the murky water. Standing, I reach for a large towel. "Up you go."

Leila stands, and I offer her my hand so that she can step out of the bath. I fold the towel around her and reach for a smaller one and towel-dry her hair.

She smells better, although, in spite of the scented bath oil, the foul odor of her clothes still pervades the bathroom.

"Come." I take her out and leave her on the sofa in the sitting area. "Stay there."

Back in the bathroom, I grab my jacket, and from the pocket extract my phone. I call Flynn's cell number. He answers immediately.

"Christian."

"I have Leila Williams."

"With you?"

"Yes. She's in a bad way."

"You're in Seattle?"

"Yes. In Ana's apartment."

"I'll be right there."

I give him Ana's address and hang up. I collect her clothes and head back to the living room. Leila is sitting where I left her, staring at the wall.

I go through the kitchen drawers and find a trash bag. Checking the pockets of Leila's coat and the slacks, I find nothing but used tissues. I dump her clothes in the trash bag, knot it, and leave it by the front door.

"I'll find you some clean clothes."

"Her clothes?" Leila says.

"Clean clothes."

In Ana's room, I find some sweatpants and a plain T-shirt. I hope Ana doesn't mind, but I think Leila's need is greater.

She's still on the sofa when I return.

"Here. Put these on." I place the clothes beside her and move to the sink at the kitchen counter. I fill a glass with water and, once she's dressed, offer it to her.

She shakes her head.

"Leila, drink this."

She takes the glass and has a sip.

"And another. Just sips," I say.

She takes another sip.

"He's gone," she says, and her face contorts with pain and grief.

"I know. I'm sorry."

"He was like you."

"Was he?"

"Yes."

"I see."

Well, that explains why she sought me out.

"Why didn't you call me?" I sit down beside her.

She shakes her head and tears well in her eyes once more, but she doesn't answer my question.

"I've called a friend. He can help you. He's a doctor."

She's exhausted and remains impassive, but her tears trickle down her face, and I feel at a loss.

"I've been looking for you," I tell her.

She says nothing but starts shaking, violently.

Shit.

There's a throw on the armchair. I drape it over her shoulders. "Cold?"

She nods. "So cold." She snuggles into the blanket and I head back into Ana's room to find her hair dryer.

I plug it into the socket beside the sofa and sit down. I take a cushion and place it on the floor between my feet.

"Sit. Here."

Leila gets up slowly, pulls the blanket around her, and sinks onto the cushion between my legs, facing away from me.

The high-pitched whir of the hair dryer disrupts the silence between us as I gently dry her hair.

She sits quietly. Not touching me.

She knows she can't. She knows she's not allowed.

How many times have I dried her hair? Ten? Twelve times?

I can't remember the exact number so I concentrate on my task.

Once her hair is dry, I stop. And it's quiet in Ana's apartment again. Leila leans her head against my thigh, and I don't stop her.

"Do your folks know you're here?" I ask.

She shakes her head.

"Have you been in touch with them?"

"No," she whispers.

She was always close to her parents.

"They'll be worried about you."

She shrugs. "They're not speaking."

"To you? Why not?"

She doesn't answer.

"I'm sorry it didn't work out with your husband."

She says nothing, but there's a knock on the door.

"That'll be the doctor." I stand and go to open the door. Flynn enters, followed by a woman in scrubs.

"John, thanks for coming." I'm relieved to see him.

"Laura Flanagan, Christian Grey. Laura is our head nurse."

When I turn, Leila is now sitting on the sofa, still wrapped in the throw.

"This is Leila Williams," I say.

Flynn crouches down beside Leila. She gazes at him, her expression blank.

"Hello, Leila," he says. "I'm here to help you."

The nurse hovers in the background.

"Those are her clothes." I point to the trash bag by the front door. "They need burning."

The nurse nods and picks up the trash bag.

"Would you like to come with me to a place where we can help you?" Flynn asks Leila. She says nothing, but her subdued brown eyes seek mine.

"I think you should go with the doctor. I'll come with you."

Flynn frowns but keeps his counsel.

Leila looks from me to him and nods.

Good.

"I'll take her," I tell Flynn, and reach down and lift her into my arms. She weighs nothing. She closes her eyes and rests her head against my shoulder as I carry her down the stairs. Taylor is waiting for us.

"Mr. Grey, Ana's gone home—" he says.

"Let's talk about it later. I've left my jacket upstairs."

"I'll bring it."

"Can you lock up? The keys are in my jacket."

"Yes, sir."

Outside in the street I put Leila into Flynn's car and climb in beside her. I fasten her seatbelt as Flynn and his colleague sit up front. Flynn starts the car and pulls out into the rush-hour traffic.

As I stare out of the window, I hope that Ana is back at Escala. Mrs. Jones will feed her, and when I get home she'll be there waiting for me. The thought is comforting.

FLYNN'S OFFICE AT THE private psychiatric clinic on the outskirts of Fremont is spartan compared to his office downtown: two sofas, one armchair. No fireplace. That's it. I pace the length of the small room, waiting for him. I'm itching to get back to Ana. She must have been terrified. My phone has died, so I haven't been able to call her or Mrs. Jones to check on Ana's well-being. My watch says it's nearly eight. I glance out of the window. Taylor is parked and waiting in the SUV. I just want to go home.

Back to Ana.

The door opens and Flynn enters. "I thought you'd have left by now," he says.

"I need to know she's okay."

"She's a sick young woman, but she's calm and cooperative. She wants help, and that's always a good sign. Please sit. I need a few details from you."

I sit down on the chair and he takes a seat on one of the couches.

"What happened today?"

I explain all that took place in Ana's apartment prior to his arrival.

"You gave her a bath?" he says, surprised.

"She was filthy. The stench was . . ." I stop and shudder.

"Okay. We can talk about that at another time."

"Is she going to be okay?"

"I think so, though you can't medicate against grief. It's a natural process. But I'll dig a little deeper and find out what we're dealing with here."

"Anything she needs," I state.

"That's very generous of you, considering she's not really your problem."

"She came to me."

"She did," he acknowledges.

"I feel responsible."

"You shouldn't. I'll update you when I know more."

"Great. And thanks again."

"I'm just doing my job, Christian."

TAYLOR IS BROODING ON the way home. I know he's mad that Leila slipped through the cracks once more, in spite of the measures we have in place; Ana's apartment was swept by security this morning. I say nothing. I'm tired and anxious to get back to Escala. Ana's purse and cell phone are still in the car, and Taylor has informed me that she went home with Ethan. The thought is displeasing. So I picture her snuggled in the armchair in the library, asleep, a book in her lap. Alone.

I'm impatient. I want to get home to my girl.

AS WE PULL INTO the garage, Taylor reminds me, "We should review our security requirements now that Miss Williams has been found."

"Yes. I don't think we'll be needing the guys."

"I'll talk to Welch."

"Thanks." He parks and I'm out of the car in an instant, headed right to the elevator. I don't wait for him.

As soon as I step into my apartment, I sense Ana's not home. My place has a ringing emptiness about it.

Where the hell is she?

Ryan is monitoring the CCTV. He looks up when I enter Taylor's office.

"Mr. Grey?"

"Did Miss Steele come home?"

"No, sir."

"Fuck." I thought she might have been and gone. I turn and head for my study. She doesn't have her purse or her phone? Why hasn't she come home? Part of me wants to send the entire team combing the city looking for her. But where do I start?

I could call Kavanagh. Taylor says she left with him.

Shit. Ethan and Ana.

The idea does not sit well with me.

I don't have his number. I contemplate calling Elliot to have him ask Kate for her brother's number, but it's after midnight in Barbados. With a frustrated sigh, I stare out at the city skyline. The sun is sinking into the sea off the Olympic Peninsula, reflecting the last of the light into my apartment. It's ironic that all this week I've been looking at this view and wondering where Leila might be. Now I'm wondering about Ana. It's getting dark. Where is she?

She's left you, Grey.

No. I'm not willing to believe that.

Mrs. Jones knocks on the door.

"Mr. Grey?"

"Gail."

"You found her."

I frown. Ana?

"Miss Williams," she clarifies.

"In a sense. She's in the hospital, where she needs to be."

"Good. Would you like something to eat?"

"No. Thanks. I'll wait for Ana."

She studies me for a moment. "I've made some mac and cheese. I'll leave it in the fridge."

Mac and cheese. My favorite.

"Okay. Thanks."

"I'm going to retire to my room now."

"Good night, Gail."

She gives me a sympathetic smile and leaves.

I check the time: 9:15.

Damn it. Ana. Come home.

Where is she?

Gone.

No.

I dismiss the thought and sit down at my desk and activate my computer. I have a few e-mails, but try as I might, I cannot concentrate. My concern for Ana is growing. Where is she?

She'll be back soon.

She will.

She has to come back.

I call Welch and leave a message that Leila has been found and is now getting the help she needs. I end the call and get up, unable to stay seated. It's been one hell of an evening.

Perhaps I should read.

In my bedroom, I pick up the book I've been reading and take it back into the living room. And wait. And wait.

Ten minutes later, I throw the book onto the sofa beside me.

I'm restless and the uncertainty about Ana's whereabouts is becoming unbearable.

I head into Taylor's office. He's there with Ryan.

"Mr. Grey."

"Can you send one of the guys to Ana's place? I want to check if she's returned to her apartment."

"Of course."

"Thanks."

I head back to the sofa and pick up my book again. I keep glancing at the elevator. But it remains quiet.

Empty.

Like me.

Empty except for my growing unease.

She's gone.

She's left you.

Leila frightened her off.

No. I can't believe that. It's not her style.

It's me. She's had enough.

Having said she'd move in, she's now reneged.

Fuck.

I get up and begin pacing. My phone buzzes. It's Taylor. Not Ana. I quash my disappointment and take the call. "Taylor."

"The apartment's empty, sir. No one here."

There's a ping. The elevator. I turn and Ana walks a little unsteadily into the living room.

"She's here," I snap at Taylor and hang up. Relief. Anger. Hurt.

All combine in a rush of emotions that threaten to overwhelm me. "Where the fuck have you been?" I bark at her. She blinks and steps back. She's flushed.

"Have you been drinking?" I ask.

"A bit."

"I told you to come back here. It's now fifteen after ten. I've been worried about you."

"I went for a drink or three with Ethan while you attended to your ex." She spits out the last word like venom.

Hell. She's mad.

She continues. "I didn't know how long you were going to be with her." She lifts up her chin with a look of righteous indignation.

What?

"Why do you say it like that?" I ask, confused by her response. Did she think I *wanted* to be with Leila?

Ana looks down and stares at the floor, avoiding eye contact.

She hasn't come completely into the room.

What's going on?

My anger subsides as anxiety ripples through my chest.

"Ana, what's wrong?"

"Where's Leila?" She looks around the room, her expression chilly.

"In a psychiatric hospital in Fremont." Where the hell does she *expect* Leila to be? "Ana, what is it?" I take a couple of cautious steps toward her, but she stands her ground, distant and aloof, and doesn't reach for me.

"What's wrong?" I press her.

She shakes her head. "I'm no good for you," she says.

My scalp tingles, pricked by fear. "What? Why do you think that? How can you possibly think that?"

"I can't be everything you need."

"You are everything I need."

"Just seeing you with her—"

Christ. "Why do you do this to me? This is not about you, Ana. It's about her. Right now, she's a very sick girl."

"But I felt it. What you had together."

"What? No." I reach for her and she steps back, away from me, her cool eyes on mine, assessing me, and I don't think she likes what she sees . . .

"You're running?"

My anxiety rises, tightening my throat.

She looks away and her brow furrows, but she says nothing.

"You can't," I whisper.

"Christian, I—" She stops and I think she's struggling to say her good-byes. She's going. I knew it would happen. But so soon?

"No. No!" I'm on the edge of the abyss once more.

I can't breathe.

This is it, what I'd predicted from the beginning.

"I . . ." Ana mutters.

How do I stop her? I look around the room, for help. What can I do?

"You can't go. Ana, I love you!" It's my last-minute pitch to save this deal, to save us.

"I love you, too, Christian, it's just—"

The vortex is sucking me under.

She's had enough.

I've driven her away.

Again.

I feel dizzy. I put my hands on my head, trying to contain the pain that slices through me. My despair is carving a hole in my chest that gets bigger and bigger and bigger. It's going to take me down. "No. No."

Find your happy place.

My happy place.

When was it easier?

Easier to wear my pain on the outside.

Elena is standing over me. In her hands, she holds a thin cane. The welts on my back burn. Each throbbing with pain as my blood thrums through my body.

I'm on my knees. At her feet.

"*More, mistress.*"

Quiet the monster.

More. Mistress.

More.

Find your happy place, Grey.

Make your peace.

Peace. Yes.

No.

A tidal wave rises inside my body, crashing and breaking within me, but as it recedes it sucks the fear away.

You can do this.

I drop to my knees.

I take a deep breath and place my hands on my thighs.

Yes. Peace.

I'm in a landscape of calm.

I give myself to you. All of me. I'm yours to do with as you wish.

What will she do?

I look straight ahead, and I'm aware that she's watching me. In the far distance, I hear her voice.

"Christian, what are you doing?"

I inhale slowly, filling my lungs. Fall is in the air. *Ana.*

"Christian! What are you doing?" The voice is closer, louder, more high-pitched.

"Christian, look at me!"

I look up. And wait.

She's beautiful. Pale. Worried.

"Christian, please, don't do this. I don't want this."

You must tell me what you want. I wait.

"Why are you doing this? Talk to me," she pleads.

"What would you like me to say?"

She gasps. It's a soft sound and it stirs memories of happier times with her. I shut those down. There is only now. Her cheeks are wet. Tears. She wrings her hands.

And suddenly she's on her knees, facing me.

Her eyes are on mine. The outer rings of her irises are indigo. They lighten toward the middle to the color of a cloudless summer sky. But her pupils are expanding, a deep black darkening each center.

"Christian, you don't have to do this. I'm not going to run. I've told you and told you and told you, I won't run. All that's happened. It's overwhelming. I just need some time to think. Some time to myself. Why do you always assume the worst?"

Because the worst happens.

Always.

"I was going to suggest going back to my apartment this evening. You never give me any time—time to just think things through."

She wants to be on her own.

Away from me.

"Just time to think," she continues. "We barely know each other, and all this baggage that comes with you. I need. I need time to think it through. And now that Leila is . . . well, whatever she is . . . she's off the streets and not a threat. I thought. I thought—"

What did you think, Ana?

"Seeing you with Leila . . ." She closes her eyes as if in pain. "It was such a shock. I had a glimpse into how your life has been . . . and . . ." She rips her gaze from mine and looks down at her knees. "This is about me not being good enough for you. It was an insight into your life, and I am so scared you'll get bored with me, and then you'll go, and I'll end up like Leila, a shadow. Because I love you, Christian, and if you leave me, it will be like a world without light. I'll be in darkness. I don't want to run. I'm just so frightened you'll leave me."

She's scared of the darkness, too.

She's not going to run.

She loves me.

"I don't understand why you find me attractive," Ana whispers. "You're, well, you're you and I'm—" She looks at me, troubled. "I just don't see it. You're beautiful and sexy and successful and good and kind and caring—all those things—and I'm not. And I can't do the things you like to do. I can't give you what you need. How could you be happy with me? How can I possibly hold you? I have never understood what you see in me. And seeing you with her, it brought all that home."

She raises her hand and wipes her nose that's blotchy and pink from crying.

"Are you going to kneel here all night? Because I'll do it, too!"

She's mad at me.

She's always mad at me.

"Christian, please, please. Talk to me."

Her lips would be soft. They are always soft after she's been crying. Her hair frames her face and my heart expands.

Could I love her any more?

She has all the qualities she says she doesn't. But it's her compassion I love most.

Her compassion for me.

Ana.

"Please," she says.

"I was so scared," I whisper. *I'm scared now.* "When I saw Ethan arrive outside, I knew someone had let you into your apartment. Both Taylor and I leapt out of the car. We knew, and to see her there like that with you—and armed. I think I died a thousand deaths, Ana. Someone threatening you. All my worst fears realized. I was so angry, with her, with you, with Taylor, with myself." I'm haunted by the vision of Leila and her gun. "I didn't know how volatile she would be. I didn't know what to do. I didn't know how she'd react." I stop, remembering Leila's surrender. "And then she gave me a clue; she looked so contrite. And I just knew what I had to do."

"Go on," Ana prompts.

"Seeing her in that state, knowing that I might have something to do with her mental breakdown—"

A memory from years ago surfaces, unwelcome—Leila smirking as she deliberately turned her back on me, knowing the consequences. "She was always so mischievous and lively. She might have harmed you. And it would have been my fault."

If anything happened to Ana . . .

"But she didn't," Ana says. "And you weren't responsible for her being in that state, Christian."

"I just wanted you gone. I wanted you away from the danger, and . . . You. Just. Wouldn't. Go." My exasperation returns and I glare at Ana. "Anastasia Steele, you are the most stubborn woman I know." I close my eyes and shake my head. What am I going to do with her?

If she stays.

She's still kneeling in front of me when I open my eyes.

"You weren't going to run?" I ask.

"No!" Now she sounds exasperated.

She's not leaving me. I take a deep breath. "I thought—" I stop. "This is me, Ana. All of me, and I'm all yours. What do I have to do to make you realize that? To make you see that I want you any way I can get you. That I love you."

"I love you, too, Christian, and to see you like this is—" She pauses as she chokes back tears. "I thought I'd broken you."

"Broken? Me? Oh no, Ana. Just the opposite."

You make me whole.

Reaching out, I take her hand in mine. "You're my lifeline," I whisper.

I need you.

I kiss each of her knuckles before pressing my palm against the palm of her hand.

How can I make her see what she means to me?

Let her touch me.

Touch me, Ana.

Yes. And before I overthink it, I take her hand and place it on my chest, over my heart.

I'm yours, Ana.

The darkness expands inside my rib cage and my breathing quickens. But I control my fear. I need her more. I drop my hand, leaving hers in place, and concentrate on her lovely face. Her compassion is there, reflected in her eyes.

I see it.

She flexes her fingers so I briefly feel her nails through my shirt. Then she removes her hand.

"No." My response is instinctive, and I press her hand to my chest. "Don't."

She looks bewildered, but then she shuffles closer so our knees are touching. She reaches up.

Shit. She's going to undress me.

And I'm filled with dread. I can't breathe. With one hand she awkwardly undoes the first button. She flexes the fingers trapped beneath my hand and I let her go. Using both hands, she makes light work of my buttons, and when she pulls open my shirt I gasp, and my breathing returns and starts to accelerate.

Her hand hovers over my chest. She wants to touch me. Skin to skin. Flesh to flesh. Reaching deep within myself and relying on years of control, I steel myself for her touch.

Ana hesitates.

"Yes," I whisper my encouragement and tilt my head to one side.

Her fingertips are feather-light on my sternum, stirring my chest hair. My fear rises in my throat, leaving a knot I can't swallow. Ana removes her hand, but I grab it, pressing it against my skin. "No, I need to." My voice is low and strained.

I must do this.

I'm doing it for her.

She flattens her palm on me, then traces a line with her fingertips to my heart. Her fingers are gentle and warm, but they're searing my skin. Marking me. I'm hers. I want to give her my love, and my trust.

I'm yours, Ana.

Whatever you want.

I'm aware I'm panting, dragging air into my lungs.

Ana shifts, her eyes darkening. She runs her fingers over me again and then places her hands on my knees and leans forward.

Fuck. I close my eyes. This will be hard to bear. I tilt my head up. Waiting. And I feel her lips, with acute tenderness, plant a kiss over my heart.

I groan.

It's excruciating. It's hell. But it's Ana, here, loving me.

"Again," I whisper. She leans in and kisses me above my heart. I know what she's doing. I know where she's kissing me. She does it again, and then again. Her lips landing soft and gentle on each of my scars. I know where they are. I know where they've been since the day they were burned into my body. And here she is, doing what no one's ever done. Kissing me. Accepting me. Accepting this dark, dark side of me.

She's slaying my demons.

My brave girl.

My beautiful brave girl.

My face is wet. My vision is blurred. But I feel my way to her and pull her into my arms, my hands in her hair. I turn her face up to mine and claim her lips. Feeling her. Consuming her. Needing her. "Oh, Ana," I whisper in veneration as I worship her mouth. I pull her down onto the floor and she cups my face and I don't know if the wet is from her tears or mine.

"Christian, please don't cry. I meant it when I said I'd never leave you. I did. If I gave you any other impression, I'm so sorry. Please, please forgive me. I love you. I will always love you."

I look down at her, trying to accept what she's just said.

She says she loves me, that she will always love me.

But she doesn't know me.

She doesn't know the monster.

The monster is not worthy of her love.

"What is it?" she says. "What is this secret that makes you think I'll run for the hills? That makes you so determined to believe I'll go? Tell me, Christian, please?"

She has a right to know. As long as we are together, this will always be an obstacle between us. She deserves the truth. Against my better judgment, I have to tell her.

I sit up and cross my legs and she sits up, too, staring at me. Her eyes are round and fearful, reflecting my feelings exactly.

"Ana." I pause and take a deep breath.

Tell her, Grey.

Get it out. Then you'll know.

"I'm a sadist, Ana. I like to whip little brown-haired girls like you because you all look like the crack whore—my birth mother. I'm sure you can guess why." The words tumble out of my mouth in a rush like they've been ready and waiting for days.

She remains impassive. Still. Quiet.

Please, Ana.

Finally, she speaks, and her voice is a frail whisper. "You said you weren't a sadist."

"No, I said I was a Dominant. If I lied to you, it was a lie of omission. I'm sorry." I can't look at her. I'm ashamed. I stare down at my fingers. Like she does. But she remains mute, so I'm forced to look at her. "When you asked me that question, I had envisioned a very different relationship between us," I add.

It's the truth.

Ana's eyes widen, and suddenly she covers her face with her hands. She can't bear to look at me.

"So it's true," she whispers, and when she removes her hands, her face is alabaster. "I can't give you what you need."

What? "No. No. No. Ana. No. You can. You do give me what I need. Please believe me."

"I don't know what to believe, Christian. This is so fucked up." Her voice is choked with emotion.

"Ana, believe me. After I punished you and you left me, my worldview changed. I wasn't joking when I said I would avoid ever feeling like that again. When you said you loved me, it was a revelation. No one's ever said it to me before, and it was as if I'd laid something to rest—or maybe you'd laid it to rest, I don't know. Dr. Flynn and I are still in deep discussion about it."

"What does that all mean?"

"It means I don't need it. Not now."

"How do you know? How can you be so sure?"

"I just know. The thought of hurting you in any real way, it's abhorrent to me."

"I don't understand. What about rulers and spanking and all that kinky fuckery?"

"I'm talking about the heavy shit, Anastasia. You should see what I can do with a cane or a cat."

"I'd rather not."

"I know. If you wanted to do that, then fine, but you don't and I get it. I can't do all that shit with you if you don't want to. I told you once before, you have all the power. And now, since you came back, I don't feel that compulsion at all."

"When we met, that's what you wanted, though?"

"Yes, undoubtedly."

"How can your compulsion just go, Christian? Like I'm some kind of panacea, and you're—for want of a better word—cured? I don't get it."

"I wouldn't say 'cured.' You don't believe me?"

"I just find it—unbelievable. Which is different."

"If you'd never left me, then I probably wouldn't feel this way. Your walking out on me was the best thing you ever did for us. It made me realize how much I want you, just you, and I mean it when I say I'll take you any way I can have you."

She stares at me. Impassive? Confused? I don't know.

"You're still here. I thought you would be out of the door by now."

"Why? Because I might think you're a sicko for whipping and fucking women who look like your mother? Whatever would give you that impression?" she snaps.

Fuck.

Ana has her claws out, and she's sinking them into me.

But I deserve it. "Well, I wouldn't have put it quite like that, but yes."

She's angry, maybe? Hurt, possibly? She knows my secret. My dark, dark secret. And now I await her verdict.

Love me.

Or leave me.

She closes her eyes. "Christian, I'm exhausted. Can we discuss this tomorrow? I want to go to bed."

"You're not going?" I can't believe it.

"Do you want me to go?"

"No! I thought you would leave once you knew."

Her expression is softer, but she still looks confounded.

Please don't go, Ana.

Life will be unbearable if you go.

"Don't leave me," I whisper.

"Oh, for crying out loud—no!" she shouts, startling me. "I am not going to go!"

"Really?" Unbelievable. She astonishes me, even now.

"What can I do to make you understand I will not run? What can I say?" She's exasperated.

And to my surprise an idea springs to mind. An idea so wild and out of my comfort zone that I wonder where it came from. I swallow. "There is one thing you can do."

"What?" she snaps.

"Marry me."

Her mouth drops open, and she gapes at me.

Marriage, Grey? Have you taken leave of your senses?

Why would she want to marry you?

She's stunned but then her lips part and she giggles. She bites her lip—I think it's to try and stop herself. But she fails. She flops down on the floor and her giggling turns to peals of laughter that echo through my living room.

This is not the reaction I was expecting.

Her laughter becomes hysterical. She drapes her hand across her face and I think she might be sobbing.

I don't know what to do.

Gently I lift her arm off her face and wipe her tears with the back of my knuckles. I try for something light. "You find my proposal amusing, Miss Steele?"

She sniffles and, reaching up, caresses my cheek.

Again, not what I expected.

"Mr. Grey," she whispers. "Christian. Your sense of timing is without doubt . . ." She stops, her eyes searching mine as if I'm a crazy fool. And maybe I am, but I need to know her answer.

"You're cutting me to the quick here, Ana. Will you marry me?"

Slowly she sits up and places her hands on my knees. "Christian, I've met your psycho ex with a gun, been thrown out of my apartment, had you go thermonuclear Fifty on me—"

Fifty?

I open my mouth to plead my case, but she holds up her hand to stop me, so I remain mute.

"You've just revealed some quite frankly shocking information about yourself, and now you've asked me to marry you."

"Yes, I think that's a fair and accurate summary of the situation."

"Whatever happened to delayed gratification?" she asks, confounding me once more.

"I got over it, and I'm now a firm advocate of instant gratification. Carpe diem, Ana."

"Look, Christian, I've known you for about three minutes, and there's so much more I need to know. I've had too much to drink, I'm hungry, I'm tired, and I want to go to bed. I need to consider your proposal just as I considered that contract you gave me. And"—she pauses and purses her lips—"that wasn't the most romantic proposal."

Hope stirs in my chest. "Fair point well made, as ever, Miss Steele. So, that's not a no?"

She sighs. "No, Mr. Grey, it's not a no, but it's not a yes, either. You're only doing this because you're scared and you don't trust me."

"No, I'm doing this because I've finally met someone I want to spend the rest of my life with. I never thought that would happen to me."

And that's the truth, Ana.

I love you.

"Can I think about it, please? And think about everything else that's happened today? What you've just told me? You asked for patience and faith. Well, back at you, Grey. I need those now."

Faith and patience.

I lean forward and smooth a wayward lock behind her ear. I would wait an eternity for her answer, if it meant that she didn't leave me.

"I can live with that." Leaning forward again, I give her a swift kiss.

She doesn't recoil.

And I feel a brief sense of relief. "Not very romantic, eh?"

She shakes her head, her expression solemn.

"Hearts and flowers?" I ask.

She nods and I give her a smile.

"You're hungry?"

"Yes."

"You didn't eat."

"No, I didn't eat," she says without rancor, and sits back on her heels. "Being thrown out of my apartment after witnessing my boyfriend interacting intimately with his ex-submissive considerably suppressed my appetite." She places her hands on her hips.

I get to my feet, still amazed that she's here. I hold out my hand. "Let me fix you something to eat."

"Can't I just go to bed?" She puts her hand in mine and I help her to her feet.

"No, you need to eat. Come."

I lead her a few feet to a barstool, and once she's sat down I explore the fridge.

"Christian, I'm really not hungry."

I ignore her as I look through the contents of the fridge. "Cheese?" I offer.

"Not at this hour."

"Pretzels?"

"In the fridge? No," she says.

"You don't like pretzels?"

"Not at eleven thirty. Christian, I'm going to bed. You can rummage around in your refrigerator for the rest of the night if you want. I'm tired, and I've had far too interesting a day. A day I'd like to forget." She slides off the stool just as I find the dish Mrs. Jones prepared earlier this evening.

"Macaroni and cheese?" I hold it up.

Ana gives me a sideways look. "You like macaroni and cheese?" she asks.

Like? I love mac and cheese. "You want some?" I try and tempt her.

Her smile says all she needs to say.

I pop the bowl into the microwave and press heat.

"So, you know how to use the microwave, then?" Ana teases. She's back on the barstool.

"If it's in a packet, I can usually do something with it. It's real food I have a problem with."

I set up two place mats, plates, and cutlery.

"It's very late," Ana says.

"Don't go to work tomorrow."

"I have to go to work tomorrow. My boss is leaving for New York."

"Do you want to go there this weekend?"

"I checked the weather forecast, and it looks like rain," she says.

"Oh, so what do you want to do?"

The microwave pings. Our supper is ready.

"I just want to get through one day at a time right now. All this excitement is . . . tiring."

Using a cloth, I remove the steaming bowl from the microwave and place it on the kitchen counter. It smells delicious, and I'm pleased that my appetite has returned. Ana dishes a spoonful onto each plate as I take my seat.

It's staggering that she's still with me, in spite of all I've told her. She's so . . . strong. She never disappoints. Even when facing Leila, she kept her cool.

She takes a bite of her food, as do I. It's exactly how I like it.

"Sorry about Leila," I mutter.

"Why are you sorry?"

"It must have been a terrible shock for you, finding her in your apartment. Taylor swept through it earlier himself. He's very upset."

"I don't blame Taylor."

"Neither do I. He's been out looking for you."

"Really? Why?"

"I didn't know where you were. You left your purse, your phone. I couldn't even track you. Where did you go?"

"Ethan and I just went to a bar across the street. So I could watch what was happening."

"I see."

"So, what did you do with Leila in the apartment?"

"You really want to know?" I ask.

"Yes," she replies, but in a tone that makes me think she's not sure. I hesitate, but she glances at me once more and I have to be honest. "We talked, and I gave her a bath. And I dressed her in some of your clothes. I hope you don't mind. But she was filthy."

Ana remains mute and turns away from me. My appetite vanishes.

Shit. I shouldn't have told her.

"It was all I could do, Ana," I try to explain.

"You still have feelings for her?"

"No!" I close my eyes as a vision of Leila, sad and waiflike, comes to mind. "To see her like that—so different, so broken. I care about her, one human being to another." I let go of the image and turn to Ana.

"Ana, look at me."

She stares at her untouched food.

"Ana."

"What?" she whispers.

"Don't. It doesn't mean anything. It was like caring for a child, a broken, shattered child."

She closes her eyes, and for a horrid moment I think she's going to burst into tears. "Ana?"

She stands and takes her plate to the sink and scrapes the contents into the trash.

"Ana, please."

"Just stop, Christian! Just stop with the 'Ana, please'!" she shouts with exasperation and starts to cry. "I've had enough of all this shit today. I'm going to bed. I'm tired and emotional. Now let me be." She storms out of the kitchen toward the bedroom, leaving me with cooling, congealing macaroni and cheese.

Shit.

I put my head in my hands and rub my face. I can't believe I asked Ana to marry me. And she didn't say no. But she didn't say yes, either. She may never say yes.

In the morning, she'll wake and come to her senses.

The day started so well. But it's been a train wreck since this evening, since Leila.

Well, at least *she's* safe and getting the help she needs.

But at what cost? *Ana?*

She now knows everything.

She knows I'm a monster.

But she's still here.

Focus on the positive, Grey.

My appetite has gone the same way as Ana's, and I'm exhausted. It's been an emotional evening. I get up from the kitchen counter. I've experienced more in the last half hour than I would have thought possible.

This is what she does to you, Grey. She makes you feel.

You know you're alive when you're with her.

I can't lose her. I've only just found her.

Confused and overwhelmed, I deposit my plate in the sink and head to my bedroom.

It will be *our* bedroom if she says yes.

Outside the bathroom, I hear a stifled noise. She's weeping. I open the door and she's on the floor, curled up in the fetal position, wearing one of my T-shirts and sobbing. The sight of her in such despair is like a swift kick to my gut that leaves me breathless. It's intolerable.

I crawl onto the floor. "Hey," I murmur, as I pull her into my lap. "Please don't cry, Ana, please." She snakes her arms around me and clings to me, but her crying shows no sign of abating.

Oh, baby.

Gently I stroke her back, thinking about how much more her tears affect me than Leila's did.

Because I love her.

She's brave and strong. And this is how I reward her, by making her cry.

"I'm sorry, baby," I whisper, holding her, and I start to rock to and fro as she weeps. I kiss her hair. Eventually, her crying subsides and she shudders, racked with dry sobs. I stand with her in my arms, carry her to the bedroom, and lay her down on the bed. She yawns and closes her eyes while I strip out of my pants and shirt. Leaving my underwear on, I slip into a T-shirt and switch off the lights. In bed, I hold her close. Within seconds, her breathing deepens and I know she's asleep. She's exhausted, too. I dare not move for fear of waking her. She needs sleep.

In the dark I try to make some sense of all that has occurred this evening. So much has happened. Too much, too much . . .

Leila stands before me. She's a waif and her stench makes me take a step back.

The stench. No.

The stench.

He smells. He smells of nasty. And dirt. It makes sick come into my mouth.

He's mad. I hide under the table. *There you are, you little prick.*

He has cigarettes.

No. I call my mommy. But she doesn't hear me. She lies on the floor.

Smoke comes out of his mouth.

He laughs.

And he holds my hair.

The burn. I scream.

I don't like the burn.

Mommy is on the floor. I sleep beside her. She is cold. I
cover her with my blankie.

He's back. He's mad.

Crazy. Stupid. Bitch.

Get out of my way, you stupid fucking runt. He hits me and I
fall.

He goes. He locks the door. And it's Mommy and me.

And then she's gone. Where is Mommy? Where is Mommy?

He holds the cigarette in front of me.

No.

He takes a puff.

No.

He presses it against my skin.

No.

The pain. The smell.

No.

"Christian!"

My eyes flick open. There's light. *Where am I?* My bedroom.

Ana's out of bed, holding my shoulders, shaking me.

"You left, you left, you must have left," I mumble incoherently.
She sits down beside me. "I'm here," she says, and lays her palm
on my cheek.

"You were gone."

I only have nightmares when you're not here.

"I just went for a drink. I was thirsty."

Closing my eyes, I rub my face, trying to separate fact from
fiction. She hasn't left. She's looking down at me: kind, kind Ana.
My girl. "You're here. Oh, thank God." I pull her down beside me
on the bed.

"I just went to get a drink," she says, as I wrap my arms around
her. She strokes my hair and my cheek. "Christian, please. I'm
here. I'm not going anywhere."

"Oh, Ana." My mouth claims hers. She tastes of orange
juice . . . sweetness and home.

My body responds as I kiss her, her ear, her throat. I tug her bottom lip with my teeth as I caress her body. My hand pushing up the T-shirt she's wearing. She trembles as I cup her breast and she moans into my mouth as my fingers find her nipple. "I want you," I whisper.

I need you.

"I'm here for you. Only you, Christian."

Her words light a fire inside me. I kiss her again.

Please never leave me.

She grabs my T-shirt and I move so that she can pull it off. I pull her upright while kneeling between her legs and drag off her T-shirt. She looks up at me, her eyes dark and full of hunger and longing. Holding her face, I kiss her, and we sink onto the mattress. Her fingers tangle in my hair as she kisses me back, matching my fervor. Her tongue in my mouth, eager to please.

Oh, Ana.

Suddenly, she pulls back and pushes against my arms. "Christian. Stop. I can't do this."

"What? What's wrong?" I murmur against her throat.

"No, please. I can't do this, not now. I need some time, please . . ."

"Oh, Ana, don't overthink this," I whisper, as my anxiety returns. I'm fully awake. She's rejecting me. *No.* I'm desperate. I tug her earlobe with my teeth and her body bows under my touch and she gasps. "I'm just the same, Ana. I love you and I need you. Touch me. Please." I stop and rub my nose against hers and stare down at her, holding my weight on my arms as I wait for her response.

Our relationship rests on this moment.

If she can't do this . . .

If she can't touch me.

If I can't have her.

I wait.

Please, Ana.

Tentatively, she reaches up and places her hand on my chest.

Heat and pain spiral across my chest as the darkness unleashes its claws. I gasp and close my eyes.

I can do this.

I can do this for her.

My girl.

Ana.

She runs her hand up to my shoulder, her fingertips scalding my skin. I groan; I want this so much and I dread it so much.

To dread your lover's touch. *What kind of fuckup am I?*

She pulls me down to her and moves her hands to my back, holding me. Her palms on my flesh. Branding me. My strangled cry is half groan, half sob. I bury my face in her neck, hiding, seeking solace from the pain, but kissing her, loving her, as her fingers cross the two scars on my back.

It's almost unbearable.

I kiss her, feverishly, losing myself in her tongue and her mouth as I fight my demons, using only my lips and my hands. They skim over her body while her hands move over mine.

The darkness is swirling, trying to dislodge her, but Ana's fingers are on me. Caressing me. Feeling me. Gentle. Loving. And I steel myself against my fear and the pain.

I trail my lips down to her breasts and close them around one nipple, tugging until it's hard and standing at attention. She groans as her body rises to meet mine and she scrapes her fingernails across the muscles on my back. It's too much. Fear erupts in my chest, hammering my heart. "Oh, fuck, Ana," I cry out and stare down at her. She's panting, eyes bright and brimming with sensuality.

This is turning her on.

Fuck.

Don't overthink this, Grey.

Man up. Go with it.

Taking a deep breath to slow my pounding heart, I skate my hand down her body, over her belly, to her labia. I cup her and my fingers are wet with her anticipation. Easing them inside her, I circle them and she pushes her pelvis up to meet my hand.

"Ana." Her name is an invocation. I release her and sit up, and her hands fall away so she's no longer touching me. I feel relieved and bereft at once. I remove my boxers, freeing my cock, and lean over to the bedside table for a condom. I hand it to her. "You want to do this? You can still say no. You can always say no."

"Don't give me a chance to think, Christian." She's breathless. "I want you, too." She rips open the foil with her teeth and slowly, with trembling fingers, slides it onto me.

Her fingers on my erection are torture. "Steady. You are going to unman me, Ana."

She gives me a quick, possessive smile, and when she's done I stretch over her. But I need to know she wants this, too. I roll us both over, quickly.

"You, take me," I whisper, staring up at her.

She licks her lips and sinks down on me, taking me, inch by inch.

"Ah." I tilt my head back and close my eyes.

I'm yours, Ana.

She grabs my hands and starts to move, up and down.

Oh, baby.

Leaning forward, she kisses my chin and runs her teeth over my jaw.

I'm going to come.

Shit.

I still her with my hands on her hips.

Slow, baby. Please, let's take this slow.

Her eyes are full of passion and excitement.

And I steel myself once more. "Ana, touch me, please."

Her eyes widen with sheer delight and she spreads her hands on my chest. It's blistering. I cry out and thrust deep inside her.

"Ah," she whimpers, and her fingernails trail through my chest hair. Tantalizing me. Teasing me. But the darkness is pushing at each point of contact, determined to rupture my skin. It's so painful, so intense, tears spring to my eyes, and Ana's face blurs in a watery vision.

I twist so that she's underneath me. "Enough. No more, please."

She reaches up and clasps my face in her hands, wiping my tears, then pulling me down so that her lips are on mine. I drive into her. Trying to find my equilibrium, but I'm lost. Lost to this woman. Her breath is at my ear: Short. Panting. She's reaching. She's close. But she's holding back.

"Let go, Ana," I whisper.

"No."

"Yes," I plead, and I shift and roll my hips, filling her.

She moans, loud and clear, her legs tensing.

"Come on, baby, I need this. Give it to me."

We need this.

She lets go, convulsing around me and crying out while she wraps her arms and legs around my body and I find my release.

HER FINGERS ARE IN my hair while my head rests on her chest. She's here. She didn't leave, but I can't shake the feeling that I nearly lost her again. "Don't ever leave me," I whisper. Above me, I feel her move her head, her chin lifting in that mulish way she has. "I know you're rolling your eyes at me," I add, pleased that she's doing so.

"You know me well." There's humor in her tone.

Thank God.

"I'd like to know you better."

"Back at you, Grey," she says, and asks me what torments me when I sleep.

"The usual."

She insists that I tell her more.

Oh, Ana, do you really want to know?

She remains silent. Waiting.

I sigh.

"I must be about three, and the crack whore's pimp is mad as hell again. He smokes and smokes, one cigarette after another, and he can't find an ashtray."

Does she really want this shit in her head? The burn. The smell. The screaming.

She tenses beneath me.

"It hurt," I mutter. "It's the pain I remember. That's what gives me nightmares. That, and the fact that she did nothing to stop him."

Ana's hold on me tightens.

I lift my head, meeting her eyes. "You're not like her. Don't ever think that. Please."

She blinks a couple of times and I lay my head on her chest again.

The crack whore was weak. *No, Maggot. Not now.*

She killed herself. Abandoning me.

"Sometimes in the dreams she's just lying on the floor. And I think she's asleep. But she doesn't move. She never moves. And I'm hungry. Really hungry. There's a loud noise and he's back, and he hits me so hard, cursing the crack whore. His first reaction was always to use his fists or his belt."

"Is that why you don't like to be touched?"

I close my eyes and hold her tighter. "That's complicated." I nuzzle the space between her breasts, surrounding myself with her essence.

"Tell me," she asks.

"She didn't love me." She can't have loved me. She didn't protect me. And she left me. Alone. "I didn't love me. The only touch I knew was . . . harsh. It stemmed from there."

I never had a mother's loving touch, Ana.

Never.

Grace respected my boundaries.

I still don't know why.

"Flynn explains it better than I can."

"Can I see Flynn?" she asks.

"Fifty Shades rubbing off on you?" I try to lighten the mood.

"And then some." Ana squirms. "I like how it's rubbing off right now."

I love her levity, and if she can joke about this, there's hope. "Yes, Miss Steele, I like that, too." I kiss her and stare into the warm depths of her eyes. "You're so precious to me, Ana. I was serious about marrying you. We can get to know each other then. I can look after you. You can look after me. We can have kids if you want. I will lay my world at your feet, Anastasia. I want you, body and soul, forever. Please think about it."

"I will think about it, Christian. I will. I'd really like to talk to Dr. Flynn, though, if you don't mind."

"Anything for you, baby. Anything. When would you like to see him?"

"Sooner rather than later."

"Okay. I'll make the arrangements in the morning." I glance at the clock: 3:44. "It's late. We should sleep." I switch off the light and pull her to me so we're spooning. I only spoon with Ana. I nuzzle her neck. "I love you, Ana Steele, and I want you by my side, always. Now go to sleep."

I'M WOKEN BY A commotion. Ana is leaping over me and onto the floor and heading for the bathroom.

She's leaving?

No.

I check the time.

Shit. It's late. I think this is the latest I've ever slept. She's going to work. Shaking my head, I call Taylor through the internal phone system.

"Good morning, Mr. Grey."

"Taylor, good morning. Could you take Miss Steele to work today?"

"With pleasure, sir."

"She's rather late."

"I'll wait for her outside the front door."

"Great."

"Come back for me."

"Will do, sir."

I sit up, and Ana hurries out of the bathroom, drying herself and gathering her clothes at the same time. It's quite the floor show, especially when she dons a pair of black lace panties and a matching lace bra.

Yes. I could watch this all day.

"You look good. You can call in sick, you know," I offer.

"No, Christian, I can't. I am not a megalomaniac CEO with a beautiful smile who can come and go as he pleases."

Beautiful smile? Megalomaniac? I grin. "I like to come as I please."

"Christian!" she sputters, and throws the towel at me.

I laugh. She's still here and I don't think she hates me. "Beautiful smile, huh?"

"Yes. You know the effect you have on me." She wraps her watch strap around her wrist and stops to fasten it.

"Do I?"

"Yes, you do. The same effect you have on all women. Gets really tiresome, watching them all swoon."

"Does it?" I can't hide my amusement.

"Don't play the innocent, Mr. Grey, it really doesn't suit you." She yanks her hair up into a ponytail and puts on a pair of high-heeled shoes.

Baby's in black. She looks sensational.

She bends down to kiss me good-bye and I can't resist. I pull her down onto the bed.

Thank you for still being here, Ana.

"What can I do to tempt you to stay?" I whisper.

"You can't," she grumbles, and makes a feeble effort to fight me off. "Let me go."

I pout and she grins. Outlining my lips with her finger, she smiles, leans up, and kisses me. I close my eyes and enjoy the feel of her lips on mine.

I release her. She needs to go. "Taylor will take you. Quicker than finding somewhere to park. He's waiting outside the building."

"Okay. Thank you," she says. "Enjoy your lazy morning, Mr. Grey. I wish I could stay, but the man who owns the company I work for would not approve of his staff ditching just for hot sex." She picks up her purse.

"Personally, Miss Steele, I have no doubt that he would approve. In fact, he might insist on it."

"Why are you staying in bed? It's not like you."

Crossing my hands behind my head, I lean back and give her a broad smile. "Because I can, Miss Steele."

She shakes her head in mock disgust. "Laters, baby." She blows me a kiss and hurries out the door. I hear her footsteps clatter down the hallway and then all is quiet.

Ana's left for the day.

And I miss her already.

I grab my phone with the intention of writing an e-mail to her. But what should I say? I told her so much last night—I don't want to frighten her off with any more . . . revelations.

Keep it simple, Grey.

From: Christian Grey
Subject: Missing you
Date: June 15 2011 09:05
To: Anastasia Steele

Please use your BlackBerry.

x

Christian Grey
CEO, Grey Enterprises Holdings, Inc.

I look around my bedroom and ponder how empty it feels without her. I type an e-mail to her personal account. I need to make sure she's using her phone, because I don't want anyone at SIP reading our e-mails.

From: Christian Grey
Subject: Missing you
Date: June 15 2011 09:06
To: Anastasia Steele

My bed is too big without you.

Looks like I'll have to go to work after all.

Even megalomaniac CEOs need something to do.

x

Christian Grey
Twiddling His Thumbs CEO, Grey Enterprises Holdings,
Inc.

I hope that will elicit a smile. I press send, then call Flynn's office. I leave a message. If Ana wants to see Flynn, she should see Flynn. With that done, I climb out of bed and head into the bathroom. After all, I do have a meeting with the mayor today.

I'M RAVENOUS AFTER YESTERDAY evening's events. I never ate dinner. Mrs. Jones has prepared a full breakfast for me—eggs, bacon, ham, hash browns, waffles, and toast. Gail has gone to town; she's in her element. While I'm eating, I get a response from Ana. Her work e-mail!

From: Anastasia Steele
Subject: All Right for Some
Date: June 15 2011 09:27
To: Christian Grey

My boss is mad.

I blame you for keeping me up late with your . . . shenanigans.

You should be ashamed of yourself.

Anastasia Steele
Assistant to Jack Hyde, Editor, SIP

Oh, Ana, I'm more ashamed of myself than you will ever know.

From: Christian Grey
Subject: Shenaniwhatagans?
Date: June 15 2011 09:32
To: Anastasia Steele

You don't have to work, Anastasia.

You have no idea how appalled I am at my shenanigans.

But I like keeping you up late ;)

Please use your BlackBerry.

Oh, and marry me, please.

Christian Grey
CEO, Grey Enterprises Holdings, Inc.

Mrs. Jones is hovering about in the background while I eat my breakfast.

"More coffee, Mr. Grey?"

"Please."

Ana's response comes through on my phone.

From: Anastasia Steele
Subject: Living to make
Date: June 15 2011 09:35
To: Christian Grey

I know your natural inclination is toward nagging, but just stop.

I need to talk to your shrink.

Only then will I give you my answer.

I am not opposed to living in sin.

Anastasia Steele
Assistant to Jack Hyde, Editor, SIP

For fuck's sake, Ana!

From: Christian Grey
Subject: BLACKBERRY
Date: June 15 2011 09:40
To: Anastasia Steele

Anastasia, if you are going to start discussing Dr. Flynn, then USE YOUR BLACKBERRY.

This is not a request.

Christian Grey
Now Pissed CEO, Grey Enterprises Holdings, Inc.

My phone rings, and it's Flynn's PA. He can see me tomorrow evening at 7:00. I ask her to have Flynn call me; I'll need to ask him about bringing Ana to the session.

"I'll see if I can schedule a call later."

"Thanks, Janet."

I also want to know how Leila is this morning.

I send another e-mail to Ana's account. This time my tone is a little softer.

From: Christian Grey
Subject: Discretion
Date: June 15 2011 09:50
To: Anastasia Steele

Is the better part of valor.

Please use discretion . . . your work e-mails are monitored.

HOW MANY TIMES DO I HAVE TO TELL YOU THIS?

Yes. Shouty capitals as you say. USE YOUR BLACKBERRY.

Dr. Flynn can see us tomorrow evening.

x

Christian Grey
Still Pissed CEO, Grey Enterprises Holdings, Inc.

I hope that will please her.

"Two for dinner?" Gail asks.

"Yes. Mrs. Jones. Thanks."

I take a last swig of coffee and set my cup down. I like bantering with Ana over breakfast. If she marries me, she could be here every morning.

Marriage. A wife.

Grey, what were you thinking?

What changes will I need to make if she agrees to marry me? I get up and stroll to the bathroom. I stop by the stairway to the upper floor. On impulse, I head up the stairs to the playroom. Unlocking the door, I step inside.

My recent memory of this room is not a good one.

Well, you are one fucked-up son of a bitch.

Ana's words haunt me. A vision of her tearstained, anguished face comes to mind. I close my eyes. Suddenly I'm empty and aching, feeling a remorse so deep it cuts through sinew and bone. I never want to see her that unhappy again. Last night she was sobbing; she cried her heart out, but this time she let me comfort her. That's a huge difference from last time.

Isn't it?

I gaze around the room. What will become of it, I wonder?

I've had some amazing times in here . . .

Ana on the cross. Ana shackled to the bed. Ana on her knees.

I like your kinky fuckery.

I sigh and my phone buzzes. It's a text from Taylor. He's outside waiting for me. With a last lingering look at what was once my safe place, I shut the door.

MY MORNING IS UNEVENTFUL, but there's a certain excitement running through GEH. It's not often that I host delegations to the company, but the mayor's visit is causing a buzz throughout the building. I get through a few early meetings and all seems in place.

At 11:30, when I'm back in my office, Andrea puts Flynn through to me.

"John, thanks for calling me."

"I assumed you wanted to talk about Leila Williams, but I noticed that you're in my schedule and I'm seeing you tomorrow evening."

"I asked Ana to marry me."

John says nothing.

"You're surprised?" I ask.

"Frankly, no."

That's not what I expect him to say. But I let it go.

He continues. "Christian, you're impulsive. And you're in love. What did she say?"

"She wants to talk to you."

"She's not my patient, Christian."

"But I am, and I'm asking you."

He's silent for a moment. "Okay," he says eventually.

"Please, tell her whatever she wants to know."

"If that's what you wish."

"I do. How's Leila?"

"She had a comfortable night and was forthcoming this morning. I think I can help her."

"Good."

"Christian." He pauses. "Marriage is a serious commitment."

"I know."

"Are you sure that's what you want?"

It's my turn to pause. Spend the rest of my life with Ana . . . "Yes."

"It's not all rainbows and unicorns," John says. "It's hard work."

Rainbows? Unicorns? What the hell!

"I've never shied away from hard work, John."

John laughs. "That's true. I'll see you both tomorrow."

"Thanks."

MY PHONE BUZZES, AND it's another text from Elena.

ELENA

Can we do dinner?

Not at the moment, Elena. I just can't deal with her at this time. I press delete. It's after midday and I realize I've heard nothing more from Ana. I type a quick e-mail.

From: Christian Grey
Subject: Crickets
Date: June 15 2011 12:15
To: Anastasia Steele

I haven't heard from you.

Please tell me you are okay.

You know how I worry.

I will send Taylor to check!

x

Christian Grey
Overanxious CEO, Grey Enterprises Holdings, Inc.

My next meeting is lunch with the mayor and his delegation. They want a tour of the building, and my PR guy is beside himself. Sam's all about raising the profile of the company, though sometimes I think it's about elevating his own profile.

Andrea knocks and opens the door. "Sam's here, Mr. Grey," she says.

"Show him in. Oh, can you update the contacts on my phone?"

"Sure." I hand her my phone and she stands aside to let Sam enter. He gives me a supercilious smile and starts a run-through of the various photo opportunities he's planned for the tour. Sam is a pretentious man and a recent hire I'm beginning to regret.

There's a knock on the door and Andrea pokes her head around. "I have Anastasia Steele on your phone. But I can't bring it to you—it's downloading your contacts, and I'm not brave enough to stop it mid-sync."

I leap up, ignoring Sam, and follow her to her desk. She hands me the phone, which is on such a short cable I have to bend over her computer.

"Are you okay?" I ask.

"Yes, I'm fine," Ana replies. *Thank goodness.*

"Christian, why wouldn't I be okay?"

"You're normally so quick at responding to my e-mails. After what I told you yesterday, I was worried." I keep my voice low. I don't want Andrea or the new girl to hear me.

"Mr. Grey." Andrea is holding her phone to her neck and trying to get my attention. "The mayor and his delegation are in reception downstairs. Shall I ask them to come up?"

"No, Andrea. Tell them to wait."

She looks stricken. "I think it's too late; they're on their way."

"No. I said wait."

Shit.

"Christian, you're obviously busy. I only called to let you know that I'm okay, and I mean that, just very busy today. Jack has been cracking the whip. Er . . . I mean—" She stops.

What an interesting choice of words.

"Cracking the whip, eh? Well, there was a time when I would have called him a lucky man. Don't let him get on top of you, baby."

"Christian!" she scolds.

And I grin. I like shocking her. "Just watch him, that's all. Look, I'm glad you're okay. What time should I pick you up?"

"I'll e-mail you."

"From your BlackBerry," I emphasize.

"Yes, Sir."

"Laters, baby."

"Bye."

I glance up and see the elevator is climbing to the executive floor. The mayor is on his way.

"Hang up," she says, and I hear the smile in her voice.

"I wish you'd never gone to work this morning."

"Me, too. But I am busy. Hang up."

"You hang up." I grin.

"We've been here before," she says in that teasing tone she has.

"You're biting your lip."

She inhales, quickly.

"You see, you think I don't know you, Anastasia. But I know you better than you think."

"Christian, I'll talk to you later. Right now, I really wish I hadn't left this morning, too."

"I'll wait for your e-mail, Miss Steele."

"Good day, Mr. Grey."

She hangs up as the elevator doors open.

BY 3:45 I'M BACK in my office. The mayor's visit was a success and a PR windfall for GEH. Andrea buzzes me.

"Yes?"

"I have Mia Grey on the line for you."

"Put her through."

"Christian?"

"Hi."

"We're having a party for your birthday on Saturday and I want to invite Anastasia."

"Whatever happened to 'Hello? How are you?'"

Mia makes a dismissive noise. "Spare me one of your lectures, big brother."

"I'm busy on Saturday."

"Cancel it. It's happening."

"Mia!"

"No ifs or buts. What's Ana's number?"

I sigh and stay silent.

"Christian!" she shouts down the phone.

Jesus. "I'll text it to you."

"No bailing. You'll disappoint Mom and Dad and me and Elliot!"

I sigh. "Whatever, Mia."

"Great! See you then. Bye." She hangs up and I stare at the phone with frustrated amusement. My sister is a pain in the ass. I hate birthdays. Well, my birthday. Reluctantly, I text Mia Ana's number, knowing that I'm unleashing the force that is my little sister on an unsuspecting victim.

I go back to reading a report.

When I finish, I check my e-mail and there's one from Ana.

From: Anastasia Steele
Subject: Antediluvian
Date: June 15 2011 16:11
To: Christian Grey

Dear Mr. Grey
When, exactly, were you going to tell me?

What shall I get my old man for his birthday?

Perhaps some new batteries for his hearing aid?

A x

Anastasia Steele
Assistant to Jack Hyde, Editor, SIP

Mia is as good as her word. She hasn't wasted any time. I have some fun with my response.

From: Christian Grey
Subject: Prehistoric
Date: June 15 2011 16:20
To: Anastasia Steele

Don't mock the elderly.

Glad you are alive and kicking.

And that Mia has been in touch.

Batteries are always useful.

I don't like celebrating my birthday.

x

Christian Grey
Deaf as a Post CEO, Grey Enterprises Holdings, Inc.

From: Anastasia Steele
Subject: Hmmm.
Date: June 15 2011 16:24
To: Christian Grey

Dear Mr. Grey
I can imagine you pouting as you wrote that last sentence.

That does things to me.

A xox

Anastasia Steele
Assistant to Jack Hyde, Editor, SIP

Her reply makes me laugh out loud, but what do I have to do to make her use her phone?

From: Christian Grey
Subject: Rolling Eyes
Date: June 15 2011 16:29
To: Anastasia Steele

Miss Steele
WILL YOU USE YOUR BLACKBERRY!!!

x

Christian Grey
Twitchy Palmed CEO, Grey Enterprises Holdings, Inc.

I await her answer. It does not disappoint.

From: Anastasia Steele
Subject: Inspiration
Date: June 15 2011 16:33
To: Christian Grey

Dear Mr. Grey
Ah . . . your twitchy palms can't stay still for long, can they?

I wonder what Dr. Flynn would say about that?

But now I know what to give you for your birthday—and I hope it makes me sore . . .

;)

A x

Finally, she's using her phone. And she wants to be sore. My mind goes into overdrive imagining the possibilities this presents. I shift in my seat as I type my response.

From: Christian Grey
Subject: Angina
Date: June 15 2011 16:38
To: Anastasia Steele

Miss Steele
I don't think my heart could stand the strain of another e-mail like that, or my pants for that matter.

Behave.

x

Christian Grey
CEO, Grey Enterprises Holdings, Inc.

From: Anastasia Steele
Subject: Trying
Date: June 15 2011 16:42
To: Christian Grey

Christian
I am trying to work for my very trying boss.

Please stop bothering me and being trying yourself.

Your last e-mail nearly made me combust.

x

P.S.: Can you pick me up at 6:30?

From: Christian Grey
Subject: I'll Be There
Date: June 15 2011 16:47
To: Anastasia Steele

Nothing would give me greater pleasure.

Actually, I can think of any number of things that would give
me greater pleasure, and they all involve you.

x

Christian Grey
CEO, Grey Enterprises Holdings, Inc.

TAYLOR AND I PULL up outside her office at 6:27. I should only have a few minutes to wait.

I wonder if she's had any thoughts about my proposal. Of course, she needs to talk to Flynn first. Perhaps he'll tell her not to be a fool. The thought depresses me. I wonder if our days are numbered. But she knows the worst and she's still here. I think there's room for hope. I check my watch—6:38—and stare at the door of her office building.

Where is she?

Suddenly she's in the street, the door swinging behind her. But she doesn't head toward the car.

What gives?

She stops, looks around, and slowly sinks to the ground.

Fuck.

I open the car door and notice out of the corner of my eye that Taylor is doing the same.

We both rush to Ana, who is sitting on the sidewalk, looking faint. I sink down beside her. "Ana, Ana! What's wrong?" I pull her into my lap to check what's wrong, holding her head between my hands. She closes her eyes and sags against me as if in relief. "Ana." I grasp her arms and shake her. "What's wrong? Are you sick?"

"Jack," she whispers.

"Fuck." Adrenaline sweeps through my body, leaving a murderous fury in its wake. I glance up at Taylor. He nods and disappears into the building. "What did that sleazeball do to you?"

Ana giggles. "It's what I did to him." And she doesn't stop laughing. She's hysterical. I'm going to kill him.

"Ana!" I give her a shake. "Did he touch you?"

"Only once," she whispers, and her giggling stops.

Rage fuels my muscles as I stand holding her in my arms. "Where is that fucker?" From inside the building we can hear muffled shouts. I set Ana on her feet. "Can you stand?"

She nods. "Don't go in. Don't, Christian."

"Get in the car."

"Christian, no." She clasps my arm.

"Get in the goddamned car, Ana."

I'm going to kill him.

"No! Please!" she begs. "Stay. Don't leave me on my own."

I drag my hand through my hair, trying and failing to hang on to my temper while the muffled shouting inside SIP intensifies. Abruptly it stops.

I pull out my phone.

"Christian, he has my e-mails," Ana says in a whisper.

"What?"

"My e-mails to you. He wanted to know where your e-mails to me were. He was trying to blackmail me."

I think I'm going to have a coronary.

That motherfucking asshole.

"Fuck!" I growl, as I call Barney.

"Hello—"

"Barney. Grey. I need you to access the SIP main server and wipe all Anastasia Steele's e-mails to me. Then access the personal data files of Jack Hyde and check they aren't stored there. If they are, wipe them."

"Hyde? H.Y.D.E."

"Yes."

"All of them?"

"All of them. Now. Let me know when it's done."

"Will do."

I hang up and dial Roach's number.

"Jerry Roach."

"Roach. Grey."

"Good evening—"

"Hyde. I want him out. Now."

"But—" Roach blusters.

"This minute. Call security. Get him to clear his desk immediately or I will liquidate this company first thing in the morning."

"Is there a reason—" Roach tries again.

"You already have all the justification you need to give him his pink slip."

"You've read his confidential file?"

I ignore his question. "Do you understand?"

"Mr. Grey, I completely understand. Our HR director is always defending him. I'll see to it. Good evening."

I hang up, feeling somewhat mollified, and turn to Ana. "Black-Berry!"

"Please don't be mad at me."

"I am so mad at you right now," I snap. "Get in the car."

"Christian, please—"

"Get in the fucking car, Anastasia, or so help me I'll put you in there myself."

"Don't do anything stupid, please," she says.

"Stupid!" I see red. "I told you to use your fucking BlackBerry. Don't talk to me about stupid. Get in the motherfucking car, Anastasia—now!"

"Okay." She holds up her hands. "But, please, be careful."

Stop shouting at her, Grey.

I point to the car.

"Please be careful," she whispers, again. "I don't want anything to happen to you. It would kill me."

And there it is. She cares. Her affection for me is plain in her words and in her kind, concerned expression.

Calm down, Grey. I take a deep breath.

"I'll be careful," I say, and I watch her walk to the Audi and climb in. Once she's in the car, I turn on my heel and stride into the building.

I have no idea where to go, but I follow Hyde's voice.

His irritating, whiny voice.

Taylor is standing outside an executive office, beside what must be Ana's desk. Inside, Hyde is on the phone and a security guard stands over him with his arms crossed.

"I don't give a fuck, Jerry." Hyde is protesting into the phone. "The woman is a pricktease."

I've heard enough.

I storm into his office.

"What the—" Hyde says, shocked to see me. He has a cut over his left eye and a purplish bruise is forming on his cheek. I suspect Taylor has been administering his own brand of discipline. I reach down to the phone cradle and press the hook, ending his call.

"Well, look what the fucking cat dragged in," Hyde says and sneers. "The boy fucking wonder."

"Pack your things. Get out. And she may not press charges."

"Fuck you, Grey. I'll be pressing charges against that little bitch, for kicking me in the balls in a completely unprovoked attack—and I'll be sending your goon here down for assault, too. Hi, handsome," he calls to Taylor, and blows him a kiss.

Taylor remains stoic.

"I won't tell you again," I state, glaring at the cocksucker.

"Like I said, fuck you. You can't come in here throwing your fucking weight around."

"I own this company. You are surplus to requirements. Get out while you can still walk." My tone is low.

The color drains from Hyde's face.

Yeah. Mine. Fuck you, Hyde.

"I knew it. I knew something shady was going on. That little bitch your spy?"

"If you mention Anastasia once more, if you even think about her, if you even think about thinking about her, I will end you."

His eyes narrow. "You like it when she kicks you in the balls?"

I hit him square on the nose and he topples backward and smacks his head on the shelves behind him before he slumps onto the floor.

"You mentioned her. Get up. Clear your desk. And get out. You're fired."

Blood is pouring from his nose.

Taylor steps into his office with a box of tissues and places them on the desk for Hyde.

"You saw him," Hyde whines to the security guard.

"I saw you fall," the security guard says. The name on his badge is M. Mathur. *Good job.*

Hyde struggles onto his feet and grabs a handful of tissues to stem his nosebleed. "I'm pressing charges. She attacked me." Hyde continues to snivel, but he begins to put his belongings in the box.

"Three hushed-up harassment cases in New York and Chicago and the two warnings you've had here. I don't think you'd get very far."

He regards me with dark eyes and unadulterated, feral hatred.

"Pack your things. You're done," I spit.

Turning, I head out of his office to wait with Taylor while Hyde packs up his stuff. I need to distance myself.

I want to kill him.

He takes forever, but he does it in silence. He's mad. Real mad. I can almost smell his blood boiling. He gives me the occasional poisonous glance, but I remain impassive. The sight of his messed-up face gives me some satisfaction.

Eventually he's done and he picks up the box. Mathur follows him out of the building.

"Are we finished here, Mr. Grey?" Taylor asks.

"For now."

"I found him groveling on the floor, sir."

"Really?"

"Miss Steele appears to know how to defend herself."

"She's always full of surprises. Let's go."

We follow Hyde out of the building and both of us head to the Audi. Because Ana is already in the front seat, Taylor gives me the key and I slide into the driver's seat. Taylor gets into the back.

Ana is quiet as I pull out into the traffic.

I don't know what to say to her.

The car phone rings.

"Grey," I answer.

"Mr. Grey, Barney here."

"Barney, I'm on speakerphone, and there are others in the car."

"Sir, it's all done. But I need to talk to you about what else I found on Mr. Hyde's computer."

"I'll call you when I reach my destination. And thanks, Barney."

"No problem, Mr. Grey." He hangs up and I stop at a red light.

"Are you talking to me?" Ana asks.

I glance at her. "No," I mutter. I'm still too mad. I told her he was trouble. And I told her to use her phone for e-mail. I was right about everything. I feel vindicated.

Grey, grow up, you're behaving like a child.

Flynn's words circle my brain. *I've long held the belief that you never really had an adolescence—emotionally speaking. I think you're experiencing it now.*

I glance across at her in the hope I can say something amusing, but she's staring out of the window. I'll wait until we get home.

OUTSIDE ESCALA, I OPEN Ana's car door while Taylor climbs into the driver's seat.

"Come," I say, and she takes my hand.

While we wait for the elevator, Ana whispers, "Christian, why are you so mad at me?"

"You know why."

As we enter the elevator, I punch the code into the keypad. "God, if something had happened to you, he'd be dead by now. As it is, I'm going to ruin his career so he can't take advantage of young women anymore, miserable excuse for a man that he is." If anything had happened to her . . . *Leila yesterday. Hyde today. Hell.*

Slowly she sinks her teeth into her lower lip while staring at me.

"Jesus, Ana!" I pull her to me and twist so that she's pinned in the corner of the elevator. Tugging her hair, upturning her face, I capture her lips with mine and pour my fear and desperation into my kiss. Her hands grasp my biceps as she returns my kiss, her tongue seeking mine. I pull back and we're both breathless. "If anything had happened to you. If he'd harmed you—" I shudder. "BlackBerry. From now on. Understand?"

She nods, her expression earnest, and I straighten up and release her. "He said you kicked him in the balls."

"Yes."

"Good."

"Ray is ex-Army. He taught me well."

"I'm very glad he did. I'll need to remember that." As we exit the elevator, I take her hand and we walk through the foyer and into the living room. Mrs. Jones is in the kitchen cooking. It smells good.

"I need to call Barney. I won't be long."

Sitting down at my desk, I pick up the phone.

"Mr. Grey."

"Barney, what did you find on Hyde's computer?"

"Well, sir, it was a little unsettling. There are articles and photographs of you, your mom and dad, and your brother and sister, all stored in one folder called 'Greys.'"

"That's odd."

"That's what I thought."

"Could you send me what he has?"

"Yes, sir."

"And keep this between us for now."

"Will do, Mr. Grey."

"Thanks, Barney. And go home."

"Yes, sir."

Barney's e-mail arrives almost immediately, and I open the "Greys" folder. Sure enough, there are online articles about my parents and their charitable work; articles on me, my company, *Charlie Tango* and the Gulfstream; and photographs of Elliot, my parents, and me taken, I assume, from Mia's Facebook page. And last, two photos of Ana and me—at her graduation and at the photographer's exhibition.

What the hell would Hyde want with all that shit? It makes no sense. I know he has a thing for Ana, that's consistent with his modus operandi. But my family? Me? It's like he's obsessed with us. Or maybe it's all about Ana? This is weird. And frankly disturbing. I resolve to call Welch in the morning to discuss. He can investigate further and get me some answers.

I close the e-mail, and sitting in my inbox are a couple of final acquisition agreements from Marco. I need to read them tonight—but first some dinner.

"Evening, Gail," I call out to her when I'm back in the living room.

"Good evening, Mr. Grey. Dinner in ten, sir?"

Ana is sitting at the kitchen counter with a glass of wine. After dealing with that asshole, I think she's earned it. I'll join her. I retrieve the open bottle of Sancerre and pour one for myself.

"Sounds good," I respond to Gail and raise my glass to Ana. "To ex-military men who train their daughters well."

"Cheers," she says, but she looks a little crestfallen.

"What's wrong?"

"I don't know if I still have a job."

"Do you still want one?"

"Of course."

"Then you still have one."

She rolls her eyes, and I smile and take another sip of my wine.

"So, did you talk to Barney?" she asks, as I take a seat beside her.

"I did."

"And?"

"And what?"

"What did Jack have on his computer?"

"Nothing important."

Mrs. Jones places our food in front of us. Chicken pot pie. One of my favorites.

"Thanks, Gail."

"Enjoy, Mr. Grey. Ana," she says pleasantly, and departs.

"You're not going to tell me, are you?" Ana persists.

"Tell you what?"

She sighs and purses her lips, then takes another bite of her meal.

The contents of Jack's computer are not something I want Ana to worry about.

"José called," she says, changing the subject.

"Oh?"

"He wants to deliver your photos on Friday."

"A personal delivery." Why is the artist doing this and not the gallery? "How accommodating of him."

"He wants to go out. For a drink. With me."

"I see."

"And Kate and Elliot should be back."

I put my fork down on my plate. "What exactly are you asking?"

"I'm not asking anything. I'm informing you of my plans for Friday. Look, I want to see José, and he wants to stay over. Either he stays here or he can stay at my place, but if he does, I should be there, too."

"He made a pass at you."

"Christian, that was weeks ago. He was drunk, I was drunk, you saved the day—it won't happen again. He's no Jack, for heaven's sake."

"Ethan's there. He can keep him company."

"He wants to see me, not Ethan," Ana says.

I scowl at her.

"He's just a friend," she continues.

She's already endured Hyde—what if Rodriguez gets drunk and tries his luck again with Ana? "I don't like it."

Ana takes a deep breath; she's trying to keep her cool. "He's my friend, Christian. I haven't seen him since his show. And that was too brief. I know you don't have any friends, apart from that god-awful woman, but I don't moan about you seeing her."

What has Elena got to do with this? And I'm reminded that I haven't responded to her texts.

"I want to see him," she continues. "I've been a poor friend to him."

"Is that what you think?" I ask.

"Think about what?"

"Elena. You'd rather I didn't see her?"

"Exactly. I'd rather you didn't see her."

"Why didn't you say?"

"Because it's not my place to say. You think she's your only friend." She's exasperated. "Just as it's not your place to say if I can or can't see José. Don't you see that?"

She has a point. If he stays here, then he can't make a pass at her. Can he?

"He can stay here, I suppose. I can keep an eye on him."

"Thank you! You know, if I am going to live here, too . . ." Her voice trails off.

Yes. She'll need to invite her friends here. Jesus. I hadn't thought about that.

"It's not like you haven't got the space." She waves a hand in the general direction of my apartment.

"Are you smirking at me, Miss Steele?"

"Most definitely, Mr. Grey." She gets up and clears both of our plates.

"Gail will do that," I say as she sashays over to the dishwasher. But I'm too late.

"I've done it now."

"I have to work for a while."

"Cool. I'll find something to do."

"Come here."

She steps between my legs and puts her arms around my neck. I hold her close against me. "Are you okay?" I whisper into her hair.

"Okay?"

"After what happened with that fucker? After what happened yesterday?" I lean back and study her expression.

"Yes," she replies, solemn and emphatic.

To try to reassure me?

I tighten my arms around her. What a weird couple of days this has been. Too much too fast, maybe. And my old life impinging on my new one. She still hasn't responded to my marriage proposal. Perhaps I shouldn't push her for an answer right now.

She holds me close and, for the first time since this morning, I feel calm and centered. "Let's not fight." I kiss her hair. "You smell heavenly as usual, Ana."

"So do you." She kisses my neck.

Reluctantly, I release her and stand. I have to read those agreements. "I should only be a couple of hours."

MY EYES ARE TIRED. I rub my face and pinch the bridge of my nose, and glance out of the window. It's getting dark, but I've finished going through both documents. I've made notes and forwarded them to Marco.

Now it's time to find Ana.

Maybe she'd like to watch TV or something. I loathe TV, but I'd sit with her and watch a film.

I expect to find her in the library, but she's not there.

Maybe she took a bath?

No. She's not in the bedroom or the ensuite.

I decide to check the sub's room but on my way there I notice that the playroom door is open. Looking inside, I see Ana is sitting on the bed, gazing with distaste at all the canes. With a grimace she looks away.

I should get rid of them.

I lean against the doorframe in silence and watch her. She slips from the bed onto the couch, her hands running over the soft leather. She spies the chest of drawers, rises, makes her way toward it, and opens the top drawer.

Well, this is unexpected.

From the chest, she pulls out a large butt plug and, fascinated, examines it, then tests the weight in her hand. It's a little big for a newcomer to anal pleasure, but I'm mesmerized by her captivated expression. Her hair is a little damp and she's wearing sweatpants and a T-shirt.

No bra.

Nice.

Glancing up, she spots me by the door. "Hi," she says, all breathy and nervous.

"What are you doing?"

She blushes. "Um, I was bored and curious."

"That's a very dangerous combination." I wander into the room to join her. Leaning over, I glance at the open drawer to see what else is inside. "So, what exactly are you curious about, Miss Steele? Perhaps I could enlighten you."

"The door was open," she says hastily. "I—" She stops, looking guilty.

Put her out of her misery, Grey.

"I was in here earlier today, wondering what to do with it all. I must have forgotten to lock it."

"Oh?"

"But now here you are, curious as ever."

"You're not mad?"

"Why would I be mad?"

"I feel like I'm trespassing. And you're always mad at me."

Am I? "Yes, you're trespassing, but I'm not mad. I hope that one day you'll live with me here, and all this"—I wave my hand around the room—"will be yours, too. That's why I was in here today. Trying to decide what to do." I watch her expression, thinking about what she's just said. I'm mostly angry at myself, not her. "Am I angry with you all the time? I wasn't this morning."

She smiles. "You were playful. I like playful Christian."

"Do you, now?" I ask, raising an eyebrow and returning her smile. I love her compliments.

"What's this?" She holds up the toy she's been examining.

"Always hungry for information, Miss Steele. That's a butt plug."

"Oh." She looks surprised.

"Bought for you."

"For me?"

I nod.

"You buy new, er . . . toys . . . for each submissive?"

"Some things. Yes."

"Butt plugs?"

Definitely. "Yes."

She eyes it warily and places it back in the drawer.

"And this?" She waves some anal beads at me.

"Anal beads."

She runs them through her fingers—intrigued, I think.

"They have quite an effect if you pull them out mid-orgasm," I add.

"This is for me?" she asks, referring to the beads. She keeps her voice low, as if she doesn't want to be overheard.

"For you."

"This is the butt drawer?"

I stifle my chuckle. "If you like."

She turns a lovely shade of pink and closes it.

"Don't you like the butt drawer?" I tease.

"It's not top of my Christmas-card list."

There's her smart mouth. She opens the second drawer. Oh, this will be fun. "Next drawer down holds a selection of vibrators."

She shuts it quickly. "And the next?"

"That's more interesting."

Slowly she opens the next one down. She picks out a toy and shows it to me.

"Genital clamp." Hastily, she puts it back in the drawer and chooses something else. I remember they were a hard limit for her. "Some of these are for pain, but most are for pleasure," I reassure her.

"What's this?"

"Nipple clamps—that's for both."

"Both? Nipples?"

"Well, there are two clamps, baby. Yes, both nipples, but that's not what I meant. These are for both pleasure and pain." I take them from her. "Hold out your little finger."

She complies, and I clamp the clip to the tip of her finger. Her breath catches. "The sensation is very intense, but it's when taking them off that they are at their most painful and pleasurable." She removes the clip. "I like the look of these." Her voice is now husky, making me smile.

"Do you, now, Miss Steele? I think I can tell."

She nods and places the clips back in the drawer. I lean forward and remove another set for her consideration.

"These are adjustable." I hold them up to demonstrate.

"Adjustable?"

"You can wear them very tight, or not. Depending on your mood."

Her eyes move from the clamp to my face and she licks her lower lip. She pulls out another toy. "This?" She's intrigued.

"That's a Wartenberg pinwheel." I pop the adjustable clamps back in the drawer.

"For?"

I take it from her. "Give me your hand. Palm up." She does, and I run the spiky wheel over the center of her hand.

"Ah!" She gasps.

"Imagine that over your breasts."

She snatches her hand away, but the quick fall and rise of her chest reveals her excitement.

This is turning her on.

"There's a fine line between pleasure and pain, Anastasia." I place the pinwheel back in the drawer.

She's looking at the other contents. "Clothespins?"

"You can do a great deal with a clothespin."

But I don't think it would be your thing, Ana.

She leans against the drawer, closing it.

"Is that all?" This is turning me on, too—I should take her downstairs.

"No." She shakes her head, and, opening the fourth drawer, she retrieves one of my favorite devices. "Ball gag. To keep you quiet," I inform her.

"Soft limit."

"I remember. But you can still breathe. Your teeth clamp over the ball." Taking it from her, I demonstrate with my hands how a ball gag fits into a mouth.

"Have you worn one of these?" she asks, curious as ever.

"Yes."

"To mask your screams?"

"No, that's not what they're about."

She cocks her head to one side, perplexed.

"It's about control, Anastasia. How helpless would you be if you were tied up and couldn't speak? How trusting would you have to be, knowing I had that much power over you? That I had to read your body and your reaction rather than hear your words? It makes you more dependent, puts me in ultimate control."

"You sound like you miss it." Her voice is barely audible.

"It's what I know."

"You have power over me. You know you do."

"Do I? You make me feel . . . helpless."

"No," she counters, shocked, I think. "Why?"

"Because you're the only person I know who could really hurt me."

You hurt me when you left.

I tuck her hair behind her ear.

"Oh, Christian. That works both ways. If you didn't want me—" A tremor runs through her and she gazes down at her fingers. "The last thing I want to do is hurt you. I love you."

She strokes my face with both her hands and I savor her touch. It's both arousing and comforting. I drop the ball gag back into the drawer and fold her in my arms. "Have we finished show-and-tell?"

"Why? What did you want to do?" Her tone is suggestive.

I kiss her gently and she presses her body against mine, making her intention clear. She wants me. "Ana, you were nearly attacked today."

"So?" she breathes.

"What do you mean, 'so'?" I feel a rush of annoyance.

"Christian, I'm fine."

Are you, Ana?

I pull her closer, squeezing her. "When I think of what might have happened—" I bury my face in her hair and breathe.

"When will you learn that I'm stronger than I look?"

"I know you're strong." *You put up with me.* I kiss her and release her.

She pouts and to my surprise reaches down and fishes out another toy from the drawer. *I thought we were done?* "That's a spreader bar with ankle and wrist restraints," I tell her.

"How does it work?" She looks up at me through her lashes.

Oh, baby. I know that look.

"You want me to show you?" I close my eyes, briefly imagining her shackled and at my mercy. It's arousing.

Very arousing.

"Yes, I want a demonstration. I like being tied up."

"Oh, Ana," I whisper. *I want to. But I can't in here.*

"What?"

"Not here."

"What do you mean?"

"I want you in my bed, not in here. Come." I take the bar and her hand and lead her out of the room.

"Why not in there?"

I stop on the stairs. "Ana, you may be ready to go back in there, but I'm not. Last time we were in there, you left me. I keep telling you—when will you understand? My whole attitude has changed as a result. My whole outlook on life has radically shifted. I've told you this. What I haven't told you is—" I pause, searching for the right words. "I'm like a recovering alcoholic, okay? That's the only comparison I can draw. The compulsion has gone, but I don't want to put temptation in my way. I don't want to hurt you."

And I can't trust you to tell me what you will and won't do.

She frowns. "I can't bear to hurt you because I love you," I add. Her eyes soften, and before I can stop her she launches herself at me, so I have to drop the spreader bar to prevent us both from toppling down the stairs. She pins me to the wall, and because she's standing on the step above me, we are lip to lip. She cups my face with both her hands and kisses me, pushing her tongue in my mouth. Her fingers are in my hair as she molds her body to mine. Her kiss is passionate, forgiving, and unrestrained.

I groan and gently push her away. "Do you want me to fuck you on the stairs?" I growl. "Because right now, I will."

"Yes," she says.

I look at her dazed expression. She wants this, and I'm tempted, as I've never fucked on the stairs, but it will be uncomfortable.

"No. I want you in my bed." Scooping her up over my shoulder, I'm gratified by her squeal of delight. I smack her hard on her backside and she squeals again and laughs. Stooping, I pick up the spreader bar and carry it and Ana through the apartment to the bedroom, where I set her on her feet and drop the spreader bar on the bed.

"I don't think you'll hurt me," she says.

"I don't think I'll hurt you, either." I take her head in my hands and kiss her, hard, exploring her mouth with my tongue. "I want you so much. Are you sure about this, after today?'

"Yes. I want you, too. I want to undress you."

Shit. She wants to touch you, Grey.

Let her.

"Okay." I managed this yesterday.

She reaches for my shirt button and my breathing halts as I endeavor to bring my fear under control.

"I won't touch you if you don't want me to."

"No. Do. It's fine. I'm good."

I steel myself, preparing for the confusion and fear that comes with the darkness. As she undoes one button and her fingers slide down to the next, I watch the concentration on her face, her beautiful face. "I want to kiss you there," she says.

"Kiss me?" My chest?

"Yes."

I inhale sharply as she undoes the next button. She looks up at me, then slowly, slowly, slowly leans forward.

She's going to kiss me.

I hold my breath and watch her, terrified and fascinated at once, as she plants a gentle, sweet kiss on my chest.

The darkness remains quiet.

She undoes the final button and pulls my shirt apart. "It's getting easier, isn't it?"

I nod. It is. Much easier. She pushes my shirt off my shoulders so it drops to the floor. "What have you done to me, Ana? Whatever it is, don't stop." I pull her into my embrace and move my hands into her hair, gripping it and tugging her head back so I can kiss and nip her throat.

She groans, and her fingers are in my waistband, undoing my button and my fly.

"Oh, baby," I whisper, and kiss her behind her ear where her pulse beats a fast, steady rhythm of need. Her fingers brush my erection, and abruptly she drops to her knees.

"Whoa!"

Before I can draw a breath, she tugs at my pants and wraps her lips around my eager cock.

Fuck.

She closes her mouth around me and sucks, hard.

I cannot take my eyes off her mouth.

Around me.

Drawing me in.

Out.

She sheaths her teeth and squeezes.

"Fuck." I close my eyes, cradling her head and flexing my hips so that I move deeper and deeper into her mouth.

She taunts me with her tongue.

And moves her mouth up and down.

Again and again.

I tighten my grip on her head.

"Ana," I warn, and try to step back.

She clamps down on my cock and grabs my hips.

She's not going to let me go.

"Please." And I don't know if I want her to stop or carry on. "I'm gonna come, Ana."

She's merciless. Her mouth and tongue skilled. She's not going to stop.

Oh, fuck.

I climax into her mouth, holding her head to steady myself.

When I open my eyes, she's gazing up at me in triumph. She smiles and licks her lips.

"Oh, so this is the game we're playing, Miss Steele?" I reach down and pull her to her feet and my lips find hers. With my tongue in her mouth, I taste her sweetness and my saltiness. It's heady. I groan. "I can taste myself. You taste better." I find the hem of her T-shirt and lift it over her head, then I pick her up and toss her on the bed. Grabbing the hem of her sweatpants, I yank them off in one move so she's naked. I take my clothes off, keeping my eyes on hers. They darken, getting larger and larger until I'm naked, too. I stand over her. She's a nymph sprawled out on the bed, her hair a chestnut halo, her eyes warm and welcoming.

My cock recovers, growing and growing as I appreciate every inch of my girl.

Yeah. She's gorgeous.

"You are one beautiful woman, Anastasia."

"You are one beautiful man, Christian, and you taste mighty fine." Her smile is sexy and coquettish.

I give her a wicked grin.

I am going to take my revenge on Miss Steele.

Grabbing her left ankle, I strap the cuff around it, keeping my eyes on hers the whole time. "We'll have to see how you taste. If I recall, you're a rare, exquisite delicacy, Miss Steele."

I grasp her right ankle and cuff that, too. While holding the bar, I stand back to admire my handiwork, happy that she's secure and that the straps aren't too tight. "The good thing about this spreader is it expands," I inform her. I push down on the clip and tug outward, and the bar extends, forcing her legs farther apart.

Ana gasps.

"Oh, we're going to have some fun with this, Ana." Reaching down, I grab the bar and twist it quickly so that Ana flips onto her front. "See what I can do to you?" I twist again and flip her onto her back.

Her breasts rise and fall as she pants.

"These other cuffs are for your wrists. I'll think about that. Depends if you behave or not."

"When do I not behave?" Her voice is husky with desire.

"I can think of a few infractions." I run my fingers up the soles of her feet and she writhes. "Your BlackBerry, for one."

"What are you going to do?"

"Oh, I never disclose my plans."

She has no idea how hot she looks right now. Slowly I crawl up the bed until I'm between her legs.

"Hmm. You are so exposed, Miss Steele," I whisper, our eyes locked together as I run my fingers up her legs, making small circles. "It's all about anticipation, Ana. What will I do to you?"

She tries to wriggle beneath me, but she's trapped.

My fingers travel higher, to her inner thighs. "Remember, if you don't like something, just tell me to stop." I lean down and kiss her belly, my nose ringing her navel.

"Oh, please, Christian."

"Oh, Miss Steele. I've discovered you can be merciless in your amorous assaults upon me. I think I should return the favor." I kiss her belly and my lips move south. My fingers north.

Slowly, I ease my fingers inside her. She jerks her pelvis up to embrace them.

I moan. "You never cease to amaze me, Ana. You're so wet." Her pubic hair tickles my lips, but I persist and my tongue finds her clitoris pert and eager for attention.

"Ah," she cries, and braces against her restraints.

Oh, baby, you're mine.

I swirl my tongue around and around and move my fingers in and out, rotating slowly. She arches off the bed, and from the corner of my eye I see her clutching the sheets.

Absorb the pleasure, Ana.

"Oh, Christian," she cries out.

"I know, baby." I gently blow on her.

"Ah! Please!" she pleads.

"Say my name."

"Christian," she exclaims.

"Again."

"Christian, Christian, Christian Grey," she shouts.

She's close.

"You are mine," I whisper, and suck and flick her with my tongue.

She cries out as she comes around my fingers, and while she's in the throes of her orgasm, I crawl back and flip her over onto her stomach and pull her into my lap.

"We're going to try this. If you don't like it, or it's too uncomfortable, tell me and we'll stop."

She's breathless and dazed.

"Lean down, baby. Head and chest on the bed."

She complies immediately and I tug her hands backward and cuff each to the bar next to her ankles.

Oh, man. Her ass is in the air; she's breathing heavily. Waiting. For me.

"Ana, you look so beautiful."

I grab a condom and quickly rip open the packet and roll it on.

I run my fingers down her spine and pause over her ass. "When you're ready, I want this, too." I brush my thumb over her anus, and she tenses and gasps. "Not today, sweet Ana," I reassure her, "but one day. I want you every way. I want to possess every inch of you. You're mine."

Moving on, I ease my finger inside her. She's still wet, and I kneel up behind her and bury myself in her.

"Aagh! Gently," she cries.

I still. *Shit.* I hold her hips. "You okay?"

"Gently," she says. "Let me get used to this."

Gently. I can do gently.

I ease back and then slowly forward, filling her. She groans and I ease back and ease forward. Again.

And again.

And again.

Take it slow.

"Yes, good, I've got it now," she murmurs.

I groan and move a little faster. She starts mewling with each thrust. And I go faster still. She scrunches up her eyes and opens her mouth, breathing in a gulp of air with each thrust.

Fuck. This is exquisite.

I close my eyes and tighten my fingers on her hips and lose myself in her.

Over and over.

Until I feel her pulling me inside.

She cries out and comes, taking me with her so I climax inside her, calling out her name. "Ana, baby."

I collapse beside her feeling utterly, utterly spent, and lie for a moment, relishing my release. I cannot leave Ana trussed up so, sitting up, I unbuckle her from the spreader bar. She curls up beside me while I rub the life back into her ankles and wrists. When she wiggles her fingers and toes, I lie back down, pulling her against me. She mumbles something unintelligible and I realize she's asleep.

I kiss her forehead, tug the duvet over her, and I sit up and watch her. Taking a strand of her hair, I rub it between my fingers.

So soft.

I curl the tendril around my index finger.

See, I'm tied to you, Ana.

I kiss the end of her hair and sit back and look out at the darkening sky. I know on the ground it will be dark, but up here, the last vestiges of the day are staining the sky pink and orange and opal. We're still in the light.

That's what she's done.

Brought light into my life.

Light and love.

But she still hasn't given me an answer.

Say yes, Ana.

Be my wife.

Please.

She stirs and opens her eyes. "I could watch you sleep forever, Ana." I kiss her forehead once more.

She gives me a drowsy smile and closes her eyes.

"I never want to let you go."

"I never want to go," she rambles. "Never let me go."

"I need you," I whisper, and her lips lift in a tender smile as her breathing evens out.

She's asleep.

Grandpa is laughing. Mia has fallen down on her butt. She's a baby.

Mia. Mommy and Daddy sit on a blanket. We are in the orchard.

My favorite place.

Elliot is running between the trees.

I lift up Mia and she walks again. Shaky steps.

But I am behind her. Watching her. Walking with her.

I keep her safe.

We have a picnic.

I like picnics.

Mommy makes apple pie.

Mia walks to the blanket. And everyone cheers.

Thank you, Christian.

You take such good care of her, Mommy says.

Mia is a baby. She needs someone to watch over her, I tell Mommy.

Grandpa looks at me.

He's talking now?

Yes.

Well, that's just great. Grandpa looks at Mommy.

He has tears in his eyes. But he's happy. Happy tears.

Elliot runs past us. He has a football.

Let's play.

Mind the apples.

I look up and behind a tree Jack Hyde is watching us.

I wake. Instantly. My heart racing. Not from fear, but because I was startled by something in my dream.

What was it?

I can't remember. It's light outside, and Ana is fast asleep beside me. I check the time. It's nearly 6:30. I woke up before the alarm. That hasn't happened for a while—not with my dreamcatcher beside me. The radio comes to life, but I switch it off and snuggle up to Ana, nuzzling her neck.

She stirs.

"Morning, baby," I whisper, grazing her earlobe. I run my hand up to her breast and gently caress her, feeling her nipple harden beneath my palm. She stretches beside me and I trace her skin to her hip and hold her close. My erection sits in the cleft of her behind.

"You're pleased to see me," she says, and wiggles, squeezing my dick.

"I'm very pleased to see you." My fingers skate over her belly to her sex and I caress her, there and everywhere, as I remind her that there are advantages to waking up together. She's warm, willing, and ready when I reach over to the bedside table, grab a condom, and lie on top of her, taking my weight on my elbows. I ease her legs apart, then kneel up and rip open the foil packet. "I can't wait until Saturday."

She looks up at me eagerly. "Your party?"

"No. I can stop using these fuckers." I roll the condom on.

"Aptly named." She giggles.

"Are you giggling, Miss Steele?"

"No," she says, trying and completely failing to keep a straight face.

"Now is not the time for giggling." I stare her down, daring her to giggle again.

"I thought you liked it when I giggle."

"Not now. There's a time and a place for giggling. This is neither. I need to stop you, and I think I know how."

Slowly, I ease into her.

"Ah," she says in my ear.

And we make sweet, unhurried love.

No more giggling.

DRESSED AND ARMED WITH a coffee and a large trash bag from Mrs. Jones, I head up to my playroom. I have one duty to perform while Ana has her shower.

I open the door, step inside, and set down my coffee. It took months to design and source everything for this room. And now I don't know when or if I'll use it again.

Don't dwell, Grey.

I face the reason I'm here—in the corner, my canes. I have several, from all over the world. I run my fingers over my favorite, fashioned from rosewood and the finest leather. I bought it in London. The others are made from bamboo, plastic, carbon fiber, wood, and suede. Carefully, I load them all into the trash bag.

I'm sorry to see them go.

There, I've admitted it to myself.

Ana is never going to enjoy these, it's just not her thing.

What is your thing, Anastasia?

Books.

It will never be canes.

I lock up the room and head to my study. Once there, I pack the canes in a closet to be dealt with at a later date, but for now, she won't have to see them again.

At my desk, I finish my coffee, aware that Ana will be ready for breakfast shortly. But before I join her in the kitchen, I call Welch.

"Mr. Grey?"

"Good morning. I wanted to talk to you about Jack Hyde."

ANA IS BEAUTIFUL AND elegant in gray when she enters the kitchen for breakfast. She should wear skirts more often; she has great legs. My heart swells. With love. With pride. And humility. It's a new and exciting feeling that I hope I never take for granted.

"What would you like for breakfast, Ana?" Gail asks her.

"I'll just have some granola. Thank you, Mrs. Jones." She sits beside me at the counter, her cheeks pink.

I wonder what she's thinking about? This morning? Last night? The spreader bar?

"You look lovely," I offer.

"So do you." Her smile is demure. Ana hides her inner freak well.

"We should buy you some more skirts. In fact, I'd love to take you shopping."

She doesn't seem overly impressed with this idea. "I wonder what will happen at work today," she says, and I know she's referring to SIP to change the subject.

"They'll have to replace the sleazeball," I mutter, but when, I don't know. I've placed a moratorium on any hiring until we've conducted a staff audit.

"I hope they take on a woman as my new boss."

"Why?"

"Well, you're less likely to object to me going away with her," she says.

Oh, baby, you'd appeal to women, too.

Mrs. Jones places my omelet in front of me, distracting me from my brief and extremely enjoyable fantasy of Ana with another woman.

"What's so funny?" Ana asks.

"You are. Eat your granola, all of it, if that's all you're having."

She purses her lips but picks up a spoon and devours her breakfast.

"Can I take the Saab today?" she asks when she finishes the last spoonful.

"Taylor and I can drop you at work."

"Christian, is the Saab just for decoration in the garage?"

"No." Of course not.

"Then let me drive it to work. Leila's no longer a threat."

Why is everything a battle?

It's her car, Grey.

"If you want," I concede.

"Of course I do."

"I'll come with you."

"What? I'll be fine on my own."

I try a different tack. "I'd like to come with you."

"Well, if you put it like that," Ana acquiesces with an accepting nod.

ANA IS BEAMING. SHE'S so delighted with the car. I'm not sure she's concentrating on what I'm saying. I show her the ignition on the center console.

"Strange place," she says, but she's practically bouncing in her seat and touching everything.

"You're quite excited about this, aren't you?"

"Just smell that new-car smell. This is even better than the Submissive Special. Um, the A3," she says quickly.

"Submissive Special?" I try not to laugh. "You have such a way with words, Miss Steele." I sit back. "Well, let's go." I wave her in the direction of the exit.

Ana claps her hands, starts the car, and pops the gearshift into drive. If I had known how thrilled she would be about driving this car, I might have relented and let her drive it sooner.

I love seeing her this happy.

The Saab glides up to the barrier and Taylor follows us out onto Virginia Street in the Q7.

This is the first time Ana has ever driven us anywhere, the first time she's driven me. As a driver, she's confident and seems adept; however, I'm not an easy passenger. This I know. I don't like being driven at all, except by Taylor. I prefer to be in the driver's seat.

"Can we have the radio on?" she asks, as we pull up at a stop sign.

"I want you to concentrate."

She snaps back, "Christian, please, I can drive with music on."

Choosing to ignore her attitude, I switch on the radio. "You can play your iPod and MP3 discs as well as CDs on this," I inform her.

The sound of The Police fills the car: a golden oldie, "King of Pain." I turn it down—it's too loud.

"Your anthem," Ana says with an impish grin.

She's making fun of me. Again.

"I have this album, somewhere," she says.

And I remember she mentioned "Every Breath You Take" in an e-mail; the stalker's anthem, she called it. She's funny—at my expense. I shake my head because she was right. After she left me, I did loiter outside her apartment during my morning run.

She's gnawing at her bottom lip. Is she worried about my reaction? About Flynn? What he might say? "Hey, Miss Smart Mouth. Come back." She stops abruptly at the red light. "You're very distracted. Concentrate, Ana. Accidents happen when you don't concentrate."

"I'm just thinking about work."

"Baby, you'll be fine. Trust me."

"Please don't interfere—I want to do this on my own. Please. It's important to me," she says.

Me? Interfere? Only to protect you, Ana.

"Let's not argue, Christian. We've had such a wonderful morning. And last night was—" Her cheeks pink. "Heaven."

Last night. I close my eyes and see her ass in the air. I move in my seat as my body reacts. "Yes. Heaven." And I realize that I've said it out loud. "I meant what I said."

"What?"

"I don't want to let you go."

"I don't want to go," she says.

"Good." I relax a little. *She's still here, Grey.*

ANA DRIVES INTO THE SIP parking lot and parks the Saab.

Ordeal over.

She's not that bad a driver.

"I'll walk you to work. Taylor will take me from there," I offer, as we climb out of the car. "Don't forget we're seeing Flynn at seven this evening." I hold out my hand for her. She presses the remote, locking the car, and gives the Saab a fond look before taking my hand.

"I won't forget. I'll compile a list of questions for him."

"Questions? About me? I can answer any questions you have about me."

Her smile is indulgent. "Yes, but I want the unbiased, expensive charlatan's opinion."

I fold her into my arms, my hands cupping hers and holding them behind her back. "Is this a good idea?" I stare into her startled eyes. They soften and she offers to forgo seeing Flynn. She shakes one of her hands loose from my grip and tenderly strokes my face. "What are you worried about?"

"That you'll go."

"Christian, how many times do I have to tell you—I'm not going anywhere. You've already told me the worst. I'm not leaving you."

"Then why haven't you answered me?"

"Answered you?"

"You know what I'm talking about, Ana."

She sighs and her expression clouds. "I want to know that I'm enough for you. That's all."

"And you won't take my word for it?" I release her.

When will she realize she's all I'll ever want?

"Christian, this has all been so quick," she says. "And by your own admission, you're fifty shades of fucked up. I can't give you what you need. It's just not for me. But that makes me feel inadequate, especially seeing you with Leila. Who's to say that one day you won't meet someone who likes doing what you do? And who's to say you won't, you know, fall for her? Someone much better suited to your needs." She looks away.

"I knew several women who like doing what I like to do. None of them appealed to me the way you do. I've never had an emotional connection with any of them. It's only ever been you, Ana."

"Because you never gave them a chance. You've spent too long locked up in your fortress. Look, let's discuss this later. I have to go to work. Maybe Dr. Flynn can offer us his insight."

She's right. We shouldn't be discussing this in a parking lot. "Come." I hold out my hand, and together we walk to her office.

TAYLOR PICKS ME UP in the Audi, and on our way to Grey House, I contemplate my conversation with Ana.

Am I locked in a fortress?

Maybe.

I stare out of the window. Commuters hurry to work, wrapped up in minutiae of their daily lives. Here, in the back of my car, I'm removed from it all. I've always been that way. Removed: isolated as a child or isolating myself as I grew up, walled off in a fortress.

I've been scared of feeling.

Feeling anything except my anger.

My constant companion.

Is that what she means? If it is, it's Ana who's given me the key to escape. And all that's holding her back is Flynn's opinion.

Maybe once she's heard what he has to say, she'll say yes.

A guy can hope.

I allow myself a brief moment to see what real optimism feels like . . .

It's terrifying.

It could end badly. Again.

My phone buzzes. It's Ana. "Anastasia. You okay?"

"They've just given me Jack's job—well, temporarily," she says, with no preamble at all.

"You're kidding."

"Did you have anything to do with this?" Her tone is accusatory.

"No. No, not at all. I mean, with all due respect, Anastasia, you've only been there for a week or so—and I don't mean that unkindly."

"I know," she says, and she sounds demoralized. "Apparently, Jack really rated me."

"Did he, now?" I'm so glad that asshole is out of her life. "Well, baby, if they think you can do it, I'm sure you can. Congratulations. Perhaps we should celebrate after we've seen Flynn."

"Hmm. Are you sure you had nothing to do with this?"

Does she really think I'd lie to her? Maybe because of my confession last night?

Or maybe they've given her the job because I won't let them recruit outside the company.

Hell.

"Do you doubt me? It angers me that you do."

"I'm sorry," she says quickly.

"If you need anything, let me know. I'll be here. And Anastasia?"

"What?"

"Use your BlackBerry."

"Yes, Christian."

I ignore her sarcastic tone and, shaking my head, I take a deep breath. "I mean it. If you need me, I'm here."

"Okay," she says. "I'd better go. I have to move offices."

"If you need me. I mean it."

"I know. Thank you, Christian. I love you."

Those three little words.

They used to terrify me and now I can't wait to hear her say them.

"I love you, too, baby."

"I'll talk to you later."

"Laters, baby."

Taylor pulls up outside Grey House.

"José Rodriquez will be delivering some portraits to Escala tomorrow," I inform him.

"I'll let Gail know."

"He's staying the night."

Taylor checks me in the rearview mirror, surprised, I think. "Tell Gail that, too," I add.

"Yes, sir."

AS THE ELEVATOR SHOOTS up to my floor, I allow myself a brief fantasy about married life. It's weird, this *hope*. Something I'm not used to. I imagine taking Ana to Europe, to Asia; I could show her the world. We could go anywhere and everywhere. I could take her to England; she'd love that.

And we'd return home to Escala.

Escala? Maybe my apartment has too many memories of other women. Perhaps I should buy a house that would be ours alone, where we can create our own memories.

But keep Escala. It's handy for downtown.

The elevator doors open.

"Good morning, Mr. Grey," the new girl says.

"Good morning—" I can't remember her name.

"Coffee?"

"Please. Black. Where's Andrea?"

"She's around." New Girl smiles and scurries off to make my coffee.

AT MY DESK, I start perusing houses on the Web. Andrea knocks and enters a few minutes later with my coffee. "Good morning, Mr. Grey."

"Andrea, good morning. I'd like you to send some flowers to Anastasia Steele."

"What would you like to send?"

"She's had a promotion. Maybe some roses. Pink and white."

"Okay."

"And can you get me Welch on the line?"

"Yes, sir. Do you remember that you're seeing Mr. Bastille today at Escala, not here?"

"Oh, yes. Thanks. Who has the gym booked here?"

"The yoga club, sir."

I make a face.

She stifles her smile. "Ros would like a word, too."

"Thanks."

AFTER MY CALLS, I go back to looking at houses online. I remember when I bought my apartment at Escala, a broker did it all for me—and it was bought off-plan. It seemed like a great investment, so I didn't look further.

Now I'm getting sucked into real-estate websites, looking at property after property. It's addictive.

I've coveted the big houses on the shores of the Sound for all the years that I've sailed. I think I'd like a home that looks out across the water. I grew up in a house like that; my parents live on the shores of Lake Washington.

A family house.

Family.

Kids.

I shake my head. Not for a long time. Ana's young. She's only twenty-one. We have years before we have to think about kids.

What kind of father would I be?

Grey, don't dwell.

I'd like to find a plot of land and build a house. Make it ecologically sustainable. Elliot could build it for me. A couple of the listings meet my criteria; one of the homes looks out across the Sound. The house is old, built in 1924, and has only come on the market in the last few days. The photographs are spectacular. Especially at twilight. For me, it will be all about the view. We can knock this house down and start again.

I check what time the sun will set this evening: 9:09 p.m.

Maybe I could get an appointment to see the house at dusk one night this week.

Andrea knocks and enters.

"Mr. Grey, I have a choice of flowers here." She places some printouts on my desk.

"This one." It's a huge basket of white and blush roses. Ana will love it. "And can you get me in to see this house? I'll e-mail you the link. I'd love to do an evening around sunset as soon as possible."

"Sure. What would you like to say on the card?"

"Put the florist through to me when you've ordered the flowers, and I'll tell her directly."

"Very good, Mr. Grey." Andrea exits.

Three minutes later she puts through the florist, who cheerily asks me to dictate a message for the card. "Congratulations, Miss Steele. And all on your own! No help from your overfriendly, neighborhood, megalomaniac CEO. Love, Christian."

"Got that. Thank you, sir."

"Thank you."

I go back to looking at houses online, and I know that I'm distracting myself from the anxiety I feel about Ana's appointment with Flynn later today. *Displacing*. That's what Flynn would call it. But my happiness hangs in the balance.

And houses are distracting.

What will Flynn say?

After half an hour of looking at houses and not doing any work, I give in and call Flynn.

"You've caught me between patients. Is it urgent?" he says.

"I was calling to find out about Leila."

"She had another comfortable night. I hope to see her later this afternoon. And I'm seeing you, too, yes?"

"Yes. With Ana."

There's a moment of silence between us, and I know this is one of John's tricks. He doesn't speak, hoping I will fill in the ensuing silence.

"Christian, what is it?"

"This evening. Ana."

"Yes."

"What will you say?"

"To Ana? I don't know what she's going to ask me. But whatever she asks, I'll give her the truth."

"That's what I'm worried about."

He sighs. "I have a different perception of you than you have of yourself, Christian."

"I'm not sure whether to be reassured or not."

"I'll see you this evening," he responds.

LATER THAT AFTERNOON I'M back from my meeting with Fred and Barney and I'm about to click on another real-estate agent's website when I notice an e-mail from Ana. I haven't heard from her all day. She must be busy.

From: Anastasia Steele
Subject: Megalomaniac . . .
Date: June 16 2011 15:43
To: Christian Grey

. . . is my favorite type of maniac. Thank you for the beautiful
flowers. They've arrived in a huge wicker basket that makes
me think of picnics and blankets.

x

She's using her phone. Finally!

From: Christian Grey
Subject: Fresh Air
Date: June 16 2011 15:55
To: Anastasia Steele

Maniac, eh? Dr. Flynn may have something to say about that.

You want to go on a picnic?

We could have fun in the great outdoors, Anastasia . . .

How is your day going, baby?

Christian Grey
CEO, Grey Enterprises Holdings, Inc.

From: Anastasia Steele
Subject: Hectic
Date: June 16 2011 16:00
To: Christian Grey

The day has flown by. I have hardly had a moment to myself
to think about anything other than work. I think I can do this!
I'll tell you more when I'm home.

Outdoors sounds . . . interesting.

Love you.

A x

P.S.: Don't worry about Dr. Flynn.

How does she know that I'm fretting about him?

From: Christian Grey
Subject: I'll try . . .
Date: June 16 2011 16:09
To: Anastasia Steele

. . . not to worry.

Laters, baby. x

Christian Grey
CEO, Grey Enterprises Holdings, Inc.

In the gym at Escala, Bastille is on a roll, but I get a couple of kicks in and knock him on his ass.

"Something is eating you, Grey. Same girl?" he sneers, as he springs off the floor.

"None of your goddamn business, Bastille."

We circle each other, looking for an opportunity to take each other down.

"Ah! I love that you have a woman in your life giving you a hard time. When do I get to meet her?"

"I'm not sure that's going to happen."

"Keep your left up, Grey. You're vulnerable."

He comes at me with a front kick, but I feint and skip left, avoiding him.

"Good move, Grey."

AFTER MY SHOWER, I get a text from Andrea.

> **ANDREA PARKER**
> Realtor can see you this evening.
> 8:30 p.m.
> Is that okay?
> Her name is Olga Kelly.

> Great!
> Thanks.
> Please text me the address.

I WONDER WHAT ANA will make of the house. Andrea sends me the address and the access code to the front gates. I memorize the code and find the house on Google Maps. While I'm working out a route from Flynn's place to the house, my phone rings. It's Ros. I stare out of the balcony window as she gives me some good news.

"Fred has come back to me. Kavanagh is a go," she says.

"Ros, that's great."

"He has a few technical issues that he wants his people to discuss with our people. He'd like a meeting tomorrow morning. Breakfast. I've told Andrea."

"Tell Barney and we'll go from there," I respond, and I turn away from the view of Seattle and the Sound to find Ana watching me.

"Will do. I'll see you tomorrow."

"Good-bye." I hang up and stride over to meet my girl, who looks sweet and shy as she stands on the threshold of the living room. "Good evening, Miss Steele." I kiss her and hold her close. "Congratulations on your promotion."

"You've showered."

"I've just had a workout with Claude."

"Oh."

"Managed to knock him on his ass twice." It's a memory to be savored.

"That doesn't happen often?"

"No. Very satisfying when it does. Hungry?"

She shakes her head and seems worried.

"What?" I ask.

"I'm nervous. About Dr. Flynn."

"Me, too. How was your day?" I release her.

"Great. Busy. I couldn't believe it when Elizabeth, our HR person, asked me to fill in. I had to go to the senior editors' lunch meeting and I managed to get two of the manuscripts I was championing considered."

She doesn't stop. She's excited. Her eyes are shining; she's passionate about what she's been doing. It's a pleasure to behold.

"Oh—there's one more thing I should tell you. I was supposed to have lunch with Mia."

"You never mentioned that."

"I know, I forgot. I couldn't make it because of the meeting, and Ethan took her out to lunch instead."

The beach bum, with my sister. I'm not sure how I feel about that. "I see. Stop biting your lip."

"I'm going to freshen up," she says quickly, before I can ask her any more about Kavanagh and my baby sister.

I've never really thought about my sister dating. There was that guy at the ball, but she didn't seem particularly interested in him.

"I USUALLY RUN HERE from home," I mention, as I park the Saab. "This is a great car."

"I think so, too. Christian . . . I—"

My gut tightens.

"What is it, Ana?"

"Here." From her purse she hands me a small dark box wrapped in a ribbon. "This is for you for your birthday. I wanted to give it to you now—but only if you promise not to open it until Saturday, okay?"

I swallow to contain my relief. "Okay."

She takes a deep, nervous breath. Why is she anxious about this? I shake it. It sounds small and plastic. What the hell has she given me?

I look up at her.

Whatever it is, I'm sure I'm going to love it. I give her a broad smile.

My birthday is on Saturday. She will be here on that day—or so this gift implies. Doesn't it?

"You can't open it until Saturday," she says, waving a finger at me.

"I get it. Why are you giving this to me now?" I place it in my inside pocket.

"Because I can, Mr. Grey."

"Why, Miss Steele, you stole my line."

"I did. Let's get this over with, shall we?"

FLYNN STANDS AS WE enter his office. "Christian."

"John." We shake hands. "You remember Anastasia?"

"How could I forget? Anastasia, welcome."

"Ana, please," she says, as they shake hands. He directs us toward his sofas.

I wait for Ana to sit down, admiring the fit of the navy dress she's changed into, and I take the other sofa but sit close to her. Flynn takes his usual chair. I place my hand on Ana's and give her hand a squeeze.

"Christian has requested that you accompany him to one of our sessions," Flynn says. "Just so you know, we treat these sessions with absolute confidentiality—"

He stops when Ana interrupts. "Oh—um, I've signed an NDA," she says quickly.

Shit.

I release her hand.

"A nondisclosure agreement?" Flynn gives me a puzzled look.

I shrug but say nothing.

"You start all your relationships with women with an NDA?" he asks me.

"The contractual ones, I do."

Flynn stifles a smile. "You've had other types of relationships with women?"

Shit.

"No," I respond, amused by his reaction. He knows this.

"As I thought." Flynn turns his attention back to Ana. "Well, I guess we don't have to worry about confidentiality, but may I suggest that the two of you discuss this at some point? As I understand, you're no longer entering into that kind of contractual relationship."

"Different kind of contract, hopefully," I say, with a look at Ana.

She blushes.

"Ana. You'll have to forgive me, but I probably know a lot more about you than you think. Christian has been very forthcoming."

She glances at me.

"An NDA? That must have shocked you," Flynn continues.

"Oh, I think the shock of that has paled into insignificance, given Christian's most recent revelations," she says, and her voice is low and husky.

I shift in my seat.

"I'm sure. So, Christian, what would you like to discuss?"

I shrug. "Anastasia wanted to see you. Perhaps you should ask her."

But Ana is staring at a box of tissues on the coffee table in front of her.

"Would you be more comfortable if Christian left us for a while?" Flynn asks her.

What?

Ana's eyes dart to me. "Yes," she says.

Fuck.

But?

Shit.

I stand up. "I'll be in the waiting room."

"Thank you, Christian," Flynn says. I give Ana a long look, trying to tell her I'm ready for this commitment that I want to make to her. Then I stalk out of the room, closing the door behind me.

Flynn's receptionist Janet looks up, but I ignore her and wander into the waiting room, where I flop into one of the leather armchairs.

What will they discuss?

You, Grey. You.

Closing my eyes, I lean back and try to relax.

Blood thrums through my ears, a thump, thump, thump that's impossible to ignore.

Find your happy place, Grey.

I'm in the orchard with Elliot. We're kids. We're running through the trees. Laughing. Picking apples. Eating apples. Grandpa is watching us. Laughing too.

We're in a kayak with Mom. Dad and Mia are ahead of us. We're racing Dad.

Elliot and I are paddling with all our twelve-year-old fury. Mom is laughing. Mia splashes us with her paddle.

"Fuck! Elliot!" We're on a Hobie Cat. He has the tiller and we're flying the hull, tearing downwind across Lake Washington.

Elliot whoops with joy as we trapeze over the side of the hull. We're wet. Exhilarated. And fighting the wind.

I'm making love to Ana. Breathing in her scent. Kissing her throat, her breast.

My body responds.

Fuck. No. I open my eyes and stare at the utilitarian brass chandelier on the white ceiling, and shift in my seat.

What are they talking about?

I get up and start pacing. But I sit down again and leaf through one of the *National Geographic* magazines, the only publication that Flynn offers in his waiting room.

I can't concentrate on any of the articles.

Nice photographs, though.

I can't bear this. I pace once more. Then sit down and check the address of the house that we're going to visit. And if Ana doesn't like what she hears from Flynn and doesn't want to see me again? I'll just have to get Andrea to cancel.

I get up, and before I know what I'm doing I'm outside, walking away from the conversation. The conversation about me.

I WALK THREE TIMES around the block and return to Flynn's office. Janet says nothing as I stride past her, knock on the door, and enter.

Flynn gives me a benevolent smile. "Welcome back, Christian," he says.

"I think time is up, John."

"Nearly, Christian. Join us."

I sit down beside Ana and place my hand on her knee. She gives nothing away, and that's frustrating, but she doesn't pull her knee out of my reach.

"Did you have any other questions, Ana?"

She shakes her head.

"Christian?"

"Not today, John."

"It may be beneficial if you both come again. I'm sure Ana will have more questions."

If that's what she wants. If that's what it takes. I clasp her hand and her eyes meet mine.

"Okay?" I ask gently.

She nods and gives me a reassuring smile. I hope the squeeze I give her hand lets her know how relieved I am. I turn to Flynn.

"How is she?" I ask him, and he knows I'm referring to Leila.

"She'll get there," he says.

"Good. Keep me updated as to her progress."

"I will."

I turn to Ana. "Should we go and celebrate your promotion?"

Her shy nod is a relief.

WITH MY HAND ON the small of her back, I escort Ana out of the office. I'm anxious to hear what was discussed. I need to know if he put her off.

"How was that?" I ask, aiming for nonchalance, as we walk out onto the street.

"It was good."

And? I'm dying here, Ana.

She looks at me and I have no idea what she's thinking. It's unnerving, and annoying. I scowl.

"Mr. Grey. Please don't look at me that way. Under doctor's orders I am going to give you the benefit of the doubt."

"What does that mean?"

"You'll see."

Will she marry me or not? Her winsome smile doesn't give me any clues.

Hell. She's not going to tell me. She's leaving me hanging. "Get in the car," I snap, and I open her door.

Her phone rings and she gives me a wary look before answering. "Hi," she says enthusiastically.

Who is it?

"José," she mouths at me, answering my unspoken question. "Sorry I haven't called you. Is it about tomorrow?" she says to him, but without looking away from me. "Well, I'm actually staying with Christian right now, and if you want to, he says you can stay at his place."

Oh yes. He's delivering the stunning photographs of Ana, his love letters to her.

Embrace her friends, Grey.

She frowns and turns away, crossing the sidewalk to lean against the building.

Is she okay? I watch her carefully. Waiting.

"Yes. Serious," she answers, her expression stern.

What's serious?

"Yes," she responds, and then she scoffs, indignant, "Of course I am . . . You could pick me up from work . . . I'll text you the address . . . Six?" She grins. "Cool. I'll see you then." She hangs up and walks back toward the car.

"How's your friend?" I ask.

"He's well. He'll pick me up from work, and I think we'll go for a drink. Would you like to join us?"

"You don't think he'll try anything?"

"No!"

"Okay." I hold my hands up. "You hang out with your friend, and I'll see you later in the evening. See? I can be reasonable."

She purses her lips—amused, I think. "Can I drive?"

"I'd rather you didn't."

"Why, exactly?"

"Because I don't like to be driven."

"You managed this morning, and you seem to tolerate Taylor driving you."

"I trust Taylor's driving implicitly."

"And not mine?" she exclaims, and puts her hands on her hips. "Honestly, your control-freakishness knows no bounds. I've been driving since I was fifteen."

I shrug. I want to drive.

"Is this my car?"

"Of course it's your car."

"Then give me the keys, please. I've driven it twice, and only to and from work. Now you're having all the fun." She folds her arms, standing firm, stubborn as ever.

"But you don't know where we're going."

"I'm sure you can enlighten me, Mr. Grey. You've done a great job of it so far." And just like that she defuses the moment. She's the most disarming person I've ever met. She won't answer me. She's left me hanging, and I want to live the rest of my life with her.

"Great job, eh?" I ask through my smile.

She flushes. "Mostly, yes." And her eyes are alight with amusement.

"Well, in that case." I hand her the keys and open the driver's door for her.

I take a deep breath as she pulls into the traffic. "Where are we going?" she asks, and I have to remind myself that she hasn't lived in Seattle long enough to know her way around.

"Continue along this street."

"You're not going to be more specific?" she asks.

I give her a slight smile.

Tit for tat, baby.

She narrows her eyes.

"At the light, turn right," I say.

She stops rather too suddenly, throwing us both forward, then indicates and moves on.

"Steady. Ana!"

Her mouth sets in a grim line.

"Left here." Ana puts her foot down and we speed up the street. "Hell! Gently, Ana." I grab the dashboard. "Slow down!" She's doing thirty-eight through the neighborhood!

"I am slowing down!" she shouts as she brakes.

I sigh and get to the heart of what I want to talk about, trying and failing to sound casual. "What did Flynn say?"

"I told you. He says I should give you the benefit of the doubt." Ana signals to pull over.

"What are you doing?"

"Letting you drive."

"Why?"

"So I can look at you."

I laugh. "No, no. You wanted to drive. So you drive, and I'll look at you."

She turns to say something to me.

"Keep your eyes on the road!" I shout.

She screeches to a halt just before a traffic light, releases her seatbelt, and storms out of the car, slamming the door.

What the hell?

She stands on the sidewalk with arms crossed in what's both a defensive and combative pose, glaring at me. I scramble out after her. "What are you doing?" I ask, completely thrown.

"No. What are *you* doing?"

"You can't park here." I point to the abandoned Saab.

"I know that."

"So why have you?"

"Because I've had it with you barking orders. Either you drive or you shut up about my driving!"

"Anastasia, get back in the car before we get a ticket."

"No."

I run my hands through my hair. What's got into her?

I look down at her. I'm at a loss. Her expression changes, softening. Damn it, is she laughing at me? "What?" I ask.

"You."

"Oh, Anastasia! You are the most frustrating female on the planet." I throw my hands in the air. "Fine. I'll drive."

She grabs my jacket and tugs me against her body. "No. You are the most frustrating man on the planet, Mr. Grey."

She looks up at me with guileless blue eyes that pull me under and I'm drowning and I'm lost. Lost in a different way. I put my arms around her, holding her close. "Maybe we're meant for each other, then." She smells amazing. I should bottle this.

Soothing. Sexy. Ana.

She hugs me hard and rests her cheek against my chest.

"Oh. Ana, Ana, Ana." I kiss her hair and hold her.

It's weird, embracing in the street.

Another first. No. A second. I held her on the street near Esclava.

She moves and I release her, and without saying a word, I open the passenger door and she gets in the car.

At the wheel, I start the car and pull into the traffic. There's a Van Morrison song playing over the sound system and I hum along as we head toward the on-ramp for I-5. "You know, if we had gotten a ticket, the title of this car is in your name," I tell her.

"Well, good thing I've been promoted. I can afford the fine."

And I hide my amusement as we head north on I-5.

"Where are we going?" she asks.

"It's a surprise. What else did Flynn say?"

"He talked about FFFSTB or something."

"SFBT. The latest therapy option."

"You've tried others?"

"Baby, I've been subjected to them all. Cognitivism, Freud, functionalism, Gestalt, behaviorism. You name it, over the years I've done it."

"Do you think this latest approach will help?"

"What did Flynn say?"

"He said not to dwell on your past. Focus on the future—on where you want to be."

I nod, but I don't understand why she hasn't accepted my proposal.

That's where I want to be.

Married.

Perhaps he said something to discourage her. "What else?" I ask, trying to get an inkling of what he might have said to dissuade her.

"He talked about your fear of being touched, although he called it something else. And about your nightmares and your self-abhorrence." I turn to meet her gaze.

"Eyes on the road, Mr. Grey," she scolds.

"You were talking forever, Anastasia. What else did he say?"

"He doesn't think you're a sadist."

"Really?" Flynn and I have differing views on this. He cannot step into my shoes. He doesn't really understand.

Ana continues. "He says that that term's not recognized in psychiatry. Not since the nineties."

"Flynn and I have differing opinions on this."

"He said you always think the worst of yourself. I know that's true. He also mentioned sexual sadism—but he said that was a lifestyle choice, not a psychiatric condition. Maybe that's what you're thinking about."

Ana, you have no idea.

You will never know the depths of my depravity.

"So, one talk with the good doctor and you're an expert."

She sighs. "Look, if you don't want to hear what he said, don't ask me," she says.

Fair point, Miss Steele.

Grey. Stop hounding the girl.

She turns her attention to the passing cars.

Damn.

"I want to know what you discussed," I say in a tone that I hope sounds conciliatory. I leave I-5 and head west on Northwest Eighty-fifth Street.

"He called me your lover."

"Did he, now? Well, he's nothing if not fastidious about his terms. I think that's an accurate description. Don't you?"

"Did you think of your subs as lovers?"

Lovers? Leila? Susannah? Madison? Each of my submissives comes to mind.

"No. They were sexual partners. You're my only lover. And I want you to be more."

"I know. I just need some time, Christian. To get my head around these last few days."

I look over at her.

Why didn't she say that earlier?

I can live with that.

Of course I can give her some time.

I'd wait until time stands still, for her.

I RELAX AND ENJOY the drive. We're in the suburbs of Seattle, but heading west toward the Sound. I think I've timed this appointment just right and we'll catch the sunset over Puget Sound.

"Where are we going?" she asks.

"Surprise."

She gives me a curious smile and turns to take in our surroundings through the window.

Ten minutes later I spy the corroded white metal gates that I recognize from the photograph I've seen online. I pull in at the bottom of an impressive driveway and punch the security code into the keypad. With a creaky groan, the heavy gates swing open.

I glance at Ana.

Will she like this place?

"What is it?" she asks.

"An idea." I steer the Saab through the gates.

The driveway is longer than I thought. To one side there's an overgrown meadow. It's big enough to install a tennis court or basketball court—or both.

"Hey bro, let's shoot some hoops."

"Elliot, I'm reading."

"Reading is not going to get you laid."

"Fuck off."

"Hoops. Come on, man," he whines.

Reluctantly, I abandon my tattered copy of Oliver Twist *and follow him out to the yard.*

ANA LOOKS STUNNED AS we arrive at the grand entrance portico and I park beside a BMW sedan. The house is sprawling and actually quite imposing from the outside.

I cut the engine, and Ana's baffled.

"Will you keep an open mind?" I ask.

She arches a brow. "Christian, I've needed an open mind since the day I met you."

And I can't disagree. She's right. As ever.

The realtor is waiting inside the large vestibule. "Mr. Grey." She greets me warmly and we shake hands.

"Miss Kelly."

"Olga Kelly," she announces to Ana.

"Ana Steele," she responds.

The realtor steps aside. The house smells a little musty from what must be months of disuse. But I'm not here to look at the interior. "Come." I direct Ana and take her hand. Having studied the floor plans at length I know where I want to go and how to get there. I lead her from the vestibule through an archway into an inner hallway, past a grand staircase, and into what was once the main living room.

There are several open French doors on the far side, which is great because the place needs airing. Tightening my hold on Ana's hand, I take her through the nearest door, onto the terrace outside.

The view is every bit as arresting and dramatic as the photographs suggested: the Sound in all its glory at dusk. Already there are lights twinkling from the distant shores of Bainbridge Island, where we sailed last weekend, and beyond that, the Olympic Peninsula.

There is so much sky and the sunset is astounding.

Ana and I stand hand in hand and stare, enjoying the spectacular view. Her face is radiant. She loves it.

She turns to look at me. "You brought me here to admire the view?"

I nod.

"It's staggering, Christian. Thank you," she says, and stares once more at the opal sky.

"How would you like to look at it for the rest of your life?" My heart starts hammering.

This is one hell of a pitch, Grey.

Her face whips to mine. She's startled.

"I've always wanted to live on the coast," I explain. "I sail up and down the Sound, coveting these houses. This place hasn't been on the market long. I want to buy it, demolish it, and build a new house—for us."

Her eyes grow impossibly large.

"It's just an idea," I whisper.

She looks over her shoulder into the old living room. "Why do you want to demolish it?" she asks.

"I'd like to make a more sustainable home, using the latest ecological techniques. Elliot could build it."

"Can we look around the house?"

"Sure." I shrug. Why does she want to look around?

I follow Ana and the realtor as she gives us the tour. Olga Kelly is in her element as she takes us through the numerous rooms, describing the features of each. Why Ana wants to see the whole house is a mystery to me.

As we file up the sweeping staircase, she turns to me. "Couldn't you make the existing house more ecological and self-sustaining?"

This house?

"I'd have to ask Elliot. He's the expert in all this."

Ana likes *this* house.

Keeping the house wasn't what I had in mind.

The realtor takes us into the master suite. It has full-height windows opening onto a balcony that looks out at the spectacular view. We both pause for a moment and stare at the darkening sky, and the last traces of the sun that can still be seen. It's a glorious vista.

We wander through the rest of the bedrooms; there are many, and the last overlooks the front of the house. The realtor suggests that the meadow might be a suitable place for a paddock and stables.

"The paddock would be where the meadow is now?" Ana asks, looking dubious.

"Yes," the realtor replies.

Back downstairs, we make our way through to the terrace once more and I rethink my plans. The house wasn't what I imagined living in, but it looks well built and solid enough and with a comprehensive update, it could serve our needs. I glance at Ana.

Who am I kidding?

Wherever Ana is, that's my home.

If this is what she wants . . .

Outside on the terrace, I hold her. "Lot to take in?" I ask.

She nods.

"I wanted to check that you liked it before I bought it."

"The view?"

I nod.

"I love the view, and I like the house that's here."

"You do?"

"Christian, you had me at the meadow," she says with a shy smile.

This means she's not leaving.

Surely.

I cup her face, my fingers in her hair, and pour all my gratitude into one kiss.

"THANKS FOR LETTING US look around," I say to Miss Kelly. "I'll be in touch."

"Thank you, Mr. Grey. Ana," she says, eagerly shaking hands with each of us.

Ana likes it!

My relief is palpable as we climb into the Saab. Olga has switched on the external lights and the driveway is edged with winking lamps. The house is growing on me. It has a sprawling, grand quality to it. I'm sure Elliot can work his magic on the place and make it more ecologically sustainable.

"So, you're going to buy it?" Ana asks when we're on our way back to Seattle.

"Yes."

"You'll put Escala on the market?"

"Why would I do that?"

"To pay for—" She stops.

"Trust me, I can afford it."

"Do you like being rich?"

I want to scoff. "Yes. Show me someone who doesn't."

She chews her finger.

"Anastasia, you're going to have to learn to be rich, too, if you say yes."

"Wealth isn't something I've ever aspired to, Christian."

"I know. I love that about you. But then again, you've never been hungry."

In the periphery of my vision, I see her turn and look at me, but I can't make out her expression in the darkness.

"Where are we going?" she asks, and I know she's changing the subject.

"To celebrate."

"Celebrate what, the house?"

"Have you forgotten already? Your acting-editor role."

"Oh yes."

"Where?"

"Up high at my club." They'll still be serving food at this hour, and I'm hungry.

"Your club?"

"Yes. One of them."

"How many do you belong to?"

"Three."

Please don't ask me about them.

"Private gentleman's clubs? No women allowed?" she teases, and I know she's laughing at me.

"Women allowed. At all of them." Especially one. A Dominant's haven. Though I haven't been for a while.

She gives me an inquisitive look.

"What?" I ask.

"Nothing," she says.

I LEAVE THE CAR with the valet and we travel up to The Mile High Club at the top of Columbia Tower. Our table isn't ready immediately, so we sit at the bar.

"Cristal, ma'am?" I hand Ana a glass of chilled champagne.

"Why, thank you, Sir." She stresses the last word and bats her eyelashes at me. She moves her legs, drawing my attention to them. Her dress is hiked up, exposing a little more of her thigh.

"Are you flirting with me, Miss Steele?"

"Yes, Mr. Grey, I am. What are you going to do about it?"

Oh, Ana. I love when you throw down the gauntlet.

"I'm sure I can think of something," I murmur. Carmine, the maître d', gives me a wave. "Come—our table's ready."

I step back and hold out my hand while she gracefully slips off the barstool, and I follow. Her ass looks great in this dress.

Ah. A wicked idea pops into my mind.

Before she sits down at our table, I touch her elbow. "Go and take your panties off," I whisper in her ear. "Go." Now.

She inhales quickly, and I remember the last time she went pantyless and how she turned the tables on me then; maybe she will again. She gives me a haughty look, but without saying a word hands me her glass of champagne and saunters to the ladies' restroom.

While I wait at the table I scan the menu. It reminds me of our dinner in the private room at The Heathman. I summon the waiter and hope that Ana won't give me a hard time because I'm ordering her meal.

"Can I help you, Mr. Grey?"

"Please. A dozen Kumamotos, to start. And then two orders of the sea bass with hollandaise sauce and sautéed potatoes. And a side of asparagus."

"Very good, sir. Would you like anything from the wine list?"

"Not right now. We'll stick to the champagne."

The waiter scuttles off and Ana appears, a secret smile playing on her lips.

Oh, Ana. She wants to play . . . but I'm not going to touch her. Yet.

I want to drive her crazy.

Standing, I motion to the seat. "Sit beside me." She slides in and I join her, mindful not to sit too close. "I've ordered for you. I hope you don't mind." Careful not to touch her fingers with mine, I give her back her glass of champagne.

She fidgets beside me but takes a sip of the Cristal.

The waiter returns with the oysters on ice. "I think you liked oysters last time you tried them."

"Only time I've tried them." Her breathing stalls. She's . . . eager.

"Oh, Miss Steele—when will you learn?" I tease, taking an oyster from the dish. I lift my hand from my thigh and she leans back in anticipation of my touch, but I reach for some lemon.

"Learn what?" she whispers, as I squeeze lemon juice over the shellfish.

"Eat." I hold the shell up to her mouth. She parts her lips and I rest the shell on her bottom lip. "Tip your head back slowly."

With a smoldering look, she does as she's told and I tip the oyster into her mouth. She closes her eyes in appreciation, and I help myself to one.

"Another?" I ask.

She nods, and this time I add a little mignonette sauce, and still I don't touch her. She swallows and licks her lips.

"Good?"

She nods.

I eat another, then feed her one more.

"Hmm . . ." she says, and the sound resonates the length of my cock.

"Still like oysters?" I ask, as she swallows the final one.

She nods again.

"Good."

I place my hands on my thighs, flexing my fingers, and I'm gratified when she shifts beside me. But as much as I want to, I refrain from touching her. The waiter tops off our champagne and clears our plates. Ana squeezes her thighs together and rubs her hands over them. And I think I hear a frustrated sigh.

Oh, baby. Craving my touch?

The waiter returns with our entrées.

Ana eyes me with suspicious recognition as the food is placed on the table. "A favorite of yours, Mr. Grey?"

"Most definitely, Miss Steele. Though I believe it was cod at The Heathman."

"I seem to remember we were in a private dining room then, discussing contracts."

"Happy days. This time I hope to get to fuck you." I reach for my knife and she fidgets beside me. I take a bite of sea bass.

"Don't count on it," she mutters, and I know without looking that she's pouting.

Oh, playing hard to get, Miss Steele?

"Speaking of contracts," she continues. "The NDA."

"Tear it up."

"What? Really?"

"Yes."

"You're sure I'm not going to run to *The Seattle Times* with an exposé?"

I laugh, knowing how shy she is. "No. I trust you. I'm going to give you the benefit of the doubt."

"Ditto," she says.

"I'm very glad you're wearing a dress."

"Why haven't you touched me, then?"

"Missing my touch?" I tease.

"Yes," she exclaims.

"Eat."

"You're not going to touch me, are you?"

"No." I hide my amusement.

She looks outraged.

"Just imagine how you'll feel when we're home," I add. "I can't wait to get you home."

"It will be your fault if I combust here on the seventy-sixth floor." She sounds pissed.

"Oh, Anastasia. We'd find a way to put the fire out."

She narrows her eyes and takes a bite of her supper. The sea bass is delicious, and I'm hungry. She wriggles in her seat and her dress rides up a little, exposing more of her skin. She takes another bite, then puts down her knife, and runs her hand up the inside of her thigh, her fingertips drumming as she does.

She's toying with me. "I know what you're doing."

"I know that you know, Mr. Grey. That's the point." She takes an asparagus stalk between her fingers and, with a sideways glance at me, dips the spear into the hollandaise sauce and swirls it around and around.

"You're not turning the tables on me, Miss Steele." I take the asparagus from her. "Open your mouth."

She opens her mouth and runs her tongue across her bottom lip.

Tempting, Miss Steele. Very tempting.

"Wider," I command, and she bites her bottom lip but complies, easing the stalk into her mouth and sucking.

Fuck.

It might as well be my cock.

She moans quietly and takes a bite and reaches for me.

I stop her with my other hand. "Oh no you don't, Miss Steele." I brush my lips across her knuckles. "Don't touch," I scold, and place her hand on her knee.

"You don't play fair."

"I know." I raise my champagne glass. "Congratulations on your promotion, Miss Steele." We clink glasses.

"Yes, kind of unexpected," she says, looking a little discouraged. Does she doubt herself? I hope not.

"Eat." I change the subject. "I am not taking you home until you've finished your meal, and then we can really celebrate."

"I'm not hungry. Not for food."

Ana. Ana. So easily distracted.

"Eat, or I'll put you across my knee, right here, and we'll entertain the other diners."

She shifts in her seat, making me think a spanking might be welcome, but her pursed lips tell a different story. Picking up an asparagus stalk, I dip the head into the hollandaise. "Eat this," I tempt her.

She does, keeping her eyes on me.

"You really don't eat enough. You've lost weight since I've known you."

"I just want to go home and make love."

I grin. "So do I, and we will. Eat up."

She sighs as if in defeat and starts tucking into her food. I follow her example. "Have you heard from your friend?" I ask.

"Which one?"

"The guy staying in your apartment."

"Oh, Ethan. Not since he took Mia out for lunch."

"I'm doing some work with his and Kate's father."

"Oh?"

"Yes. Kavanagh seems like a solid guy."

"He's always been good to me," she answers, and my earlier thoughts about a hostile takeover of Kavanagh's business recede.

She finishes her supper and places her knife and fork on her plate.

"Good girl."

"What now?" she asks, her expression needy.

"Now? We leave. I believe you have certain expectations, Miss Steele. Which I intend to fulfill to the best of my ability."

"The best of your a-a-bility?" she stutters.

I grin and stand up.

"Don't we have to pay?"

"I'm a member here. They'll bill me. Come, Anastasia, after you." I step aside, and Ana gets up from the table and pauses beside me to smooth her dress down over her thighs.

"I can't wait to get you home." I follow her out of the restaurant and stop to talk to the maître d'.

"Thanks, Carmine. Superb as always."

"You're welcome. Mr. Grey."

"And can you call down to have the car brought to the front?"

"No problem. Good night."

As we get into the elevator I take Ana's elbow and steer her toward the far corner. I stand behind her and watch as other couples get in.

Hell.

Linc, Elena's ex, joins us, wearing a shit brown suit.

What an asshole.

"Grey," he acknowledges me. I nod, and I'm relieved when he turns around. The fact that he's here, only inches away, makes what I'm about to do even more exciting.

The doors close and I kneel quickly, pretending to do up my shoelace. I place my hand around Ana's ankle, and as I stand, I skim my hand up her calf, past her knee, and her thigh, to her ass. Her naked ass.

She tenses and I slide my left arm around her waist and pull her to me while my fingers skate down her ass, to her sex. The elevator stops at another floor and we shuffle back as one to let more people on board. But I'm not interested in them. Slowly I brush her clitoris, once, twice, thrice, and then move my fingers back to her heat. "Always so ready, Miss Steele," I whisper as I inch my middle finger inside her. I hear her faint gasp. "Keep still and quiet," I warn, so only she can hear me. Slowly I move my finger in and out, on and on, as my excitement grows. She grabs the arm I have around her waist and she squeezes. Holding on. Her breathing accelerates, and I know she's trying to keep quiet as I silently torment her with my fingers.

The sway of the elevator as it stops to pick up more passengers adds to the rhythm. She sags against me, then pushes her ass against my hand, wanting more. Faster.

Oh, my greedy, greedy girl.

"Hush," I breathe, and nuzzle her hair. I ease a second finger inside her and continue to pump them in and out. She tips her head back against my chest, exposing her throat. I want to kiss her, but that would draw too much attention to what we're doing. Her grip on me tightens.

Damn. I'm bursting. My jeans are too fucking tight. I want her, but now really is not the place.

Her fingers dig into me.

"Don't come. I want that later," I whisper, and I splay my hand on her belly and press down, knowing that this will emphasize everything she's feeling. Her head is lolling against my chest and she's biting down on her bottom lip.

The elevator stops.

There's a loud ping and the doors open on the first floor.

Slowly I withdraw my hand as the passengers exit, and I kiss the back of her head.

Well done, Ana.

She did not give us away.

I hold her for a moment longer.

Linc turns and nods as he leaves with a woman who I assume is his present wife. When I'm sure Ana is able to stand, I release her. She gazes up at me, her eyes dark and smoky with lust.

"Ready?" I ask, then slip both of my fingers briefly into my mouth. "Mighty fine, Miss Steele." I give her a wicked grin.

"I can't believe you just did that," she whispers, breathless and arousing.

"You'd be surprised what I can do, Miss Steele." Reaching out, I neaten her hair, pushing it behind her ear. "I want to get you home, but maybe we'll only make it as far as the car." I give her a quick smile, check that my jacket is covering the front of my jeans, then take her hand and lead her out of the elevator. "Come," I bid her.

"Yes, I want to."

"Miss Steele!"

"I've never had sex in a car," she says, as her heels echo on the marble floor. I stop and tip her head up so that we are eye to eye.

"I'm very pleased to hear that. I have to say I'd be very surprised, not to say mad, if you had."

"That's not what I meant," she huffs.

"What did you mean?"

"Christian, it was just an expression."

"The famous expression, 'I've never had sex in a car.' Yes, it just trips off the tongue." And I'm teasing her, she's so easy to provoke.

"Christian, I wasn't thinking. For heaven's sake, you've just . . . um, done that to me in an elevator full of people. My wits are scattered."

"What did I do to you?"

She purses her lips. "You turned me on, big-time. Now take me home and fuck me."

I laugh, taken aback. I had no idea she could be quite so crude. "You're a born romantic, Miss Steele." I take her hand and we head to the valet, who has the Saab parked up and ready. I give him a large tip and open the passenger door for Ana.

"So you want sex in a car?" I ask, as I switch on the ignition.

"Quite frankly, I would have been happy with the lobby floor."

"Trust me, Ana, so would I. But I don't enjoy being arrested at this time of night, and I didn't want to fuck you in a restroom. Well, not today."

"You mean there was a possibility?"

"Oh yes."

"Let's go back."

I turn to look at her earnest expression. She's so unexpected sometimes. I start to laugh, and soon we are both laughing. It's cathartic after the build-up of sexual tension. I place a hand on her knee, caressing her and she stops laughing and looks at me with large, dark eyes.

I could fall into them and never come back. She's so beautiful.

"Patience, Anastasia," I whisper and we move off, heading up Fifth Avenue.

She's silent but restless as we drive back but she gives me the occasional come-hither look through her dark lashes.

I know that look.

Yes. Ana. I want you, too.

In every way . . . Please say yes.

The Saab glides into a parking space in Escala's garage. I switch off the engine, thinking about her wish for sex in a car. I have to admit it's not something I've done, either. She's biting her lip, her expression . . . wanton.

Groin-tighteningly wanton.

Gently, I release her lip with my fingers. I love that she wants me as much as I want her. "We will fuck in the car at a time and place of my choosing," I whisper. "Right now, I want to take you on every available surface of my apartment."

"Yes," she says, even though it's not a question. I lean toward her and she closes her eyes and puckers her lips, offering me a kiss. Her cheeks are slightly flushed.

I take a quick look around the car.

We could.

No.

She opens her eyes, waiting impatiently.

"If I kiss you now, we won't make it into the apartment. Come." Resisting the urge to jump her, I climb out of the car, and together we wait for the elevator.

I hold her hand, stroking her knuckles with my thumb. Setting up a rhythm that I hope to repeat with my dick in a few minutes.

"So, what happened to instant gratification?" she asks.

"It's not appropriate in every situation, Anastasia."

"Since when?"

"Since this evening."

"Why are you torturing me so?"

"Tit for tat, Miss Steele."

"How am I torturing you?"

"I think you know."

And I watch as realization dawns on her face.

Yes, baby.

I love you. And I want you to be my wife.

But you won't tell me your answer.

"I'm into delayed gratification, too," she whispers, and gives me a shy smile.

She *is* torturing me!

I tug her hand and pull her into my arms, and my fingers wrap around her nape and I angle her head so I can look into her eyes. "What can I do to make you say yes?" I beg her.

"Give me some time, please," she says. I groan and my lips are on hers, my tongue seeking hers. The elevator doors open and we shuffle in, maintaining our embrace. And she's lit from within. Her hands are on me. Everywhere. In my hair. Around my face. On my ass. And she's kissing me back with such passion.

I burn for her.

Pushing her against the wall, reveling in the fervor of her kiss, I pin her with my hips and my erection. I have one hand in her hair and one on her chin.

"You own me," I whisper against her mouth. "My fate is in your hands, Ana."

She pushes my jacket off my shoulders and the elevator stops and opens and we are in the foyer. I notice that the usual flowers are missing from the foyer table.

Fucking A.

Foyer table, surface number one!

I press Ana against the wall and she finishes the job and pushes my jacket off me onto the floor. My hand runs up her thigh, taking the hem of her dress with it while we kiss. I boost her skirt higher.

"First surface here," I murmur, and lift her suddenly. "Wrap your legs around me."

She does as she's told and I lay her down on the hall table. From my jeans pocket I fish out a condom and hand it to Ana and undo my fly.

Her fingers impatiently open the packet.

Her enthusiasm is arousing.

"Do you know how much you turn me on?"

"What? No. I . . ." She's breathless.

"Well, you do. All the time." I grab the packet from her hands and roll on the condom while staring at her. Her hair is cascading over the edge of the table and she's staring up at me, her eyes brimming with want.

I move between her legs and lift her ass off the table, spreading her legs farther apart. "Keep your eyes open. I want to see you." I take both her hands and slowly sink into her.

It takes all my willpower to keep my eyes open on hers. She's exquisite.

Every fucking inch of her.

She closes her eyes and I thrust hard into her. "Open," I urge, and I tighten my hold on her hands.

She cries out but opens her eyes. They are wild and blue and beautiful. Slowly I pull out of her, then sink into her again. She watches me.

Her eyes on me.

God, I love her.

I move faster. Loving her. The only way I really know how.

Her mouth opens, slack, wide, beautiful. And her legs tense around me.

This is going to be quick.

And she comes around me, taking me with her.

She calls out through her climax.

"Yes, Ana!" I cry. And come and come and come.

I collapse on her, release her hands, and rest my head on her chest. I close my eyes. She cradles my head, running her fingers through my hair as I catch my breath. I look up at her. "I'm not finished with you yet," I whisper, and I kiss her and disengage myself.

Hastily, I do up my fly and lift her off the table.

We stand in the foyer holding each other. We're under the careful watch of the women in my Madonna and Child paintings that line the walls.

I think they approve of my girl.

"Bed," I whisper.

"Please," she says. And I take her to bed and make love to her once more.

SHE COMES, RIDING ME hard, and I hold her upright as I watch her spiral out of control.

Fuck, it's erotic.

She's naked, her breasts bouncing, and I let go, climaxing inside her, my head back, my fingers digging into her hips. She flops down on my chest, panting hard.

As I recover my breath, I run my fingers down her back, dewy with her sweat.

"Satisfied, Miss Steele?"

She mumbles her agreement. Then she looks up at me; her expression is a little dazed, but she angles her head.

Shit. She's going to kiss my chest.

I take a deep breath and she plants a soft, warm kiss on my chest.

It's okay. The darkness is quiet. Or gone. I don't know.

I relax and roll us onto our sides.

"Is sex like this for everyone? I'm surprised anyone ever goes out," she says, with a sated smile.

She makes me feel ten feet tall. "I can't speak for everyone, but it's pretty damned special with you, Anastasia." My lips touch hers.

"That's because you're pretty damned special, Mr. Grey." She caresses my face.

"It's late. Go to sleep." I kiss her and pull her to me so that we're spooning, her back to my front, and I tug up the comforter.

"You don't like compliments." Her voice is drifting. She's tired.

No. I'm not used to them.

"Go to sleep, Anastasia."

"I loved the house," she mutters.

That means she might say yes. I grin into her hair and nuzzle her. "I love you. Go to sleep."

And I close my eyes as her scent fills my nostrils.

A house. A wife. What more do I need? Please say yes, Ana.

Ana's cry drags me from my sleep. Opening my eyes, I wake. She's beside me and I think she's asleep. "Flying too close," she whimpers. The early-morning light bleeds pink and bright between the blinds, illuminating her hair. "Icarus," she says.

Leaning up on my elbow, I check to see if she's asleep. I haven't heard her talk in her sleep for a while. She turns over so that she's facing me. "Benefit of the doubt," she says. And her face relaxes.

Benefit of the doubt?

Is this about me?

She said it yesterday. She said she was going to give me the benefit of the doubt.

It's more than I deserve.

Much more than you deserve, Grey.

I plant a chaste kiss on her forehead, switch off the alarm before it wakes her, and get out of bed. I have an early-morning meeting to discuss Kavanagh's fiber-optic requirements.

In the shower, I think about my schedule for the day. I have Kavanagh. Then I fly down to WSU via Portland with Ros. Drinks in the evening with Ana and her photographer friend.

And I'll put an offer on that house today. Ana says she loved it. I grin as I rinse the shampoo from my hair.

Just give her time, Grey.

IN MY CLOSET, I slip on my pants and notice my jacket from yesterday slung over the chair. I fish through the pockets and grab Ana's present. It still produces a tantalizing rattle.

I slip it into my inside pocket, pleased that it will rest close to my heart.

You're getting sentimental in your old age, Grey.

SHE'S STILL CURLED UP asleep when I check on her before I leave. "Gotta go, baby." I kiss her neck. She opens her eyes and turns over to face me. In her drowsy state, she smiles up at me, then her expression changes.

"What time is it?"

"Don't panic. I have a breakfast meeting."

"You smell good," she whispers. She stretches out beneath me and encircles my neck with her hands. Her fingers trail in my hair. "Don't go."

"Miss Steele, are you trying to keep a man from an honest day's work?"

She gives me a sleepy nod, her eyes a little dazed. Desire blooms in my body; she looks so damn sexy. Her smile is captivating and it takes all my self-control not to strip off my clothes and slip back into bed. "As tempting as you are, I have to go." I kiss her and stand. "Laters, baby." I leave before I change my mind and cancel the meeting.

Taylor looks troubled when I join him in the garage.

"Mr. Grey. I have a problem."

"What is it?"

"My ex-wife called. My daughter may have appendicitis."

"Is she in the hospital?"

"They're admitting her now."

"You should go."

"Thank you. I'll drop you at work first."

"Thanks. I appreciate it."

TAYLOR IS DEEP IN thought when we pull up outside Grey House.

"Let me know how she is."

"I may not be back until tomorrow morning."

"It's fine. Go. I hope Sophie's okay."

"Thank you, sir."

I watch him zoom off. He's seldom preoccupied . . . but this is family. Yes. Family comes first. Always.

Andrea is waiting for me when I step out of the elevator.

"Good morning, Mr. Grey. Taylor called. I'll arrange a driver for you here and in Portland."

"Good. Everyone here?"

"Yes. In your boardroom."

"Great. Thanks, Andrea."

THE MEETING GOES WELL. Kavanagh looks refreshed, no doubt from his recent vacation in Barbados, where he met my brother for the first time. He says he likes him. Considering Elliot's fucking his daughter, that's a good thing.

When they left, Kavanagh and his people seemed satisfied with our conversation. Now all that remains is to haggle over the price of the contract. Ros will have to take the lead on that with cost projections from Fred's division.

Andrea has laid out the usual breakfast spread; I grab a croissant and head back to my office with Ros. "What time do you want to leave?" Ros asks me.

"Our driver will pick us up at ten."

"I'll see you in the foyer downstairs," Ros confirms. "I'm excited. I've never been in a helicopter."

Her grin is infectious.

"I found a house yesterday and I want to buy it. Will you handle the details?"

"As your lawyer, sure, of course I will."

"Thanks. I owe you."

"You will." She laughs. "See you downstairs."

I stand alone inside my office, feeling elated. I'm buying a house. The Kavanagh contract will be a great boost to the company. And I had a wonderful evening with my girl. At my desk, I send her an e-mail.

From: Christian Grey
Subject: Surfaces
Date: June 17 2011 08:59
To: Anastasia Steele

I calculate that there are at least 30 surfaces to go. I am looking forward to each and every one of them. Then there's the floors, the walls—and let's not forget the balcony.

After that there's my office . . .

Miss you. x

Christian Grey
Priapic CEO, Grey Enterprises Holdings, Inc.

I take a look around my office. Yes, there's a lot of potential here: the sofa, the desk. Andrea knocks on the door and enters with my coffee. I marshal my wayward thoughts, and my body.

She places the coffee on my desk. "More coffee."

"Thank you. Can you get the realtor for the house I saw yesterday on the line?"

"Sure thing, sir."

My discussion with Olga Kelly is brief. We agree on a price to take back to the seller, and I give her Ros's details so we can move quickly with inspections if the offer is accepted.

I check my e-mail. And I'm pleased to see a response from Ana to my earlier missive.

From: Anastasia Steele
Subject: Romance?
Date: June 17 2011 09:03
To: Christian Grey

Mr. Grey
You have a one-track mind.

I missed you at breakfast.

But Mrs. Jones was very accommodating.

A x

Accommodating?

From: Christian Grey
Subject: Intrigued
Date: June 17 2011 09:07
To: Anastasia Steele

What was Mrs. Jones accommodating about?

What are you up to, Miss Steele?

Christian Grey
Curious CEO, Grey Enterprises Holdings, Inc.

From: Anastasia Steele
Subject: Tapping Nose
Date: June 17 2011 09:10
To: Christian Grey

Wait and see—it's a surprise.

I need to work . . . let me be.

Love you.

A x

From: Christian Grey
Subject: Frustrated
Date: June 17 2011 09:12
To: Anastasia Steele

I hate it when you keep things from me.

Christian Grey
CEO, Grey Enterprises Holdings, Inc.

From: Anastasia Steele
Subject: Indulging you
Date: June 17 2011 09:14
To: Christian Grey

It's for your birthday.

Another surprise.

Don't be so petulant.

A x

Another surprise? When I pat down my jacket pocket, I'm reassured by the presence of the box that Ana's given me.

She's spoiling me.

ROS AND I ARE in the car on the way to Boeing Field. My phone flashes. It's a text from Elliot.

> ELLIOT
> Hey, asshole. Bar. This evening.
> Kate's getting in touch with Ana.
> You'd better be there.

> **Where are you?**

> ELLIOT
> Layover Atlanta
> Missed me?

> **No.**

> ELLIOT
> Yeah you have. Well I'm back and
> you're getting your beer on tonight Bro.

It's been a while since I went drinking with my brother and at least I won't be alone with Ana and her photographer friend.

> **If you insist.**
> **Safe travels.**

ELLIOT
Laters dude.

Our flight to Portland is uneventful, though it's a revelation how giddy Ros can be. She's like a kid in a candy store during the flight. Fidgeting. Pointing. Nonstop commentary on everything she sees. It's a side of Ros I never knew existed. Where's the cool, collected lawyer I know? I'm reminded how quietly appreciative Ana was when I first took her up in *Charlie Tango*.

When we land, I pick up a voice mail from the realtor. The seller has accepted my offer. They must want a quick sale.

"What?" asks Ros.

"I've just bought that house."

"Congratulations."

AFTER A LENGTHY MEETING with the president and vice president of economic development at WSU in Vancouver, Ros and I are in conversation with Professor Gravett and her postgraduate team. The professor is in full flow. "We've been able to isolate the DNA of the microbe that's responsible for nitrogen fixation."

"What does that mean, exactly?" I ask.

"In layman's terms, Mr. Grey, nitrogen fixation is essential for soil diversity, and as you know, diverse soils recover from shocks like drought far more quickly. We can now study how to activate the DNA in the microbes that live in the soil in the sub-Saharan region. In a nutshell, we'll be able to get the soil to hold its nutrients for far longer, making it more productive per hectare."

"Our results will be published in the *Soil Science Society of America Journal* in a couple of months. We're sure to double our funding once the article comes out," Professor Choudury says. "And we'll need to get your input on potential funding sources that align with your philanthropic objectives."

"Of course," I say, offering my support. "As you know, I think your work here should be shared broadly to benefit as many people as possible."

"We've kept that goal front and center in all that we're doing."

"Good to hear."

The president of the university nods in agreement. "We're very excited about this discovery."

"It is quite the achievement. Congratulations, Professor Gravett, and to your team."

She glows in response to the compliment. "Thanks to you."

Embarrassed, I glance at Ros, and it's as if she can read my mind. "We should be going," she says to the group, and we push our chairs back.

The president shakes my hand. "Thank you for your continued support, Mr. Grey. As you've seen, your contribution to the environmental sciences department makes a huge difference to us."

"Keep up the good work," I say. I'm anxious to get back to Seattle. The photographer will be delivering those photographs to Escala, and then seeing Ana. I'm fighting my jealous impulses and, so far, successfully keeping them under control. But I will be happier when we set back down at Boeing Field and I join them both at the bar. In the meantime, I have a surprise for Ros.

OUR TAKEOFF IS SMOOTH; I pull back the collective and *Charlie Tango* ascends like a graceful bird into the air above the Portland heliport. Ros smiles with girlish delight. I shake my head; I had no idea she could be this excitable, but then again, I always feel a rush on takeoff. Once I've finished talking to the tower, Ros's disembodied voice asks over my headset, "How is your private merger going?"

"Good, thanks."

"Hence the house?"

"Yeah. Something like that."

She nods and we fly in silence over Vancouver and WSU, homebound toward my goal.

"Did you know Andrea was getting married?" I ask her. This has bothered me since I found out.

"No. When?"

"Last weekend."

"She kept that quiet." Ros sounds surprised.

"She says that she didn't tell me because of our non-fraternization policy. I didn't know we had one."

"It's a standard clause within our employment contracts."

"Seems a little harsh."

"She's married someone in-house?"

"Damon Parker."

"Engineering?"

"Yes. Can we help him with a green card? I believe he's on an H-1B visa at the moment."

"I'll look into it. Though I'm not sure there are any shortcuts."

"I'd appreciate it, and I have a surprise for you." I veer a few degrees northeast and we fly for about ten minutes. "There!" I point toward the barnacle on the horizon that will become Mount St. Helens as we get closer.

Ros actually squeals with delight. "You changed the flight plan?"

"Just for you."

As we fly nearer, the mountain looms over the landscape. It looks like a child's drawing of a volcano, tipped with snow, craggy at the top, and nestled within the lush green forest of Gifford National Park.

"Wow! It's so much bigger than I thought," says Ros as we get nearer.

It's an impressive sight.

I bank slowly and we circle the crater, which is no longer complete. The north wall has gone, a casualty of the 1980 eruption. It looks eerily deserted and otherworldly from up here; the scars of the last eruption are still obvious, running down the mountain, displacing the forest and defacing the landscape beneath it.

"This is amazing. Gwen and I have been meaning to bring the kids to see this place. I wonder if it will erupt again?" Ros speculates, as she snaps photos with her phone.

"I have no idea, but let's head home now that you've seen it."

"Good idea, and thank you." Ros gives me a grateful smile, her eyes shining.

I veer west following the South Fork Toutle River. We should

DARKER 463

be back at Boeing Field in forty-five minutes, which will give me plenty of time to join Ana, the photographer, and Elliot for drinks.

Out of the corner of my eye I see the master caution light flicker.

What the fuck?

The fire light in the engine T-handle flashes, and *Charlie Tango* dips.

Shit. We have a fire in engine one. I take a deep breath but smell nothing. Quickly, I execute an S-turn to see if I can see smoke. A trail of gray fog lingers in our flight path.

"What's wrong? What is it?" Ros asks.

"I don't want you to panic. We have a fire in one of the engines."

"What!" She clutches her purse and her seat. I shut engine number one down and blow the first fire bottle while deciding whether to land or carry on with one engine. *Charlie Tango* is equipped to fly with a single engine . . .

I want to get home.

I give the landscape a quick sweep, looking for a safe place to land, should we need to. We're a little low, but I can see a lake in the distance—Silver Lake, I think. It's clear of trees at the southeast end.

I'm about to radio a distress signal when the second engine fire light flashes.

Motherfucking hell!

My anxiety balloons and I clench my fingers around the collective.

Fuck. Focus, Grey.

Smoke filters into the cabin and I open my windows and quickly check all the instrument stats. The dash is lighting up like fucking Christmas. And it may be that the electronics are failing. I have no choice. We're going to have to land. And I have a split second to decide whether to kill the engine or keep it going to get us down.

I hope to Christ I can do this. Sweat beads on my brow and I dash it away with my hand. "Hang on, Ros. This is going to get rough."

Ros makes a wailing sound, but I ignore her.

We're low. Too low.

But maybe we have time. That's all I need. Some time. Before she blows.

I lower the collective and reduce the throttle to idle and we autorotate, diving down, and I'm trying to maintain speed to keep the rotors spinning. We hurtle toward the ground.

Ana. Ana? Will I see her again?

Fuck. Fuck. Fuck.

We're close to the lake. There's a clearing. My muscles burn as I fight to hold the collective in place.

Fuck.

I see Ana in a kaleidoscope of images like the photographer's portraits: laughing, pouting, pensive, stunning, beautiful. *Mine.*

I can't lose her.

Now! Do it, Grey.

I flare—pitching *Charlie Tango*'s nose up and dipping the tail to reduce the forward speed. The tail clips some treetops. By some miracle, *Charlie Tango* stays in line as I increase the throttle. We crash-land, tail first, on the edge of the clearing, the EC135 skidding and bumping across the terrain before she comes to a complete stop, in the middle of the clearing, the rotors whipping branches off some nearby fir trees. I activate the second fire bottle, shut down the engine and the fuel valves, and apply the rotor brake. I switch off all electrics, lean across and punch the buckle on Ros's harness so it releases, lean farther, and open the door. "Get out! Stay low!" I roar, and push her so that she scuttles out of her seat and falls out to the ground. I grab the fire extinguisher beside me, scramble out my side, and run to the back of the cabin to spray CO_2 over the smoking engines. The fires are quickly subdued and I take a step back.

Ros, bedraggled and deeply shaken, stumbles over to me as I stand and stare with horror at *Charlie Tango*, my pride and joy. In an uncharacteristic show of emotion, Ros throws her arms around me and I freeze. It's only then that I notice she's sobbing.

"Hey. Hey. Hush. We're down. We're safe. I'm sorry. I'm sorry." I hold her for a moment to calm her down.

"You did it," she chokes out. "You did it. Fuck. Christian. You got us down."

"I know." And I can't quite believe we're both in one piece. I step away from her and hand her a handkerchief from my pocket.

"What the hell happened?" she says as she wipes away her tears.

"I don't know." I'm stumped. What the fuck happened? Both engines? But I've no time for this now. She could blow. "Let's move away. I've done an emergency shutdown on all the systems, but there's enough fuel on board to give Mount St. Helens a run for her money should it go up."

"But my stuff—"

"Leave it."

We're in a small clearing, the tops of some of the fir trees now missing. The smell of fresh pine, jet fuel, and acrid smoke is in the air. We shelter under the trees at what I assume is a safe distance from *Charlie Tango*, and I scratch my head.

Both engines?

It's rare for both to go. Bringing *Charlie Tango* down intact and using the fire extinguisher means her engines are preserved and we can find out what went wrong.

But a postmortem and crash analysis is for another time, and for the FAA. Right now, Ros and I have to decide what to do.

I wipe my forehead with my jacket sleeve, and I realize I'm sweating like a fucking pig.

"At least I have my purse and my phone," Ros mutters. "Shit. I don't have a signal." She holds her phone skyward, searching for service. "Do you? Will someone come and rescue us?"

"I didn't have time for a distress call."

"That's a no, then." Her face falls.

I grab my phone from my inside pocket, and I'm cheered when I hear the rattle of Ana's gift, but I don't have time to think about that, now. I just know I have to get back to her.

"When I don't report in, they'll know we're missing. The FAA has our flight plan." My phone has no signal either but I check the GPS on the off chance that it's working and set to our current position.

"Do you want to stay or go?"

Ros looks nervously around at our rugged surroundings. "I'm a city girl, Christian. There are all kinds of wild animals out here. Let's go."

"We're on the south side of the lake. We're a couple of hours from the road. Maybe we can get help there."

Ros starts in heels but is barefoot by the time we hit the road and it makes our progress slow. Fortunately, the ground is soft, but not so the road.

"There's a visitors' center along here." I inform her. "We could get help there."

"They're probably closed. It's after five," Ros says, her voice wavering. We're both sweating and in need of water. She's had enough, and I'm beginning to wish we'd stayed near *Charlie Tango*. But who knows how long it would have taken for the authorities to find us?

My watch says 5:25 p.m.

"Do you want to stay here and wait?" I ask Ros.

"No way." She hands me her shoes. "Can you?" She makes a snapping-twig motion with her fists.

"You want me to break the heels off? They're Manolos."

"Please, just do it."

"Okay." Feeling that my manhood is on trial, I use all my strength to snap off the first heel. It gives after a moment or two, as does the second. "Here. I'll get you a new pair when we're home."

"I'll hold you to that."

She puts on her shoes once more and we set off down the road.

"How much money do you have?" I ask.

"On me? About two hundred dollars."

"I have about four hundred. Let's see if we can hitch a ride."

WE MAKE FREQUENT STOPS to rest Ros's feet. I offer to carry her at one point, but she refuses. She's quiet but resilient. I'm grateful that she's held it together and not succumbed to panic, but I don't know how long that will last.

We're taking a rest break when we hear the thumping rumble

of a semi. I stick my thumb out in the hopes that the vehicle will stop. Sure enough, we hear a grinding of gears and the gleaming rig comes to a standstill a few feet away, the engine rumbling on, growling, waiting for us.

"Looks like we got a ride." I flash a grin at Ros, trying to keep her buoyant. Her smile is thin, but it's a smile. I help her to her feet and almost carry her to the passenger door. A bearded young guy in a Seahawks cap opens the passenger door from the inside. "You folks okay?" he asks.

"We've had better days. Where you heading?"

"I'm taking this empty box back to Seattle."

"That's where we're going. Will you give us a ride?"

"Sure thing. Climb aboard."

Ros frowns and whispers, "I would never do this if I was on my own." I help Ros to scramble up and I follow her into the cab. It's clean and smells of new car and pine forest, though I suspect that's from the air freshener hanging from a hook on the dash.

"What you folks doing down here?" the guy asks, as Ros settles on the comfortable-looking couch at the back of the cabin. It looks brand-new.

I glance at Ros, who gives me a small shake of her head.

"We're lost. You know." I keep my answer vague.

"Okay," he says, and I know he doesn't believe us, but he puts the beast into gear and we rumble off in the direction of Seattle.

"Name's Seb," he says.

"Ros."

"Christian."

He leans over and shakes our hands in turn. "You guys thirsty?" he asks.

"Yes," we both say at once.

"Back of the cabin there's a small fridge. Should find some San Pellegrino in there."

San Pellegrino?

Ros retrieves two bottles and we drink gratefully. I never knew sparkling water could taste so good.

I notice a microphone hanging from above.

"CB radio?" I ask.

"Yep. But it's not working. It's new. Damn thing." He gives it a frustrated knock with his knuckles. "Whole rig is new. This is her maiden voyage."

That's why he's driving so slowly.

I check the time. It's 7:35. My phone is dead. As is Ros's. *Damn.*

"Do you have a mobile?" I ask Seb.

"No way. I want my ex-wife to leave me alone. When I'm out in the cab it's just me and the road."

I nod.

Fuck. Ana might be worried. But I'll worry her more if I tell her what's happened before she sees me. And she's probably at the bar. With José Rodriguez. I hope Elliot and Katherine will keep an eye on him.

Feeling glum and a little helpless, I stare out at the scenery. We'll shortly be on I-5, and on our way home.

"You guys hungry? I have some kale and quinoa wraps in the fridge left over from my lunch."

"That's mighty hospitable. Thank you, Seb."

"You folks mind a little music while we drive?" he asks when we've finished his lunch.

Oh, hell.

"Sure," says Ros, but I hear her uncertainty.

Seb has Sirius on his radio and he turns it to a jazz station. The mellow notes of Charlie Parker's saxophone playing "All the Things You Are" fill the cab.

"All The Things You Are."

Ana. Is she missing me?

I'm on the road with a kale-and-quinoa-eating trucker who listens to cool jazz. This is not how I expected my day to go. I give Ros a brief look. She's sunk onto the couch and is fast asleep. I breathe a sigh of relief and close my eyes.

If I hadn't been able to land.

Jesus. Ros's family would have been devastated.

Both engines?

What is the likelihood?

And *Charlie Tango* had just had all her routine checks.

Something doesn't add up.

The rumble of the truck goes on and on and on. Billie Holiday is singing. Her voice is soothing, like a lullaby. "You're My Thrill."

Charlie Tango is hurtling to the ground.

I'm pulling back on the collective.

No. No. No.

There's a woman screaming.

Screaming.

Ana. Screaming.

No.

There's smoke. Choking smoke.

And we're hurtling down.

I can't stop this.

Ana is screaming.

No. No. No.

And *Charlie Tango* hits the ground.

Nothing.

Black.

Silence.

Nothing.

I wake suddenly, gasping. It's dark, except for the occasional light on the freeway. I'm in the cab.

"Hey." It's Seb.

"Sorry, I must have fallen asleep."

"No problem. You two must be bushed. Your friend is still asleep." Ros is out on the couch behind us.

"Where are we?"

"Allentown."

"What? Great." I peer out and we're still on I-5, but the lights of Seattle are in the distance. Cars whiz past us. This has to be the slowest piece of transport I have ever traveled in. "Where are you heading in Seattle?"

"The docks. Pier 46."

"Right. Could you drop us in town? We can pick up a cab."

"No problem."

"So have you always done this?"

"No. I've done a little of everything. But this truck. This one is mine and I'm working for myself."

"Ah. An entrepreneur."

"Exactly."

"I do a little of that myself."

"One day I'd like to own a fleet of these." He slaps his hands on the wheel.

"I hope you do."

SEB DROPS US AT Union Station.

"Thank you. Thank you. Thank you," says Ros as we climb out of his truck.

I hand him four hundred dollars.

"I can't take your money, Christian," Seb says, holding up his hand and refusing the cash.

"In that case, here's my card." From my wallet, I give him my card. "Call me. And we can talk about the fleet you want to own."

"Sure thing," says Seb, without looking at my card. "Nice meeting you folks."

"Thanks. You're a lifesaver." And with that, I shut the door and we wave him away.

"Can you believe that guy?" Ros asks.

"Thank God he turned up. Let's get a cab."

IT TAKES US TWENTY minutes to get to Ros's place, which, fortunately, is near Escala.

"Next time we go to Portland, can we take the train?"

"Sure thing."

"You did good, Christian."

"So did you."

"I'll call Andrea and let her know we're safe."

"Andrea?"

"She can call your family. I'm sure they're worried. I'll see you tomorrow at your birthday party."

My family? They don't worry about me. "See you then."

She leans across and kisses my cheek. "Good night." I'm touched. It's the first time she's ever done that.

I watch her walk through the courtyard of her apartment building.

"Ros!" I hear Gwen's screech as she comes barreling out of the double doors of the entryway and scoops Ros up in her embrace.

I wave and order the cab to take me around the corner.

THERE ARE PHOTOGRAPHERS OUTSIDE of my apartment building. Something must be going on. I pay the driver, get out of the cab, and keep my head down as I walk through the front door.

"There he is!"

"Christian Grey."

"He's here!"

The flashes dazzle me, but I manage to get inside relatively unscathed. Surely they're not here for me? Maybe they are, or is it someone else who's in the building tonight that's worthy of this kind of attention? Fortunately, the elevator is free. Once inside, I take off my shoes and socks. My feet are sore, and it's a relief to be barefoot. I look at my shoes. I probably won't wear them again.

Poor Ros. She's going to have some blisters tomorrow.

I don't imagine Ana will be home. She's probably still at the bar. I'll go find her once I've swapped the battery on my phone, changed my shirt, and maybe had a shower. I take off my jacket as the doors to the elevator open and step into the foyer.

The television is blaring from the TV room.

Odd.

I wander into the living room.

My family are all gathered here.

"Christian!" Grace shrieks, and she races toward me like a tropical storm, so I'm forced to drop my jacket and shoes in time to catch her. She wraps her arms around my neck and kisses me vigorously on my cheek, and hugs me. Hard.

What the hell?

"Mom?"

"I thought I'd never see you again," Grace rasps.

"Mom, I'm here," I reassure her, bemused. Can't she see I'm fine?

"I died a thousand deaths today." Her voice cracks on the last word and she begins to sob. I hold her tighter in my arms. I've never seen her like this. My mom. Holding me. It feels good. "Oh, Christian," she sobs, and she hugs me like she'll never let me go as she weeps into my neck. Closing my eyes, I rock her gently.

"He's alive! Shit, you're here!" My dad comes out of Taylor's office, followed by Taylor. Carrick barrels toward Mom and me and embraces us both.

"Dad?"

Then Mia joins us. Hugging us all.

Jesus!

A family huddle.

When did this ever happen?

Never!

Carrick pulls away first, and he's wiping his eyes.

He's crying?

Mia and Grace step back. "Sorry," Grace says.

"Hey, Mom, it's okay," I say, uncomfortable with all this unwarranted attention.

"Where were you? What happened?" she cries, and puts her head in her hands, still weeping.

"Mom." I pull her into my arms and kiss her head and hold her once more. "I'm here. I'm good. It's just taken me a hell of a long time to get back from Portland. What's with the welcoming committee?" I look up, and there she is. Wide-eyed and beautiful. Tears streaming down her face. My Ana.

"Mom, I'm good," I tell Grace. "What's wrong?"

She holds my face and addresses me as if I'm still a child.

"Christian, you've been missing. Your flight plan—you never made it to Seattle. Why didn't you contact us?"

"I didn't think it would take this long."

"Why didn't you call?"

"No power in my cell."

"You didn't stop. Call collect?"

"Mom, it's a long story."

"Oh, Christian! Don't you ever do that to me again! Do you understand?"

"Yes, Mom." I wipe her tears with my thumbs and give her another hug. It feels good to hold the woman who saved me.

She steps back and Mia hugs me. Hard. And then she slaps me hard on my chest.

Ow.

"You had us so worried!" she shouts through her tears. I comfort her and calm her with the fact that I'm here now.

Elliot, looking nauseatingly tanned and healthy from his holiday, hugs me.

Christ. Et tu, brute? He slaps me hard on my back.

"Great to see you," he says, loud and gruff. His voice full of emotion.

A lump forms in my throat.

This is my family.

They care. They fucking care.

They were all worried about me.

Family first.

I step back and look at Ana. Katherine stands behind her, stroking her hair. I can't hear what she says. "I'm going to say hi to my girl now," I tell my parents, before I lose it. My mother gives me a teary smile, and she and Carrick step aside. I walk toward Ana and she uncurls herself from her seat on the sofa. She's a little unsteady when she stands. I think she's making sure that I'm real. She's still crying, but suddenly she bolts toward me and into my arms.

"Christian!" she sobs.

"Hush," I whisper, and, holding her close, I'm relieved to feel her small, delicate frame pressed against me. I'm grateful for everything that she is to me.

Ana. My love.

I bury my face in her hair and inhale her sweet, sweet scent. She raises her beautiful, tearstained face to me and I plant a quick kiss on her soft lips. "Hi," I whisper.

"Hi," she says, hoarse and husky.

"Miss me?"

"A bit." She sniffles.

"I can tell." I wipe her tears away with my fingers.

"I thought. I thought—" She sobs.

"I can see. Hush. I'm here. I'm here." I hold her close and kiss her again. Her lips are always so tender when she's been crying.

"Are you okay?" she asks, and her hands are on me. Everywhere, it feels. But I don't mind; I welcome her touch. The darkness is long gone.

"I'm okay. I'm not going anywhere."

"Oh, thank God." She wraps her arms around my waist and holds me.

Damn. I need a shower. But she doesn't seem to care.

"Are you hungry? Do you need something to drink?" she asks.

"Yes."

She tries to step back, but I'm not ready to release her. I hold her and extend a hand to the photographer, who's hovering.

"Mr. Grey," says José.

"Christian, please."

"Christian, welcome back. Glad you're okay, and, um—thanks for letting me stay."

"No problem." *Just keep your hands off my girl.*

Gail interrupts us. She looks a mess. She's been crying, too.

Shit. Mrs. Jones? It rocks me to my soul.

"Can I get you something, Mr. Grey?" She's dabbing her eyes with a tissue.

"A beer, please, Gail. Budvar, and a bite to eat."

"I'll get it," Ana says.

"No. Don't go." I tighten my arm around her.

The Kavanagh kids are next: Ethan and Katherine. I shake his hand and give Katherine a peck on the cheek. She looks well. Barbados and Elliot obviously agree with her. Mrs. Jones returns and hands me a beer. I refuse the glass and take a long draft of Budvar.

It tastes so good.

All these people are here for me. I feel like the long-lost prodigal son.

Perhaps I am . . .

"Surprised you don't want something stronger," says Elliot. "So, what the fuck happened to you? First I knew was when Dad called me to say the chopper was missing."

"Elliot!" Grace admonishes him.

"Helicopter!" For fuck's sake, Elliot. I hate the word "chopper." He knows that. He grins, and I find myself grinning back at him.

"Let's sit and I'll tell you." I sit down with Ana beside me and the clan joins us. I take a long draft of my beer and spot Taylor in the background. I give him a nod and he nods back.

Thank God he's not crying. I don't think I could cope with that.

"Your daughter?" I ask him.

"She's fine now. False alarm, sir."

"Good."

"Glad you're back, sir. Will that be all?"

"We have a helicopter to pick up."

"Now? Or will the morning do?"

"Morning, I think, Taylor."

"Very good, Mr. Grey. Anything else, sir?"

I shake my head and raise my bottle to him. I can brief him in the morning. He gives me a warm smile and leaves us.

"Christian, what happened?" Carrick asks.

Sitting on the sofa I begin to regale them with the executive summary of my crash landing.

"A fire? Both engines?" Carrick is shocked.

"Yep."

"Shit! But I thought—" Dad continues.

"I know," I interrupt him. "It was sheer luck I was flying so low."

Ana shudders beside me and I put my arm around her. "Cold?" I ask her, and she squeezes my hand and shakes her head.

"How did you put out the fire?" asks Katherine.

"Extinguisher. We have to carry them—by law," I answer, but she's so brusque. I don't tell her that I used the fire bottles.

"Why didn't you call or use the radio?" Mom asks.

I explain that I had to switch everything off because of the fire. With the electronics out, I couldn't radio and we had no cell coverage. Ana tenses beside me. I lift her onto my lap.

"So how did you get back to Seattle?" Mom says, and I tell them about Seb.

"Took forever. He didn't have a cell, weird but true. I didn't realize." I look around at the concerned faces of my family and stop at Mom's.

"That we'd worry? Oh, Christian! We've been going out of our minds!" She's pissed, and for the first time I feel a tad guilty. Flynn's lecture on strong familial ties for adoptees comes to mind.

"You've made the news, bro," says Elliot.

"Yeah. I figured that much when I arrived to this reception, and the handful of photographers outside. I'm sorry, Mom—I should have asked the driver to stop so I could phone. But I was anxious to be back."

Grace shakes her head. "I'm just glad you're back in one piece, darling."

Ana sags against me. She must be tired.

"Both engines?" Carrick mutters again, with disbelief.

"Go figure." I shrug and run my hand down Ana's back. She's sniffling again.

"Hey," I murmur, and tilt her chin up. "Stop with the crying."

She wipes her nose with her hand. "Stop with the disappearing," she says.

"Electrical failure. That's odd, isn't it?" Carrick won't leave it alone.

"Yes, crossed my mind, too, Dad. But right now I'd just like to go to bed and think about all that shit tomorrow."

"So, the media know that Christian Grey has been found safe and well," Katherine comments, looking up from her phone.

Well, they snapped me coming home. "Yes. Andrea and my PR people will deal with the media. Ros called her after we dropped her home."

Sam will be in his fucking element with all that attention.

"Yes, Andrea called me to let me know you were still alive," Carrick says with a grin.

"I must give that woman a raise," I mutter. "Sure is late."

"I think that's a hint, ladies and gentlemen, that my dear bro needs his beauty sleep." Elliot gives me a teasing wink.

Fuck off, bro.

"Cary, my son is safe," Mom announces. "You can take me home now."

"Yes. I think we could use the sleep," Carrick replies, smiling down at her.

"Stay," I offer. There's enough room.

"No, sweetheart, I want to get home. Now that I know you're safe."

I ease Ana onto the couch and stand as everyone starts making a move. Mom hugs me once more and I embrace her.

"I was so worried, darling," she whispers.

"I'm okay, Mom."

"Yes. I think you are," she says, and gives Ana a quick look and a smile.

After some lengthy good-byes, we usher my family, Katherine, and Ethan into the elevator. The doors close and it's just me and Ana in the foyer.

Shit. And José. He's hovering in the hallway.

"Look. I'll turn in. Leave you guys," he says.

"Do you know where to go?" I ask.

He nods. "Yeah, the housekeeper—"

"Mrs. Jones," Ana says.

"Yeah, Mrs. Jones, she showed me earlier. Quite a place you have here, Christian."

"Thank you," I respond, and place my arm around Ana and kiss her hair. "I'm going to eat whatever Mrs. Jones has put out for me. Good night, José." I turn and leave him with my girl.

He'd be a fool to try anything now.

And I'm hungry.

Mrs. Jones hands me a ham-and-cheese sandwich with lettuce and mayo.

"Thank you," I tell her. "Go to bed."

"Yes, sir," she says with a sweet smile. "I'm glad you are back with us." She leaves, and I wander into the living area and watch Rodriguez and Ana.

I finish my sandwich as he hugs her. He closes his eyes.

He adores her.

Can't she tell?

She waves him off, then turns and sees me watching her. She walks toward me, then stops and stares.

I drink her in. She's crumpled and tearstained, and she's never looked more beautiful to me. She's a welcome, welcome sight.

She's home.

My home.

My throat burns.

"He's still got it bad, you know," I murmur, to distract myself from my intense emotion.

"And how would you know that, Mr. Grey?"

"I recognize the symptoms, Miss Steele. I believe I have the same affliction."

I love you.

Her eyes grow larger. Serious. "I thought I was never going to see you again," she whispers.

Oh, baby. The knot in my throat tightens. "It wasn't as bad as it sounds." I try to reassure her. She collects my jacket and shoes from where they lie on the floor and walks toward me.

"I'll take that," I say, retrieving my jacket.

And we stand there, regarding each other.

She's really here.

She was waiting for me.

For you, Grey. When I thought no one would ever wait for me. I pull her into my arms.

"Christian," she chokes, and she starts crying again.

"Hush." I kiss her hair. "You know, in the few seconds of sheer terror before I landed, all my thoughts were of you. You're my talisman, Ana."

"I thought I'd lost you," she says. And we stand. In silence. Holding each other. I remember dancing with her in this very room.

Witchcraft.

That was a moment to remember. *Like now.* And I never want to let her go.

She drops my shoes, and it startles me when they bump on the floor.

"Come and shower with me." I'm filthy from my marathon trek.

"Okay." She looks up at me but doesn't release me. I tip her chin back.

"You know, even tearstained, you are beautiful, Ana Steele." I kiss her tenderly. "And your lips are so soft." I kiss her again, taking everything she has to offer. She runs her fingers through my hair.

"I need to put my jacket down," I whisper.

"Drop it," she orders, against my lips.

"I can't."

Leaning back, she cocks her head, bemused.

I let her go. "This is why." And from the inside pocket I pull out her present to me.

Ana glances at her watch and takes one step back as I drape my jacket over the couch and place the box on top.

What's going on?

"Open it," she whispers.

"I was hoping you'd say that. This has been driving me crazy."

Her smile is broad and she bites her lip, and if I'm not mistaken she's a little nervous.

Why?

I give her a reassuring smile, unwrap the box, and open it.

Nestled inside is a keychain that shows a pixelated picture of Seattle that flashes on and off. I take it out of the box, wondering what the significance might be, but I'm lost. I have no idea.

I look to Ana for a clue.

"Turn it over," she says.

I do. And the word "YES" flashes on and off.

Yes.

Yes.

YES.

One simple word. One profound meaning.

A life-changer.

Right here. Now.

My heartbeat spikes and I gawk at her, hoping this means what I think it means.

"Happy birthday," she whispers.

"You'll marry me?"

I don't believe it.

She nods.

I still don't believe it. "Say it." I need to hear it from her lips.

"Yes, I'll marry you."

Joy bursts in my heart—in my head, in my body, in my soul. It's exhilarating. It's overwhelming. Brimming with elation, I lunge forward and gather her in my arms and swing her around, laughing as I do. She clutches my biceps, her eyes shining, as she laughs, too.

I stop, set her on her feet, and grab her face and kiss her. My lips tease hers and she opens for me, like a flower: my sweet Anastasia.

"Oh, Ana," I whisper, in adoration, my lips brushing the corner of her mouth.

"I thought I'd lost you," she says, and she looks a little dazed.

"Baby, it will take more than a malfunctioning 135 to keep me away from you."

"135?"

"*Charlie Tango.* She's a Eurocopter EC135, the safest in its class."

But not today.

"Wait a minute." I hold up the keychain. "You gave this to me before we saw Flynn."

Her smile is a little smug as she nods.

What?

Anastasia Steele!

"I wanted you to know that whatever Flynn said, it wouldn't make a difference to me."

"So all yesterday evening, when I was begging you for an answer, I had it already?" I'm feeling breathless—giddy, even—and a little pissed off.

What the hell?

I don't know whether to be angry or celebratory. She confounds me, even now.

Well, Grey, what are you going to do about it?

"All that worry," I murmur darkly. She gives me an impish grin and shrugs once more. "Oh, don't try and get cute with me, Miss Steele. Right now, I want—"

I had the answer all the time.

I want her.

Here.

Now.

No. Wait.

"I can't believe you left me hanging."

She watches my expression as I construct a plan. Something worthy of such audacity. "I believe some retribution is in order, Miss Steele." My voice is low. Ominous.

Ana takes a cautious step back. Is she going to run? "Is that the game? Because I will catch you." Her smile is playful and infectious. "And you're biting your lip," I add.

She takes another step back and turns to run, but I pounce and grab her. She squeals and I hoist her over my shoulder, and head for my—no, *our*—bathroom.

"Christian!" She swats my behind.

I swat hers back. Hard.

"Ow!" she yelps.

"Shower time," I declare, as I carry her down the corridor.

"Put me down!" She squirms on my shoulder but my arm is locked over her thighs. What's really making me smile are her gasps and giggles. She's enjoying this.

As am I.

My grin is as broad and as wide as the Puget Sound when I open the bathroom door. "Fond of these shoes?" I ask. They look expensive.

"I prefer them to be touching the floor." Her words are strangled, and I think she's feigning outrage and trying not to laugh at the same time.

"Your wish is my command, Miss Steele." I pull off both her shoes and they clatter onto the tiles. By the vanity I empty my pockets: phone, keys, wallet, but most precious of all is my new keychain. I don't want to get it wet. With my pockets empty, I march into the shower, carrying Ana over my shoulder.

"Christian!" she cries. Ignoring her, I turn on the water and it cascades over us both, but mostly over Ana's backside. It's cold. She shrieks and laughs at once, and writhes on my shoulder.

"No! Put me down!" she says between giggles. She swats me once more, and I take pity.

Releasing her, I let her wet, clothed body slide down the length of mine.

She's flushed. Her eyes bright and beautiful. She's captivating.

Oh, baby.

You said yes.

I cup her face and kiss her, my lips tender on hers. I worship her mouth, cherishing her. She closes her eyes and accepts my kiss, kissing me back with a sweet hunger under the streaming shower.

The water is warmer now and her hands move to my soaking shirt. She tugs its hem from my pants. And I groan in her mouth, but I can't stop kissing her.

I can't stop loving her.

I won't stop loving her.

Ever.

Slowly, she begins to unbutton my shirt, and I reach for the zipper at the back of her dress. I slide it down, feeling her warm flesh beneath my fingertips.

Oh. The feel of her. I want more. I kiss her hard, my tongue exploring her mouth.

She moans and suddenly yanks my shirt open, the buttons flying off and landing in the shower.

Whoa.

Ana!

She tugs my shirt over my shoulders and pushes me against the tiles. But she can't remove it. "Cuff links." I hold up my wrists. Her fingers make light work of each, and she lets them fall to the floor, followed by my shirt. Her feverish fingers reach for my waistband.

Oh no.

Not yet.

Grasping her shoulders, I spin her around, giving me easier access to her zipper. I complete its journey to its bottom and pull her dress down, just below her breasts. Her arms are still in the sleeves, restricting her movement.

I like that.

Smoothing her wet hair away from her neck, I lean forward, and with my tongue, I taste the water running off her skin, from her neck to her hairline.

She tastes so good.

I run my lips along the length of her shoulder, kissing and sucking, as my arousal strains against my zipper. She braces her hands on the tiles and groans while I kiss my favorite spot beneath her ear. Gently, I unhook her bra and push it down, then cup her breasts in my hands. I moan my appreciation. She has great tits.

Responsive, too.

"So beautiful," I whisper in her ear. She rolls her head to one side, exposing her neck and throat, and she pushes her breasts into the palms of my hands. She reaches around, still trapped by her dress, and she finds my erection.

Sucking in a breath, I push my impatient cock into her hands. The feel of her fingers through the soaking fabric is erotic.

Gently, I tug on her nipples, first between my thumb and forefinger, then pinch them between my fingers. She whimpers, loud and clear, as they harden and lengthen under my touch.

"Yes," I whisper.

Let me hear you, baby.

I turn her around and capture her lips with mine, peeling off her dress and her underwear until she's naked before me; her clothes a sodden mess at our feet.

She grabs the body wash and squirts some into her hand. Gazing up at me, asking for permission, she waits.

Okay. We're doing this.

I take a deep breath and nod.

With aching tenderness, she places her hand on my chest. I freeze and slowly she rubs in the soap, skimming small circles on my skin. The darkness is quiet.

But I'm tense.

Everywhere.

Damn it.

Relax, Grey.

She means you no harm.

After a beat, I clasp her hips and watch her face. Her concentration. Her compassion. It's all there. My breathing accelerates. But it's cool. I can cope.

"Is this okay?" she asks.

"Yes." I squeeze the word out.

Her hands flow across my body to wash my underarms, my ribs, down over my belly, and down farther, to the waistband of my pants.

I exhale. "My turn." Moving us out of the shower stream, I reach for the shampoo. I squirt some onto her head and begin massaging the soap into her hair. She closes her eyes and makes an appreciative noise deep in her throat.

I chuckle, and it's cathartic. "You like?"

"Hmm . . ."

"Me, too." I kiss her forehead and continue kneading her scalp. "Turn around." She obeys immediately, and I continue to wash her hair. When I'm done, her head is covered in suds. I ease her under the shower once more. "Lean your head back."

Ana complies, and I rinse out all the soap.

There is nothing I love more than taking care of my girl.

In every way.

She turns around and grabs the waistband of my pants. "I want to wash all of you," she says. I hold up my hands in surrender.

I'm yours, Ana. Take me.

She undresses me, freeing my erection—and my pants and boxers join the rest of our clothes on the shower floor.

"Looks like you're pleased to see me," she says.

"I'm always pleased to see you, Miss Steele."

We beam at each other while she grabs and soaps a sponge. She surprises me a little when she starts at my chest, and she works her way down to my ready cock.

Oh yes.

She drops the sponge and her hands are on me.

Fuck.

I close my eyes as she tightens her fingers around me. I flex my hips and groan. This is exactly how to spend the early hours of a Saturday morning after a near-death experience.

Wait.

I open my eyes and pin her with my gaze. "It's Saturday." I grasp her waist and pull her against my body and kiss her.

No more condoms.

My hand, wet and slick with soap, travels down her body, over her breasts, her belly, down to her sex. I tease her with my fingers while I consume her mouth and her tongue, keeping her head in place with my other hand.

I slip my fingers inside her and she moans in my mouth.

"Yes," I hiss. She's ready. I lift her, my hands on her backside. "Wrap your legs around me, baby." She does as she's told, wrapping around me like warm, wet silk. I brace her against the wall.

We're skin on skin.

"Eyes open. I want to see you." She peers up at me, her pupils large and full of need. Slowly I sink into her, keeping my eyes on hers. I pause. Holding her on me. Holding her up. Feeling her.

"You are mine, Anastasia."

"Always."

Her answer makes me feel ten feet tall.

"And now we can let everyone know, because you said yes."

Leaning down, I kiss her and ease out of her, taking my time. Savoring her. She closes her eyes and tilts back her head as we move together.

Us.

Together.

As one.

I speed up. Needing more. Needing her. Enjoying her. Loving her. Her small cries spur me on, telling me she's climbing higher and higher. With me. Taking me.

She cries out when she comes, her head back against the wall, and I follow her, finding my release and burying my face in her neck.

Carefully, I sink to the floor as the water stream rains down on us. I hold her face in my hands and I can see that she's crying.

Baby.

I kiss away each tear.

She shifts so her back is against mine and neither of us says anything. Our silence is golden. Quiet. After all the anxiety of this afternoon and evening, my crash landing, my marathon trek, the endless road trip, I've found some peace. I rest my chin on her head, my legs wrapped around her while I hold her in my arms. I love this woman—this beautiful, brave, young woman who will soon be my wife.

Mrs. Grey.

I grin and nuzzle her wet hair, surrendering us both to the cascading water.

"My fingers are pruny," she remarks, staring down at her hands. I take her fingers in mine and kiss each one.

"We should really get out of this shower."

"I'm comfortable here," she says.

Me, too, baby. Me, too.

She sags against me and stares, at my toes I think, and then she chuckles.

"Something amusing you, Miss Steele?"

"It's been a busy week."

"That it has."

"I thank God you're back in one piece, Mr. Grey." She's suddenly serious.

I might not have been here.

Shit.

If . . .

I swallow as my throat constricts, and an image comes to mind of the ground speeding toward me and Ros in the cockpit of *Charlie Tango*. I shudder. "I was scared," I whisper.

"Earlier?"

I nod.

"So you made light of it to reassure your family?"

"Yes. I was too low to land well. But somehow I did."

She stares at me, fear on her face. "How close a call was it?"

"Close. For a few awful seconds, I thought I'd never see you again." This feels like a dark, dark confession.

She moves and puts her arms around me. "I can't imagine my life without you, Christian. I love you so much it frightens me."

Whoa.

But I feel the same. "Me, too. My life would be empty without you. I love you so much." I tighten my arms around her and kiss her hair. "I won't ever let you go."

"I don't want to go, ever." She kisses my throat and I bend down and kiss her.

I'm getting pins and needles in my feet. "Come—let's get you dry and into bed. I'm tired and you look beat."

She lifts an eyebrow.

"You have something to say, Miss Steele?"

She shakes her head and stands, waiting for me.

We clear our clothes and I grab my cuff links. Ana dumps our soaking clothes into her sink. "I'll deal with these tomorrow," she says.

"Good idea." I wrap her in a towel and place one around my waist. As we brush our teeth at my sink, she gives me a frothy grin, and we both try not to laugh and choke on the toothpaste when I reciprocate.

I'm fourteen again.

In a good way.

I FINISH DRYING HER hair and she climbs into bed. She looks the way I feel, exhausted. I take another look at the keychain and at my favorite word ever written in the English language.

A word full of hope and possibilities.

She said yes.

I grin and join her in bed. "This is so neat. The best birthday present I've ever had. Better than my signed Giuseppe DeNatale poster."

"I would have told you earlier, but since it was going to be your birthday . . ." Ana lifts her shoulder. "What do you give the man who has everything? I thought I'd give you . . . me."

I place the keychain on my bedside table and snuggle up to Ana, pulling her into my arms. "It's perfect. Like you."

"I am far from perfect, Christian."

"Are you smirking at me, Miss Steele?"

"Maybe." She chuckles.

I can tell, Ana. Your body language gives you away.

"Can I ask you something?" she adds.

"Of course."

"You didn't call on your trip back from Portland. Was that really because of José? You were worried about me being here alone with him?"

Maybe . . .

I feel like an idiot. I thought she was at the bar having a good time. I had no idea—

"Do you know how ridiculous that is?" she says, as she turns to face me, her eyes full of reproach. "How much stress you put your family and me through? We all love you very much."

"I had no idea you'd all be so worried."

"When are you going to get it through your thick skull that you are loved?"

"Thick skull?"

"Yes. Thick skull."

"I don't think the bone density of my head is significantly higher than anywhere else in my body."

"I'm serious! Stop trying to make me laugh. I am still a little mad at you, though that's partially eclipsed by the fact that you're home safe and sound when I thought—" She stops and swallows and in a quieter tone continues. "Well, you know what I thought."

I caress her face. "I'm sorry. Okay?"

"Your poor mom, too. It was very moving, seeing you with her," she says quietly.

"I've never seen her that way."

Grace sobbing.

Mom.

Mom sobbing.

"Yes, that was really something. She's normally so self-possessed. It was quite a shock."

"See? Everyone loves you. Perhaps now you'll start believing it." She kisses me. "Happy birthday, Christian. I'm glad you're here to share your day with me. And you haven't seen what I've got for you tomorrow, um, today."

"There's more?" I'm astonished. What more could I possibly want?

"Oh yes, Mr. Grey, but you'll have to wait until then."

She cuddles up to me and closes her eyes, and in moments she's asleep. I'm amazed at how she can fall asleep so quickly.

"My precious girl. I'm sorry. I'm sorry to make you worry," I whisper, and kiss her forehead. Feeling more content than I've ever felt in my life, I close my eyes.

Ana, burnished hair and broad smiles, is with me in *Charlie Tango.*

Let's chase the dawn.

She laughs. Carefree. Young. My girl.

The light around us is golden.

She's golden.

I'm golden.

I cough. There's smoke. Smoke everywhere.

I can't see Ana. She's gone in the smoke.

And we're diving down. Down.

Hurtling fast. In *Charlie Tango.*

The ground is coming up to meet me.

I close my eyes, waiting for the impact.

It never comes.

We're in the orchard.

The trees are laden with apples.

Ana smiles, her hair free and wafting in the breeze.

She holds out two apples. A red apple. A green apple.

You choose.

Choose.

Red. Green.

I smile. And take the red apple.

The sweeter apple.

Ana takes my hand and we walk.

Hand in hand.

Past the alcoholics and addicts outside the liquor store in Detroit.

They wave and hold up their brown paper bags in salute.

Past Esclava. Elena smiles and waves.

Past Leila. Leila smiles and waves.

Ana takes my apple. She bites into it.

Mmm . . . tasty. She licks her lips.

Delicious. I love it.

I made it. With Grandpa.

Wow. You're so capable.

She smiles and whirls around, her hair flying.

I love you, she cries. *I love you, Christian Grey.*

I wake, startled by my dream. But, I'm left with a sense of contentment, when normally I'm terrified of my dreams.

The Anastasia Steele effect.

I grin and look around. She's not in bed. Before I get up, I check my charged phone. I have too many messages, mostly from Sam, but I don't want to deal with him just yet. I switch off my phone and pick up my keychain to examine it once more.

She said "Yes."

That wasn't the most romantic proposal.

She's right. She deserves better. If she wants the hearts and flowers shit, then I need to step up. I have an idea, and Google a florist near my parents' home. They're not yet open so I leave a voice mail.

Shit. I'm going to need a ring. Today.

I'll deal with that later.

In the meantime, I go looking for Ana. She's not in the bathroom. I wander toward the living room and hear her voice. She's talking to her friend. I pause. And listen.

"You really like him, don't you?" José says.

"I love him, José."

That's my girl.

"What's not to love?" José says and I think he's referring to my apartment.

"Gee, thanks!" Ana exclaims, sounding hurt.

What an asshole.

"Hey, Ana, just kidding." José tries to placate her. "Seriously, I'm kidding. You've never been that kind of girl."

No. She's not. You dick.

"Omelet good for you?" she asks him.

"Sure."

"And me," I state, striding into the kitchen, surprising them both. "José." I greet him with a nod.

"Christian." José returns my nod.

Yeah. I heard you, you fucker, disrespecting my girl.

She's giving me an odd look. She knows what I'm doing. "I was going to bring you breakfast in bed," she says. I saunter over to her, in front of the photographer, tilt up her chin, and kiss her, long, hard, and noisily.

"Good morning, Anastasia," I whisper.

"Good morning, Christian. Happy birthday." She gives me a shy smile.

"I'm looking forward to my other present," I state, and she blushes and looks nervously in Rodriguez's direction.

Oh. What does she have planned?

Rodriguez looks like he's swallowed a lemon.

Good.

"So what are your plans today, José?" I ask, keeping it polite.

"I'm heading up to see my dad and Ray, Ana's dad."

"They know each other?" I frown at this new tidbit of information.

"Yeah, they were in the Army together. They lost contact until Ana and I were in college. It's kinda cute. They're best buds now. We're going on a fishing trip."

"Fishing?" He really doesn't look the type.

"Yeah—some great catches in these coastal waters. The steelheads can grow way big."

"True. My brother Elliot and I landed a thirty-four-pound steelhead once."

"Thirty-four pounds?" José says, and he seems genuinely impressed. "Not bad. Ana's father, though, he holds the record. A forty-three-pounder."

"You're kidding! He never said." But Ray wouldn't brag. That's not his thing, just like his daughter.

"Happy birthday, by the way."

"Thanks. So, where do you like to fish?"

"All around the Pacific Northwest. Dad's favorite is the Skagit."

"Really, that's my dad's favorite, too." I'm surprised yet again.

"He prefers the Canadian side. Ray on the other hand prefers the American."

"Lead to some arguments?"

"Sure, after a beer or two." José grins and I settle in beside him at the kitchen counter. Maybe this guy's not such a dick.

"So your dad likes the Skagit. What about you?" I ask.

"I prefer coastal waters."

"You do?"

"Sea fishing is harder. More exciting. More of a challenge. I love the sea."

"I remember the seascapes in your exhibition. They were good. By the way, thanks for dropping those portraits off."

He's embarrassed by the compliment. "No problem. Where do *you* like to fish?"

We discuss at length the merits of fishing in rivers, in lakes, and at sea. He's passionate about it, too.

Ana makes breakfast and watches us—happy, I think, that we're getting along.

She pops a steaming omelet and a coffee on the counter for each of us, and sits down beside me to eat her granola. Our conversation segues from fishing to baseball, and I hope we're not boring her. We talk about the upcoming Mariners game—he's a fan—and I realize that José and I have much in common.

Including loving the same woman.

The woman who has agreed to be my wife.

I'm dying to tell him, but I behave.

Once I finish my breakfast, I change quickly into jeans and a T-shirt. When I come back into the kitchen, José is clearing his plate.

"Ana, that was delicious."

"Thank you." She colors in response to José's praise.

"I have to go. I have to drive out to Bandera and meet the old man."

"Bandera?" I ask.

"Yes, we're fishing for trout in the Mount Baker National Forest. One of the lakes near there."

"Which one?"

"Lower Tuscohatchie."

"I don't think I know that one. Good luck."

"Thanks."

"Say hi to Ray for me," Ana adds.

"Will do."

Arm in arm, Ana and I accompany José into the foyer.

"Thanks for letting me crash here." He shakes my hand.

"Anytime," I respond. And I'm surprised that I actually mean it. He seems harmless enough, like a puppy. He hugs Ana, and to my surprise, I don't want to rip his arms off.

"Stay safe, Ana."

"Sure. Great to see you. Next time we'll have a real evening out," she says, as he enters the elevator.

"I'll hold you to that." He waves from inside and the doors close.

"See, he's not so bad," Ana says.

Maybe.

"He still wants into your panties, Ana. But can't say I blame him."

"Christian, that's not true!"

"You have no idea, do you? He wants you. Big-time."

"Christian, he's just a friend, a good friend."

I hold up my hands in surrender. "I don't want to fight."

"Me neither."

"You didn't tell him we were getting married."

"No. I figured I ought to tell Mom and Ray first."

"Yes, you're right. And I . . . um, I should ask your father."

She laughs. "Oh, Christian—this isn't the eighteenth century."

"It's traditional."

And I never thought I'd have to ask any father for his daughter's hand in marriage. Give me this moment. Please.

"Let's talk about that later," she says. "I want to give you your other present."

Another present?

Nothing can top the keychain.

Her smile is mischievous and her teeth sink into her lower lip.

"You're biting your lip again." I tug gently at her chin. She gives me her coy look but she squares her shoulders, takes my hand, and drags me back into the bedroom.

From under the bed, she produces two wrapped gift boxes.

"Two?"

"I bought this before the, um . . . incident yesterday. I'm not sure about it now." She gives me one of the parcels, but she looks anxious about it.

"Sure you want me to open it?"

She nods.

I tear off the wrapping.

"*Charlie Tango*," Ana whispers.

Inside the box are the parts for a little wooden helicopter. But the bit that blows me away is the rotor. "Solar-powered. Wow." What a thoughtful gift. And from deep in my past, a memory surfaces. My first Christmas. My first proper Christmas with Mom and Dad.

My helicopter can fly.
My helicopter is blue.
It flies around the Christmas tree.

It flies over the piano and lands in the middle of the white.
It flies over Mommy and flies over Daddy.
And flies over Lelliot as he plays with his Legos.

With Ana watching, I sit down and start to assemble it. It snaps together easily, and I hold the little blue copter in my hand.

I love it.

I beam at Ana and go over to the balcony window, where I watch the rotors start to spin under the warm rays of the sun. "Look at that. What we can already do with this technology." I hold the helicopter at eye level, watching how easily solar energy is converted to mechanical energy. The rotors spin and spin, faster and faster.

Wow. All this in a child's toy.

There is so much more that we could do with this simple technology. The challenge is how to store this energy. Graphene is the way to go . . . but can we build efficient enough batteries? Batteries that charge quickly and hold their charge—

"You like it?" Ana interrupts my thoughts.

"Ana, I love it. Thank you." I grab her and kiss her and we watch the rotors spin. "I'll add it to the glider in my office." I move my hand out of the light and the rotors slow and come to a complete stop.

We move in the light.

We slow in the shadows.

We stop in the dark.

Hmm. Philosophical, Grey.

This is what Ana has done for me. She's dragged me into the light and I quite like it.

I place *Charlie Tango Mark II* on the chest of drawers. "It'll keep me company while we salvage *Charlie Tango*."

"Is it salvageable?"

"I don't know. I hope so. I'll miss her, otherwise."

Ana eyes me speculatively.

"What's in the other box?" I ask.

"I'm not sure if this present is for you or me."

"Really?"

She hands me the second box. It's heavier and has a substantial rattle. Ana flicks her hair over her shoulder and shifts from foot to foot.

"Why are you so nervous?"

She seems excited and a little embarrassed, too. "You have me intrigued, Miss Steele. I have to say I'm enjoying your reaction. What have you been up to?" I remove the lid of the box and on top of some tissue is a small card.

On your birthday
Do rude things to me.
Please.
Your Ana x

My eyes dart to hers.

What does this mean?

"Do rude things to you?" I ask. She nods and swallows. She's nervous, and deep down I know where this is going. She's talking about the playroom.

Are you ready for this, Grey?

I rip open the tissue that conceals the box's contents and retrieve an eye mask. Okay, she wants to be blindfolded. Next are some nipple clamps. *Oh, not these.* They're vicious. Not beginner level. Beneath the clamps is a butt plug, but this one is way too big. She's enclosed my iPod, too, which pleases me. She must like my music choices. And here's my silver gray Brioni tie, so she wants to be tied up.

Last, as I suspected, there's the key to my playroom.

She's giving me the big blue eyes. "You want to play?" I ask, my voice soft and husky.

"Yes."

"For my birthday?"

"Yes." Her agreement is barely audible.

Is she doing this because she thinks I want to? Is what we do not enough for her? Am I ready for this?

"You're sure?" I prompt.

"Not the whips and stuff."

"I understand that."

"Yes, then. I'm sure."

She confounds me. Every day. I stare down at the contents of the box. Sometimes she's just bewildering. "Sex-mad and insatiable," I mutter. "Well, I think we can do something with this lot."

If this is what she wants—and her words come back to me in a swirl. She's asked me and asked me and asked me.

I like your kinky fuckery.

If I win, Christian, you'll take me back into the playroom.

Red Room, here we come.

I want a demonstration. I like being tied up.

I place the items back in the box.

We could have some fun.

And that spark of anticipation flares and ignites in my gut. I haven't felt it since we did our last scene in the playroom. I regard her through narrowed eyes and hold out my hand. "Now," I state. I'll see how willing she really is.

She puts her hand in mine.

Okay, then, we're doing this.

"Come." I have a million things to do since yesterday's crash landing, but I don't give a fuck. It's my birthday and I'm going to have some fun with my fiancée.

Outside the playroom, I pause. "You're sure about this?"

"Yes," she says.

"Anything you don't want to do?"

She's thoughtful for a moment. "I don't want you to take photos of me."

Why the hell would she say that? Why would I want to take pictures of her?

Grey. Of course you would, if she'd let you.

"Okay," I agree, concerned about what has motivated this question. Does she know? That's impossible.

I unlock the door, feeling apprehensive and excited at once—like the first time I brought her in here. I usher her in and close the door.

For the first time since she left me, the room is welcoming.

I can do this.

Placing the gift box on the chest of drawers, I remove the iPod, place it in its dock, and set the Bose sound system so the track plays over the speakers. Eurythmics. Yes. This song came out the year before I was born. It has a seductive beat. I love it. Yeah, I think Ana will like it. Setting it to repeat, I hear the track begin. It's a little loud so I lower the volume a tad.

When I turn to her, she's in the middle of the room, watching me, a hungry, wanton expression on her face. Her teeth are toying with her lower lip, and her hips are swinging in time to the beat of the music.

Oh, Ana, you sensual creature.

I amble over to her and gently tug her chin, releasing her lip. "What do you want to do, Anastasia?" I whisper, and plant a chaste kiss at the corner of her mouth, keeping my fingers on her chin.

"It's your birthday. Whatever you want," she breathes and her darkening eyes flick up to mine, full of promise.

Fuck.

She might as well be addressing my cock.

I skim my thumb across her bottom lip. "Are we in here because you think I want to be in here?"

"No. I want to be in here, too."

She is a siren.

My siren.

In that case, let's begin with the basics. "Oh, there are so many possibilities, Miss Steele. But let's start with getting you naked." I jerk the sash of her robe, undoing it, and it falls open revealing her silk nightdress.

I step back, and sit down on the arm of my chesterfield sofa. "Take your clothes off. Slowly."

Miss Steele loves a challenge.

She slips the robe off and lets it fall like a cloud onto the floor, while her eyes stay on me. I'm hard. Instantly, as desire sweeps through my body. I run my finger over my lips to keep my hands off her.

She lifts both straps of her nightgown off her shoulders, watching me, watching her, and then drops them so her gown floats down her body to join the robe on the floor. She is naked before me in all her glory.

It makes a difference, her eyes on me.

It's more exciting because I can't hide anymore.

I have an idea, and stroll over to the chest of drawers to retrieve my tie from her gift box. Running it through my fingers, I walk back to where she's patiently waiting. "I think you're underdressed, Miss Steele." I place it around her neck and quickly tie it in a half Windsor, but I leave the wider end long. My fingers brush her neck and she gasps, and I let the long end fall so that it skims the top of her pubic hair. "You look mighty fine now, Miss Steele." I give her a swift kiss. "What shall we do with you now?" I murmur. Taking the tie in my hand, I tug it sharply and she's forced into my arms. Her naked body against mine is like an incendiary device. My fingers are in her hair. My mouth is on hers and with my tongue I claim her.

Hard. Insistent. I'm taking no prisoners.

She tastes of sweet Anastasia Steele. My favorite flavor.

With my other hand, I cup her behind, feeling her fine ass.

When I release her, we're both panting. Her breasts rising and falling with each breath.

Oh, baby. What you do to me.

What I want to do to you.

"Turn around," I prompt. She does so immediately, and I pull the tie from her hair and braid it. No loose hair in the playroom.

I gently pull her braid, and her head tilts up. "You have beautiful hair, Anastasia." I kiss her throat and she writhes. "You just have to say stop. You know that, don't you?" I whisper against her skin.

She nods, her eyes closed.

But damn, she looks happy.

I turn her around and take hold of the end of the tie.

"Come." I lead her over to the chest where her gift box sits, displaying its contents. "Anastasia, these objects." I hold up the butt plug. "This is a size too big. As an anal virgin, you don't want to start with this. We want to start with this." I show her my pinkie.

Her eyes grow impossibly large.

And I have to confess, one of my favorite pastimes is shocking Ana.

"Just finger. Singular," I add. "These clamps are vicious." I poke the nipple clamps. "We'll use these." From one of the drawers I take out a kinder pair. "They're adjustable."

She examines them. Fascinated. I love how she's so curious. "Clear?" I ask.

"Yes. Are you going to tell me what you intend to do?"

"No. I'm making this up as I go along. This isn't a scene, Ana."

"How should I behave?"

It's a strange question. "However you want to." And I wonder out loud if she was expecting my alter ego.

"Well, yes. I like him," she says.

"Do you, now?" I run my thumb across her lower lip, tempted to kiss it again. "I'm your lover, Anastasia, not your Dom. I love to hear your laugh and your girlish giggle. I like you relaxed and happy, like you are in José's photos. That's the girl that fell into my office. That's the girl I fell in love with.

"But, having said all that, I also like to do rude things to you, Miss Steele, and my alter ego knows a trick or two. So do as you're told and turn around."

She obeys, her face glowing with excitement.

I love you, Ana.

Simple.

I take what I need from the drawers, then arrange all the toys on the top. "Come." I tug the tie and lead her to the table. "I want you to kneel up on this." Gently I lift her onto the table, and she folds her legs beneath her and kneels in front of me.

We are nose to nose. She stares at me with shining eyes.

I run my hands down her thighs and at the knees gently pull her legs apart so that I can see my goal.

"Arms behind your back. I'm going to cuff you."

I show her the leather elbow cuffs and lean around her to put them on. She turns and runs her parted lips along my jaw, her tongue teasing my stubble. I close my eyes and for a moment revel in the contact, suppressing a groan.

Pulling back, I admonish her, "Stop. Or this will be over far quicker than either of us wants."

"You're irresistible."

"Am I, now?"

She nods, looking impertinent.

"Well, don't distract me, or I'll gag you."

"I like distracting you."

"Or spank you," I warn. She grins. "Behave," I scold her, and stand back and beat the cuffs across my palm.

It could so easily be your ass, Ana.

She looks modestly down at her knees. "That's better." I try again, and this time succeed in putting them on. I ignore her running her nose over my shoulder, but I thank God for our shower in the early hours of the morning.

The cuffs on, her back arches a little. Her breasts now prominent and begging to be touched. "Feel okay?" I ask as I admire her.

She nods.

"Good." From my back pocket I take the mask. "I think you've seen enough now." I slide it over her head and over her eyes.

Her breathing accelerates.

And I step back and drink her in.

She looks smoking hot.

Back at the drawers, I gather the items I need and slip off my T-shirt. I keep my jeans on, even though they are a little uncomfortable, because I don't want her distracted by my impatient dick.

In front of her once more, I open the small glass bottle that contains my favorite massage oil and wave it under her nose. Infused with cedarwood, argan, and sage, it's body-safe, and its fragrance reminds me of a crisp, fall day after the rain.

"I don't want to ruin my favorite tie," I mutter, as I undo it and pull it gently off Ana's body. She squirms as the material floats up her body, teasing her.

I fold my tie and place it beside her. Her anticipation is almost palpable. Her body is humming with impatience. It's arousing.

I pour a little oil on my hands and rub them together, warming the oil. She's listening to what I'm doing. I love heightening her senses. Gently, I caress her cheek with my knuckles and run them down her jaw.

She startles when I touch her, but she leans into my hand. I start massaging the oil into her skin—her throat, her clavicle, and along her shoulders. I knead the muscles beneath and let my hands glide in small circles across her chest, avoiding her breasts. She bows backward, pressing them toward me.

Oh no, Ana. Not yet.

I move my fingers down her sides, rubbing in the oil in slow, measured strokes in time to the music. She groans and I don't know if it's from pleasure or frustration. Maybe a little of both.

"You are so beautiful, Ana," I whisper, my lips close to her ear. I run them along her jaw as my hands work their magic. I move them beneath her breasts, over her belly, down to my goal. I kiss her quickly and inhale her scent, now mixed with the oil, down her neck and throat.

"And soon you'll be my wife, to have and to hold."

She inhales sharply.

"To love and to cherish." My hands continue. "With my body, I will worship you."

She throws her head back and moans as my fingers run through her pubic hair to her clitoris. Slowly I palm her, teasing her and spreading oil over her where she's wet already.

It's intoxicating.

I lean over to pick up a bullet vibrator. "Mrs. Grey."

She moans.

"Yes," I whisper, continuing my ministrations with my hand. "Open your mouth." She's already panting, but she opens her mouth farther and I slip the small vibrator inside. It's attached to a chain and can be worn as jewelry if so required. "Suck. I'm going to put this inside you."

She stills.

"Suck," I repeat, and remove my hands from her body.

She flexes her knees and makes a frustrated grunt. Smiling, I pour more oil onto my palms and finally cup her breasts. "Don't stop," I warn, as I gently roll her stiffening nipples between my thumbs and forefingers. They harden and lengthen some more under my touch. "You have such beautiful breasts, Ana."

She moans, and I gather one of the nipple clamps in one hand. Trailing my lips from her throat toward her breast, I stop and carefully attach a clamp.

Her garbled groan is my reward as I bring her trapped nipple to full attention with my lips. She writhes under my touch, shifting from side to side, and I clamp the remaining nipple. Ana's groan is just as loud this time. "Feel it," I insist, and I lean back to take in the beautiful sight.

"Give me this." I remove the vibrator from her mouth and my hand skims down her back toward her backside and between her buttocks. She tenses and rises up on her knees. "Hush, easy," I reassure her and kiss her neck as my fingers continue to stroke between the fine, fine cheeks of her ass.

I glide my other hand down the front of her body and start palming her clitoris once more, then ease my fingers into her. "I'm going to put this inside you," I murmur. "Not here." And my fingers circle her anus, spreading the oil. "But here." And I move the fingers of my other hand slowly into and out of her vagina.

"Ah!" she responds.

"Hush now." I stand and slide the vibrator inside her. Capturing her face with my hands, I kiss her, then click the small remote.

When the vibrator starts, she gasps and jolts up on her knees. "Ah!"

"Easy," I whisper against her lips, stifling her gasp. I tug gently on each of the clamps in turn.

She cries out. "Christian, please!"

"Hush, baby. Hang in there."

You can do this, Ana.

She's panting now and dealing with all the stimulation. I'm sure it's intense. "Good girl." I soothe her.

"Christian," she says, and she sounds a little frantic.

"Hush, feel it, Ana. Don't be afraid." I place my hands on her waist, holding her. *I'm right here, baby. I've got this. You've got this.*

I dip my little finger into the open pot of lube and slowly I move my hands down her back to her ass, watching her reaction; checking that she's okay. I massage her skin and knead her ass, her stunning ass, and I slip one hand between her buttocks.

"So beautiful." Gently, I push my finger inside her ass so that I feel the vibrator buzzing through her body. She tenses and I move my finger slowly, easing in and out while my teeth graze her chin. "So beautiful, Ana."

She gasps, then groans and kneels up a little higher, and I know she's close. Her lips start to move, but whatever she's saying, it's soundless. Suddenly she screams as her orgasm strikes. With my free hand I release first one, then the other nipple clamp, and she cries out.

I hold her close as her body pulses through her climax, still easing my finger in and out of her.

"No," she shouts, and I know she's had enough.

I remove my finger and the vibrator while keeping her in my arms. She sags against me, but her body is still convulsing. Deftly I unstrap the cuffs on one arm and she falls forward against me. Her head rolling on my shoulder as her intense climax begins to subside.

Her legs must be aching. She groans as I lift her and carry her to the bed, where I lay her faceup on the satin sheets. Using the remote, I switch off the music, then remove my jeans, freeing my raging erection. I start to rub the back of her legs, her knees, her calves, and then her shoulders, and I remove the cuffs. Lying down beside her, I peel off her mask and find her eyes are scrunched closed. With tenderness I untie her braid, freeing her hair. Leaning forward, I kiss her on the lips. "So beautiful," I say.

She opens one dazed eye.

"Hi." I smile down at her.

She grunts in response.

"Rude enough for you?"

She nods and gives me a sleepy grin.

Ana, you never fail.

"I think you're trying to kill me."

"Death by orgasm. There are worse ways to go."

Like plunging to your death in *Charlie Tango*.

She reaches up and caresses my face and my dispiriting thought disappears. "You can kill me like this anytime," she says. Taking her hand, I kiss her knuckles. I'm so proud of her. She never lets me down in here. She cups my face between her hands and kisses me.

I stop, pulling back. "This is what I want to do," I whisper. From beneath the pillow, I pull out the remote and change the song. I press the button, knowing it will play on repeat, and ease Ana onto her back. "The First Time Ever I Saw Your Face"—Roberta Flack's classic fills the room. "I want to make love to you," I murmur. My lips seek and find hers, and her fingers entwine in my hair.

"Please," Ana breathes, and her sensitized body rises to meet mine, opening up for me as I gently ease into her, and we make slow, sweet love.

I watch her fall apart in my arms and her climax takes me with her. I let go, pouring myself into her, throwing my head back and calling out her name in wonder.

I love you, Ana Steele.

I hold her to me. I never want to let her go.

My joy is complete. Have I ever been this happy?

As I come back to planet earth, I smooth her hair from her face and look down at the woman I love.

She's crying.

"Hey." I clasp her head in my hands. Did I hurt her? "Why are you crying?"

"Because I love you so much," she says, and I close my eyes, letting her words wash over me.

"And I you, Ana. You make me . . . whole." I kiss her once more as the music stops, and gather the sheet and wrap it around us both. She looks glorious; her hair is a mess and her eyes are luminous in spite of her tears. She's so full of life.

"What do you want to do today?" she asks.

"My day is made, thank you." I kiss her.

"Mine, too."

I love Ana's inner freak; she's never far away. And I think of the plans that I have for her later. I hope they will make her day, too. "Well, I should call my head of PR. But frankly, I'd like to remain in this bubble with you."

"About the crash?"

"I'm playing hooky."

"It is your birthday, Mr. Grey. You're allowed. And I like having you to myself." She leans up and grazes her teeth against my jaw. She looks happy, and free, if a little tired. "I love your music choices. Where do you find them?"

"I'm glad you like them. Sometimes, when I can't sleep I'll either play the piano or trawl iTunes."

"I don't like to think about you unable to sleep and on your own. It sounds lonely," Ana says, her compassion showing.

"To be honest, I never felt lonely until you left. I didn't realize how miserable I was."

She cups my face. "I'm sorry."

"Don't apologize, Ana. What I did was wrong."

She puts her finger over my lips. "Hush," she says. "I love you just the way you are."

"That's a song."

She laughs and she changes the subject; asking me about work.

"WE'VE COME A LONG way," Ana says, caressing my face.

"We have."

She looks wistful all of a sudden.

"What are you thinking about?" I ask.

"The photo shoot that José did. Kate. How in command she was. And how hot you looked."

"Hot?" *Me?*

"Yeah. Hot. And Kate was all: Sit here. Do this. Do that." Her impersonation of Kavanagh is spot on. I laugh.

"To think it could have been her who came to interview me. Thank the Lord for the common cold." I kiss the tip of her nose.

"I believe she had the flu, Christian," she scolds, and unconsciously trails her fingers through my chest hair. It's weird, but I think she's driven the darkness away. I don't even flinch. "All the canes have gone," she says, as she glances around the playroom. I tuck a stray strand of hair behind her ear.

"I didn't think you'd ever get past that hard limit."

"No, I don't think I will." She turns and stares at the whips, paddles, and floggers on the wall.

"You want me to get rid of them, too?" I ask.

"Not the crop . . . the brown one. Or that suede flogger." She gives me a coy smile.

"Okay, the crop and the flogger. Why, Miss Steele, you're full of surprises."

"As are you, Mr. Grey. It's one of the things I love about you." She kisses the corner of my mouth.

Suddenly I need to hear this from her, because I still can't quite believe it. "What else do you love about me?"

Her eyes soften with her affection. "This," she says, and traces her finger across my lips, tickling them. "I love this, and what comes out of it, and what you do to me with it. And what's in here." She strokes the side of my head. "You're so smart and witty and knowledgeable, competent in so many things. But most of all, I love what's in here." She presses her palm against my chest. "You are the most compassionate man I've ever met. What you do. How you work. It's awe-inspiring."

"Awe-inspiring?" I repeat her last words, not quite believing them but loving them anyway. A slow smile tugs at my mouth, but before I can say anything she launches herself at me.

ANA DOZES FOR A few minutes, in my arms. I lie staring up at the ceiling, enjoying her weight on me. Could I be any more content? I don't think so. She wakes when I kiss her forehead.

"Hungry?" I ask.

"Hmm, famished."

"Me, too."

She puts her arm on my chest and studies me. "It's your birthday, Mr. Grey. I'll cook you something. What would you like?"

"Surprise me." I run my hand down her back. "I should check my BlackBerry for all the messages I missed yesterday." I sigh when I sit up. I could spend all day with her in here.

"Let's shower," I say.

She grins and together, wrapped in one red sheet, we head down to the bathroom.

Once Ana is dressed she takes all the wet clothes from last night out of her sink and heads out the door. Wearing a tiny blue dress, she's all legs.

Too much leg.

Well at least it's just us.

And Taylor.

I stop shaving for a moment. "Leave them for Mrs. Jones," I call after her. She glances over her shoulder and smiles.

FEELING BUOYANT, I SIT down at my desk. Ana is working in the kitchen, and I have a ton of e-mails and messages to get through. Most are from Sam, annoyed that I've not called him. But there are others . . . moving messages from my mother, from Mia, my dad, and Elliot, all begging me to call. It's painful to hear their concern.

And Elena.

Shit.

Ana's hesitant voice is next.

Hi . . . um . . . it's me. Ana. Are you okay? Call me. Her concern is obvious. My heart constricts as it becomes blindingly clear that I've put her and my family through hell.

Grey, you're an idiot.

You should have called.

I save all the messages bar Elena's and return to the most important voice mail, from the florist in Bellevue. I call them back to outline my requirements, and I'm relieved that they can help me, given such short notice.

Then I call my favorite jewelry store. Okay, the only jewelry store I know. I purchased Ana's earrings there, and it looks like they'll be able to help me with the ring.

If I were a superstitious man I would say that these are good omens for what's to come.

Next, I call Sam.

"Mr. Grey, where have you been?" He's pissed. Tough.

"Busy."

"The press has been all over the helicopter story. There are several TV news and print outlets that want an interview—"

"Sam—draw up a statement. Tell them Ros and I are fine. And send it through to me for approval. I'm not interested in doing any interviews. Print, TV, or otherwise."

"But, Christian, this is a great opp—"

"The answer's no. Get me the statement."

He's silent for a moment, publicity whore that he is. "Yes, Mr. Grey," he says, tight-lipped. I hear, and ignore, his reluctance, but I'm beginning to think I need a new PR person. His credentials were seriously overstated when we checked his references.

"Thanks, Sam." I hang up.

I buzz Taylor on the internal phone system.

"Good afternoon, Mr. Grey."

"What news?"

"I'll come down, sir."

Taylor tells me that *Charlie Tango* has been found, and that a recovery crew is on its way with an FAA official and someone from Airbus, *Charlie Tango*'s manufacturer.

"I hope they'll be able to provide some answers."

"I'm sure they will, sir," says Taylor. "I've e-mailed you a list of people you should call."

"Thanks. There's one more thing. I'm going to need you to pop down to this store." I explain what I've discussed with the jeweler. Taylor gives me a broad grin.

"With pleasure, sir. Will that be all?"

"For now, yes. And thanks."

"You're most welcome, and happy birthday." He gives me a nod and leaves.

I pick up the phone and start making my way through Taylor's list of calls.

While I'm on the phone giving a report to the FAA, an e-mail from Ana pops up.

From: Anastasia Steele
Subject: Lunch
Date: June 18 2011 13:12
To: Christian Grey

Dear Mr. Grey
I am e-mailing to inform you that your lunch is nearly ready.

And that I had some mind-blowing, kinky fuckery earlier today.

Birthday kinky fuckery is to be recommended.

And another thing—I love you.

A x
(Your fiancée)

I'm sure Mrs. Wilson on the other end of the phone at the FAA can hear my smile. With one finger, I type a response.

From: Christian Grey
Subject: Kinky Fuckery
Date: June 18 2011 13:15
To: Anastasia Steele

What aspect was most mind-blowing?

I'm taking notes.

Christian Grey

Famished and Wasting Away After the Morning's Exertions CEO, Grey Enterprises Holdings, Inc.

P.S.: I love your signature.

P.P.S.: What happened to the art of conversation?

I conclude the phone call with Mrs. Wilson and leave my study to find Ana.

She's concentrating hard. I tiptoe up to the kitchen counter as she types into her phone. She presses send, looks up, and jumps when she sees me smirking at her. I bound around the kitchen island, pull her into my arms, and kiss her, taking her by surprise once more. "That is all, Miss Steele," I say when I release her, and I stroll back into my study feeling ridiculously pleased with myself.

Her e-mail is waiting.

From: Anastasia Steele
Subject: Famished?
Date: June 18 2011 13:18
To: Christian Grey

Dear Mr. Grey

May I draw your attention to the first line of my previous e-mail informing you that your lunch is indeed almost ready . . . so none of this famished and wasting away nonsense. With regard to the mind-blowing aspects of the kinky fuckery . . . frankly—all of it. I'd be interested in reading your notes. And I like my bracketed signature, too.

A x

(Your fiancée)

P.S.: Since when have you been so loquacious? And you're on the phone!

I call my mom to tell her about the flowers.

"Darling, how are you? Recovered? It's all over the press."

"I know, Mom. I'm fine. I have something to tell you."

"What?"

"I've asked Ana to marry me. She's said yes."

My mother is stunned into silence.

"Mom?"

"Christian, I'm sorry. That's wonderful news," she says, but she sounds a little hesitant.

"I know this is sudden."

"Are you sure, darling? Don't get me wrong, I adore Ana. But this is so soon and she's the first girl—"

"Mom. She's not the first girl. She's the first one you've met."

"Oh."

"Exactly."

"Well, I am delighted for you. Congratulations."

"There's one more thing."

"What is it, love?"

"I'm having some flowers delivered, for the boathouse."

"Why?"

"Well, my first proposal was pretty crap."

"Oh, I see."

"And, Mom—don't tell anyone else. I want it to be a surprise. I plan to make an announcement this evening."

"As you wish, darling. Mia is in charge of deliveries for the party. Let me find her."

I wait for what feels like an eternity.

Come on, Mia.

"Hey, big brother. Thank God you are still with us. What gives?"

"Mom tells me you are coordinating deliveries for my party. How big is this bash, anyway?"

"After your near-death experience, we're celebrating."

Oh, hell.

"Well, I have a delivery coming for the boathouse."

"Yes? What?"

"From the Bellevue Florist."

"Why? What for?"

Christ, she can be annoying. I look up and Ana is standing in her short, short dress staring at me. "Just let them in and leave them alone. Do you understand, Mia?"

Ana cocks her head to one side, listening.

"Okay. Don't get your panties in a wad. I'll send them to the boathouse."

"Good."

Ana mimes eating.

Food. Great.

"I'll see you later," I say to Mia and hang up. "One more call?" I ask Ana.

"Sure."

"That dress is very short."

"You like it?" Ana pirouettes in the doorway and her skirt flares up, providing a tantalizing glimpse of her lacy underwear.

"You look fantastic in it, Ana. I just don't want anyone else to see you like that."

"Oh!" She looks upset. "We're at home, Christian. No one but the staff."

I don't want to upset her. I nod as graciously as I can manage and she turns and heads back to the kitchen.

Grey, get a grip.

The next call I have to make is to Ana's father. I have no idea what he's going to say when I ask him for his daughter's hand in marriage. From Ana's file, I get Ray's mobile number. José said he was fishing. I just hope he's somewhere with a signal.

No. He isn't. The call goes to voice mail. "Ray Steele. Leave a message."

Short and to the point.

"Hi, Mr. Steele, it's Christian Grey here. I'd like to talk to you about your daughter. Please call me." I give him my number and hang up.

What did you expect, Grey?

He's in the wilds of the Mount Baker Park.

While I have Ana's file on my desk, I decide to deposit some money into her bank account. She'll have to get used to having money.

"Twenty-four thousand dollars!"

"Twenty-four thousand dollars, to the lovely lady in silver, going once, going twice. Sold!"

I chuckle, remembering her audacity at the auction. I wonder what she'll make of this. I'm sure it will be an interesting discussion. On my computer, I transfer fifty thousand dollars to her account. It should show up within the hour.

My stomach growls. I'm hungry. But my phone starts ringing. It's Ray. "Mr. Steele. Thank you for calling back—"

"Is Annie okay?"

"She's fine. More than fine. She's great."

"Thank the Lord. What can I do for you, Christian?"

"I know you're fishing."

"I'm trying. Not catching much today."

"I'm sorry to hear that." This is more nerve-racking than I anticipated. My palms are sweating and Mr. Steele says nothing, cranking my anxiety up a notch.

Supposing he says no? This is not something I've considered.

"Mr. Steele?"

"I'm still here, Christian, waiting for you to get to the point."

"Yes. Of course. Um. I called because, um, I'd like your permission to marry your daughter." The words tumble out like I've never negotiated or clinched a deal in my life. What's more, they're met with a resounding silence.

"Mr. Steele?"

"Put my daughter on the line," he says, giving nothing away.

Shit.

"Just a minute." I dart out of my study to where Ana is waiting, and hold out the phone to her. "I have Ray for you."

Her eyes widen with shock. She takes the phone and covers the mouthpiece. "You told him!" she squeaks.

I nod.

She takes a deep breath, and removes her hand from the mouthpiece. "Hi, Dad."

She listens.

She seems calm.

"What did you say?" she asks, and listens again, her eyes on me. "Yes. It is sudden. Hang on." She gives me another unreadable look and heads to the other end of the room and out onto the balcony, where she continues her conversation.

She starts pacing up and down, but she stays close to the window.

And I'm helpless. All I can do is watch her.

Her body language gives nothing away. Suddenly, she stops and beams. Her smile could light Seattle. He's either said yes . . . or no.

Hell.

Damn it, Grey. Stop with the negative.

She says something else. And she looks like she's going to cry.

Shit. That's not good.

She stomps back and she shoves the phone at me, looking several shades of pissed off.

Nervously, I put the phone to my ear. "Mr. Steele?" Feeling Ana's gaze on my back, I wander into my study just in case it's bad news.

"Christian, I think you ought to call me Ray. Sounds like my little girl is crazy about you and I'm not one to get in her way."

Crazy about you. My heart flips and soars.

"Well, thank you, sir."

"You hurt her in any way and I'll kill you."

"I'd expect nothing less."

"Crazy kids," he mutters. "Now you take good care of her. Annie is my light."

"She's mine, too . . . Ray."

"And good luck with telling her mother." He laughs. "Now let me get back to my fishing."

"I hope you top the forty-three-pounder."

"You know about that?"

"José told me."

"He's a talkative guy. Good day, Christian."

"It is now." I grin.

"I HAVE YOUR STEPFATHER'S rather begrudging blessing," I announce to Ana in the kitchen. She laughs and shakes her head.

"I think Ray is freaked out," she says. "I've got to tell my mom. But I'd like to do that on a full stomach." She waves in the direction of the counter where our food is waiting. Salmon, potatoes, salad, and an interesting dip. She's also selected some wine. A Chablis. "Well, this looks great." I open the wine and pour us each a small glass.

"Damn, you're a good cook, woman." I raise my glass to Ana in appreciation. Her lighthearted expression fades and I'm reminded of the expression on her face outside the playroom this morning. "Ana? Why did you ask me not to take your photo?"

Her consternation deepens, worrying me. "Ana, what is it?" My tone is sharper than I intended and she jumps.

"I found your photos," she says, as if she's committed some terrible sin.

What photos? But as I say the words, I realize exactly what she's talking about. And I feel like I'm back in my father's study, waiting for a pompous dressing-down for some infraction I've committed.

"You've been in the safe?" *How the hell did she do that?*

"Safe? No. I didn't know you had a safe."

"I don't understand."

"In your closet. The box. I was looking for your tie, and the box was under your jeans. The ones you normally wear in the playroom . . . Except today."

Fuck.

No one should see those photographs. Especially Ana. How did they get there?

Leila.

"It's not what you think. I'd forgotten all about them. That box had been moved. Those photographs belong in my safe."

"Who moved them?" Ana asks.

"There's only one person who could have done that."

"Oh. Who? And what do you mean it's not what I think?"

Confess, Grey.

You've already alluded to the depths of your depravity.

This is it, baby. Fifty shades.

"This is going to sound cold, but—they're an insurance policy."

"Insurance policy?"

"Against exposure."

I watch her face as she realizes what I mean. "Oh." She closes her eyes as if she's trying to erase what I've told her. "Yes. You're right," she says quietly. "That does sound cold." She stands and starts to clear the dishes; it's to avoid me.

"Ana."

"Do they know? The girls. The subs?"

"Of course they know."

Before she can escape to the sink, I fold her into my arms. "Those photos are supposed to be in the safe. They're not for recreational use."

They were once upon a time, Grey.

"Maybe they were when they were taken originally. But—they don't mean anything."

"Who put them in your closet?"

"It could only have been Leila."

"She knows your safe combination?"

I guess. "It wouldn't surprise me. It's a very long combination, and I use it so rarely. It's the one number I have written down and haven't changed. I wonder what else she knows and if she's taken anything else out of there." I'll check it. "Look, I'll destroy the photos. Now, if you like."

"They're your photos, Christian. Do with them as you wish." And I know she's offended and hurt.

Christ.

Ana. This was all before you.

I take her head in my hands. "Don't be like that. I don't want that life. I want our life, together." I know she struggles with not being enough for me. Maybe she thinks I want to do those things to her and photograph her.

Grey, be honest, of course you would.

But I'd never do it without her permission. I had all my submissives' consent to having their photographs taken.

Ana's wounded expression reveals her vulnerability. I thought we'd moved on. I want her as she is. She's more than enough. "Ana, I thought we exorcised all those ghosts this morning. I feel that way. Don't you?"

Her eyes soften. "Yes. Yes, I feel like that, too."

"Good." I kiss her and hold her, feeling her body relax against mine. "I'll shred them. And then I have to go to work. I'm sorry, baby, but I have a mountain of business to get through this afternoon."

"It's cool. I have to call my mother," she says, and makes a face. "Then I want to do some shopping and bake you a cake."

"A cake?"

She nods.

"A chocolate cake?"

"You want a chocolate cake?"

I grin.

"I'll see what I can do, Mr. Grey."

I kiss her once more. I don't deserve her. I hope, one day, I'll prove that I do.

ANA WAS RIGHT, the photographs are in my closet. I will have to ask Dr. Flynn to find out if Leila moved them. When I walk back into the living room, Ana's not there. I suspect she's calling her mother.

There's a certain irony in sitting at my desk and shredding these photographs: relics of my old life. The first photograph is of Susannah, bound and gagged, on her knees on the wooden floor. It's not a bad photograph, and briefly I wonder what José would make of this subject matter. The thought amuses me, but I put the first few photographs through the shredder. I turn the rest of the pile over so I can't see the images and within twelve minutes they're all gone.

You still have the negatives.

Grey. Stop.

I'm relieved to find that nothing else is missing from the safe. I turn to my computer and make a start on my e-mails. My first task is to rewrite Sam's pretentious statement about my crash landing. I edit it—it lacks clarity and detail—and I send it back to him.

Then I scroll through my text messages.

> ELENA
>
> Christian. Please call me.
> I need to hear it from your lips that you're okay.

Elena's text must have come through while I was having lunch. The rest are from late last night and yesterday.

> ROS
>
> My feet are sore.
> But all good.
> Hope you are good, too.

> SAM PUBLICITY VP
>
> I really need to talk to you.

> SAM PUBLICITY VP
>
> Mr. Grey. Call me. Urgently.

> SAM PUBLICITY VP
>
> Mr. Grey. Glad you are okay.
> Please call me asap.

ELENA

Thank God you're okay.

I just saw the news.

Please call me.

ELLIOT

Pick up the phone. Bro.

We're worried. Here.

GRACE

Where are you?

Call me. I'm worried.

So is your father.

MIA

CHRISTIAN. WTF.

CALL US. ☹

ANA

We're at the Bunker Club.

Please join us.

You've been mighty quiet Mr. Grey.

Miss you.

ELENA

Are you ignoring me?

Fuck. Just leave me alone, Elena.

TAYLOR

Sir, false alarm with my daughter.

On my way back to Seattle.

Should be there 3 p.m.

I delete them all. I know I'm going to have to deal with Elena at some point, but I don't feel like it now. I open a spreadsheet from Fred with the cost projections for the Kavanagh contract.

The smell of baking drifts into my study. The aroma is mouth-watering and evokes one of the few happy memories I have of my early childhood. It's a bittersweet feeling. The crack whore. Baking.

A movement distracts me from my thoughts and the spread-sheet I'm reading. It's Ana, standing in my study doorway. "I'm just heading to the store to pick up some ingredients," she says.

"Okay." Not dressed like that, surely?

"What?"

"You going to put some jeans on or something?"

"Christian, they're just legs," she says dismissively, and I grit my teeth. "What if we were at the beach?" she says.

"We're not at the beach."

"Would you object if we were at the beach?"

We'd be on a private beach. "No," I respond.

She gives me a wicked smile. "Well, just imagine we are. Laters." She turns and bolts.

What? She's running?

And before I know it, I'm out of my seat and going after her. I see a flash of turquoise exit through the main entrance at speed and I pursue her into the foyer, but she's in the elevator and the doors are closing when I catch up with her. She gives me a wave from inside and then she's gone. Her haste is such an overreaction, I want to laugh.

What did she think I'd do?

Shaking my head, I walk back to the kitchen. The last time we played tag, she left me. The thought is sobering. I stand at the fridge and pour myself some water and I spy my cake cooling on a wire rack. I bend to sniff it and my mouth waters. I close my eyes and a memory of the crack whore resurfaces.

Mommy is home. Mommy is here.

She's wearing her biggest shoes and a short, short skirt. It's red. And shiny.

Mommy has purple marks on her legs. Near her butt.

She smells good. Like candy.

"Come in, big guy, make yourself comfortable."

She's with a man. A big man with a big beard. I don't know him.

"Not now, Maggot. Mommy has company. Go play in your room with your cars. I'll bake you a cake when I'm done."

She closes her bedroom door.

I hear a ping of the elevator and I turn around expecting Ana to walk back in, but it's Taylor with two men, one holding a briefcase, the other as broad as he is tall, carrying himself like hired muscle.

"Mr. Grey." Taylor introduces the younger, smarter man, who's carrying the briefcase. "This is Louis Astoria, from Astoria Fine Jewelry."

"Ah. Thank you for coming."

"My pleasure, Mr. Grey." He's animated. His ebony eyes are warm and friendly. "I have some fine pieces to show you."

"Excellent. Let's look at these in my study. If you'd like to follow me."

I know immediately which platinum ring I want. It's not the biggest; it's not the smallest. It's the finest and most elegant ring, with a four-carat diamond of the highest quality, grade D, and internally flawless clarity. It's beautiful, oval in shape, in a simple setting. The others are too fussy or too gaudy—not right for my girl.

"You've made a fine choice, Mr. Grey," he says, as he pockets my check. "I'm sure your fiancée will love it. And we can get it resized if necessary."

"Thank you again for coming. Taylor will see you out."

"Thank you, Mr. Grey." He hands me the ring box and leaves my study with Taylor. I take one more look at the ring.

I really hope she likes it. I place it in my desk drawer and sit down. I wonder if I should call Ana, just to say hi, but dismiss the idea. Instead I listen to her message once more. *Hi . . . um . . . it's me. Ana. Are you okay? Call me.*

Just hearing her voice is enough. I return to my work.

WHILE I'M ON THE phone with the Airbus engineer, I stare out of the window at the sky. It's the same blue as Ana's eyes. "And the Eurocopter specialist is due Monday afternoon?"

"He's flying from Marseilles-Provence near our headquarters in Marignane, to Paris, then to Seattle. It's the earliest we can get him there. We're fortunate that our base in the Pacific Northwest is at Boeing Field."

"Good. Just keep me informed."

"We'll have our people all over the aircraft as soon as she arrives here."

"Tell them that I'll need their initial findings either Monday evening or Tuesday morning."

"Will do, Mr. Grey."

I hang up and turn back to my desk.

Ana is standing in the doorway, watching me, looking pensive and a little worried.

"Hi," she says, and she enters my study and walks around my desk until she's standing in front of me. I want to ask her why she ran, but she preempts me. "I'm back. Are you mad at me?"

I sigh and lift her into my lap. "Yes," I whisper.

You ran from me, and the last time you did that, you left me.

"I'm sorry. I don't know what came over me." She curls into me, and rests her hand and her head against my chest. Her weight is a comfort.

"Me, neither. Wear what you like." I place my hand on her knee just to reassure her, but as soon as I touch her, I want more. My desire is like an electric current through my body. It jolts me awake and makes me feel alive. I run my hand up her thigh. "Besides, this dress has its advantages."

She looks up, her eyes smoky, and I bend to kiss her.

Our lips touch, and my tongue teases hers and my libido lights up like a solar flare. I feel it in her, too. She grabs my head between her hands, as her tongue wrestles with mine.

I groan as my body responds, growing hard. Wanting her. Needing her. I nip her lower lip, her throat, her ear. She moans into my mouth and yanks my hair.

Ana.

I unzip my pants and free my erection, and pull her astride me. Stretching her lacy underwear to the side and out of the way, I sink into her. Her hands grip the back of my chair, the creak of the leather giving her away. She stares down at me and begins to move. Up and down. Fast. Her rhythm is quick and frenetic.

There's a desperation in her movements, as if she wants to make amends.

Slow, baby, slow.

I put my hands on her hips and slow her down.

Easy. Ana. I want to savor you.

I capture her mouth and she moves at a gentler pace. But her passion is in her kiss and in her touch as she tugs my head back.

Oh, baby.

She moves faster.

And faster still.

This is what she wants. She's building. I feel it. Climbing higher and higher as she moves, faster and faster.

Ah.

She falls apart in my arms and she takes me with her.

"I LIKE YOUR VERSION of sorry," I whisper.

"And I like yours." She nuzzles my chest. "Have you finished?"

"Christ, Ana, you want more?"

"No! Your work."

"I'll be done in about half an hour." I kiss her hair. "I heard your message on my voice mail."

"From yesterday."

"You sounded worried."

She hugs me. "I was. It's not like you not to respond."

I kiss her once more and we sit in quiet, peaceful togetherness. I hope she always sits in my lap like this. She fits perfectly.

Finally, she shifts. "Your cake should be ready in half an hour," she says as she stands.

"Looking forward to it. It smelled delicious, evocative even, while it was baking." She leans down and plants a tender kiss at the edge of my mouth.

I watch her sashay out of my study as I zip up my jeans and I feel . . . lighter. I turn and look at the view from the window. It's late afternoon and the sun is shining, although it's beginning to dip toward the Sound. There are shadows on the streets below. Down there it's already dusk, but up here the light is still golden. Maybe that's why I live here. To be in the light. I've been striving for it since I was a small boy. And it's taken an extraordinary young woman to make me realize that. Ana is my guiding light.

I'm her lost boy, now found.

ANA IS STANDING WITH a frosted chocolate cake that's adorned with a solitary flickering candle.

She sings "Happy Birthday" to me in her sweet musical voice, and I realize I've never heard her sing.

It's magical.

I blow out the candle, closing my eyes to make my wish.

I wish that Ana will always love me. And never leave me.

"I've made my wish," I inform her.

"The frosting is still soft. I hope you like it."

"I can't wait to taste it, Anastasia."

She cuts us each a slice and hands me a plate and a fork.

Here goes.

It's heavenly. The frosting is sweet, the cake moist, and the filling . . . Mmm. "This is why I want to marry you."

She giggles—relieved, I think—and watches me devour the rest of my cake.

ANA IS QUIET IN the car on the way to my parents' place in Bellevue. She stares out of the window but gives me an occasional glance. She looks sensational in emerald green.

There's little traffic tonight, and the R8 roars along the 520 bridge. About halfway across, Ana turns to me. "There was an additional fifty thousand dollars in my bank account this afternoon."

"And?"

"You don't—"

"Ana, you're going to be my wife. Please. Let's not fight about this."

She takes a deep breath and is silent for a while as we cruise just above the pink and dusky waters of Lake Washington. "Okay," she says. "Thank you."

"You're most welcome."

I breathe a sigh of relief.

See, that wasn't so hard, was it Ana?

On Monday, I'll take care of your student loans.

"READY TO FACE MY family?" I switch off the R8 ignition. We're parked in my parents' driveway.

"Yes. Are you going to tell them?"

"Of course. I'm looking forward to seeing their reactions." I'm excited. I step out of the car and open her door. It's a little cool this evening and she pulls her wrap around her shoulders. I take her hand and we head to the front door. The driveway is choked with cars, including Elliot's truck. It's a bigger party than I had anticipated.

Carrick opens the front door before I can knock.

"Christian, hello. Happy birthday, son." He takes my hand and engulfs me in a surprise hug.

This never happens. "Um . . . thanks, Dad."

"Ana, how lovely to see you again." He gives Ana a quick affectionate embrace and we follow him into the house. There's a loud clatter of heels, and I expect to see Mia running down the hallway, but it's Katherine Kavanagh. She looks mad.

"You two! I want to talk to you," she gripes.

Ana gives me a blank look and I shrug. I have no idea what Kavanagh's beef is but we follow her into the empty dining room. She shuts the door and turns on Ana. "What the fuck is this?" she hisses and waves a piece of paper at her. Ana takes it from her and reads it. Almost immediately she blanches and her startled eyes meet mine.

What the hell?

Ana steps between me and Katherine.

"What is it?" I ask, feeling anxious.

Ana ignores me and addresses Kavanagh. "Kate! This has nothing to do with you." Katherine is surprised by her reaction.

What the fuck are they talking about?

"Ana, what is it?"

"Christian, would you just go, please?"

"No. Show me." I hold out my hand and reluctantly she passes the piece of paper to me.

It's her e-mail response to the contract.

Shit.

"What's he done to you?" Katherine asks, ignoring me.

"That's none of your business, Kate." Ana sounds exasperated.

"Where did you get this?" I ask.

Kavanagh blushes. "That's irrelevant." But I stare at her and she continues. "It was in the pocket of a jacket, which I assume is yours, that I found on the back of Ana's bedroom door." She scowls at me, ready for battle.

"Have you told anyone?" I ask.

"No! Of course not," she snaps, and has the gall to look offended.

Good. I walk over to the fireplace and taking a lighter from the small porcelain bowl on the mantelpiece I set fire to the corner of the printout and let it float, burning, into the grate. Both women are silent, watching me.

Once it's reduced to ashes, I turn my attention back to them.

"Not even Elliot?" Ana asks.

"No one," Katherine says, and she sounds emphatic. She looks a little puzzled and maybe hurt. "I just want to know you're okay, Ana," she says, concerned.

Unseen by them both, I roll my eyes.

"I'm fine, Kate. More than fine. Please, Christian and I are good, really good—this is old news. Please ignore it," Ana pleads with her.

"Ignore it?" she says. "How can I ignore that? What's he done to you?"

"He hasn't done anything to me, Kate. Honestly—I'm good."

"Really?" she asks.

For fuck's sake.

I wrap my arm around Ana and stare at Katherine, trying and

probably failing to keep the animosity out of my expression. "Ana
has consented to be my wife, Katherine."

"Wife!" she exclaims, her eyes widening in disbelief.

"We're getting married. We're going to announce our engagement this evening," I inform her.

"Oh!" Katherine stares at Ana, stunned. "I leave you alone
for sixteen days, and this happens? It's very sudden. So yesterday,
when I said—" She stops. "Where does that e-mail fit into all this?"

"It doesn't, Kate. Forget it—please. I love him and he loves me.
Don't do this. Don't ruin his party and our night," Ana begs.

Katherine's eyes fill with tears.

Shit. She's going to cry.

"No. Of course I won't. You're okay?"

"I've never been happier," Ana whispers, and my heart quickens.

Katherine grabs her hand, even though I still have my arm
wrapped around Ana.

"You really are okay?" she asks, her voice full of hope.

"Yes." Ana sounds happier and she shrugs out of my hold to
hug her.

"Oh, Ana—I was so worried when I read this. I didn't know
what to think. Will you explain it to me?" she asks.

"One day, not now."

"Good. I won't tell anyone. I love you so much, Ana, like my
own sister. I just thought—" She shakes her head. "I didn't know
what to think. I'm sorry. If you're happy, then I'm happy." Katherine looks at me. "I'm sorry. I don't mean to intrude."

I give her a nod. Maybe she does care about Ana, but how
Elliot puts up with her I'll never know.

"I really am sorry. You're right, it's none of my business," she
whispers to Ana. There's a knock that startles us all, and my mom
pokes her head around the door.

"Everything okay, darling?" Mom asks, looking directly at me.

"Everything's fine, Mrs. Grey," Katherine offers.

"Fine, Mom," I respond.

She expresses her relief as she enters the room. "Then you won't mind if I give my son a birthday hug." She gives us all a broad smile and walks into my waiting arms. I hold her close. "Happy birthday, darling," she says. "I'm so glad you're still with us."

"Mom, I'm fine." I look into her warm hazel eyes and they're shining with maternal love.

"I'm so happy for you," she says, and she holds her palm against my cheek.

Mom. I love you.

She steps out of my embrace. "Well, kids, if you've all finished your tête-à-tête, there's a throng of people here to check that you really are in one piece, Christian, and to wish you a happy birthday."

"I'll be right there."

Mom looks from Katherine to Ana, satisfied, I think, that nothing is amiss. She winks at Ana as she holds open the door for all of us. Ana takes my hand.

"Christian, I really do apologize," Katherine says.

I acknowledge her with the briefest of nods and we walk into the hallway.

"Does your mother know about us?" asks Ana.

"Yes."

Ana raises her eyebrows. "Oh. Well, that was an interesting start to the evening."

"As ever, Miss Steele, you have a gift for understatement." I kiss her knuckles and we step into the living room.

A deafening, spontaneous round of applause erupts as we enter.

Shit. So many people! Why so many people? My family. Kavanagh's brother, Flynn and his wife. Mac! Bastille. Mia's friend Lily and her mother. Ros and Gwen. Elena.

Elena catches my attention with a little salute while she applauds. I'm distracted by my mom's housekeeper. She's carrying a tray of champagne. I squeeze Ana's hand and let it go as the applause dies down.

"Thank you, everyone. Looks like I'll need one of these." I take two flutes, and hand a glass to Ana.

I raise my glass in tribute to the room. Everyone moves forward, overzealous and eager to greet me because of yesterday's accident. Elena is first to reach us, and I take Ana's free hand. "Christian, I was so worried." Elena kisses me on both cheeks before I have a chance to react. Ana tries to free her hand but I tighten my hold on her.

"I'm good, Elena," I respond.

"Why didn't you call me?" She sounds aggravated, her eyes searching mine.

"I've been busy."

"Didn't you get my messages?"

I let go of Ana's hand and put my arm around her shoulder, instead pulling her to me.

Elena gives Ana a smile. "Ana," she purrs. "You look lovely, dear."

"Elena. Thank you." Ana's tone is saccharine and insincere.

Could this be any more awkward?

I catch Mom's eye and she frowns, looking at the three of us.

"Elena, I need to make an announcement," I tell her.

"Of course," she says, with a brittle smile.

I ignore her. "Everyone," I call out, and I wait for the hum in the room to die down. When I have everyone's attention, I take a deep breath. "Thank you for coming today. I have to say I was expecting a quiet family dinner, so this is a pleasant surprise." I shoot Mia a pointed look and she waves at me. "Ros and I"—I give Ros and Gwen a nod—"we had a close call yesterday." Ros raises her glass to me. "So, I'm especially glad to be here today to share with all of you my very good news. This beautiful woman"—I look down at my girl beside me—"Miss Anastasia Rose Steele, has consented to be my wife, and I'd like you all to be the first to know."

My announcement is met with a few gasps, a cheer, and another spontaneous round of applause. I turn to Ana, who looks flushed and beautiful, tip her chin up and give her a swift, chaste kiss. "You'll soon be mine."

"I am already."

"Legally," I mouth at her, with a wicked grin.

She chuckles.

Mom and Dad are the first to congratulate us.

"Darling boy. I've never seen you this happy." Mom kisses my cheek and wipes a tear and then gushes over Ana.

"Son, I'm so proud," Carrick says.

"Thanks, Dad."

"She's a lovely girl."

"I know."

"Where is the ring?" exclaims Mia as she hugs Ana.

Ana gives me a startled look.

"We're going to choose one together." I glare at my little sister. She's such a pain in the ass sometimes.

"Oh, don't look at me like that, Grey!" Mia scoffs, and she folds her arms around me. "I'm so thrilled for you, Christian," she says. "When will you get married? Have you set a date?"

"No idea, and no we haven't. Ana and I need to discuss all that."

"I hope you have a big wedding here!" Her persistence is overwhelming.

"We'll probably fly to Vegas tomorrow."

She looks pissed, but thankfully I'm saved by Elliot, who gives me bear hug.

"Way to go, bro." He slaps me on the back, hard.

Elliot turns to Ana and Bastille claps me on my back, too. Harder.

"Well, Grey, I did not see this coming. Congratulations, man." He pumps my hand.

"Thank you, Claude."

"So, when will I start training your fiancée? The thought of her kicking you onto your backside fills me with hope and joy."

I laugh. "I've given her your schedule, I'm sure she'll be in touch."

Lily's mother, Ashley, congratulates me, but she's a little frosty. I hope she and Lily steer clear of my fiancée.

I rescue Ana from Mia as Dr. Flynn and his wife approach. "Christian," says Flynn, holding out his hand, and we shake.

"John. Rhian." I give his wife a kiss.

"Glad you're still with us, Christian," Flynn says. "My life would be most dull—and penurious—without you."

"John!" Rhian scolds him, and I introduce her to Anastasia.

"Delighted to meet the woman who has finally captured Christian's heart," Rhian says warmly to Ana.

"Thank you," she replies.

"That was one googly you bowled there, Christian." Flynn shakes his head in amused disbelief.

What?

"John—you and your cricket metaphors." Rhian scolds him again, wishes me a happy birthday and congratulates us, and soon she and Ana are deep in an animated conversation.

"That was quite the announcement, given your audience," John says, and I know he's referring to Elena.

"Yes. I'm sure she wasn't expecting that," I answer.

"We can talk about it later."

"How's Leila?"

"She's good, Christian, responding well to treatment. Another couple of weeks and we can consider an outpatient program."

"That's a relief."

"She's interested in our art therapy classes."

"Really? She used to paint."

"So she said. I think these classes could really help."

"Great. Is she eating?"

"Yes. Her appetite's fine."

"Good. Ask her something for me."

"Of course?"

"I need to know if she moved some photography I had in my safe."

"Ah. Yes. She told me about that."

"She did?"

"You know how mischievous she can be. Her intention was to rattle Ana."

"Well, it worked."

"We can discuss that later, too."

We're joined by Ros and Gwen, whom I introduce to Ana.

"I'm so glad to finally meet you, Ana," says Ros.

"Thank you. Have you recovered from your ordeal?"

Ros nods and Gwen puts her arm around her. "It was quite something," Ros continues. "How Christian managed to land safely was a miracle. He's an excellent pilot."

"It was luck, and I wanted to get home to my girl," I respond.

"Of course you did. And having met her, who can blame you?" says Gwen.

Grace announces that dinner is served in the kitchen.

Taking Ana's hand, I give it a quick squeeze to see how she's holding up, and we follow the guests through to the kitchen. Mia ambushes Ana in the hallway, holding two cocktail glasses, and I know she's up to no good.

Ana gives me a brief panicked look but I let her go, watching as they enter the dining room. Mia closes the door behind them.

In the kitchen, Mac approaches me to offer his congratulations.

"Please, Mac, call me Christian. You're at my engagement party."

"Heard about the crash." He listens intently as I give him the grisly details.

My mother has set out a feast with a Moroccan theme. I load a plate while Mac and I shoot the breeze about *The Grace*.

As I help myself to a second portion of lamb tagine, I wonder what the hell Ana and Mia are doing? I decide to go and rescue Ana but outside the dining room, I hear her shouting. "Don't you dare tell me what I'm getting myself into!"

Shit. What gives?

"When will you learn? It's none of your goddamned business!" Ana rages.

I try to open the door, but someone is in the way. The person moves and the door swings open. Ana is bristling with anger. Her complexion reddening. She's shaking with fury. Elena stands before her, drenched in what must have been Ana's drink. I shut the door and stand between them.

"What the fuck are you doing, Elena?" I snarl.

I told you to leave her alone.

She wipes her face with the back of her hand. "She's not right for you, Christian."

"What?" I yell and I'm so loud that I'm sure I've startled Ana because Elena jumps, too. But I don't give a fuck.

I've warned her. And warned her.

"How the fuck do you know what's right for me?"

"You have needs, Christian," she says, her voice softer, and I know she's trying to placate me.

"I've told you before, this is none of your fucking business." I'm surprised by my own vehemence. "What is this?" I scowl at her. "Do you think it's you? You? You think you're right for me?"

Elena's expression hardens, her eyes like flint. She stands taller and steps toward me. "I was the best thing that ever happened to you," she hisses, with unrestrained arrogance. "Look at you now. One of the richest, most successful entrepreneurs in the United States. Controlled, driven, you need nothing. You are master of your universe."

She's going there.

Fuck.

I step back. Disgusted.

"You loved it, Christian, don't try and kid yourself. You were on the road to self-destruction, and I saved you from that, saved you from a life behind bars. Believe me, baby, that's where you would have ended up. I taught you everything you know, everything you need."

I cannot remember a time when I've felt such rage. "You taught me how to fuck, Elena. But it's empty, like you. No wonder Linc left."

She gasps. Shocked.

"You never once held me. You never once said you loved me."

Her ice-blue eyes narrow. "Love is for fools, Christian."

"Get out of my house," Grace commands in a cold fury.

The three of us jump and turn to see my mother, an avenging angel, standing on the threshold of the room. She fixates on Elena, and if looks could kill, Elena would be a small mound of ash on the floor.

I look from Grace to Elena, her color now drained from her face. And as Grace stalks toward her, Elena seems powerless to move or say anything while under my mother's withering glare. Grace slaps her hard across her face, astonishing us all. The sound resonates off the walls. "Take your filthy paws off my son, you whore, and get out of my house—now!" Grace seethes through gritted teeth.

Fuck. Mom!

Elena clutches her cheek in shock. She blinks rapidly, staring at Grace, then turns and abruptly leaves the room, not bothering to close the door behind her.

Mom turns to me, and I cannot look away.

I see hurt and anguish written all over her face.

She says nothing as we stare at each other, and an oppressive and unbearable silence fills the room.

Finally she speaks. "Ana, before I hand him over to you, would you mind giving me a minute or two alone with my son?" It's not a request.

"Of course," Ana whispers. I watch Ana leave and close the door.

Mom glowers at me, saying nothing, looking at me as though she's seeing me for the first time.

Seeing the monster she reared but did not create.

Shit.

I'm in big trouble. My scalp prickles in acknowledgment and I feel the blood drain from my face.

"How long, Christian?" she says, her voice low. And I know that tone—it's the calm before the storm.

How much did she hear?

"A few years," I mumble. I don't want her to know. I don't want to tell her. I don't want to hurt her and I know it will. I've known that since I was fifteen.

"How old were you?"

I swallow and my heart rate accelerates like a Formula One engine. I have to be careful here. I don't want to cause trouble for Elena. I study Mom's face, trying to judge how she'll react. Should I lie to her? Could I lie to her? And part of me knows I lied to her every time I saw Elena and told her I was studying with a friend.

Mom's eyes are piercing. "Tell me. How old were you when this all started?" she says through clenched teeth. It's the voice that I've only heard on rare occasions, and I know I'm doomed. She will not stop until she has an answer.

"Sixteen," I whisper.

She narrows her eyes and cocks her head to one side.

"Try again." Her voice is chillingly quiet.

Hell. How does she know?

"Christian," she warns, prompting me.

"Fifteen."

She closes her eyes like I've stabbed her, her hand flying to her mouth as she stifles a sob. When she opens them, they're filled with pain and unshed tears.

"Mom . . ." I try to think of something to say to take that pain away. I step toward her and she holds up her hand to stop me.

"Christian. I am so mad at you right now. I suggest you don't come any closer."

"How did you know? That I lied," I ask.

"For heaven's sake, Christian—I'm your mother," she snaps and dashes a fallen tear from her cheek.

I feel myself blushing, feeling stupid and slightly piqued at the same time. Only my mom can make me feel this way. My mom. And Ana.

I thought I was a better liar.

"Yes, you should look shamefaced. How long did this go on for? How long did you lie to us, Christian?"

I shrug. I don't want her to know.

"Tell me!" she insists.

"A few years."

"Years! Years!" she shouts, making me cringe. She so rarely shouts.

"I can't believe it. That *fucking* woman."

I gasp. I have never heard Grace swear. Ever. It shocks me.

She turns and paces to the window. I stay standing. Paralyzed. Speechless.

Mom just cursed.

"And to think, all the times she's been here . . ." Grace groans and puts her head in her hands. I cannot stand by any longer. I step toward her and wrap my arms around her. This is so new to me, holding my mom. I pull her to my chest, and she starts to weep quietly.

"I've already thought you dead this week, and now this," she sobs.

"Mom—it's not what you think."

"Don't even try it, Christian. I heard you, I heard what you said. That she taught you to fuck."

She's said it again!

I flinch—this isn't her. She doesn't swear. It's mortifying to think I have something to do with this. The thought of hurting Grace is excruciating. I'd never want to hurt her. She saved me. And all at once I'm overwhelmed by my shame and my remorse.

"I knew something happened when you were fifteen. She was the reason, wasn't she? The reason you suddenly calmed down, seemed to focus? Oh, Christian. What did she do to you?"

Mom! Why is she overreacting? Do I tell her that Elena brought me under control? I don't have to tell her how. "Yes," I murmur.

She groans again. "Oh, Christian. I've gotten drunk with that woman, spilled my soul to her so many nights. And to think . . ."

"My relationship with her has nothing to do with your friendship."

"Don't give me that bullshit, Christian! She abused my trust. She abused my son!" Her voice cracks, and once more she buries her face in her hands.

"Mom—it didn't feel like that."

She stands back and swats me around the head, making me duck.

"Words fail me, Christian. Fail me. Where did I go wrong?"

"Mom, this is not your fault."

"How? How did it start?" She holds her hand up and continues hurriedly. "I don't want to know that. What will your father say?"

Fuck.

Carrick will go batshit.

Suddenly I'm fifteen again, dreading another of his interminable lectures on personal responsibility and acceptable behavior. Christ, that's the last thing I want.

"Yes, he'll be mad as hell," Mom interjects, correctly interpreting my expression. "We knew something had happened. You changed overnight—and to think it was because you got laid by my best friend."

Right now, I want the floor to swallow me up.

"Mom—it's been, it's done, it's gone. She did me no harm."

"Christian, I heard what you said. I heard her cold response. And to think . . ." She puts her head in her hands once more. Suddenly her eyes fly up to meet mine, and widen in horror.

Fuck. What now?

"No!" she breathes.

"What?"

"Oh no. Tell me it's not true, because if it is—I'll find your father's old pistol and I'll shoot the bitch."

Mom!

"What?"

"I know that Elena's tastes run to the exotic, Christian."

For the second time this evening, I feel slightly dizzy. *Shit.* She must not know this.

"It was just sex, Mom," I mutter quickly—let's shut that down right now. No way am I exposing my mother to that part of my life.

She narrows her eyes at me. "I don't want the sordid details, Christian. Because that's what this is—nasty, sordid, squalid. What kind of woman does that to a fifteen-year-old boy? It's disgusting. To think of all the confidences I've shared with her. Well, you can be sure she'll never set foot in this house again." She presses her lips together in determination. "And you should cease all contact with her."

"Mom, um . . . Elena and I run a very successful business together."

"No, Christian. You cut your ties with her."

I stare at her, speechless. How can she tell me what to do? I'm twenty-eight years old, for fuck's sake.

"Mom—"

"No, Christian—I'm serious. If you don't, I will go to the police."

I pale. "You wouldn't."

"I will. I couldn't stop it then, but I can now."

"You're just real mad, Mom, and I don't blame you—but you're overreacting."

"Don't tell me I'm overreacting," she yells. "You are *not* going to have any kind of relationship with someone who can abuse a troubled, immature child! She should come with a health warning." She's glowering at me.

"Okay." I hold my hands up defensively and she seems to compose herself.

"Does Ana know?"

"Yes, she does."

"Good. You shouldn't start your married life with secrets." She frowns as if she's speaking from personal experience. Vaguely, I wonder what that's about, but she recovers herself.

"I'd be interested to hear what she thinks of Elena."

"She's kind of in your camp."

"Sensible girl. You've fallen on your feet with her, at least. A lovely young woman who's the right age. Someone you can find happiness with."

My expression softens.

Yes. She makes me happier than I ever thought possible.

"You are to end it with Elena. Cut all ties. You understand?"

"Yes, Mom. I could do that as a wedding present to Anastasia."

"What? Are you crazy? You'd better think of something else! That's hardly romantic, Christian," she scolds.

"I thought she'd like that."

"Honestly, men! You have no idea sometimes."

"What do you think I should give her?"

"Oh, Christian." She sighs, then offers me a small wan smile. "You really haven't taken in a word, have you? Do you know why I'm upset?"

"Yes, of course."

"Tell me, then."

I gaze at her and sigh. "I don't know, Mom. Because you didn't know? Because she's your friend?"

She reaches up and gently strokes my hair, like she used to when I was small. The only place she would touch me, because it was the only place I let her.

"For all those reasons and because she abused you, darling. And you are so deserving of love. You're so easy to love. You always have been."

There's a burning sensation at the back of my eyes.

"Mom," I whisper.

She puts her arms around me, calmer now, and I hug her in return.

"You'd better go find your bride-to-be. I'm going to have to tell your father when the party's over. No doubt he'll want to talk to you, too."

"Mom. Please. Do you have to tell him?"

"Yes, Christian, I do. And I hope he gives you hell."

Fuck.

"I'm still mad at you. But madder at her." Her face loses all trace of humor. I'd never realized how scary Grace could be.

"I know," I murmur.

"Go on, off you go. Find your girl." She releases me, steps back, and rubs her fingers under her eyes to wipe away her smudged makeup. She looks beautiful. This wonderful woman, who truly loves me, like I love her.

I take a deep breath. "I didn't mean to hurt you, Mom."

"I know. Go."

I lean down and gently kiss her forehead, surprising her.

I walk out of the room to find Ana.

Shit. That was heavy.

ANA'S NOT IN THE kitchen.

"Hey, bro, want a beer?" Elliot asks.

"In a minute. I'm looking for Ana."

"She come to her senses and run off?"

"Fuck off, Lelliot."

She's not in the sitting room.

She wouldn't leave, would she?

My room? I vault up the first flight of stairs, then up the second. She's standing on the landing. I reach the top step and stop when we are eye to eye.

"Hi."

"Hi," she answers.

"I was worried—"

"I know," she interrupts me. "I'm sorry. I couldn't face the festivities. I just had to get away, you know. To think." She caresses my face and I lean my cheek into her touch.

"And you thought you'd do that in my room?"

"Yes."

Stepping up beside her, I reach out to her and we hold each other. She smells amazing . . . soothing, even. "I'm sorry you had to endure all that."

"It's not your fault, Christian. Why was she here?"

"She's a family friend."

"Not anymore. How's your mom?"

"Mom is pretty fucking mad at me right now. I'm really glad you're here, and that we're in the middle of a party. Otherwise I might be breathing my last."

"That bad, huh?"

Complete overreaction.

"Can you blame her?" Ana asks.

I consider this for a moment. Her best friend fucking her son.

"No."

"Can we sit?"

"Sure. Here?"

Ana nods and we both sit down at the top of the stairs.

"So, how do you feel?" she asks.

I let out a deep breath.

"I feel liberated." I shrug and it's true. It's like a weight has been lifted. No more worrying about what Elena thinks.

"Really?"

"Our business relationship is over. Done."

"Will you liquidate the salon business?"

"I'm not that vindictive, Anastasia. No. I'll gift them to her. I'll talk to my lawyer Monday. I owe her that much."

She gives me a quizzical look. "No more Mrs. Robinson?"

"Gone."

Ana grins. "I'm sorry you lost a friend."

"Are you?"

"No," she says, sardonically.

"Come." I stand and offer her my hand. "Let's join the party in our honor. I might even get drunk."

"Do you get drunk?"

"Not since I was a wild teenager." We walk down the stairs. "Have you eaten?"

Ana looks guilty. "No."

"Well, you should. From the look and smell of Elena, that was one of my father's lethal cocktails you threw on her."

"Christian, I—"

I hold up my hand. "No arguing, Anastasia. If you're going to drink and toss alcohol on my exes, you need to eat. It's rule number one. I believe we've already had that discussion after our first night together."

An image of her lying comatose on my bed at The Heathman comes to mind. We stop in the hallway and I caress her face, my fingers skimming her jaw. "I lay awake for hours and watched you sleep," I whisper. "I might have loved you even then." Leaning down I kiss her, and she melts against me.

"Eat." I motion toward the kitchen.

"Okay," she says.

I CLOSE THE DOOR, having bid farewell to Dr. Flynn and his wife.

Finally. I can be alone with Ana. It's just the family left. Grace has had too much to drink and is in the den, murdering "I Will Survive" on the Karaoke machine with Mia and Katherine.

"Do you blame her?" Ana asks.

I narrow my eyes. "Are you smirking at me, Miss Steele?"

"I am."

"It's been quite a day."

"Christian, recently, every day with you has been quite a day."

"Fair point well made, Miss Steele. Come. I want to show you something." I lead her through the hall into the kitchen.

Carrick, Elliot, and Ethan Kavanagh are arguing about the Mariners.

"Off for a stroll?" Elliot taunts us as we head to the French doors, but I give him the finger and otherwise ignore him.

Outside, it's a mild night. I usher Ana up the stone steps to the lawn, where she takes off her shoes and pauses for a moment to admire the view. The half-moon is high above the bay, illuminating a bright silvery path across the water. Seattle is lit up and twinkling as a backdrop.

We walk, hand in hand, toward the boathouse. It's lit inside and out and the beckoning light is our guide.

"Christian, I'd like to go to church tomorrow," Ana says.

"Oh?"

When was the last time I was in church? I recall her background information; I don't remember her being religious.

"I prayed you'd come back alive and you did. It's the least I could do."

"Okay." Maybe I'll go with her.

"Where are you going to put the photos José took of me?"

"I thought we might put them in the new house."

"You bought it?"

I stop. "Yes. I thought you liked it."

"I do. When did you buy it?"

"Yesterday morning. Now we need to decide what to do with it."

"Don't knock it down. Please. It's such a lovely house. It just needs some tender loving care."

"Okay. I'll talk to Elliot. He knows a good architect; she did some work on my place in Aspen. He can do the remodeling."

Ana smiles, then chuckles with amusement.

"What?" I ask.

"I remember the last time you took me to the boathouse."

Oh yes. I was in the moment. "Oh, that was fun. In fact—" I stop and scoop her up over my shoulder and she squeals.

"You were really angry, if I remember correctly," Ana observes while she bounces on my shoulder.

"Anastasia, I'm always really angry."

"No, you're not."

I swat her behind and slide her down my body when I get to the door of the boathouse. I take her head in my hands. "No, not anymore." My lips and tongue find hers and I pour all the anxiety that I'm feeling into a passionate kiss. She's breathless and panting when I release her.

Okay. I hope she likes what I have planned. I hope it's what she wants. She deserves the world. She looks a little intrigued and caresses my face, running her fingers along my cheek, to my jaw and chin. Her index finger pauses over my lips.

Showtime, Grey.

"I've something to show you in here." I open the door. "Come." I take her hand and lead her to the top of the stairs. Opening the door, I glance inside, and it all looks good. I step aside to let Ana go first, and I follow her into the room.

She gasps at the sight that greets her.

The florists have gone to town. There are wild meadow flowers everywhere, in pinks and whites and blues, all lit by tiny fairy lights and soft pink lanterns.

Yes. This will do.

Ana is stunned. She whips around and gapes at me.

"You wanted hearts and flowers."

She stares at me in disbelief.

"You have my heart." And I wave at the room.

"And here are the flowers," she murmurs. "Christian, it's lovely." Her voice is hoarse and I know she's close to tears.

Plucking up my courage, I lead her farther into the room. In the center of the arbor, I sink onto one knee. Ana catches her breath, and her hands fly to her mouth. From my inside jacket pocket, I pull out the ring and hold it up for her.

"Anastasia Steele. I love you. I want to love, cherish, and protect you for the rest of my life. Be mine. Always. Share my life with me. Marry me."

She is the love of my life.

It will only ever be Ana.

Her tears start to fall in earnest but her smile eclipses the moon, the stars, the sun, and all the flowers in this boathouse.

"Yes," she says.

Taking her hand, I slip the ring on her finger; it fits perfectly.

She looks down at it in wonder. "Oh, Christian," she sobs, her legs buckle and she falls into my arms. She kisses me, offering me everything, her lips, her tongue, her compassion, her love. Her body is pressed to mine. Giving, like she always does.

Sweet, sweet Ana.

I kiss her back. Taking what she has to offer, and giving in return. She's taught me how.

This woman who has dragged me into the light. This woman who loves me in spite of my past, in spite of my wrongdoings. This woman who's agreed to be mine for the rest of her life.

My girl. My Ana. My love.

E L James

DARKER

After twenty-five years working in TV, E L James decided to pursue her childhood dream, and set out to write stories that readers would fall in love with. The result was the sensuous romance *Fifty Shades of Grey* and its two sequels, *Fifty Shades Darker* and *Fifty Shades Freed*, a trilogy that went on to sell more than 150 million copies worldwide in 52 languages. In 2015 she published the best seller *Grey*, the story of *Fifty Shades of Grey* from the perspective of Christian Grey.

In 2012, E L James was named one of *Time* magazine's "Most Influential People in the World," one of Barbara Walters's "Ten Most Fascinating People of the Year," and *Publishers Weekly*'s "Person of the Year." She went on to work as a producer on the film adaptations of her trilogy for Universal Pictures; *Fifty Shades of Grey*, the film, broke box-office records all over the world in 2015. Its 2017 sequel, *Fifty Shades Darker*, proved equally popular with fans of Ana and Christian's story, and the concluding film, *Fifty Shades Freed*, will be released in 2018.

E L James lives with her husband, the novelist and screenwriter Niall Leonard, their two sons, and their two dogs in West London, where she is working on new novels and movie projects.

THE OTHER SIDE
OF THE STORY

GREY

E L JAMES

FIFTY SHADES OF GREY AS TOLD BY CHRISTIAN